One

T*he microwave chimed* the completion of its reheat cycle. Emma Merrigan, her hand safely encased in a mitt that resembled a bright red calico lobster with button eyes, removed the last two portions of the weekend's stew. One nice thing about stew: Not even the most modern technology could keep it from tasting better the second time around.

Em decanted supper onto a pair of plates, garnished them with the dark green leaves of a warm spinach salad, and carried the plates out of the kitchen.

"You look awful," her mother announced as Emma set the plates on the dining table.

Em let the words roll off her back without comment or reaction. Life with her mother—life in Eleanor Graves' general vicinity—was an endless stream of non sequiturs. Emma had a mouthful of soft, sweet carrots when Eleanor erupted again.

"I'm not kidding, Emma—you look perfectly awful."

Em swallowed hard. She'd come a long way since that night, more than a year and a half ago, when Eleanor had reentered her life after a half-century's absence. Never mind that her mother hadn't looked a day over twenty-five that inauspicious evening and looked even younger now. Eleanor would never be "Mom," or even "Mother," but she'd gradually become a friend, except when she slipped and said something utterly uncalled for, something utterly Eleanor.

"I'm tired," Emma replied deliberately.

"There's no reason for you to be tired. There's no good reason for one of Orion's Children to ever be tired."

Orion's Children—that was a phrase Eleanor had stumbled upon last year to describe herself, her daughter, and a few thousand other humans. Let ordinary folk have the traditional zodiac, Orion's Children were predators who walked across time hunting humanity's curses. Emma had adopted the phrase, but in a more restrictive sense. She used it only for Eleanor and herself and the small group, both hunters and ordinary folk, who shared their secrets.

Conveniently, Eleanor's variety of Orion's Children could hunt curses while their bodies racked up beauty sleep, which meant, as Eleanor had claimed, there was no good reason for a diligent hunter—and Emma was diligent; she bestirred herself to the wasteland hunting ground at least six nights out of any seven and had never missed more than two nights in a row—to sport the hollow, smudge-circled eyes Em saw whenever she looked in a mirror.

"You're not tired," Eleanor corrected when Em had failed to rise to her bait. "You're worn out."

"There's a difference?" Em asked, not that she believed there was or could be. But rampant curiosity, which she'd nicknamed her "engineering gene" because she'd inherited it from her late father, a tenured engineering professor, had always been her downfall.

Eleanor smiled triumphantly. "Of course. Tired's in the body. If you're hunting, by definition you're getting plenty of sleep; you're not tired. Worn out's in the mind, in the

Down
Time

Lynn Abbey

ACE BOOKS, NEW YORK

THE BERKLEY PUBLISHING GROUP
Published by the Penguin Group
Penguin Group (USA) Inc.
375 Hudson Street, New York, New York 10014, USA
Penguin Group (Canada), 10 Alcorn Avenue, Toronto, Ontario M4V 3B2, Canada
(a division of Pearson Penguin Canada Inc.)
Penguin Books Ltd., 80 Strand, London WC2R 0RL, England
Penguin Group Ireland, 25 St. Stephen's Green, Dublin 2, Ireland (a division of Penguin Books Ltd.)
Penguin Group (Australia), 250 Camberwell Road, Camberwell, Victoria 3124, Australia
(a division of Pearson Australia Group Pty. Ltd.)
Penguin Books India Pvt. Ltd., 11 Community Centre, Panchsheel Park, New Delhi—110 017, India
Penguin Group (NZ), Cnr. Airborne and Rosedale Roads, Albany, Auckland 1310, New Zealand
(a division of Pearson New Zealand Ltd.)
Penguin Books (South Africa) (Pty.) Ltd., 24 Sturdee Avenue, Rosebank, Johannesburg 2196, South Africa

Penguin Books Ltd., Registered Offices: 80 Strand, London WC2R 0RL, England

DOWN TIME

An Ace Book / published by arrangement with the author

PRINTING HISTORY
Ace edition / April 2005

ISBN: 0-441-01270-1

ACE
Ace Books are published by The Berkley Publishing Group,
a division of Penguin Group (USA) Inc.,
375 Hudson Street, New York, New York 10014.
ACE and the "A" design are trademarks belonging to Penguin Group (USA) Inc.

PRINTED IN THE UNITED STATES OF AMERICA

10 9 8 7 6 5 4 3 2 1

spirit. When was the last time you relaxed—really relaxed and let your mind float free?"

Emma shrugged. She had an answer for that question, but she didn't discuss her private life with anyone, especially her youthful, but worldly, mother. There was a man whose presence both excited and relaxed her. In her mind, he was the core of her select version of Orion's Children. His name was Blaise Raponde and he'd died in 1685—

No one, least of all Blaise himself, could explain why his essence—never speak of souls around Blaise, never say anything that smacked of religion unless you were prepped for a lengthy theological discussion—had persisted after his body's demise. Then again, once you accepted the existence of curses and the barren extra-dimensional wasteland where they congregated, reasonable explanations ceased to be a top priority. It was enough that Blaise, with his chivalrous manners, amber-pommeled sword, and outlandish clothes—the height of seventeenth-century Parisian fashion—had made himself a part of Em's life.

Together, the two of them had conjured a hideaway, a subterranean bolt-hole beneath the wasteland's weird magenta sky, where the curses couldn't interrupt their hours together. Most nights, after she'd mooted her self-set quota of curses, Emma checked in at the bolt-hole, hoping to find Blaise there waiting for her.

Talk about safe sex . . .

"See," Eleanor intruded into her daughter's silence. "You can't even remember."

"It's been a long week," Em conceded as she picked up her wine goblet and swirled the liquid against the glass. "I'll relax tomorrow."

Eleanor made a long face. "You're not going to work tomorrow? You're finally taking a Saturday off? May I quote you on that? What is it? Seven-thirty? This is the earliest you've been home for supper all week. Last night you didn't get home until eight. Tuesday, it was nearly ten, and I'll bet you had popcorn and ice cream for supper."

"You've been spying on me?" Em tried to sound indignant, but whether the word was *weary* or *tired,* it described her all too well, and her accusation fell flat.

"I keep an eye out, yes," Eleanor said without a hint of guilt or shame. "Somebody has to. You apparently don't know when to stop. When are you going to put your foot down and tell those people at the library that they don't own you? You could give notice any time, you know—take an early retirement, blow this town, and restart your life. You'll have to sooner or later. Why not now?"

An August-sunset breeze wafted through the window screen, cooling Em's face as she sipped her wine. Thank heaven Eleanor was a better tactician than strategist. She didn't expect answers to her rhetorical questions and had no idea that Emma had taken them to heart and begun to ask them herself.

This summer wasn't the first time the staff of the university's Horace Johnson Library had been dragged through a wrenching reorganization, following the surprise resignation of one director and the ascension of its next. But the last six weeks of punitive memos, preemptive transfers, and all-out turf warfare added up to the worst summer that Emma could recall.

Gene Shaunekker had been a good man to have at Horace Johnson's helm these last six years, but six years was an eternity among directors of first-tier university libraries, and Em couldn't blame Gene for leaping at the opportunity to run the works at an Ivy League institution. He'd left in early January. Emma had expected his office to remain vacant for the better part of a year, while a search committee fiddled, fumed, and reluctantly recommended. That's how they'd selected Gene. But the U's president had forgone committees and announced Gene's replacement in mid-February, leaving Em and her cronies to wonder if the switch hadn't been in the works for months before Gene's departure.

The rumor was that Margaret Patrick had been hired to shake things up in the U's library system. If the rumor were true, then Maggie—the woman prized informality while rattling the staff to its foundations—had been doing a damn good job from day one. In the first place, call it sexist or woefully old-fashioned, but Emma didn't like working for another woman, especially a woman who arrived on campus with a hired-gun's reputation for destroying morale while hacking a library's budget with a dull machete.

As director of Acquisitions, Emma had the sort of job security associated with tenured professors. No director could fire her, not without cause and a vote from the university senate, but that hadn't stopped Maggie from making Em the codirector of Acquisitions and Cataloging. Now she and a man she'd known and liked for fifteen years were locked in a turf battle neither could afford to lose. They each had a handful of years before they qualified for a fully-funded retirement. Years that might be very long indeed, if the number of hours Em felt obligated to sit behind her desk continued to grow the way it had all summer. She'd plotted the rising curve: By Christmas, she'd be living in her office twenty-four hours a day, seven days a week.

It wouldn't get that bad; something would give before then. Em only hoped it was Margaret Patrick and not her own health.

Lightning bugs circled outside the screened window, flashing their yellow green love lights. There must have been a female glowworm camped out in the branches of the evergreen shrubs banked against the townhouse walls. Later in the evening, getting on toward midnight, the ritual would be repeated in a cooler, bluer light, because Michi-

gan was one of those lucky places in North America with
two resident lightning-bug species.

Emma Merrigan knew about Michigan's lightning bugs
because she was a librarian, and librarians had access to an
endless stream of trivia. Or was it her appetite for trivia
that had pushed her into the library years ago, when the af-
tershocks of an early and misguided first marriage had left
her in need of a career?

"Cancel it," Eleanor said.

Emma sat bolt upright in shock. Her mind had been
wandering, and she didn't know where Eleanor had been
dragging their conversation, or for how long. She shook
her head as a matter of principle.

"There's no point to hunting curses when you're already out on your feet," Eleanor insisted with a grimace.
"Call the others and tell them it's off for tonight."

So, they were talking about the regularly Friday-night
gathering of Orion's Children.

"I'll be fine once we get started," Em assured her
mother. "I won't carry any of this to the wasteland, you
know that."

"What I know is that you haven't . . . yet. There's always a first time. I'm the first to admit you've put together
a good team, and we've been carving nicely through
rogues and curses, but that's all the more reason not to
push things when you're not up to par."

"I wouldn't drag you into the wasteland if I thought
there was risk."

Eleanor was the senior curse hunter at the dining table,
but thanks to a horrific stint as the captive of rogues and
leaching curses, Eleanor was phobic about translating herself into the wasteland. She relied on Emma to get her
there and bring her home to her body again. Em strongly
suspected that it wasn't a sense of curse-hunting duty that
brought Eleanor to her daughter's home to hunt each Fri-

day night, but a desire—a need—to experience the translation.

For hunters, *Think Young* wasn't an advertising slogan;
it was a cardinal rule. Each time they translated themselves
from the curse-ridden wasteland to ordinary reality,
hunters remade themselves according to an internalized
image of self. Eleanor's flawless skin, her smooth, un-
blemished hands all needed regular translation to retain
their youthfulness. Even Emma, who had made no deliberate changes in her fifty-ish appearance, had recently realized that she was less dependent on her assortment of
reading glasses and no longer needed to cover the roots of
her graying hair with applications of permanent dye.

At least she worked for her perks, chasing dozens of
curses each night, annihilating them with beams of laser-
like light, shot from the star of a ruby ring that had once
belonged to her maternal grandmother.

On Fridays, though, Orion's Children hunted rogues.
Rogues were the most dangerous form of curses, a curse
with a body, often several bodies, and an ability to slice
through time and reality that was, if anything, superior to
anything that Emma and her allies possessed. Rogues had
an unquenchable appetite for misery, and they stopped at
nothing to satisfy it.

"What's one Friday night without a rogue hunt?"
Eleanor wheedled. "Call Matt and Nancy and tell them
you're beat to the bone and you're taking the week off.
God, Emma, it's not as if the rogue won't be there next Friday or the Friday after that."

Emma shook her head. Rogues, with their time-hopping
and body-hopping, were harder to track and trap than
Eleanor implied, but they were also creatures of habit and
Blaise Raponde's prey of choice. The rogue Blaise had tar-
geted for this week's hunt was, by his own admission, a
lazy, habit-ridden creature. Maybe he'd picked an easy tar-

get because he'd noticed that his partner wasn't as sharp as she could be?

"I'll call Nancy," she agreed, then corrected herself. "It's too late, they'll be out having dinner."

"Cell phone?" Eleanor said, turning the question into an exasperated reminder.

Emma might be the last person in America who still associated phones with places, not people. She shook her head. "No, they're civilized. They wouldn't want to field a nonemergency call in a restaurant."

"You can't remember the number," Eleanor chided, then recited it from memory.

"I know the number," Em insisted honestly. "I'm just not going to bother them, and everyone near them, with a silly phone call during their dinner. We've made our plans; we'll see them through."

Em picked at her cooling stew.

"Will you at least agree that you need to take a break, if not tonight, then sometime soon?"

Once again, the back of Emma's mind sizzled with the idea that she was being set up. "I don't know, maybe," she conceded before stabbing one of the smaller chunks of potato. "This isn't the first time the library's been turned upside down by an idiot director. Sooner or later, the place rights itself. Entrenched bureaucracy always wins in the end, and with my seniority, I'm entrenched with the best. It's a matter of waiting it out, of being patient." She swallowed the potato and shook her head. "I just don't seem to have the patience I used to have."

It was the closest Emma had come to telling anyone—including herself—that the job she'd held and enjoyed for years had become a millstone. For a moment, she was lightheaded from the revelation. Her hands and feet seemed to belong to another body. She wasn't sure her fingers could find the stem of her goblet or guide the glass to her mouth.

If Eleanor had pressed for confidences or confessions, Em would have been defenseless, but Eleanor—thank heaven—was working from a different script.

"Didn't you schedule a week's vacation for September?"

Em seized the glass stem. "Third week," she admitted. Little more than a month away, though, just then; five weeks might well have been an eternity.

"Then I've got just the ticket for you."

Eleanor smiled triumphantly then reached beneath the table for something she'd stashed on the seat of another chair. Emma wasn't sure what she expected, but it wasn't an inch-high stack of glossy brochures, each featuring sparkling water and an ocean liner on the front.

"I'm not up for a cruise." Emma stifled a vision of oppressive sunlight, sweaty bodies, smarmy gigolos and giglettes, all of them her age or older. "They're not for me."

"Nonsense," Eleanor countered, opening the topmost brochure. "What more could you ask out of a vacation? You check into a hotel, and the hotel moves itself from one tourist trap to the next. Everything's paid for in advance. All you have to do is lie back and be waited on. This ship's got a French spa and four whirlpools that are open twenty-four hours a day. You get four nights of entertainment, two islands, a private beach, and all the wine you can drink— and, if we book tomorrow, a land-package that puts us up in theme-park heaven for three additional nights."

"No."

"All right." Eleanor selected a second brochure. "Here's one for five nights out of Tampa: Key West, two days at sea, and two in Mexico. If you don't want to do the beaches, you can book a tour of the Mayan ruins, and it's *still* going to cost you less per day than staying five nights at the Bower Holiday Inn."

The ruins tempted Emma. She fingered the brochure.

Even the paper was bright. She got migraines from the considerably less bright Michigan sun. And the pictures showed crowds of deeply tanned attractive folk—as if crowds were an asset.

"Usually, when I go on a vacation, I like to get away from it all."

"And where was the last time you actually got away from anything? Anything on *this* side of the Netherlands."

Em had to delve into her memory. Except for a librarians' conference in June she hadn't gone anywhere this year. The previous year, Eleanor's stints in a nursing home and rehab had eaten through Em's banked vacation time. And the year before that, the year Eleanor had shown up on her doorstep, was also the year that her father had died.

"In June I went to Chicago for a long weekend."

"That doesn't count. You were delivering a paper on databases."

"Wrong, that was last December, a different organization, and in Saint Louis. June was the Higher Learning Librarians, and I didn't have to do anything except stay awake and listen."

"That's what I thought. You need a vacation." Eleanor pushed another of the brochures toward Emma's hand.

This paper had an eye-soothing matte finish, and the front pictures, in addition to the obligatory ship-in-profile, included a less-than-bronzed woman reclining in a shaded, comfortable-looking chair, a tall, tropical drink beside her, and no one else in sight, as the sun set in a wash of orange and amber.

"This is probably the most expensive of the lot," Emma said as she dragged the brochure closer and flipped it open.

"So what if it is? The tourist industry isn't exactly going gangbusters these days and, pardon me for pointing this out to you . . . *again* . . . but, in addition to your salary, your savings, and whatever you inherited from your father, you've got a trust fund that's been accumulating nicely for the last fifty years. Live a little, why don't you? Be reckless . . . damn the torpedoes, and reserve an *outside* cabin."

Emma jerked her hand away from the brochure. Had it been that obvious that she'd been looking at the dimensions of the cheapest, interior, hugging-the-water-line cabin? When had Eleanor—oblivious and self-absorbed Eleanor—gotten to know her so well?

"But, alone . . . it would be—" Dawn broke slowly, belatedly over Emma Merrigan's universe. "You mean the two of us—you and I—we should take a cruise together."

"It had crossed my mind."

"Oh."

"I don't snore, Emma, and it wouldn't be a bad idea for you and I to, you know, claim a bit of quality, mother-daughter time."

Em stared silently at her mother's flawless face, her maroon-tipped, auburn hair—still quite avant-guard for Bower, Michigan. No question which of them would be passing for mother and which for daughter.

You could change that, said the voice at the back of Emma's mind, the conscientious voice she'd called her mother-voice all the years when Eleanor hadn't been a factor in her life. Em shook the notion away.

"Why? We're all the family either one of us has!"

Eleanor reached for the brochure. Em put her hand down with weight and kept it in front of her.

"It's not you. It's not anything. A cruise isn't the vacation I would have thought of, but maybe you've got a point. Maybe I need to check into a moving hotel and let the world come to me. Heaven knows I don't have the energy for anything more strenuous. If you can, get some more information about these guys—" She flipped the brochure over, looking for a name. " 'Fantabulous Cruises.' The *Excitation* and *Marvelocity.* Good grief, it sounds like a bubblegum rock band. You'd think both ships would turn pink with shame."

"It's a first-class—"

"No. No, I'm sure it is. What else do I need to know? When it leaves . . . where it goes? Do I have to dress for dinner? Let me know. Try to make it all fit into the third week of September; I don't want to have to beg to change my vacation time. If the price isn't too outlandish."

"Don't worry about the cost. Don't worry about a thing. I'll take care of it all."

Em realized there'd be no backing down—Eleanor could be decisive and efficient when it served her purpose. She was committing herself to a cruise, details to be provided later.

A cruise with Eleanor.

She must be more tired—more weary—than she'd thought.

Eleanor babbled about the *Excitation* and her sister ship's many amenities. Emma let the words pass unhindered into her mind. She was thinking about the picture: alone with a tropical sunset. If Eleanor could deliver that image . . .

A car with mismatched headlights drove slowly past the townhouse. As it passed beneath the street lamp Em made out the lines of an ancient Escort. "Unless I'm mistaken and there's another car with one regular headlight and one xenon headlight cruising the neighborhood, Matt's here, and he's having trouble finding a parking space."

"He's early!" Eleanor complained.

She pushed away from the table and bolted up the stairs to Emma's solitary bathroom, missing the sour look her daughter directed at her back.

"I really should have seen it coming," Emma muttered to herself as she gathered the dishes.

Matt Barto was a computer geek in the best sense of the word. He'd quickly surpassed anything Em could teach him about the library's patched-together systems and their semi-independence from the university's all-encompassing network. He kept their computers running better than any of the last four sys-admins who'd come and gone without leaving a lasting impression in either the computer systems or Emma's memory.

She liked him. Indeed, there'd been a time—before her life became complicated—when she'd begun to like him more than seemed wise or appropriate, which was why, probably, she found Eleanor's behavior so unsettling.

If wishes were horses then Matt Barto would be hunting curses with Orion's Children. The talent—the *wyrd* as Eleanor called it—did sometimes crop up unannounced in the general population of humanity, but it wasn't hiding in Matt's genes. He was one of three ordinary people who knew what Emma and her mother were. The second was Nancy Amstel. Em couldn't have kept her curse hunting a secret from Nancy, who'd been her best friend since elementary school, or from John, Nancy's husband and the third secret sharer. But, if she'd had a choice—if she'd known what the *wyrd* meant—she would have kept it from Matt.

And she surely would have kept Eleanor away from him!

Clearing the table, Em quickly forgot about cruising on the *Excitation* and began counting the reasons a romance between her mother and her friend was a Bad Idea of the highest order. She turned the hot water on full blast and rinsed the dishes with extra vigor. A few more swipes with a soapy sponge and she could have set them directly in the drying rack, but she loaded them into the dishwasher anyway and, since it already held her dishes from Tuesday, Wednesday, and Thursday, dialed up a full wash cycle.

The machine was purring politely when Em strode out of the kitchen and into the scene, where Eleanor and Matt stood in the doorway between the living room and front hall, wrapped in each other's arms like lovers caught by mistletoe at Christmas. Em turned smartly on her heels before they noticed her. She neatened the dish towels and, though the trash can was only half full, knotted the plastic liner and carried it out to the larger can outside the back door.

The storm door slammed behind her, not entirely by accident, and by the time Em returned to the living room the couple had unentwined. Matt offered her a few sheets of paper.

"Based on what you told me, I couldn't find much—and nothing definite. Funny, isn't it? You'd think it would be easier to pinpoint a bar when you had its name and the makes and models of the cars parked outside, but it wasn't. I maybe narrowed it down to a dive on the Baltimore waterfront."

Emma took the paper. "It's really just for curiosity's sake," she admitted. "It's nice to know the where and when, but it's not like we need it, not like there're signposts saying this way to the nineteen-thirties, or turn left here for seventeenth-century Paris."

For a moment Matt's envy showed so clearly on his face that it hurt, and Emma wanted to shove her mother against the nearest wall. Even if Eleanor's motives were pure as the driven snow, the sooner Matt Barto walked away from Orion's proverbial Children, the better. In the meantime, and despite Eleanor's manifest disinterest, Em engaged Matt in a conversation about Maggie Patrick's latest cost-cutting, morale-deadening innovations. Matt, who approached office politics with the same naïveté the rest of the world brought to their computers, was admitting that he was beginning to worry that his days in the library basement, surrounded by servers and free from I-Tech's supervision, were numbered, when Nancy knocked on the front door.

Fifteen minutes later, the four of them were sitting cross-legged (full lotus for Nancy, who'd been taking yoga classes for years) on the carpet. Emma took her mother's hands between her own and began the utterly simple exercise of imagining a coin spinning, falling slowly.

Heads! she thought to herself, and heads it was. The living room was gone, replaced by the wasteland's barren, alien vistas.

Eleanor knelt an arm's length in front of her, looking exactly as she'd looked in the living room. Emma, on the other hand, had translated her clothing from the T-shirt and lightweight jeans that were her off-hours summer uniform to a vaguely medieval dress that covered her arms to the wrist and her legs to the ankles. The dress was a Friday-night concession. Blaise Raponde was too much the gentleman—and too much alone—to object to twenty-first-century styles, but he preferred his lover in more traditionally feminine attire. She'd completely ruled out corsets and all the other figure-modifying devices of his time, but indulged him on Fridays with clothing inspired by stained glass windows and pre-Raphaelite paintings. The other nights she stuck to T-shirts and jeans.

Em looked quickly to her right where a lustrous black stone broke through the parched, dark ground some ten feet away. The stone was the second-fastest way back to her body—Nancy back in Bower and a strategically placed ice cube were the fastest—but so long as Em could get her palms on the way-back stone, she need fear no wasteland rogue or flaming curse.

"A little farther off than usual, aren't we?" Eleanor sniped.

Emma shrugged. "A little," she conceded when she'd risen to her feet. The bolt-hole exerted a magnetic pull on her mind. She guessed it was a quarter mile away, and, true, she usually brought them in quite a bit closer, but a quarter of a mile was nothing in a reality where walking was the only means of transportation. "Maybe this time Harry will be there before us," she mused as she set a good pace in the bolt-hole's direction.

"Harry's not coming."

"What!?" Em spun around to confront her mother. The black stone was still ten feet to her right, maintaining a relative position to its creator in its inexplicable but reliable way.

"I called him this afternoon—about something else entirely—but I knew how weary you were, that you needed a rest—if not an outright vacation. If you must know, he was the one who suggested that, strictly speaking, tonight wasn't necessary—"

"He suggested; you agreed?" Emma raked her hair. If she hadn't been weary before, she was now; and Eleanor was the last person she wanted to share her weariness with.

"I told him I couldn't imagine that you wouldn't agree. It didn't occur to me, or him, that you'd be all damn-the-torpedoes, full-speed ahead."

"We could have called him again, before we left. Let him know we were still on."

Eleanor shook her head from side to side. "He and James were headed out for a quiet dinner in the City. Some new place serving four star's worthy of Provençal cuisine. Trust me, you wouldn't want to interrupt that, even if you could."

To the extent that Emma had assembled Orion's Children as a team for hunting curses and rogues, Harry Graves was one of its members; that didn't mean she was completely comfortable with him. Harry was, by all accounts, the financial wizard who handled the legal affairs for just about every other American curse hunter, enabling them to transfer assets from one carefully crafted identity to the next. He was also the most ancient of the curse hunters that Emma was aware of. He'd been around longer than Blaise Raponde, dead or alive. To hear him tell the tale, Harry had applied his real-world *wyrd* for the winning side in the Revolution.

Lately, Harry wanted to apply them on Emma's behalf.

Em knew she'd eventually have to give in. Harry was almost as good as he thought he was, and she didn't know the first thing about crafting an alternate identity that would survive government scrutiny in the post–9-11 world. But she was holding out. Switching identities meant watching her friends grow old without her, and she didn't want to face that devil even one day sooner than necessary.

Harry Graves could stand in for the devil. After Eleanor walked out on Emma and her father in the early Fifties, she'd wound up married to Harry Graves. Emma had the sense that the marriage had been a sort of penance for both of them, for undefined crimes and indiscretions that, maybe, included abandoning a baby; or, maybe not. Typically, Emma hadn't been able to get a straight answer out of either of them regarding the current state of their marriage. Not that she wasted a lot of time asking questions; they were both reflexive liars.

All the curse hunters were. Lying went with the territory. Emma had gotten pretty good at fabrication herself.

Compared with Harry and Eleanor, Eleanor and Matt were practically the same age. And, compared with Emma herself, Harry looked more like a slightly older brother than a step-father. No wonder she felt chronologically adrift whenever she thought about him.

"Okay, that means we've got to improvise," Em said as she started walking again.

"Improvise, or turn around."

Emma didn't dignify that comment with a response, except to dig her heels into the crumbling ground and walk faster. She'd finalized her improvisations by the time they reached the shallow side of the orange-wedge depression that hid the bolt-hole. She wasn't happy with the tactics she'd concocted, but there really weren't many options.

Eleanor couldn't translate back to the absolute-present reality by herself. In an emergency Matt could pull her through with a well-placed ice cube or pinprick; that's what he was in Em's living room for. They'd tested the theory once, and it *had* worked, though Eleanor had wound up unconscious and woozy for days afterward. For practical purposes, then, Eleanor needed a hunter's help to get home and couldn't be left alone either in the wasteland or the shadows of Baltimore where Orion's Children expected to flush the rogue.

Emma was still at the apprentice stage when it came to flushing rogues. She wasn't about to try flushing one on her own, and, even if she were, she wasn't foolhardy enough to leave Blaise and Eleanor together without witnesses. Oh, they got along all right—better than she and Eleanor did, if politeness were the only measure, but many things could legitimately go wrong when a rogue came barreling onto the wasteland and Em, if push came to shove, couldn't count on her mother and her lover to help each other.

Put all the pieces together and they added up to Blaise going to Baltimore via the bolt-hole window, while she and Eleanor hiked to the wasteland point where they planned to ambush the rogue when it ran away from Blaise.

"We had some bum communications back in the here-and-now," Em explained to her lover, when the three of them were in the bolt-hole.

She deliberately hadn't mentioned Eleanor's name or role in the confusion, but Blaise glared in her mother's direction anyway. Eleanor glowered right back.

"I'll hike out to the rogue's crossover point with Eleanor." Em hadn't exactly lied when she said there were no signposts in the wasteland. There were no pillars and arrows, but it was her particular *wyrd* to know the correspondence between parched dirt and historical reality, the way plants knew sun from soil. Emma couldn't describe the point where they expected to confront the rogue—it would look no different than any other patch of wasteland dirt, but she could find it with a thought. "The two of us will be waiting when the rogue comes through."

"*If* it comes through," Blaise corrected sourly. "With only myself to drive it *au-delà,* there is a greater chance it will veer away from where we expect it."

Em decided to put a stop to the bickering. "It's the exact same chance you had for the three hundred years you hunted rogues by your lonesome. If it veers, it veers, but if it doesn't, Eleanor and I will be waiting with bells on. It *won't* get away."

Blaise sank into thought. By his own admission, three hundred years of solitude had transformed him into a more patient, pragmatic man than he'd been during his natural lifetime; and when it came to mooting curses or rogues, there was no denying the fierce determination Eleanor brought to the battlefield.

"Ah," he declared with a shrug. He reached for his coat and hat.

In those rare moments when Emma was awake before the alarm went off and she seized the opportunity to wonder how much of her life was really real and how much could be attributed to imagination or hallucination, she always came back to Blaise Raponde's clothing. She could never have imagined his dark-green damask coat with its huge lapels and incongruously striped patch pockets, or his broad-brimmed hat with its off-center array of natural and dyed feathers. They were both clearly the products of fashion in one of its more absurd moments.

Blaise's trousers were even more outlandish than his hat, being little more than balloons of damask slung from a belt and tied off at the knees like a pair of empty sausage casings. Or they had been; once Blaise had gotten a look at Harry Graves, he'd transformed his baggy pants into tailored slacks. He'd abandoned his flowing bleached linen shirts at the same time in exchange for the dark, silken turtlenecks Harry favored.

The final effect as Blaise wound a bleached-linen scarf around the turtleneck and tucked the lacy ends beneath his coat was less jarring than it might have been, but still completely beyond the reach of Em's imagination.

"When you're right, Madame Mouse, you're right."

About the time that Emma would convince herself of her lover's reality—if the alarm clock hadn't gone off—she'd hit the language wall. Though Em occasionally emitted an idiom that Blaise didn't comprehend, and he sometimes lapsed into indecipherable French, the vast bulk of their conversation occurred in colloquial American English of the early third millennium. It wasn't some mystic, magic, mental communication, either: Now that she'd had an opportunity to watch Blaise speaking to someone else—Eleanor or Harry—Em was satisfied that his lips and tongue were shaping English phrases.

How, Em would ask herself, could Blaise's clothes be so unimaginably authentic and his language so utterly familiar? Then the clock radio would begin to play, or he'd give her a kiss for luck, and all the nagging questions would recede.

Blaise picked up one of two identical foot-high hourglasses sitting on a dark-wood sideboard.

"Shall we?" he asked, flipping it over so the sand began to trickle.

Emma quickly flipped the other as Blaise headed for the leaded glass window that dominated one side of the bolthole. In yet another wasteland paradox, the window did not open onto solid dirt and rock. Most of the time it faced out on an autumnal garden Emma had copied from a painting that had hung over her bed in her childhood room, but it also functioned as a gateway into the shadow past, where curse hunters pursued their elusive prey. As Blaise approached the window, the garden scene darkened, as if the moon had overtaken the sun to cause a total eclipse. The view was midnight when Blaise lifted the latch and pulled the casement open—midnight broken by the glare of old-fashioned streetlights on damp pavement and the orange-red of a neon sign glowing somewhere just out of sight.

"*À bientôt,*" Blaise said with a grin, as he threw a leg over the windowsill.

"*À bientôt,*" Em agreed, because sometimes French was more romantic, more fun.

Blaise disappeared almost at once, the streetlights, too. The eclipse ended, and the garden reappeared. Em turned to Eleanor.

"We'd better get a move on."

Half the sand and then some had descended into the hourglass's lower bulb before Emma and her mother reached the place her gut said was the wasteland equivalent of the street Blaise had entered from the window. Though the wasteland lacked landmarks, it was not entirely featureless. The parched dirt rolled gently between hills that were, perhaps, some twenty feet high and a quarter mile apart. Em positioned herself, the hourglass, and the way-back stone on the crest of a hill. She watched as Eleanor hiked another several hundred yards to the crest of the next hill.

No sun shone in the wasteland. What little light reached the ground was filtered through the dense, magenta clouds. Hunters could see one another at a distance only by an act of will that surrounded each of them with a faintly silver nimbus. Withdraw that will, as first Emma then Eleanor did, and the women became virtually invisible in the deep, threatening twilight. The last of the sand fell unnoticed into the lower bulb while Emma—and her mother—kept watch for the rogue.

Emma knew what to look for: a brief shower of sparks followed by the emergence of a dark silhouette or a pillar of flame, depending on the shape the rogue brought to the wasteland. But she was more often Blaise's Friday-night partner, flushing rogues from their chronological lairs, and was unaccustomed to the role of ambusher. As a result, though Em spotted the sparks, Eleanor got off the first mooting blast.

And an impressive blast it was. Every hunter chose his or her weapon. After several unsuccessful experiments, Emma had settled on the ruby ring and its thin streak of red, laser-like light. Blaise coaxed a broader beam of golden light from the amber pommel of his sword. Both were potent weapons, but neither compared to the swath of flame Eleanor brought forth from the tip of a sparkling and beribboned Lucite wand.

The rogue let out an ear-splitting shriek and a gout of sticky flame that raced along the ground toward Eleanor. Emma had her wits about her then. Rising swiftly to one knee, Em imitated the snipers she'd seen in numerous movies. She braced her right arm with her left and, sighting down her forearm as if her ring were the muzzle of a rifle, she took aim at the stream of fire creeping Eleanor's way.

The ruby ring came alive on Emma's finger. Beneath magenta skies, the beam it unleashed seemed less red light than a dense ebony shadow, but there was no doubting its power. It scorched a line across the dirt that the rogue's creeping flame couldn't cross. Then, when Em was satisfied that her mother's position was secure, she brought her wrath on the white-hot body of the rogue itself.

Be gone! she thought, and *Be reduced to your component atoms, your electrons, protons, and neutrons, your quarks and your strings!*

It was easier to annihilate a rogue when it manifested as alien flame than when it appeared with one of its stolen human faces. Emma focused her wrath and concentrated on burning a dark line across the middle of the rogue's brilliant fiery pillar. She was about a third of the way through her self-appointed task when she realized that Blaise had arrived.

When all was said and done, the rogue was doomed from the moment it chose to stand against Eleanor's flame; and once Blaise added his will to the fight, the rogue withered and was quickly reduced to a charred stain on the dark ground. Emma and her companions continued to paint the stain with their chosen weapons for several moments, like firemen soaking the ruins of a three-alarm fire. Blaise stood down first, then Emma. Eleanor didn't let up until Emma shouted her name.

"We got it?" she asked after Emma and Blaise had walked into conversation distance. When she fought, Eleanor slipped into a rage as blind and timeless as any rogue's.

"Like clockwork," Em assured her.

Eleanor began to tremble. She dropped her wand and hid her face behind her hands. Had Harry been with them, he would have put his arm around Eleanor's shoulders and helped her to her feet. But Harry was off having a fancy dinner with his housemate, and Emma was late off the mark coming to her mother's aid.

"We'd better be going," she said to Blaise, who never seemed quite convinced by Eleanor's post-rogue performances.

"You'll be returning?" he countered, and when Emma nodded he began the lonely walk to the bolt-hole.

She walked close to Eleanor, who remained seated on the ground.

"That was a bad one," Eleanor whispered. "I could see its face the whole time."

Em didn't challenge the assertion. The wasteland was a subjective reality. Expectations mattered, and hunters took different memories away from the same event. Eleanor took rogues more personally than her daughter did. It was no wonder, then, if Eleanor saw them wearing faces, even faces she recognized.

"Are you ready to go home?"

Eleanor shook her head and shoulders together. "I don't know how many more of these I can handle."

If Eleanor could doubt, then Eleanor could stand. Emma braced herself and brought her mother with her as she stood. The way-back stone was in its customary position, a few feet to her right.

"You don't have to come—I mean, you're wanted and appreciated, but not if it's ripping you apart. The three of us—"

"You'd miss more than you'd moot." Eleanor took her weight onto her own feet. "And then the ones that get away will start comparing notes, and it will get even harder. You need me. You need what I bring. And, besides, I'm not talking about quitting. I won't quit until they're all gone, every last curse and rogue. It's just . . . I need—"

"A vacation?" Em asked with forged innocence.

"That would be nice."

Em dropped to her knees beside the way-back stone with a sigh. No wonder Blaise viewed Eleanor with constant suspicion. She reached her left hand back to grasp her mother's before placing her right on the stone's unnaturally smooth, cold surface.

"Brace—"

The translation was uneventful, effortless. Em was her complete, unified self again, sitting comfortably on her living room floor.

"—yourself."

The clock read 8:20. They'd been hunting rogues for barely ten minutes.

Two

Bower's transition from summer to autumn swept by in a blur, accented only by the days immediately preceding and following Labor Day. Those were the days when the students returned, or arrived for the first time, days the permanent members of the U's extended family referred to as *Eek Week*. Though the library was spared the worst of the onslaught and Em generally looked forward to the annual dose of energy the students brought with them, their presence, along with Maggie Patrick's ongoing campaign to remake the library in her own image, added hours to Em's work week.

Left to her own devices, Em would have scheduled no preparation more strenuous than a haircut for her third-week-of-September vacation. But, of course, Emma's vacation had strayed far from her devices. Once she'd nodded her head and authorized her mother to check into Fantabulous Cruises, the downward slide from Michigan to a four-night adventure aboard the *Excitation* had been inevitable. Eleanor had cheerfully done all the work except for packing Em's suitcases; and she probably would have done that, too, if Em hadn't decided to start her vacation a day early and in front of her bedroom closet.

Emma didn't remember when Eleanor suggested that they drive, rather than fly, to Florida. She certainly didn't remember agreeing to the eleven-hundred-mile road trip, but surprisingly, it turned out to be a good idea. Em had been driving her "new" car for nearly a year without driving it farther than Kalamazoo. Pointing the Integra's nose down I-75 proved more enjoyable, more invigorating than any airport-to-airport jet journey could have been, especially in the brave new era of multiple ID checks, unlocked luggage, and shoe searches. The hardest part of the drive had been getting two cabin-sized suitcases into the Integra's hatchback, and Em met that challenge on the second try.

They'd broken their trek in Kentucky, spending the night in a motel overlooking the hills and valleys of a national forest. The Kentucky trees were still wearing their summer's green, and an evening's walk to a nearby lake had been marred by mosquitoes the size of the jets they were avoiding. Still, the sunset had been spectacular, and when Emma escaped from the motel bed to the wasteland bolt-hole, Blaise commented that one day of vacation—a concept Emma had struggled to explain—had lightened his lover's mood and brightened her eyes.

They reached Port Canaveral on Florida's east coast late Saturday afternoon—too late for a tour of the Space Center, though not too late to walk up to the gate. The air was hot and thick with the threat of thunderstorms, and an impressive display of lightning did drive them back to the car, but not before Emma got to lay eyes on a for-real rocket standing at its launch pad. No matter what else happened, Eleanor's vacation had allowed Emma to draw a line through one of the many items on her lifetime to-do list.

"You were right," she admitted to her mother over an

unremarkable dinner in a NASA-themed restaurant. "I needed to get away."

"You're talking as if it's all over. The fun hasn't started yet. Just wait until tomorrow!"

Em didn't argue. She was feeling mellow, which she hadn't been in months and was almost able to imagine herself in a deck chair, sipping a frosty, bright-colored drink out of a glass sporting a little paper umbrella.

That sense of pleasant anticipation carried Em through the evening. She made her nightly trek to the wasteland, but her mind wasn't set on annihilation, and Blaise was nowhere to be found around the bolt-hole. Emma shrugged off her disappointment. For centuries, stalking rogues had been the pivot point of her lover's existence. With their weekly Friday-night hunts on hold until Em and Eleanor returned to Bower, Blaise had warned her that he might go off to do some solitary hunting.

Sunday morning, Emma followed the signs to Port Canaveral where the *Excitation* was docked. Though clearly marked, the route seemed circuitous and her attention was riveted on driving until they were in the port complex itself. The sparkling white mass of the *Excitation,* looming above the embarkation building, caught her by surprise.

"Good grief," she muttered. "It's *huge.* I've never seen a ship that big." Which, though true, didn't mean much. Michigander that she was, Em's personal exposure to saltwater vessels had been limited to the fishing boats and yachts she'd seen during infrequent childhood trips to New England. "It's got to be bigger than the *Titanic.*"

"Oh, it is. Maximum of about twenty-five hundred passengers and nearly a thousand crew." Eleanor had been doing nothing but her homework and repacking her suitcases for the last month. Her *Secret Guide to Fantabulous Cruises*—a spiral-bound collection of information she'd peeled from the Internet—lay open in her hands.

The guide was a compilation of tips and tidbits pertaining to the *Excitation* and its identical twin, the *Marvelocity*. Emma had read it twice, but Eleanor had very nearly memorized it.

"If something happens to this baby . . . But it won't. There *are* plenty of lifeboats, and no one's seen an iceberg between here and St. Thomas since the end of the Ice— Ooh, turn there!"

Em hung a left and got the car in line to disgorge its luggage to a cohort of uniformly smiling stevedores. Eleanor got out of the car with the suitcases.

"I'll get us in line for embarkation. You just remember where you park the car. They've got a lost car service, but we don't want to be late on Thursday! I want three full days at the theme parks!"

Emma nodded. In late August, Eleanor's target had shifted from a weeklong cruise on the *Excitation* to a four-day one, with three days tacked on for visiting the theme parks in nearby Orlando. Em would rather have had more time at Cape Kennedy and a visit to the Everglades, but the Everglades—at least the visitors' part of the Everglades— were a day's drive from the seaport, and the Space Center couldn't compete with Mickey Mouse, Dr. Seuss, and special-effects movies turned into roller coasters.

Em had visited the parks back when she was busy raising her second husband's children, Jeff Jr. and Laurie. The three-day stay had been one of the high points of their years as a family. She'd resisted Eleanor's change of focus on account of those memories but had given in when Eleanor insisted that she'd never seen the famous Mouse except on television.

Em handed her charge card to another smiling man in a cartoonish, striped jacket at the entrance to the long-term parking lot, then snaked among the rows of cars, most of them from Florida, looking for an empty space. She duly noted the number of the space on the back of a business card and tucked it into her wallet.

Eleanor was midway through one of more than a dozen embarkation lines when Emma caught up with her. They sailed through the question-and-answer session when they reached the counter and were directed to a neon-framed embarkation tunnel where they were questioned again, this time with an eye toward security. Their carry-ons were x-rayed, while they were wanded and questioned a third time, then it was into the second half of the neon-striped tunnel, which opened into the wide, rock-solid gangway.

A calypso band in elaborate costume welcomed Emma, Eleanor, and all the other passengers. Emma, who found the music infectiously bright, wanted to stand and listen, but Eleanor had other ideas.

"Later!" She took Emma's wrist like she was a wayward child. "They'll be playing for hours. We've got work to do. First we've got to find our way to the cabin."

Em let herself be towed away from the band. She knew their cabin number and its location on the map the travel agent had given Eleanor, but she had no clear sense of where they were. Not so for Eleanor, who marched past the elevators. "Too crowded, and we don't need them anyway. We're only two decks down."

The cabin was a pleasant surprise. Em truly thought an outside cabin was an unnecessary luxury and expense, especially as Eleanor's to-do list for the next four nights and three days left them with barely enough time to sleep. Eleanor had stood her ground and won a porthole—but what a porthole! The round window was easily four feet in diameter and dominated the far end of a partitioned room. A king-sized bed nearly filled all of the space in the near part. Even so, there was ample room for the women to slip past each other on their way to the porthole portion where a comfy sofa provided a good view of both the sea and a state-of-the-art entertainment center.

Mirrors added to the sense of spaciousness. Those parts of the interior walls that weren't mirrored were paneled in a gold-colored wood that continued into the built-in cabinets, drawers, tables, and two tiny closets. The carpets were blue, and the drapes and bedspread were nautically themed in complementary colors. The undeniably compact bathroom was fitted out with (according to Eleanor's research) creamy Italian marble that was more durable than painted wood or enamel. The whole cabin could have passed for a parlor room in a land-based hotel, except for the inch-high railings that rimmed about every flat surface and the detailed water-conservation instructions posted on the shower door.

"I like it," Emma decided when she'd finished her inspection. "It's a lot bigger than I thought it would be, and the porthole, it really makes a difference."

Eleanor wisely resisted the temptation to celebrate her victory.

They'd beaten their luggage to the cabin, but their embarkation package was waiting for them on the bed—exactly where Eleanor expected it to be.

"Do you think you can find your way to Gondolas"—that being the name of the value-added haute *Italienne* restaurant where Eleanor had determined they would eat exactly one dinner—"or would you rather make our reservations at the spa?" she asked after scattering all but one of the embarkation papers across the bed.

"I'll find my way to the restaurant."

"You're sure you don't want me to reserve something for you: a massage? How about aromatherapy? Not even a dip in the herbal bath? It's got over a hundred synchronized water jets."

Emma understood the need to book a special meal in an adults-only dining room that caught the sunset and overlooked the ocean. She was less convinced that she needed to drop a hundred or so dollars in the European spa that offered a variety of pseudo-science "therapies" and made promises that no *American* establishment would have dared.

"You're making a big mistake."

Em hated sales pressure. She looked down at the papers in her hand. They were no help: lists of Bahamian excursions and the duty-free temptations that would become available once they'd cleared U.S. waters. The welcoming calypso music, with its infectious "don't worry" melodies echoed in her mind. Without warning, her ability to resist vanished.

"All right," Em heard herself say, "sign me up for the synchronized herbal bath—"

"And a manicure?"

Em was at a loss for words: In fifty-plus years of sober, Midwestern living she'd never come close to a manicure. It was, well . . . *decadent*—not something the daughter of an engineering professor *did* with her spare time, her spare money.

"A pedicure, then? Let me pay for it— call it a late birthday present, an early Christmas gift. Emma, dear, you've got to loosen up!"

The thought of a stranger handling her feet pushed Em to the verge of panic. She capitulated to a manicure. A manicure was definitely less decadent than a pedicure.

"There, that wasn't so hard. You see, you decided to do something for yourself, and the world didn't come to an end."

Emma nodded weakly. She pocketed their meal tickets and followed the red arrows woven into the corridor carpet that pointed aft.

"Don't forget—last night, second seating. And try to get a table in the San Marco section, or the Piazza section. The sunset view's better from there. And don't worry about coming back here and waiting for me. If we meet on deck someplace, that's fine, otherwise, remember that we've got to be here at three-thirty for the disaster drill, and you've *got* to be here for that. No exceptions. They'll toss us off the boat."

Em looked at her watch: one-thirty. Two hours on her own, even if she spent them waiting in a line, sounded like a good idea. Her mother's enthusiasm was infectious, but exhausting.

Contrary to what it said in Eleanor's *Secret Guide to Fantabulous Cruises,* there was no endless line waiting to make reservations at Gondalos. A mere three people stood in front of Emma, and when her turn came, there were plenty of tables left in the San Marco section.

"Would you like special service?" the crew-woman asked as she filled out a brightly colored reservation card. "A birthday? Anniversary? We have a Romantic Evening package with champagne in collectible glasses—"

Em shook her head. "We're just two friends on vacation together."

The crew-woman—her name tag read "Renata"—smiled sagely. "We have just the thing: a Festivo Italiano package with your choice of a tropical drink in collectible glasses and a chocolate volcano for dessert. It's only twenty dollars extra for two, a real bargain."

Em thought she was appalled by the idea, but some free-radical spirit had seized control of her tongue. "Why not?" it said. "Put us down for the Festivo."

She was still wondering what had come over her when she left the restaurant.

The "don't worry" sounds of the calypso band wafted softly up from the gangway. They'd have competition soon, though. Another band was setting up its instruments beside one of the three pools Em could see from the top-deck railing. Gaggles of crewmembers in jumpsuits of various colors were erecting a buffet with military precision in the gap between two of the pools. Watching a huge bowl of shrimp pass beneath her, Em remembered that she hadn't eaten since breakfast, some six hours earlier.

Em's weren't the only eyes the shrimp bowl attracted. A crowd was already forming at the open-air buffet, a larger crowd than she cared to mingle with. But if there was one thing Eleanor and the *Secret Guide* had taught Em, it was that *Excitation* cruisers had no excuse for hunger. There were food depots scattered throughout the ship, all of them serving free food to passengers. With her ship map—already showing fuzz along the creases from the number of times Em had refolded it—firmly in hand, Em made her way down one deck to a buffet line every bit as overflowing as the one she'd seen forming between the pools, but indoors, air-conditioned, and protected from the sun.

A model of restraint, Em built herself a modest sandwich, surrounded it with small dollops of a handful of salads, and skipped desert altogether. Then, though there were empty tables all around, she carried her tray outside where she was able to find a shaded table with a view of the Atlantic Coast. She missed the novels she'd packed into her suitcase but the view up toward Cape Kennedy made up for it. Her thoughts wandered, recalling the history that rockets had made. She saw, but not quite noticed, storm clouds gathering. They darkened the eastern sky from the coastline to the horizon.

She'd finished her sandwich and was starting to think she'd acted just a little precipitously by choosing to walk past the dessert island, when Eleanor showed up bearing a tray with more than enough dessert and everything else for two.

"I'd hoped for a few more men," Eleanor announced. "A few more *unattached* men. They're young enough—no overabundance of knobby knees on this ship, thank heaven—but they all seem to be traveling with their families."

Emma, who had vetoed more than one attempt to book

passage on a singles cruise, said nothing, except to ask if she could claim the strawberries and cream.

"Go ahead. I'm only planning to sample. Just save me a bite."

The berries had the taste of forbidden fruit. Em savored every juicy bite but silently envied Eleanor's blithe ability to content herself with a forkful of chocolate-chocolate cake, another of key lime pie, a spoonful of tropically bright tira misu, the last of the strawberries, *and* most of a bowl of melting chocolate-fudge ice cream.

"Let's take a walk," Eleanor suggested.

Em raised her eyebrows. "It'd have to be a very long one to make up for what we're going to eat over the next four days."

Eleanor made a face, and they left the table behind.

They achieved a useful, if not particularly long, walk, exploring the decks and outposts where the ship's passengers could congregate, then returned to their cabin in time to hear a speaker directly above their bed summon them to the disaster drill. With two thousand other guests, the women donned their orange life vests and trekked to their designated lifeboat station.

"The ship's owners didn't like the looks of orange lifeboats," Eleanor told the dozen-plus men and women gathered by the boat, quoting her *Secret Guide* from memory. "So they got permission to paint them yellow, instead. Too bad they couldn't have done something about these things." She tugged on the straps of the bulky, but presumably reliable, vest.

To Em's dismay, her lifeboat companions were unfamiliar with the *Secret Guide* and devoured Eleanor's bits of trivia, until, after clipboard-bearing crew members had approved the passengers' formations, an all-clear was sounded. Emma let a fascinated couple with two children in tow get between her and Eleanor as they left the lifeboat.

Two large and familiar suitcases waited outside their cabin. Wrestling them inside was a challenge, but unpacking them was easier than Em had expected. She and Eleanor had already divvied up the storage space, which was more than sufficient for the paraphernalia they'd brought. When her suitcase was empty and back out in the corridor, Emma settled on the sofa at right angles to the porthole and began sorting through the books and needlework she'd brought for amusement. Eleanor rearranged her belongings among the shelves, drawers, and closets for the second or third time.

By the time Emma helped move Eleanor's suitcase into the hall, her own suitcase had vanished and it was nearly time for the *Excitation* to push itself away from its dock.

"She doesn't need help. No tugboats. No tugboats at all when we spend Wednesday on our private island. She can line herself up and scoot *sideways* . . . in or out. She can pivot, too, right around her middle."

"I know, I know. I read the guide, Eleanor. I read everything you gave me. Honest. You don't have to lecture."

Eleanor deflated. "I just want you to have fun. You need fun. You don't laugh anymore. You hardly ever smile."

"I'm having fun." Em pointed at the sofa where hobbies were strewn across the cushions and piled on the coffee table.

"I mean the kind of fun you can only have on a cruise. You could sit in your own living room sewing little flowers."

"But I don't. I haven't had time to read or work on my embroidery since I don't know when. And they're not little flowers. They're butterflies, stumpwork butterflies."

"Now who's lecturing? Come on, let's go upstairs—*topside*—and party!"

Emma laughed—it had been a long time, too long—and tapped her slacks pocket to assure herself that she had her *Excitation* passport, the little plastic rectangle that served not only as their cabin key but as a credit card for any shipboard purchases she might make.

The calypso band had reassembled itself near the stern, and toward the bow, a quartet of energetic twenty-some-things in psychedelic band uniforms played some of Em's favorite classic rock from the Sixties. Em, who usually strove not to march to the beat of anyone's drum, succumbed to the Beatles.

Beside her, Eleanor asked, "Champagne?" and despite the beverage's proven ability to give her a migraine, Emma nodded her head. Eleanor disappeared and reappeared moments later with two plastic flutes of bubbling blond alcohol.

Costumed crew people, dripping with sequins, joined the band then descended from the stage to mingle with the increasingly giddy passengers. Emma wasn't nearly tipsy enough to dance with anyone dressed up as Little Bo Peep. She faded back to the edge of the gathering and took note of the dark clouds that were mounded up over the Atlantic. No wonder the festivities seemed a touch frantic: There was a storm coming, and the *Excitation* was headed straight for it.

A nursery-rhyme melody from the ship's horn signaled the awaited moment when the lines were cast off. Em drained her champagne, set the empty flute on one of countless tables, and headed for the railing. From her vantage point overlooking the wharf, Em couldn't see if there were tugboats guiding the ship or if the *Excitation* was moving under her own power, but, sure enough, she was moving broadside through the water. Far above the waterline, Em could barely feel the engines through her feet; she felt nothing at all when the ship stopped moving sideways and began moving forward.

Eleanor joined Em at the rail, two more champagne flutes in her hands. "Pretty cool, huh?"

"Pretty cool," Em agreed, taking the flute Eleanor thrust her way. "And it better be pretty fast, too."

She gestured toward the eastern clouds just as they were laced by lightning. Thunder followed, louder than the bands and the ship's horn combined.

"Wow—I didn't even notice!"

"You don't notice the engines, either. I think that's the whole idea. This isn't a ship, it's a place that moves . . . like the whole planet's a place that moves. You don't see it. You don't feel it. Weather's just something to be plowed through and ignored."

"So you don't think we need to . . . well, go *below*?"

Emma looked from the storm to the celebration. The bands were still playing, and passengers still danced, but the second tier of crew—the visible workers in color-coded uniforms as opposed to the entertainers or the white-suited invisibles who tended the ship rather than the passengers—were harvesting food from the buffet tables. The costumed performers had already vanished. She shrugged before answering. "I think they'll tell us if we need to come in out of the rain. It's not like they haven't done this before, and the media would have a heyday if Fantabulous Cruises damaged its ships or passengers on a regular basis."

Eleanor looked relieved. "I'd better get more champagne before it all disappears. What about you?"

"I'm already two glasses past my limit."

"You can't be! We get free wine with dinner and a cordial afterward."

"Not me. My heavy drinking days ended ages ago."

Emma caught her breath. She'd gone all day without giving a thought to herself as one of Orion's Children. She'd thought of Eleanor as "mother" once or twice, but that label had been defanged—she no longer bothered herself with imagining what Eleanor *should* look like or even what she had looked like a scant year ago.

"Are you all right?" Eleanor asked, taking Em's arm.

Em nodded. "A stray thought, that's all."

She was spared the need to say more as another thunder clap, louder and sharper than the first, rolled across the *Excitation*. Now everyone noticed the clouds overhead. The passengers looked for shelter. The bolder ones joined Em and Eleanor at the rail, which was sheltered by the round-the-ship, open-air jogging track one deck up, while a greater number headed for the fully enclosed decks below. With the next thunderclap, rain began to fall—large, widely scattered raindrops that left inch-wide marks on the teak decks and were merely the advance guard for the storm that was sure to follow. Someone wisely pulled the plug on the bands, whose members dashed for a door marked "Crew Only." Invisibles, all of whom appeared more foreign than the rest of the crew, swarmed to break down the electrical equipment.

Like an army, Em mused, *a well-disciplined army.* This might be all new to the passengers, but the crew had seen it before and knew exactly what to do. Certainly the ship's officers had. The *Excitation* continued its steady progress through the channel that separated Port Canaveral from the ocean.

Dry beneath the jogging deck, Emma and Eleanor made their way forward. There were no tugs that they could see guiding the *Excitation,* only a handful of Zodiac motorized rafts buzzing around them and another all-white ship preceding them through the channel. The rain intensified; the lightning and thunder did too. It almost drowned out the monotone blasts from the horn of the third cruise ship to join the procession to the sea.

The brochures touted the Port Canaveral cruises as adventures. In truth, they were clockwork packages, scheduled down to the last available minutes. The only adventure was watching the *Excitation* and her cousins charge into weather that would have daunted the boldest sailor of any earlier era.

Emma and Eleanor stayed at their forward posts until the last channel buoy slid by the bow. A pair of officers emerged from the bridge to work fold-down control panels on either side of the forward bridge deck.

"Stabilizers," Eleanor said, quoting her *Secret Guide* again. "It'll take a forty-knot wind to rock us . . . or maybe we can make forty knots forward speed once the stabilizers are out. I'll have to check—"

The danger with memorizing something you didn't understand was that you couldn't always tell whether your quotes were accurate. Em didn't mind. The engineering gene was captivated by the least indication that human hands and human decisions, not computers, guided the *Excitation*. She inched along the rail overlooking the forward bridge deck until she found the precise spot where her view of the working officer was as good as it could be without exposing herself entirely to the rain.

By then the rain was coming down in wind-driven torrents. But there was no reason to worry. There was an interior door in easy, if not quite dry, walking distance, and with the twenty or so other stalwarts, they retreated to the underwater decor of the lobby outside the spa where Eleanor had scheduled Emma for hydrotherapy and a manicure for Monday afternoon.

"We'll surely have finished our shopping by then. Nassau's going to be our walking day, though. You really should have let me schedule you for a pedicure and foot massage. Nothing like a foot massage after a day of shopping and sightseeing."

Eleanor bent over to shake water from her copper-and-purple hair onto the pale blues and greens of the carpet, utterly oblivious to the stares of the spa employees. The short, ragged hairstyle that Eleanor favored lay closer to her head when she straightened up, but otherwise it looked no worse, or better, for its exposure to the storm. Emma wished she could say the same for her own appearance. Her hair took on a frizzy life of its own the moment it was struck by even a single raindrop. She hustled Eleanor through the double doors that connected the spa with the ship's high-priced cabins.

"I'm going to need a hair dryer before we go to dinner," she conceded when they'd descended to their own deck.

"Dinner's not the first event on our schedule. We're second seating, remember. The *Secret Guide* recommended that families take the first seating, 'cause it's easier on the kids, and the second seating for unaccompanied adults, so we don't have to deal with the families. We took their advice: Nightly entertainment first, then a leisurely dinner with the adults afterward."

When her hair was back under control, Emma zipped up her dressiest black slacks and her favorite silk blouse, a high-neck, bishop-sleeved number in satiny royal blue. She added jewelry—a gold chain necklace and hoop earrings—and was satisfied with her appearance until she looked across the cabin to Eleanor, also in black slacks and a silk blouse, albeit a fire-engine red, spaghetti-strapped, lingerie-lacy blouse.

There was not a chance in the universe that anyone would mistake them for anything but a mother and daughter combo; and no way anyone would mistake her for Eleanor's daughter.

"Ready?"

It was too late to change her clothes. Emma grabbed the tiny, beaded purse she'd borrowed from Nancy and followed Eleanor out the door.

The *Excitation*'s first-night entertainment was a somewhat incongruous cross between theme-park wholesome and Las Vegas glitz. Instantly forgettable, its first act had blurred into Em's memory before the second act began, though she'd managed to hang on to one image: the gentle sway of the proscenium curtains as the ship sliced through sea and weather.

"What did you think of the guy playing Horatio?" Eleanor asked while they waited to progress through the shopping arcade to their appointed dining room.

Horatio, Emma vaguely remembered, had been the name of the male lead in the thinly plotted spectacle. "Good voice. Lots of energy."

"And his looks?"

Emma shrugged. "Blond. Very blond, unless he was wearing a wig."

"Ach," Eleanor muttered in apparent disgust. "Why even bother to ask? They've got to be dark and broody before you'll notice them."

Em opened her mouth to protest, then shut it again: The truth stung more than she cared to admit.

They showed their plastic passport cards and were ushered to a circular table for eight, already half full. Introductions were made, and Emma made an effort to remember the names: Sarah and Jim, young newlyweds— Emma didn't expect to see much of them. Art and Gracie, an older couple who proudly announced that this was their fifth cruise aboard the *Excitation*. In short order they were joined by another Sarah, a glamorous thirty-something, traveling alone with Tiffany, her I-don't-want-to-be-here daughter, who looked to be ten or eleven; and Daniel, also thirty-something and traveling with a teen-aged daughter, whose whisper-spoken name eluded Em's hearing.

Service at the table proceeded under the watchful eye of a table captain: Draco, a Croatian whose command of the English language was better than that of his three hardworking helpers. According to Draco, answering Daniel's question, except for the command officers, the *Excitation*'s crew was made up almost entirely of foreign nationals who signed on for six-month stints. Draco was midway through his third stint and sending enough money home that he could keep his two children in private schools.

"Does the crew turn over completely at the same time?" Em asked.

Draco shook his head. "Every cruise, a few come, a few leave."

Mitya, who at that moment was putting an oversized menu into Em's hands, added that this was only her second cruise and she was still getting lost almost as often as the passengers. Eleanor asked which country she called home.

"I am Russian," she replied, which got Em thinking about the potential political fallout within a truly international crew.

Ordering dinner went smoothly, though Emma, spoiled by the variety of restaurants available to the residents of a university town, had hoped for something more exotic than the half-dozen menu offerings, four of them seafood. She settled on a bouillabaisse pasta and agreed to share her cntrée with Eleanor, who ordered steak, rare, and a baked potato, loaded. Between the departure of the menus and the arrival of the wine, Emma studied the dining room.

There were three dining rooms aboard the *Excitation*. Tonight, they were in Rocaille where the decor, from the pebbles-and-shells carpeting to the undulating white ceiling, recalled a bright-colored coral reef. Schools of holographic fish swam in the air above their heads, and probably— Emma realized belatedly—were the reason for all the fish on the menu. Tomorrow, Draco would oversee their table in Chelsea's Place, which the *Secret Guide* described as an art deco wonderland, where, over the course of their meal, the lighting would shift from white to rainbows. Tuesday, they'd be in Xanadu with cut-glass mosaics on the floor, ceilings, and walls. They were, however, sailing a *four*-night cruise, meaning Draco's dining passengers were scheduled to return to Rocaille for their last dinner at sea, which was why Eleanor, following the *Secret Guide*'s advice, had sent

Emma after fourth-night reservations at the one shipboard restaurant where Draco could not attend to their every dining need.

Em was only halfway through the appetizer of her first dinner, and already could feel twinges of guilt and disloyalty, as though Draco's children might have to leave their private school because of her mother's obsession with the *Secret Guide.* And who knew what censure might befall Mitya, who'd bobbled their wine order, mistakenly bringing Em another glass of champagne.

Half-aware, Em cast a glance around the dining room, looking for Mitya, a rangy young woman in a waiter's tuxedo with long, dark hair confined in a loose braid. Her vision snagged, instead, on a different server—a young woman who was shorter and sturdier than Mitya. The woman's hair matched Eleanor's unnatural rusty auburn; perhaps they used the same brand of dye. She was clear across the large room, yet Em would swear that the young woman's eyes were a pale gray and that they were staring at each other. Before Emma could refocus herself, an unexpected thought flashed through her mind: *There's trouble traveling with that girl.*

The thought lingered even after Em spotted Mitya hurrying across the room, a cocktail tray bearing a single wine goblet held high over her head. Emma closed her eyes: She'd ordered *white* zinfandel, the blushing non-wine, not regular dark red zinfandel, which, on top of two glasses of champagne, was sure to give her a migraine. But she wouldn't send it and Mitya back again. If Draco noticed the mistake—and he'd caught the champagne error before Mitya had set the fluted glass on the table—Em vowed she'd insist that Draco had mis-remembered her order.

And she did, earning herself a sharp, sidelong glance from their table captain.

"What was that all about?" Eleanor demanded.

"Nothing," Em said and stabbed into her Caesar salad, which had arrived during the wine contretemps.

"Well, did you order regular zinfandel? Usually you order white zin."

"I don't really remember. I should have ordered iced tea!"

The three of them—Eleanor, Draco, and Mitya—were watching her. Draco and Mitya were furtive about it, but Eleanor was plainly waiting for Emma to pick up the damned goblet. She held out until she'd finished her salad, hoping against hope that getting some food into her stomach would blunt any red-wine headache that might be waiting for her. As she tipped the glass, Em caught sight of the waitress with the rust-colored hair, and though she might be wrong about the color of her eyes, there could be no doubt that the young woman was staring at her.

Why? she wondered. *Why her? Why me?* and, just before Em broke the stare, *What troubles her?*

It was a question Emma couldn't tear free of. Her bouillabaisse was delicious—all that the *Secret Guide* had promised. The dark wine went well with the pasta's strongly herbed sauce and—thank heaven!—it wasn't going to give her a headache. Em knew when a taste would trigger a migraine the instant it touched her tongue. She put herself into being sociable, to getting to know her tablemates.

Tiffany never said a word, but Jessica, the teenager whose name Emma hadn't caught the first time, was less sullen than shy. Jessica was fascinated by Emma's job at a library and the days she spent surrounded by books.

"Do you get *paid* to do that?" Jessica asked incredulously. "Can you get *paid* to do what you want to do?"

Emma sensed there was more baggage behind those questions than she could begin to understand, but she nodded anyway—and caught sight of the copper-haired waitress a few tables behind Jessica's shoulders. The young woman was staring again, staring at Emma, true, but staring at Eleanor, too; and Eleanor was staring back.

Em shuddered. Foreboding or a stray blast from the air conditioner? She wanted to believe it was the air conditioner, but she nudged her mother instead.

"You're staring," she hissed.

Eleanor shrugged off the advice. "I was thinking," she insisted. "And looking at the walls. The patterns aren't random, you know. There're supposed to be faces—the signs of the zodiac. One on each section of the wall. They're easier to spot if you let your eyes go out of focus."

"Faces? Really?" Jessica asked. "Show me."

Eleanor described Virgo the Queen, watching from the textured wall panel nearest the table. Score another one for the *Secret Guide*. But Virgo and Sagittarius weren't the only ones watching Draco's table. Em couldn't rid herself of the sensation that she was under scrutiny, but she could resist it, at least until she'd eaten the last dollop of her berries and cream. She was headed out of the dining room, listening to Eleanor's detailed plans for the balance of the evening—

"There's some guy doing impressions at the Komedy Klub, line-dancing lessons—from the electric slide to the macarena."

Eleanor stopped short so suddenly that Em reached for her mother's wrist, thinking that she was about to faint. Her green eyes were locked and staring. Em followed them and was not at all surprised to find that Eleanor was staring at the copper-headed waitress. The young woman was barely twenty feet away, lined up with the rest of the staff, bidding the passengers to a fun-filled night.

"What's going on?" Em demanded as she stepped in front of her mother, breaking the visual connection. "Do you know that woman?"

Eleanor shook her head. "Of course not. Of all the times and places—I want a drink."

"Not half as much as I want answers. This is a curse."

Eleanor arrested the conversation with an acid-etched glower before it could be overheard, leaving Em no option but to follow her mother meekly to one of the many bars laid out in the cruise decks.

"Two, please—burgundy."

Reluctantly, Emma took the second glass when it arrived.

"Now," Eleanor said, "let's go down to the cabin and put our feet up before we go dancing."

Em didn't say a word until the heavy door had closed behind them.

"All right, what's going on?"

"If you know enough to ask the question, Emma, then you already know the answer."

Emma took a deep breath. "It's a curse. That girl waiting on tables is under a curse."

"I'd stake my life on it."

At that singularly ironic answer, Emma sank onto the sofa. "And it knows what—what—what we are?" She still had trouble, sometimes, labeling herself a curse hunter.

"She, not it. Not a rogue. Thank God for small favors: It's only a curse." Eleanor thrashed through one of her drawers. "God, I could use a cigarette right now."

"You quit over a year ago," Em snapped. "How can you be so sure it's not a rogue?"

Eleanor ignored the question, devoting her attention instead to a map of the ship. "I'm going to the sports bar. It's practically the only place on this damn ship where you can buy cigarettes and have a smoke."

"Not until you've told me how you're so sure we're not sharing this ship with a rogue."

"Didn't you read the book I left you?"

"I've got two of them," Emma shot back, referring to

the handwritten notebooks that were both guide and diary for the practicing curse hunter.

The black-bound books sat on a bookshelf in easy reach of her living room armchair. One—the one Eleanor had left behind when she'd disappeared from her daughter's life a half-century ago—was mostly blank pages and laden with arcane—not to mention poisonous and illegal—recipes where it wasn't blank. The second was a gift from Harry Graves, and it, like him, was filled to the edges with rambling thoughts that were more philosophically interesting than practically applicable. Emma had read a third handbook, more like the first than the second, but had returned it to Eleanor after she had physically recovered from her captivity among rogues and curses.

"None of them told me—really told me—how to recognize a real-time cursed human being. The best information I've gotten about that problem came from a rogue. Maleric Dunbar told me that I couldn't resist a plea for help."

"Of course you can. You're resisting it now, aren't you? We both are. We're not puppets on a string, Emma; we can make our own choices. And . . . besides . . . if that rogue hadn't come to you . . . well, it wasn't like the dining room, was it?"

Emma compared the two moments. "I guess not. I've only met two cursed people—cursed or roguish people: Malerie and Bran Mongomery. Not much of a sample for drawing conclusions. That waitress, she wasn't like either of them. I wouldn't have thought *Egad, a curse!* if I hadn't noticed that you were staring, and being stared at, too. It had crossed my mind, but I wasn't sure until you were."

"Well, mark it down. It's different for everyone. You know that, and now you know what it's like for you. That young lady's carrying a curse, and there's not a damn thing we can do about it." Eleanor picked up her purse and plastic passport. "Now, I'm going to the sports bar."

"Wait—what do you mean, there's not anything we can do about it?"

"We're on a ship!"

Em racked her memory for any mention of ships in the handbooks and resurrected nothing. "What does a ship have to do with mooting curses? Seems to me we've got a captive audience and it should be fairly straightforward."

"The ship's *moving,* Em! Slip yourself off to the Netherlands from a moving ship—a moving anything— and you'll never find yourself again afterward. Your body *moves* while you're gone."

"That's absurd. In the real world, we're all always moving. The earth spins on its axis, and it spins around the sun. The sun spins around the center of the Milky Way, and the Milky Way's still recoiling from the Big Bang. In the big picture, we're already miles away from where we were when I started this sentence. Little as I like the idea, there's some sort of connection between the real world and the wasteland. Science can't describe it—at least the science I know can't describe it—but it's real, and it's not magic. I refuse to believe in magic and I refuse to believe that *moving* matters when coming or going to the wasteland."

Eleanor scowled. "Forget the universe; your universe is what doesn't matter. The ship's the only thing that matters." She brightened. "The movement you can feel, that's what matters, okay?"

"Then we've got nothing to worry about. I can't tell if we're moving or not unless I look at the porthole."

She pointed to the circular window where rainwater droplets could be seen streaming steadily from the bow toward the stem.

"Don't argue with me over this, Emma. You may think you know all the answers, but I'm telling you the truth: Don't leave here for there from a moving object. It didn't work when horseback was the fastest you could go, and it's sure not going to work out in the middle of the ocean. Now, can I get out of here?"

Em didn't have the will for an argument; she'd drunk way more wine than she was accustomed to, and, come to think of it, she *could* feel the ship moving, plowing forward, unfazed by the weather. She held her ground, though, between Eleanor and the cabin door.

"You don't want to start smoking again—"

"Look at me!" Eleanor stretched her arm between them; her hand was trembling. "I'm shaking like a damned leaf. I want a cigarette . . . I *need* one, Emma, and, right now, I don't care about what happens tomorrow."

"Tomorrow, we see that girl again—and if you're telling the truth—"

"I am, Emma, I swear I am. The whole idea—when I thought of getting you away from Bower, I thought of a cruise, *because* the boat moves. Three days and four nights in the real world—that's what I was thinking, because that's what you needed. Mooting curses *every* night the way you do—hunting rogues on Friday because, well, never mind that. I never dreamed we'd cross paths with a curse. The odds of that! And here we are. Here *you* are. I mean, what's different for me? I'm not going anywhere. I've got my feet cast in a ton of concrete. It's all on you again, and that's exactly what I thought we could avoid by going on a cruise."

Em stared at the wall, at the bed, at her feet—everywhere except at her mother's face. "There's got to be something we can do," she said helplessly. "That girl's carrying a curse. It'll destroy her, sooner or later, and who knows who else? Malerie was right; I can't walk away."

"Booze," Eleanor replied, ignoring everything in her daughter's heartfelt conscience. "If you won't let me smoke, at least let me drink enough that I'll pass out and sleep without dreaming."

"Booze isn't the answer—"

"Good God, Em, give me a break. You're starting to sound like some holier-than-thou prig."

"I just mean I've had some of my worst nightmares coming down from an extra glass of wine."

"Now she tells me. I'm not asking you to drink with me or smoke with me. I'm just asking you to get out of my way."

Emma did get out of the way, and then she walked with Eleanor to the one elevator that rose through the ship's forward funnel, which was, in fact, a three-story celebration of world-class athleticism with eight giant screen televisions that Em could see from the front door. Each screen displayed a different sporting event, three of them American football, two European. A good many of the patrons were wearing headphones, possibly to tune into the sound stream from a particular television, more likely to drown out the anthem-rock blasting from surround-sound speakers. The air was rank with beer, and if there were any other women in the club, Emma couldn't see them for the smoke.

The sports bar was the last place Em wanted to be just then. The addition of sound and smoke to the wine she'd drunk was cocking one too many of her migraine triggers. Already she felt a familiar throbbing in her right temple, but she'd given her word to Eleanor on the way up. She was assuring herself that she had packed her migraine prescriptions when she felt a tug on her sleeve.

"Not here—"

It was clear from Eleanor's face that she was shouting, though the effect, amid the din, was barely audible and Emma's lip-reading talents weren't up to deciphering the rest of her statement. They retreated to the elevator lobby.

"Let's go outside and take a walk," Eleanor suggested.

The rain had slowed to a drizzle, but even that, considering the ship's speed, made walking on the open deck surrounding the forward funnel an uncomfortably damp encounter. The women descended exterior stairs and found themselves on the same deck where they'd watched the ship's officers man the stabilizer consoles. They found a self-serve kiosk with brimful baskets of coffee, tea, and cocoa packets. A trio of well-anchored urns rose behind the baskets, each leaking a cloud of steam from its spout. Em flipped through the teas until she found something fragrant and decaffeinated. Eleanor regarded the process with the same suspicion one of Em's cats might bring to a dead snake or a foam-filled bathtub. Then the scent of oranges and cinnamon hit her nose, and she asked for a sip.

Emma shook her head. Even behind the kiosk the wind off the bow was stiff and moist. A single layer of silk was no protection and, now that she clutched the warm cup between her palms, Em didn't want to surrender it. "Go ahead," she urged her mother, "make your own. The cup will keep your hands warm."

They found a table in a more enclosed part of the deck and towels from a courtesy cabinet that they used to swab any lingering moisture from the chairs around it.

"Malerie was right," Em repeated after a few moments of silence had passed. "I can't hear a plea for help and not respond."

"Not on a ship, Emma. Promise me you won't do anything while we're on board."

A member of the invisible crew came by to collect their discarded towels. They lowered their voices, though the odds were that the crewman didn't understand much English and they were reflexively careful not to say anything that couldn't be overheard as ordinary concern or caution.

"You can always do something once you're back on solid ground. It's not as if the problem's going to go away."

"Don't worry," Em assured her. "I never do anything when I've got a headache anyway."

"Have you got a migraine?"

"The beginnings of one—thank you for not staying in

that sports bar. This is better: the tea, the fresh air. I'll be fine. It's fading already."

"You wouldn't want to go to the Komedy Klub?"

Left to her own devices, Em's answer would have been an unequivocal no, but left to her own devices, she'd never have boarded the boat in the first place. "Why not? There's no smoking, is there? It's all part of what we paid for." The tea had cooled. She drained the cup. "Whenever you're ready."

There was nothing memorable about the Komedy Klub's comedian and his sanitized patter, but he knew how to move an audience from one bit to the next. Emma laughed at jokes she'd heard before. Laughter was good for migraines, too. She drank iced fruit-tea and felt completely sober when she and Eleanor returned to their cabin shortly after midnight.

"You won't forget your promise?" Eleanor asked from the far side of the king-sized bed they'd be sharing for the next four nights.

"Not a chance," Em replied as she turned out the light.

Three

Emma Merrigan assumed she dreamt on a regular, healthy basis. All the best research said that without regular dreams to restore the brain's chemistry, a human being went insane, and since, despite her status as founder of the curse-hunting Orion's Children, Emma was not insane, it followed logically that her brain went about its dreaming business while her mind was elsewhere.

What she hadn't done in the last two years was remember her dreams. It wasn't a great loss; Emma had never been an especially vivid or complete dreamer. The dream images she did recall were mostly snippets of childhood memory with a surreal twist. She had never, for example, dreamt of a home other than the house on Teagarden Street where she'd grown up, and when her dream-self went traveling, it returned to the beaches, campgrounds, and tourist traps she'd first visited with her father.

If there was anything that Emma missed about her unremembered dreams, it was the images of her father. She'd begun her wasteland treks while she was still mourning his death and, in those early days, would often awaken with a damp pillow beneath her cheek. That ache had faded now. Her heart no longer thudded when she summoned Arch Merrigan's face from memory or photographs, but memories and photographs were silent, unmoving. Only her dreams, Em believed, could bring back her father's laughter.

She thought of him as she settled into the surprisingly comfortable bed. If she wasn't going to do anything useful, then the least she could do was dream a memorable dream of Arch Merrigan. . . .

Not all of Emma's dreams had been comfort food for her psyche. From early childhood she'd been plagued by night terrors—not dreams, exactly, but pitch dark chasms from which she would suddenly, and barely, make her escape. As a child on Teagarden Street, Em's response to her night terrors had been to cry out for her father. Without fail, he would hurry down the carpeted hall to her room to hold her in his arms until she knew who and where she was again. Sometimes, she'd fall back to sleep in his arms, but when sleep eluded her, they'd go downstairs for warm milk and a visit to the book-lined den where, amid the most familiar surroundings imaginable, her father would patiently explain that no dream, no matter how formless or menacing, could hurt his daughter.

Em consoled herself with those words when she found herself sitting bolt upright in the darkness. The hidden space around her felt wrong, sounded wrong, and some of the longest moments of her life passed before she remembered:

Cabin. Engine. I'm on a boat. This is the place where I'm supposed to be.

She was freezing cold—another frequent consequence of a night terror. Hugging herself didn't help. Snuggling down into the blankets was scarcely better. Emma couldn't quite shake the feeling, even now that the terror itself had faded, that she was under observation.

"Eleanor?" she kept her voice to a whisper that wasn't meant to awaken and heard nothing in reply.

Somewhere between the terror and the pillow, her migraine had returned, full-blown and oppressive. The pills that would put it in retreat were in the top drawer of the dresser; she hadn't wanted to put them out on the bathroom's small shelves, where the bottle might find a way to disappear over the inch-high, seaworthy fencing that surrounded the cabin's every flat surface. A good idea—at least a reasonable one—at the time, but now Em had to ease out of the bed and across an unfamiliar room in darkness broken only by the pinprick red light of a smoke detector and the hint of gray at the drapery-covered porthole.

She found the pills by touch and quiet patience, then made her way slowly toward the bathroom. The cabin was roomy enough with the lights on, but shrank in the darkness. Em overshot the door by a good eighteen inches and added injury to insult when she stubbed her bare toe on the safety-first, pressure-sealed door's ridged metal threshold. The switch was where it should be, and she flipped it on before remembering that a roaring exhaust fan came on with the light.

Well, with any luck Eleanor was sleeping like a log. And if, by some remote chance they did something like this again, Emma was putting a flashlight at the top of her packing list.

With two of the big crimson capsules successfully transferred from the bottle to her stomach, Emma hit the switch again and made her way to the bed. The terror was history, but not the sense of observation. Em lay on her back, staring into the darkness, wondering what time it was. Her mind was starting to drift toward the wasteland, to the bolt-hole, and Blaise who, if he was there at all, never seemed to be asleep when she arrived.

She wrenched her thoughts back to the cabin. There'd come a time to test Eleanor's prohibition, maybe while they were driving back to Bower, but not now with night terrors in her memory and a migraine in her head.

Far below the cabin, the *Excitation* shifted gears. She did nothing so ungainly as shudder, but there was a difference to her almost inaudible sound, her nearly imperceptible movement. Had the stabilizers been drawn back into the hull? Was the *Excitation* cutting through the ocean like a more traditional ship? Slowing down, perhaps? The itinerary had been a bit fuzzy about the timing of their arrival in Nassau, but they were promised to be tied up at the dock before breakfast, maybe before sunrise. If she couldn't sleep, perhaps she could scout herself a good view of the docking process. The prospect of observing an ultramodern passenger ship go through its paces had been one of the reasons she'd chosen a Fantabulous cruise over all the other packages that Eleanor had proposed.

There was no way Em could slip out of the cabin without disturbing Eleanor. Her jeans were buried at the bottom of a drawer, her sneakers at the back of the closet. And though her mind seemed too active for going back to sleep, her body wasn't ready to abandon the bed. With a sigh, she pulled the covers close and set her imagination loose in the shops of Nassau.

The prospect of having her Christmas shopping done by the end of September proved more exhausting than any herd of leaping, insomniac sheep. Em was at the bottom of her sleep cycle when the tinkling of chimes filled the cabin.

"Good morning, everyone!" a pixie voiced with a clipped British accent proclaimed. "It's eight A.M. and you don't want to miss a moment of your first day in *Excitation* paradise. We've docked in Nassau. The sun is shining, the temperature is twenty-five degrees—"

Em opened her eyes. "Centigrade," she muttered. Granted, most of the crew probably thought about the weather in metric, but she was strictly Fahrenheit. The announcement told her absolutely nothing about the heat she and Eleanor would be walking into when they left the ship. On the other hand, Em thought she'd gotten to the bottom of that "we're watching you" sense that had dogged her dreams: The cabin speaker was a polished silver hemisphere protruding from the ceiling above the bed. A more paranoid passenger might assume there was a tiny camera inside; Emma convinced herself that the dome had been infinitesimally brighter than the ceiling around it.

The activities coordinator continued her recitation of departure times and meeting points for various shore excursions. Tomorrow, when they visited their second Bahamas island, Em and Eleanor would need to pay attention. They'd booked what the *Guide* described as a leisurely kayaking and authentic barbeque excursion. But today they were headed for downtown Nassau, armed with nothing but their wallets and a colorfully bound guidebook.

"The stores don't open before ten," Eleanor said from her side of the bed. "We can catch another hour's sleep."

Emma guessed Eleanor was feeling the aftereffects of the previous evening, which she, blessedly, was not. "I'm going to go off in search of breakfast. I'll be back long before ten."

Eleanor wasn't about to surrender a moment of vacation. She was up and half dressed when Em emerged from the shower. There were at least a half-dozen places to grab breakfast aboard the *Excitation*. First choice for both women was a casual indoor-outdoor buffet over the stern where they'd eaten lunch the previous day. As they entered, they promised each other to eat light—playing tourist in the tropics was no fun on an over-full stomach—and, considering the quantities and varieties of food spread over several service tables, they kept their promises. Still, Emma succumbed not only to another dish of berries and cream, but a bowl of granola and several rashers of bacon as well.

"We'd better do a lot of walking, or I'm not going to fit into the pants I want to wear tonight," she said when, fresh from the cabin and armed with all the typical tourist gear, they joined the line of disembarking passengers.

Security was obvious, but not particularly tight. Their plastic cabin keys were the ship's first line of defense. A smiling crewman—or woman, in Eleanor's case—dressed in semi-military white uniform, swiped the card through a reader then compared the readout with a picture ID. Em and Eleanor both passed inspection and were given a quick lecture of Bahamian do's and don'ts, along with the stern warning to guard the little plastic card well because without it and a photo ID, preferably from an actual passport, there was no getting back on board the *Excitation*.

Duly warned and cautious, Em returned the rectangle to her wallet—she hadn't lost her wallet since high school and didn't plan to start in Nassau. Eleanor seemed to feel that the back pocket of her jeans was the safest place for her cabin key.

Emma's new digital camera could hold more than four hundred pictures before she had to change its memory chip. She took six pictures of the *Excitation* and its wharf-mates before they came to Bahamian customs on the gated boundary between the port and the city proper, then she took another four. Her snap-happy ways must have marked her as a prime tourist, because she and Eleanor were accosted by not one but three women in the bright colors and straw hats that passed for native costuming before they'd crossed the painted-line border into the city. All the women wanted to braid their hair. Em wasn't tempted, but Eleanor, whose every hair was already divided between a rusty auburn root and a maroon tip, had to add beads and colored thread, three dollars a braid, to her look.

Em should have been forewarned when a short but furious argument in rapid island patois broke out among the ladies about which one of them would have the privilege of braiding Eleanor's hair. The biggest, loudest, and probably the oldest of the three won. She led Eleanor to a high chair under a bright red umbrella, one of perhaps a dozen in the customs courtyard. Eleanor wore her hair short; it barely covered her ears. Twenty minutes and fifty-one American dollars later, Eleanor left the chair with a fringe of aqua, purple, and gold beads dangling from her right temple. While she waited, Emma had taken four pictures of the braids in progress and another six of the *Excitation*.

There was something amiss with Emma's introduction to Bahamian paradise. At first, she thought it was the location—the shops closest to the port were the first, or last, places a cruise passenger would see, so it wasn't surprising that they were stocked with an eye for glitz and flash, not quality. Then she thought it was the crowds—the stream of passengers from the *Excitation* and the two other ships tied up in the harbor was a tide of tourists washing ashore every day. When your customers came in rich American waves, why bother with individual service or distinctive goods? But, by the time she and Eleanor had made their way through half a dozen shops, Emma was beginning to think the discord was woven into Nassau itself and the price the city paid for being dependent on tourists who would pass through the town once and once only.

Her dreams of matching the names on her Christmas shopping list with just the right island-flavored gift faded quickly. For one thing, all the prices were in American dollars and on a par with Michigan prices—at least in the rare instances where Emma could compare apples with apples. Indeed, for the items on which she could do a price comparison, she could have gotten better bargains at an average Interstate outlet mall. The more exotic items—mostly jewelry, perfumes, and leather goods that purported to be direct from Europe—sported reduction tags with 50- to 75-percent markdowns that were dog-earred and bleached by the island sun. To Emma's inexpert eye, almost everything appeared to have been made in China, regardless of whether the display case said English bone china, Italian leather, or French perfume.

The heat was a problem, too. Air conditioning in Nassau didn't mean what it meant at home, and in the stores where the thermostats were cranked down to Midwestern comfort zones, mildew mustiness hung in the air.

But they kept going, led by Eleanor's guidebook, which provided glowing descriptions of every shop they encountered. After more than an hour of futile browsing, and a change in direction that put them on the sunny side of the street, Emma was ready to call it quits, except that she wasn't going to be the wet blanket—if Eleanor was enjoying herself. And Eleanor seemed to be having a great time, though she wasn't spending any money, either.

"Oh, here's one for you!" Eleanor said, pointing to the window sign that proclaimed embroidered French linens within.

Emma smiled gamely. Lace and embroidery were among the few areas where she could judge what she was looking at, and from what she'd seen, none of the textiles in Nassau had originated anywhere near France. They'd all had the flat, overprocessed look of Chinese trade goods. The only question in Em's mind was, Had the work been done by machine or by thousands of bored, perhaps imprisoned, Chinese men and women stitching the same tired flowers day after day? It was one of those questions for which she really didn't want an answer.

The shop's linens filled one musty corner. They overflowed a mahogany cabinet that was more intriguing than all the cloth spilling out of it—not that Em had room in her townhouse for a six-by-four-foot antique cabinet, even if she could have gotten it all the way to Michigan. Though she'd lost track of Eleanor, Em made a point of going through the cellophane-wrapped (another sign that the articles had never been to France) napkins and tea towels. Idly, she looked for some mark that would prove their provenance. On one of the napkins she found a tiny oval indentation where a "made in China" label might once have been attached.

Do these people think no one can tell the difference? she asked herself.

The price, four dollars, American, would have been a steal for European textiles. It was on the high side for Chinese work . . . which said something truly unpleasant about wages in China and made Em think again that the embroiderers and crocheters were conscripts of some sort.

She glanced at the unenthusiastic sales staff, grouped silently at a central checkout counter. *They know,* she decided. *They're just going through the motions.* And she wondered if there hadn't been a time, a generation earlier, when a shop like this had actually stocked its shelves with luscious linens fit for noble beds and tables.

With that thought, Em found what had been bothering her since they'd crossed the customs plaza. Despite the three huge ships in port, trade in Nassau had seen better days, better tourists. The shops piled on the Chinese wares, because those were what they could afford to stock and sell to middle-class Americans who were keen for a bargain but not particularly knowledgeable about their purchases.

Feeling more sad than disappointed, Emma carefully returned the napkin to its stack in the cabinet. She heard someone coming up from behind and hoped it wasn't one of the shop clerks.

"Look what I've found!"

The voice was Eleanor's. Em turned around and barely swallowed a gasp. There was a small, gray cat, a ringer for her female cat, Charm, sleeping in her mother's arms.

"Isn't it cute? It's my kind of pet. No food, no poop, just

run a vacuum over it every so often or pick it up and shake it by its tail."

To Emma's dismay, Eleanor gave a vigorous demonstration of the cleaning maneuver.

"It's a cat, Eleanor," Emma said softly.

"Of course it's a cat. Does it look like a dog? Isn't it amazing how lifelike they've made it? The little nose, the ears—"

"No. It's a *cat,* Eleanor. A real cat. I don't know whether it's stuffed or freeze dried or some combination of the two, but it's a cat—it *was* a cat. The Chinese were exporting them to the U.S. I saw them in a couple of gift stores last Christmas. I was like you—I couldn't believe how soft, how just like a cat it was, and I never thought it *was* a cat, either. Then PETA and a bunch of other organizations stood up and said the Chinese were rounding up stray cats and making toys out of them. I don't think anyone had to make it illegal."

Eleanor looked down at the incredibly lifelike cat she held by the tail. "You mean—? They're going out and collecting *cats*? Maybe *stealing* them? Stealing somebody's *pet*?"

"I don't know," Em admitted. "Tell you the truth, I didn't want to know where cats stand in China or whether there are any Chinese people who think of cats as pets. I know where they stand with me, and I was afraid maybe I'd find out that the Chinese raised them primarily for meat and were selling the skins just to make extra money. Oriental cooking gets a whole lot more exotic than mu-shu pork."

With a strangled yelp, Eleanor's hand jerked open. The gray cat fell to the floor, bouncing once on its head, before coming to rest on its back. The cat was dead. It was a *thing* that had been dead for months or more. And the Chinese were entitled to their culture, to eat whatever they wanted to eat, to profit wherever they could from whatever they had. After all, didn't the Chinese keep crickets as household mascots, while Em ruthlessly crushed any of the creatures she found in her basement? Em deemed herself unable to judge anything she couldn't understand, but, even so, she felt her stomach turn over and was grateful that her breakfast was well past the point of no return.

"Mygod, mygod," Eleanor repeated, folding her hands against her breast.

Which meant that Emma had to retrieve the *thing* that was so very soft, so very taboo. She didn't ask where Eleanor had found it. She just put it down on top of the napkin she'd been looking at and said to Eleanor, "Let's leave, okay?"

Eleanor reached the shop's door first. She left it swinging for Emma to catch with her shoulder. Without speaking a word, they made their way to the nearest corner, where, without consultation, they chose a direction that led away from the commercial district.

Halfway down the block, Em broke her silence, "I could do with something cold to drink."

She expected to have to choose her restaurant carefully; she didn't expect the complete absence of eateries that met her eyes as she scanned left and right.

"Good luck. If you do find something, I'm not sure I'd trust what's inside. Except for the hotels." Eleanor opened her arms and pointed the closed guidebook at the row of large buildings at the foot of their street. Thin slices of blue harbor were barely visible between the fortress-like hotels lining the waterfront. "The book doesn't recommend any place to eat. I guess there's not much point in trying to sell food to tourists who've got twenty-four-hour, free food service."

Emma grasped her camera, then let it hang loosely on its strap again. The insight she'd just had couldn't be captured in a single image. The cruise ships and the hotels were destinations in and of themselves. Nassau, a city with

more history than all but a few of its American counterparts, was irrelevant.

"I wonder," Em asked, "how many passengers never
even leave the boat?"

"Lots, I imagine. What did Art and Gracie say last
night—that this was their fifth *Excitation* cruise? Unless
they're doing one of the package excursions, they're probably still on board."

"Probably," Emma agreed and turned the corner that
would lead them back to the customs depot.

Eleanor called her back with, "What's that standing outside that big hotel?"

"Can't say for sure—a statue of some sort. Maybe
some sort of outdoor art?"

Shopping for Christmas presents had gone bust, and
there was nowhere to go for a tall glass of iced tea. Still,
Emma wasn't quite ready to abandon Nassau. Curiosity
drew her toward the statue, which failed to resolve itself
into man, beast, or abstract art until the women had only
one street left to cross.

"Who do you suppose it is?" Em asked, once the dark
shape had become a man in colonial garb caught in energetic mid-stride.

"No idea," Eleanor snapped.

The traffic was too heavy, too unpredictable for crossing the street while reading the appropriate paragraphs
from their guidebook. It wasn't until they were standing on
the curb of the garden—little more, really, than the traffic
median separating a hotel's entrance from the busy
street—surrounding the statue, before Eleanor dared open
her book. Em couldn't tell whether the slightly-larger-
than-life statue had been carved or cast, but there was no
question that the sculptor and his model had had fun with
the project. The man in question was the very definition of
dashing, as he reached to unsheathe his sword, his weight
surging forward on one leg, his unbuttoned frock-coat

furled out behind, and an expression of wolfish intensity captured on his face. Em leaned forward a little herself to read the name written on the plaque at his feet.

"Woodes Rogers. If he were wearing a uniform, or there'd been some famous battle of Nassau harbor, I'd say he was the hero of the hour. Otherwise, the man looks a bit like a pirate—"

"Privateer," Eleanor corrected, she'd found the appropriate page in her guidebook. "And first governor of the Bahamas. It doesn't mention a battle, but he's the man who put all the other Caribbean pirates out of business."

Emma acknowledged the information with a thoughtful nod. "Send a thief to catch a thief. It's worked before."

"Says here," Eleanor continued, "that he rescued Andrew Selkirk along the way—Selkirk's the original Robinson Crusoe."

Em took a cautious step backward for a better view. "He must have been a force to be reckoned with—and whoever commissioned this statue had the sense not to make him a flat-foot politician."

"You're just a sucker for any man with a sword and long coat."

Em opened her mouth to protest and shut it quickly. Not that she couldn't easily think of a dozen differences between her lover and Woodes Rogers, but every one of them was beside the point. "It might be fun to see our pirate-governor in action," she mused finally. "To see whether the statue does him justice."

"You don't get tired of that, do you?"

"No," Em admitted. "It's not just that the world is our oyster, but the oyster has four dimensions, and Blaise and I can explore them all. Of course, the closer we get to something pivotal, the more ghost-y everything feels. Harry calls that chronological resilience. It gets to the point where it's almost like watching television. But we did manage to get into the Louvre and catch Louis the

Fourteenth going about his daily business once. Nasty-looking little man—"

"Strikes me as worse than being a tourist. At least a tourist leaves money behind."

Emma shrugged. "There's the art, and the sense that I've *seen* what historians can only imagine."

"On television. I don't understand what value you see in touristing through the past. If there's no curse nearby, there's nothing to do but gawk from the shadows. Might as well ask a wolf or lion to stop and admire the scenery."

Eleanor was a hunter through and through—a predator with no thought for anything but her prey.

Em hoisted her camera. She took several pictures of Mr. Rogers before saying, "It gives us something to share, something to talk about. You can only talk about work for so long."

"If what you're doing when you're together is talking. Plus, you've got that window. Maybe if I'd ever had a bolt-hole with a window . . ."

Em didn't want to wander down that conversational cul-de-sac. "Look, over there—a convenience store that looks like it was imported entirely from the states. I can see the Coke machine from here. Sure you wouldn't like something cold to drink? My treat," Em offered.

At two dollars each, the cans of soda pop were not the most expensive Emma had ever bought, but they might have been the most welcome. She and Eleanor drained them to the last drop and split a genuine, imported Krispy Kreme Doughnut as well before returning to the dazzling bright sidewalk. Em turned left, toward the customs depot, but Eleanor had a different suggestion.

"Our Governor Rogers was just about the last stop on my guidebook's walking tour of Nassau. If we wanted, we could do the tour in reverse. It wouldn't take more than forty-five minutes . . . an hour at the most. If you're game.

Hard to say when you might get back here . . . in the flesh, anyway."

Emma agreed and they headed right, instead, weaving along shaded streets where every other residence looked as old as the United States. Em pointed her camera through a wrought iron gate of an imposing mansion that was in need of equally imposing repairs.

"They say Michigan has a harsh climate," she said when she'd finished taking a few shots. "And that our winters are killers, but when a house gets built in Michigan, it stays built for years—for a century. You paint it once every ten years, fifteen if you're lucky. Around here, you let a house go for a season or two, and its walls are covered with mold and the wood's starting to rot."

"Nobody ever said the living's easy in the tropics."

"That's exactly what they do say—'summertime and the living is easy.' Nassau's got year-round summertime and civilization's under year-round siege."

"European civilization," Eleanor corrected.

They started walking again, uphill now, and into a district where the mansions had been converted into headquarters for government trade missions and international corporations. A few luxury cars sped by, but there was no foot traffic other than themselves. Emma wondered how much business got done on the average Nassau Monday and how many vacation suites lurked behind each corporate logo.

They climbed higher and the city's derelict fortress appeared in front of them. Without the guidebook, they wouldn't have known the brig from the powder magazine. From its stubby dark gray stone walls to its narrow parapet, the fort seemed smaller than it should have been, smaller by far than the reconstructed fort on Michigan's Mackinac Island, which Emma had visited several times on school trips. She imagined that Governor Rogers could have garrisoned his Nassau defenses quite nicely with a force of two dozen men.

The view from the fort, as defender or tourist, was spectacular. If there was a higher point on the island of New Providence, it didn't overlook Nassau harbor. One of the two other cruise ships had sailed off to other ports. The *Excitation* and one other cruise ship dominated the central portion of the harbor. Together, the two boats were as big as the shopping district Emma and Eleanor had abandoned. To the right—Em didn't know if her right was east, west, north, or south; she couldn't figure the compass points so close to noon in near-tropical latitudes—loomed something called Paradise Island, which looked like a large chunk of the Vegas strip plunked down on a Caribbean island and painted a singularly unnatural shade of salmon.

Emma had seen lavish commercials for Paradise Island on Detroit television. Naively, she'd assumed the place *was* an island unto itself—certainly the commercials had portrayed it as an all-in-one destination. They never bothered to add that downtown Nassau was within hiking distance.

Emma closed her eyes and tried to imagine the view as it might have been ten years earlier—even five years—before the colossal resort heaved into existence and when cruise ships had been both smaller and more expensive. The Nassau atmosphere would have been much different, more exclusive, probably, and, maybe, more authentic. Em could, of course, compare her imaginings with historical reality. All she'd have to do was stand in front of the wasteland window and bend her thoughts in the proper direction. She could visit her island paradise before it became Paradise Island—

With a start, Em broke out of her reverie. She turned to Eleanor and admitted: "You were right."

"About what?" her mother replied with furrows of suspicion across her forehead.

"The window is a dangerous temptation. I caught myself thinking that I wanted to see what this place looked like when it was thriving and not hanging on in the shadow of a tourist industry that packages reality. And maybe Nassau would be something to see in its prime, but ten years ago or three hundred—it wouldn't be my Nassau. My Nassau has Chinese cats, cruise ships, and that god-awful monstrosity over there. I may not want to come back to *my* Nassau, but I shouldn't kid myself that I can pick some other Nassau and call it mine."

"I was only trying to help," Eleanor said in a tone that left Emma wondering if she'd completely misunderstood her mother's earlier caution.

"You did," Em assured her and clicked off a panorama of Nassau harbor, capturing it in the fleeting moment of the absolute present. "Well, we've been to the high point. Have we seen everything there is to see?"

Eleanor consulted the guidebook. "We take the Queen's Staircase to get down from here, then there are a few old government buildings."

"Ready?"

With a nod Eleanor closed the book and they made their way out of the fort. Apparently all the walking tours went clockwise, rather than the counterclockwise trek the women were on. Though they'd entered the fort through quiet, empty streets, they left it through an ad hoc marketplace. A phalanx of carts, tables, and open cars lined the spiraling road down from the fort.

Most of the merchandise appeared to be T-shirts and straw hats, some of the latter embellished with woven straw embroidery. Before she'd started hunting curses, Emma's greatest passion had been embroidery, both as an outlet for her own creativity and as a very small-time collector. She'd always brought textiles back from her vacations, and the impulse to purchase something hand-stitched in Nassau was too strong to be easily resisted, but each time Em so much as glanced at one of the displays, a chorus of hard-sell patter erupted from the other vendors. The tactic seemed counterproductive: It would take a strongwilled tourist to brave the verbal onslaught, a strongerwilled one than her, at any rate, and Eleanor had gone positively rigid.

The women paid a price for shutting down their awareness of their surroundings. The clockwise path to the fort was easy to follow—just walk uphill. Counterclockwise offered more downhill options, and, somewhere in the second half of their descent, they made a wrong turn into a neighborhood where tourists were clearly not regular visitors. They tried backtracking, going uphill instead of down. That worked for two short blocks until they were in someone's yard, dodging chickens and a brindle dog that looked a lot stronger than the chain that held it.

"What now?" Eleanor asked when they'd retreated to an unfamiliar intersection of sidewalks and streets.

Em refused to consult the guidebook. "The harbor's that way. I think I can even see the *Excitation*'s funnels. It's broad daylight . . . we just start walking and try not to act too lost."

That might have been a good plan, had they been able to execute it, but two female tourists deep in a local neighborhood attempting point-to-point navigation were all too obviously lost. They got only a few hundred yards when a man of indeterminate age and ancestry appeared at their side. With an island lilt he offered to guide them wherever they wanted—needed—to go. After an exchange of glances that were surely undisguised, Emma said, "We're on our way to the Queen's Stairs."

The man grinned and said they'd gone far astray. He said something else, too, but between his accent and the pounding of her heart, Emma didn't catch the words. She'd gotten used to the dangers of the wasteland, but in the here-and-now, she'd seldom been more anxious than she was as they set out beside their sudden savior. Em promised herself and the mother-voice railing in the back of her head that she'd follow only so long as she was sure they were headed in the correct direction.

Soon they were back on a macadam road, walking past a sign with arrows pointing in opposite directions, one toward the fort and the other to the Queen's Staircase. Em thanked the man for his help. She even herded Eleanor a step or two in the right direction, but their guide clung to them. He began talking about his family—five children, all in school, and his wife who worked at the big hotel. Emma tried to disengage politely, but it was Eleanor who decoded the situation.

"How much do you want?" she asked bluntly.

"Five dollars, don't you t'ink? You ladies were very lost. No tellin' where you go next."

While Eleanor dug for her wallet, the man stared at Emma until she realized that five dollars was not a group rate.

"We're not doing too well," Eleanor stated the obvious when they were on their way again.

"We're fresh-off-the-boat tourists. It's our job to get fleeced . . . and I think we've done very well so far."

"You can laugh now. All I could see for a few moments was disaster."

"We'll laugh when we get home."

"No way!" Eleanor retorted. "I'm not saying a word about this to anyone, ever. I *have* traveled before, and, I swear to you, that's the first time I've been hit up for a fool."

"All right, we won't tell anyone," Em agreed, choosing the easy option. She wasn't proud of her own performance here in Nassau. Forget the last five minutes, pretending the last few hours hadn't happened would go a long way to numb her sense of being a hopeless amateur among world travelers.

At last, the Queen's Staircase opened in front of them: a lengthy series of steps hand carved, the guidebook informed them, from living stone. Beside the staircase, a stream had been transformed into a cultivated waterfall. Lush plants clung to the damp, stone walls, all of them a healthy green against dark gray stone. The waterfall stirred a breeze, which, if not cool, was at least cooler and quite inviting to a pair of upper-Midwest tourists. There were wooden benches lining the walls of the deep, narrow park at the bottom of the staircase.

"The staircase was carved by slaves in 1793 in honor of Queen Victoria who'd issued the proclamation that freed them," Eleanor read from the guidebook.

Em paused with her hand on the railing. "That book isn't worth the powder to blow it up. First it sends us to stores that sell freeze-dried cats, then it gets us lost coming out of the fort, and now it's got newly freed slaves laboring to build a memorial to an English queen—but not Queen Victoria. I don't know, maybe she did free the English slaves, but she didn't do it in 1793. She couldn't even have been alive in 1793. I mean, she was old when she died in 1901, but she wasn't *that* old."

"I bought this one because it's won all sorts of awards," Eleanor countered and flipped the book shut to flash the cover at Emma.

The movement was not overly dramatic, but it was enough to send Eleanor teetering on one of the Queen's many steps. Without thought or hesitation, Emma seized her mother's shirt sleeve. She was balanced again before she'd had a chance to panic.

Eleanor forced a laugh. "These hand-carved steps are too uneven. Back home, someone would have had them declared unsafe. We'd be taking the Queen's Escalator right about now."

"Probably," Em agreed, keeping her hand on the rail. "I

think it's past time for us to get back to the ship—before we manage to do serious damage."

But sunlight filtering through the greenery brought a subtle beauty to the narrow, rock-walled park at the bottom of the Queen's Staircase. The air was cooler, too, and scented with dew and flowers. A handful of straw-hat and T-shirt vendors displayed their wares, but they were less aggressive than their counterparts on the fortress hill. Emma surveyed them from a distance and, seeing virtually no difference among the displays, bought a hat with a rainbow of straw roses attached to the brim from the nearest cart and vendor. The T-shirts looked to be pretty much the same, as if there were one central warehouse elsewhere on the island that supplied every Bahamian peddlar with identical goods. Em picked a souvenir shirt that seemed to be printed on a slightly better grade of cotton jersey and advised Eleanor to do the same.

Eleanor, though, didn't like the design. Eleanor wanted the perfect T-shirt and was prepared to sift through every pile of shirts in the Queen's Staircase gap to find it. She was still sifting and rejecting after Emma had taken a dozen pictures looking up at the waterfall to match the dozen she'd taken looking down on it.

"I'll be over there." Em pointed to the wooden benches lining the gap.

"I've found three that would be all right, but not in my size. If I could wear a men's extra large, I'd be set."

"Take your time."

The benches were in the park's deepest shade. To Em's mind, they should have been not merely cooler, but downright cool. Her climatological instincts, honed as they were in the upper Midwest, were unreliable in the semitropics. The air around the benches was still, almost stagnant, and too warm. She'd have been better off staying closer to the waterfall, but now that she was seated, relocating was more effort than she cared to expend. Leaning back until her head touched the gray stone, Em closed her eyes and let her thoughts drift.

If the Nassau heat was oppressive to someone dressed in shorts and a loose cotton shirt, what must it have been like in the days when ladies laced themselves into boned corsets and concealed their legs beneath layers of petticoats? Not that men had had it much better. Em couldn't imagine a day in the Bahamas when Woodes Rogers would have actually needed his billowing frock coat. No wonder that the tropics had a reputation for slow living. Who wanted to move at all, when the least exertion broke a sweat, and the sweat just clung to your skin?

Slaves, Emma thought, not that they would have wanted to. They had no choice. She could hear them working on the stairs, their hammers falling deliberately and not a whit faster than necessary. Children—slaves themselves, the children of slaves—might have carried cups of water to their parents from the tumbling stream, not yet transformed into an attractively terraced waterfall. Cups? Would slaves have possessed pottery cups, or would gourds have been more likely? Perhaps seashells? Caribbean history wasn't Em's long suit, nor was the day-to-day life of eighteenth-century slaves and laborers.

Easier to imagine the middle classes: a woman making her way to the unfinished steps. Why might she visit? Her husband the architect, commissioned by Woodes Rogers— no, Rogers would have been long dead by 1793. Some other royal governor then, or maybe the distant queen herself who wanted a practical memorial: The staircase and its gap did a good job of connecting the upper and lower towns of Nassau.

The architect's pretty young wife would wear white, because it was cooler and because it was easier to bleach clothes clean than scrub them. A servant—a slave— walked beside her, carrying the parasol that protected her pale European skin. She carried a basket with lunch for her husband. Sandwiches—had the earl given his name to a meal of meat between slices of bread by 1793? Had they become popular so far from home? And would her architect drink tea, lukewarm tea, or rum? Rum was a mainstay of island trade; Em remembered that from American history in junior high.

An architect and his wife, her servant. A slave gang and . . . an overseer, with a cruel sneer on his lips and a coat meant for someone else stretched across his burly shoulders. Em could see them all parading past her mind's eye, walking along the gap as if the modern-day tourists and vendors were the stuff of dreams. The residents of colonial Nassau weren't the only ones trooping through Emma's imagination. There were other, fainter figures who didn't so much walk as drift.

"Emma?"

The drifters were gaunt and clothed in rags. They held their arms in front of them, as if reaching for something just beyond their grasp. A few of them bore serious wounds that did not seem to pain them—

"Em?"

The drifters were slaves, Em decided, a few of the many slaves who'd lived and died on the island. Not all of the slaves; that, she imagined would have filled the gap to its brim. But dozens of them, maybe scores. They were hard to count, drifting, as they did, into the rock walls, and disappearing there while replacements floated down from above.

They weren't all slaves. Here and there among the dark-skinned misery Em spotted paler creatures, equally gaunt, some of them in rags, others in more fashionable garments. Her vision snagged on one such pale drifter, a young woman with a crown of braided hair wound around her head. She wore a dark dress and long apron that had never, anywhere, been fashionable. She propped a basket of what might have been laundry against one hip and in the other hand held the hand of a towheaded child, no more than six or seven.

As the pair drifted past, the woman turned her head to return Emma's stare. Her eyes seemed very alive and, suddenly, very close. Emma had a sense that she knew those eyes—

"Emma? Are you okay?"

With great effort Emma turned her head toward the sound. There was no one there, no one she knew among the drifters or the slaves pounding stone at the end of the gap. She tried to find the pale drifter again. The woman had continued on. She and the child were nearing the rock walls. They would disappear in another step or two. The child spun around. He walked backward, smiling at Emma—

"Emma?"

Had he called her name? Em didn't think so; his lips hadn't moved. She looked right and left, even up, searching for the someone who was searching for Emma.

Out of nowhere, a hand fell on her shoulder.

"Merle Acalia Merrigan! Pay attention to me!"

Emma opened her eyes. The drifters were still there. The boy was still smiling as he vanished, but there was someone else, too—a woman with bicolored hair. The face was familiar, but elusive. Emma closed her eyes again.

"Come back here!"

The hand shook Em's shoulder so vigorously that the back of her head rattled against the stone. Pain forced her attention. She opened her eyes again. The woman with parti-colored hair bent over her. Her face was more familiar now: Eleanor. Eleanor Merrigan . . . no, Eleanor Graves. What was Eleanor Graves doing at the Queen's Staircase? Em couldn't answer that question. Her eyes began to close.

"Emma. Emma, snap out of it!"

She tried, but except for her face, she couldn't move a muscle, and even her eyelids were leaden. Eleanor Graves released Em's shoulder and pressed the back of her hand gently against Em's cheek.

"Good God, you're burning up!"

Eleanor disappeared from sight then returned, heart-beats later, to fling water from her fingertips onto Emma's face. Em dodged the droplets—a small movement, no more than an inch, but it broke the paralysis. She caught a final glimpse of the ghostly boy before he vanished in the shimmering gray walls. When they vanished, so did all the other drifters. The slaves' chant faded, then it, too, was gone.

"Where am I?" she whispered.

"Nassau. Nassau, Em. You're in Nassau, the Bahamas. You're on a cruise; we've been playing tourist."

"The Queen's Staircase." Em's awareness reformed. Her voice grew stronger with each word, and her right arm, at least, was hers again. She grasped Eleanor's wrist before her mother could spatter her again with water from the bottle they'd brought off the ship. "I'm all right now," she insisted. "I don't know what happened there. One minute I was sitting here trying not to think about how hot it is, the next—" Emma lowered her voice. "The next I was watching this place being constructed. That, and—"

Eleanor scowled. She looked the staircase gap up and down without losing the scowl. "We need to get you back to the ship. Can you walk?"

Emma thought a moment. "I'll be fine. I just lost it for a moment. Lost it or found it. But the ship's a good idea. Obviously, I'm not cut out for this climate."

It took two tries and a helping hand, but Emma left the bench and began putting one foot in front of the other again, each step steadier than the one before.

"That had to be one of the weirder moments of my life. I made myself a vision of the staircase under construction, then I added people to it—an architect and his wife—like an artist painting a picture. Then all sorts of things started drifting in. Slaves, I think, most of them. Not curses"—she made that judgment after the fact—"but there was misery enough. And a few white people. A girl and a boy. They looked very out of place; and they looked straight at me. Especially the boy."

"Heatstroke. You were on the threshold of heatstroke, that's all—and that's enough. It's my fault. I never should have made you come here. And I sure as hell should have been paying closer attention. God help me, I'm just not as sensitive as I was, and you're sensitive enough for both of us."

Em shrugged. "Sensitive enough for what?" The whole episode was sinking fast into memory, and she felt better than she had all day. "It's hot, and it's bright, but I'm enjoying myself . . . honest. Not everything, but, you know, it was kind of interesting just now. Was I making the scene up entirely, or was I looking back—looking back without benefit of the bolt-hole window? For that matter, it brings back the whole question of the accuracy of our experiences—"

"Don't talk about it!" Eleanor snapped. "Don't talk about it; don't think about it. You spend too much time thinking, Emma. You're worse than Harry. You'll wind up tying yourself in knots."

As was frequently the case, the urgency of Eleanor's warnings was all Emma needed to consider the experience more deeply. "The drifters. What were they?"

"Nothing! You're not used to the heat, and you sat in a spot where the air was stale. *Things* collect where the air is stagnant. *Things* get attracted, like mosquitoes. Tell yourself they were mosquitoes, and let it go at that."

Emma let it go, not because she thought her mother was right—Eleanor didn't get that outspoken unless there was something more important that she wasn't saying—but because they'd passed from the relative isolation of the staircase chasm to the streets of Nassau's tourist quarter. Discretion was always the better part of valor when it came to discussions about the wasteland. Especially when all the wine she'd drunk the previous evening had seemed to return to haunt her brain.

Four

An *hour alone* in the cabin while Eleanor soaked up decadence via hydrotherapy and a pedicure restored Emma completely. She took her mother's advice about forgetting her little time-shifting episode at the Queen's Stairway, not because she'd come to agree with it but because, with a little sleep behind her eyes, the sense that she was conjuring real people had faded into a dream. She was, after all, out of the habit of dreaming. The naturally surreal quality of dreams had become unfamiliar.

"When I get home, I need to spend a few more nights sleeping in my own bed," she said to the cabin, since neither of her cats was present to absorb stray bits of conversation.

After a quest for cola that took her into unfamiliar parts of the ship, Em settled into the cool, not-too-bright comfort of the cabin's nautically themed sofa. She cracked the paperback cover of the previous year's best-selling novel — the one all the book clubs and reading groups had recommended and she hadn't gotten around to reading.

She was getting into the story when Eleanor returned in an aura of herbal scents.

"Your turn—if you're feeling better."

Emma blanched. She'd managed to repress her commitment to visit the spa. Eleanor had handed her a perfectly good excuse, but using it might bring more trouble than it was worth. She slipped quickly into an ancient bathing suit—she'd still been married the last time she'd worn it—covered the teal and fuchsia diagonal strips with a knee-length T-shirt, and arrived at the spa with two minutes to spare.

A Polish girl who didn't look old enough to be working helped Emma into the aromatic hydrotherapy tub then left her there, surrounded by indirect blue green lights and faintly Polynesian music, for the contracted twenty-five minutes of bliss. Ever the skeptic, Emma expected nothing more than an expensive bath, but by the time the advertised hundred-plus hot water jets had finished cycling from her neck to the soles of her feet a few times, she'd become a convert to the religion of fast-moving water. She listened seriously to the follow-up speech about stimulation and exfoliation, nodding at all the right moments and succumbing to a ridiculously overpriced, all-natural scrub that would leave her skin younger and smoother, if she could just remember to use it after every shower.

The manicure was less successful. Emma Merrigan was a true child of the Sixties, the era of student protest, folk-rock, and the all-natural look for coeds. Not to mention that she'd sailed through her formative years with only her father for guidance. As a result, she learned more about plumbing than she had about what Arch Merrigan had labeled "war paint." Her nails had spent decades filed into utilitarian ovals of varying lengths and left pinkly naked to the world.

The petite Asian girl who studied Em's right hand then

her left shook her head sadly and said, "You not do much with them," in a tone midway between inquiry and despair.

Defensively, Em replied, "I don't bite them or break them."

"I fix," the girl promised and went to work first with a pair of nail clippers, then with an assortment of files and buffers. Emma thought the manicure was finished—and was pleased with the results—when she had, for the first time in recorded history, a matching set of nails on the tips of her fingers, but the girl was far from finished. She squirted thick oil onto Em's forearms and went to work massaging her arms from the elbow down. Tendons crackled and muscles that had been tight for years began to relax. Emma was beginning to think that manicures were another indulgence she might add to her routine back in Bower when the girl said, "Choose," and pointed to a rack of several dozen nail polish bottles.

Em obediently chose a color she liked—a dark luscious shade between plum and grape that the bottle label said was *Aubergine*—without a thought for what it would look like way down at the ends of her arms. She sensed that she'd made a mistake from the first stroke of color across her pinkie nail, then told herself she was on vacation and entitled to do something wild and experimental without her usual reluctance to attract attention. She sat quietly while the girl applied two coats of color and two more coats of other, clear liquids before positioning Em's hands in the breeze of a miniature table fan.

"Wait five minutes," she said, and Emma did.

She paid her bill—spa services were empathetically *not* included among the prepaid cruise services—and left tips she hoped were adequate. Em just missed the elevator, which meant she used her own finger, with its *Aubergine* tip, to press the "Down" button. She was sure, as only a chronically shy person can be, that everyone who joined her on the next elevator was staring at her unnaturally colored fingernails.

Eleanor did notice them before Em closed the cabin door. "Let's see!" she insisted enthusiastically.

Em displayed her hands for inspection.

"They look great! Way to go! I *really* like the color."

The compliment, coming from a woman whose hair was coppery at the roots and maroon at the ends and laced with bright-colored beads, did little to raise Emma's confidence in her sense of color, much less style.

"Let's party!" Eleanor brandished the day's activity sheet. "There's shrimp and wine on the pool deck and that calypso band you liked when we came on board. Then a Broadway revue and dinner in Chelsea's Place. If we dress now, we can go straight from the party to the theater to supper."

Courtesy of Eleanor's *Secret Guide,* Emma had packed specific outfits for each of the *Excitation*'s restaurants. For Chelsea's Place, with its Art Deco theme, she'd planned on her black slacks and a rather severe white satin blouse she'd bought on sale years earlier and never gotten around to wearing. Once dressed and wearing her war paint, she studied herself in the mirror.

Neat, presentable, and as far removed from a particular style or fashion as I can be—except for my nails. She made fists to conceal them.

"You look fine," Eleanor said.

Em returned the compliment sincerely and just a little enviously. Eleanor, in a bias-cut yellow dress and a wreath of brightly colored wooden beads for jewelry, had style to spare.

Em steered clear of both the wine and the sun, sipping diet cola in the shadow of an upper deck, while the calypso band put on a show. Eleanor kept them supplied with hors d'oeuvres that Em ate despite the distraction of her purple fingernails.

"I don't think this is me," she said to Eleanor, fanning her fingers between them after her fourth or fifth shrimp.

"Then don't think. You spend too much time inside your own head."

Em shrugged and considered the probability that her mother was right. In the spirit of cooperation, she marched into the sunlight and got herself a glass of wine that coordinated nicely with her nails.

The Broadway revue was fast-paced and exhausting, at least for the small company of singers and dancers who hoofed their way through more than a dozen musical excerpts. As with the previous night's entertainment, there was nothing knock-your-socks-off memorable about any one bit, except for the male lead from the previous night who'd done most of his singing and dancing in a pair of Robin Hood tights. Emma and Eleanor agreed he was more scenic than the scenery.

"He could eat cookies in my bed any time," Eleanor decided, and Em succumbed to giggling.

The wine was stronger this evening, or it was affecting her more. Em swore to herself that she'd have iced tea with dinner, and broke the promise without regret as she crossed the threshold of Chelsea's Place. Barring paradise, she'd found her favorite location within the *Excitation.* The colors were black and white, accented with bronze; the effect, though, was more Art Deco than postmodern stark. Layered curves swept along the walls, disguising the corners; they gave the huge room a surprising aura of intimacy. Chandeliers with lamps in the shape of lilies, that most Art Deco of flowers, were suspended above every table. The lily motif was repeated in the chairs and even the servers' table, where Draco and his minions awaited them in uniforms straight out of some sophisticated 1930s comedy.

According to the *Secret Guide*—and the cruise line's own promotional literature—Chelsea's Place was the dining room that evolved over the course of a meal into a "feast of color." Em couldn't imagine that any sort of evolution would create an improvement over the black-and-white elegance surrounding them.

The menu promised sophistication, too. Emma opted for tastes in unusual combinations: chicken braised in a persimmon-ginger sauce with a pignoli ragout, whatever that might turn out to be. Eleanor looked relieved when she found the roast beef. She ordered it end cut, medium, with a baked potato and buttered carrots, neither of which were printed on the menu. Mitya suggested wine: an unfamiliar German wine for Em, a red South African one for Eleanor, after promising that it was "very American" in character.

With the ordering taken care of, the table got down to the business of sharing their day's adventures. Despite her vow of silence, Eleanor made their walk through Nassau—including their accidental drift into the city's not-ready-for-tourists areas—sound interesting, which was more than Emma could have done on a dare. Still it was clear that their table mates, who'd gone off on day-trips, had had a more exciting day.

"Let's go to the reservations desk and see if there's anything exciting left for Wednesday on the private island," Eleanor suggested when the dinners arrived and conversation lagged.

"Even your *Secret Guide* said the island excursions were too expensive for what they delivered—that's why we didn't book any in advance. We've got our trip tomorrow: kayaking down a river. How much more exciting do you want?"

"Didn't you listen to Gracie talk about snorkeling with the dolphins? Even if they're not the best value, they've got to be better than doing nothing on our last day out. Besides, how expensive are they, really? How expensive for a once-in-a-lifetime day in paradise? Fifty dollars—even a hundred and fifty—isn't going to break either one of us."

It was disconcerting to hear Eleanor toss around a

phrase like "once in a lifetime." Em started to say that the good excursions had most likely been booked up in advance, then heard the negativity in her thoughts and kept them to herself. If she was right, then let some smiling crew member dash Eleanor's hopes; and if she was wrong? So, she spent a hundred and fifty dollars to swim with Flipper. No matter what her future held, it probably would be once in a lifetime, and it certainly would be better than their misadventures in Nassau.

"You're right. I've been trying to fight it—" Em caught sight of her plum-dark fingernails. "A vacation is an interregnum—"

Emma paid the price for working in a library as Eleanor wrinkled her nose and asked, "A what?"

"A time when the regular rules are suspended—*all* of them. And I've been trying to fight it. The smart thing to do is to lean back and let the *Excitation* work its magic and wonder. We'll be back in Michigan soon enough."

Eleanor raised her wineglass. "I'll drink to that."

They clinked, with Emma swallowing a pang of guilt with her wine. She was, after all, counting on the crew at the reservation desk to tell them that all the magic and wonder on the island Fantabulous Cruises called its own was already booked.

Conversations resumed, none of them either unpleasant or sufficiently compelling to stifle Emma's engineering gene. Their table was next to one of Chelsea's white walls, and Em's chair put her at just the right angle to spot a tight pattern of tiny dots embedded in the paint. Fiber optics, she decided, solving the mystery of where the evolving color would come from, leaving only the lesser mysteries of when and how. She kept a weather eye on the wall and was rewarded midway through her entrée.

A faint blue wave shimmered across the wall and quickly disappeared. *Very subtle,* Em approved. No one else at the table had noticed the first stirring of color. She looked beyond the table, but this was the "adult" seating and the few children, like those at Emma's table, had other things on their minds beside watching the restaurant's walls.

Then Emma caught sight of the cursed rusty-haired server. As soon as she did, the woman returned Em's accidental stare. Em lowered her eyes, but the damage was done. After an all-day absence, the young woman rose instantly to the top of her conscience. Eleanor, who was at times uncannily sensitive about such things, noticed the change at once.

"She's closer tonight. Drawn in like a moth."

Em nodded and reached for her wine.

"Ignore it, Em. There's nothing we can do."

"The boat's not moving," she whispered. "It hasn't moved all day. We could have done something. We could still *do* something instead of sitting here eating ourselves silly. Departure's not until 10:30."

"What did you just call this? An inter-something when the regular rules are off? Take your own advice and let it be."

"I'm not sure I can."

"Try. Do better than try, succeed. This isn't the time or place for righting wrongs."

"It just doesn't seem right."

"It's not right; it just is. We're on vacation and even if we weren't, we're far from our base. Didn't you read the chapters on roots? Didn't Harry talk to you about the perils of getting strung out far from home?"

Harry Graves had, in fact, pontificated on the extra danger a curse-hunter faced when he or she transited to the wasteland from an unfamiliar part of the real world, but he'd done it in the form of a debate with him presenting both sides. There were those who said a hunter should nurture a single reference point—a single root—between here and there, strengthening it with every wasteland translation. That way, if something ever went wrong, habit would guide the wayward hunter home. Of course, there were those who recommended the exact opposite: The more roots, the better, because habit itself was the enemy.

Em had hunted curses from the unfamiliarity of a hotel room during a librarians' conference. The hunt had been one of her rare failures: She hadn't kicked up a single curse all night. That wouldn't be a problem on the *Excitation*. The engineering gene—

Got distracted by a swirl of crimson working its way across the wall. The light was stronger this time, the wave slower and bolder. Art and Gracie noticed and shared their expert observations with the table. Even sullen Tiffany gasped with delight as the swirling pattern faded.

"You wait, now," Art explained, sounding a bit like Harry Graves in lecture-mode. "This is just the beginning. It gets better from here on."

Emma reserved judgment on the "better," but the light show certainly got more noticeable, though it didn't come to dominate the dining room until after the main course had been cleared. Draco, his minions, and all their counterparts disappeared with the dishes—which, alone, was a clue that something extraordinary was about to happen. The ambient lights dimmed, leaving the lily lamps as the room's sole source of light, and hidden loudspeakers came to life. A smooth-talking male voice narrated the story of Chelsea, a jazz-age chanteuse who'd gone to sea in search of a sailor who'd won her heart. Chelsea's search ended tragically with the sailor swept overboard midway across the ocean and the desolate Chelsea leaping in after him (Emma wondered if the earlier, family-oriented, seating heard a different version of the tale), but as the narrator spieled it out, Chelsea's story reached a happy conclusion' when the lovers' spirits found a new home aboard the *Excitation* (leaving Emma to ask herself who or what infused the walls of the identical Chelsea's Place on the *Excita-tion*'s sister ship, *Marvelocity*?).

Existential questions aside, the conceit worked. The creative minds behind Chelsea's Place might have a trite grasp of plot and characterization, but they were masters of entertainment. Musically, they'd come up with a blend of smokey jazz and traditional sea chanteys, then enhanced their sound with the best visual effects technology could produce and money could buy. Emma was grinning as broadly as anyone in the dining room when the staff made its triumphant reappearance bearing trays of desserts high above their shoulders, each tray sprouting a rainbow flambé.

Eleanor, who'd ordered one of Chelsea's special flaming desserts, reported that bright green hadn't improved the taste of her crisp-coconut ice-cream concoction. Emma graciously offered her mother a small portion of her bitter chocolate cheesecake.

"I told you not to order anything that had to be set on fire first."

"But it sounded so pretty on the menu," Eleanor replied, sneaking her spoon into Emma's territory and stealing a much larger chunk of cheesecake.

With Eleanor in the lead, they were among the first passengers to leave the dining room and the fourth in line at the reservations desk. By the time they were face-to-face with smiling Johan, they knew there were only two unfilled private-island excursions: a five minute parasailing experience over the bay or scuba-diving for rank beginners. Since neither of them were interested in diving and the lesson was actually the more expensive of the offerings, they handed their plastic passports over for parasailing reservations.

"I hope we know what we're doing," Em laughed as they walked away from the desk.

"We don't need to. Fantabulous Cruises has never lost

a passenger. Now, we've got choices: the piano bar, disco karaoke, or the trivia challenge with a three hundred-dollar jackpot."

Emma said she didn't care where they went, so long as they were leaning against the deck rails when the time came for the *Excitation* to begin its island hop to Freeport. "I want to see this ship do a one-eighty turn and leave the harbor all by itself."

Eleanor chose the trivia challenge, because they could enter as a team, and "You know more trivial things than anyone I know, excluding Harry, of course." But the night's challenge theme was Music of the Nineties, and Emma came up short somewhere between Seattle Grunge and Boy-Bands of Orlando. They were eliminated at the end of the second round.

The piano player was on a break and, by mutual consent, karaoke was not a viable option, which sent the women back to their cabin. They changed into more comfortable clothes and had claimed two deck chairs on the starboard side of the pool deck well before the disembarkation festivities of food, fireworks, and classic rock were scheduled to begin. Eleanor went off in search of beverages, wine for her, diet cola for Emma, while Emma looked out on Nassau and gradually lost herself in her thoughts.

She was somewhere between the hundreds of lights of Nassau and the millions of books housed in the Horace Johnson Library when Eleanor jostled her elbow with a cold, damp glass.

"Soft drinks cost as much as wine, so I got you wine."

"Not only am I turning into a lush, I can feel my clothes getting smaller by the hour!" But Em took the tumbler-shaped glass and sipped gratefully.

"I was watching you on my way back. You weren't thinking of slipping off, were you?"

"Not even close. I don't even remember what I was

thinking about. Something to do with what the library would look like if all the books were lamps."

Eleanor wrinkled her nose. "Just so long as you stick to the here and now."

"I'm not reckless," Em countered, not adding that she left recklessness to her mother, who had an impressive record of impulsive decisions, including her decision to abandon her infant daughter. "It bothers me that we can't do anything. Mooting curses is our responsibility. I feel uncomfortable shirking it, that's all."

"You take it all too seriously. I suppose that's my fault for leaving you."

Eleanor leaned against the teak rail and toyed with her glass. Em said nothing. This wasn't the first time Eleanor had made a remark that cut uncannily close to something Em hadn't said. She'd asked Eleanor—Harry and Blaise, too—if telepathy played any role in a curse-hunter's life. They'd each emphatically insisted it didn't, which left Emma thinking that her moods must be extremely transparent.

"There's never been any *need* to go off mooting every night. Nobody does; nobody expects you to. A couple of times a month . . . once a week, or when the watchers put out a call that something major's broken loose." The watchers were hunters with a special sensitivity to the movement of large-scale curses and rogues. Nearly two years ago, it had been watchers who'd noticed Emma when she'd made her first blundering forays into the wasteland. "It doesn't need to be an obsession. No one thinks we can moot all the curses—and, even if we could, tomorrow morning some bitter old pill is going to shrivel up and die and make a curse in the process."

"It's not like that," Em said softly. "The ones I've seen, they're mostly ordinary people."

"Even more so if it's ordinary people letting loose. We can't make the world a better place and, for all their malice, it's not curses—or rogues—that make it a worse one."

"We ignore time—we can remake ourselves. Look at Harry. Look in the mirror, for heaven's sake. I don't know what I want out of the future, but it seems only right that I've got to start paying for it now."

Eleanor tried spinning her glass between her fingers and nearly lost it overboard. "You make yourself sound very high-minded. My experience . . . my long experience is that nobody's all that good or high-minded. There's always something else, something simpler . . . something like a *man.*"

On reflex, Emma looked over both shoulders before stating, "Blaise has nothing to do with this."

"Point one: He's already obsessed, longtime obsessed. With good reason, no denying that, and it's not as though there's much else he can do with his time . . . except wait for you to show up. That quota system you've come up with: so many little curses every night, so many middling ones, one big one or rogue every Friday come Hell or high water. You've got an itch in your conscience, Emma dear, and you're scratching it with curses."

"Don't be ridiculous," Em snapped quickly, too quickly for even her own satisfaction. For all her faults, Eleanor wasn't a stupid woman, and her tendency to see the world in simple, sharp patterns often yielded simple, sharp insights. "If anything, Blaise has gotten less obsessed about rogues since we've all started hunting them together."

"I believe that's called codependency."

"You've been watching too much *Oprah.* I'm not obsessed; I'm not high-minded; and I'm not codependent. All I say is that we're privileged, and even if we can't possibly make the world a perfect place, or even a curse-less place, we still need to give back. A few hours each night isn't asking too much. It's not as if we're losing any sleep."

Eleanor tightened her eyebrows in calculation. "You

should talk to Harry about the Puritans sometime. Perpetual penance doesn't work. You'll just get ground down because you can't ever give back enough."

There was a glint in Eleanor's eyes and an unusual hardness in her tone that brought Em up short. She'd gotten to know the woman calling herself Eleanor Graves tolerably well over the past months, and it was easy to believe the myth that she was the person she seemed to be, but Eleanor Graves had been Eleanor Merrigan for half a century and Eleanor Baker when she'd been born decades before that. Emma knew virtually nothing about Eleanor Baker or the lessons Miss Baker learned when she truly was a young woman.

"I'll think about it," she promised. "I'll try to take a longer view of the whole situation."

Eleanor let the subject drop, and they lapsed into silence, which lasted only until the calypso band began playing. Minutes later, the fireworks began in a cascade of red, green, and magnesium white that preceded the ship as it departed Nassau's harbor. Between the music and the lights and, especially, the wine, Emma banished the past and the future from her thoughts. She dwelt in the present, sampling the buffet, even dancing with Eleanor until the music stopped.

"Good grief, it's nearly one A.M.," she realized after a glance at her watch.

"And the world didn't come to an end."

"I think I'll get a good night's sleep tonight," Em predicted.

But Emma's predictive ability failed. She lay on her back, staring at the ceiling, then on her side, watching the red display on the cabin clock slip past 2:00.

Eleanor's breathing was deep and regular, yet she roused when Emma eased out of the bed. "You okay?" she asked huskily.

"Can't sleep. I'm going to get dressed and take a walk . . . the promenade deck's open all night."

"Be careful."

Em made light of her mother's concern, chiding her with, "Don't worry. I'm not going to fall in."

She found clothes she'd shed earlier in the day—cruising was all about changing clothes—and dressed without turning on the light. The corridor outside their cabin was dim and quiet, as it hadn't been since their arrival. She took the stairs to the promenade deck—it was only two flights up. The invisible crew was out and about with a variety of cleaning implements. They scrupulously took no notice of a stray passenger as she walked across the lobby to the port side doors.

Except for an elderly couple leaning side-by-side against the railing, Em would have had the port-side deck to herself. The couple was a good distance away, well beyond earshot, but Emma wanted to be alone. She crossed the lobby a second time to the starboard side, and found what she was looking for: splendid isolation with not even an invisible crew member going about the business of keeping the *Excitation* clean.

She's right, Emma conceded after she'd settled in against the rail.

The moon was on the other side of the ship; probably why the other midnight ramblers had chosen the port-side promenade, but the moon's light cast a line of diamond reflections all the way to the starboard horizon. Em appreciated the scene a moment before getting into an argument with herself.

She could *be right. It's possible Blaise colors everything I do and think—at least everything I do and think about the wasteland . . .*

Em chewed on that thought, looking for ways to refute its essential truth.

I've fallen in love with a ghost . . . no, he's not even a ghost. If the wasteland isn't real . . . if the whole notion of mooting curses is a form of mass hysteria with no basis in reality, then I'm in love with a figment of my own imagination . . . in love with myself.

She shivered, and not from cold.

I . . . I think there's something wrong . . . I'm afraid there's something wrong with me—that two divorces and the prospect of growing old by myself—

But my mother—my very own mother—has grown young, not old. I've watched *her do it. My closest friends have watched her do it. We can't all be mad. Or could we? Isn't that exactly what mass hysteria is? A little mass—the friends of Emma Merrigan . . .*

If I'm not crazy—if I really am going to live a very long time—

Another shiver. Em let go of the ship's rail and wrapped her arms tightly around herself.

There is a price. There has to be a price for everything . . . for being one of Orion's Children. And, especially, for Blaise, the man of my dreams . . . literally. And the only price I can pay is hunting curses, mooting as many as I can. Call it karma—if I don't risk it all, then it all will go sour . . .

She's right—Call it by another name, but perpetual penance's a formula for disaster . . . suicide. I'm losing my place here, in the absolute present. I need to get rooted again, or I'm going to drift into disaster.

Morbidly, Emma imagined a moment, deep in the future, when, maybe, she'd find herself standing in moonlight on another ship. If the fall didn't kill her—these modern cruise ships soared as high as a ten-story building above the water—the sea surely would.

Em had been born with a vivid imagination. When she imagined something, really imagined it in all its dimensions, it would hover like a hologram before her eyes. She saw a body falling, thought nothing of it, blinked, and be-latedly realized it hadn't been her imagination at all.

Time thickened around Emma Merrigan. She felt each *thudding* beat of her heart, each neuron firing, each muscle twitching as her hands moved ever-so-slowly to the rail and her body leaned ever-so-cautiously into moonlit space and saw . . . churning foam. The *Excitation* wasn't pulling as much speed as she had on her overnight course from Port Canaveral to Nassau, but she wasn't drifting, either—

And what thought had just crossed her mind—*If the fall didn't kill her?*

Bleakest irony overwhelmed Emma. An eternity un-wound before Em could string a thought together. She looked left and right. Far to the stern, an invisible manned a mop; but most of the invisibles weren't fluent in English, and Em knew, at that moment, she wasn't fluent, either. Then it came to her like second nature: Dial 9-1-1. There were telephones in every cabin . . . and one hung on the wall beside the door behind her. A ship didn't have a po-lice department or EMS services, but surely a live person would—and did—respond to a 9-1-1 call.

"Somebody jumped," Em stammered. "I just saw some-one jump into the ocean."

Silence—disbelief? The *Excitation* billed itself as a place where dreams, not nightmares, came true. Then, in a softened tone almost as quavery as her own, the man asked, "Where are you?"

"The promenade deck, port . . . no, the starboard side, about in the middle."

"And the . . . *accident* you saw happened?"

"Above me. I saw him go by." Em checked her mem-ory—yes, the face, the hair, the body type, and light shirt tucked firmly into dark slacks: The jumper had been male.

"Ah . . . ah . . . *stay there.* I—I have to tell . . . Some-one will be there. Stay where you are."

The line went dead. Emma took a step toward the rail,

then retreated as though catastrophe might be contagious. There were chairs and benches all around her, but she stayed by the phone, numb from the inside out, until a young man in a crisp, white pseudo-military uniform came through the doors. He took one look at Em and seemed to know she was the one he needed to talk to.

"Second Officer Lee Sobecy," he said in lightly accented but perfect English that might have had its origin in Australia. He offered his hand, which Em took and held longer than she usually held a handshake.

Officer Sobecy asked her name; Em found her voice. It was barely a whisper, but that was enough on the quiet deck.

"You saw something fall overboard?"

"A man," Em corrected. "He was dark-haired and wearing dark slacks and, maybe, a white polo shirt. A light shirt, anyway. What are you going to do? What *can* you do?"

He almost shook his head, but caught himself. "We're checking the other decks above here—to see if anyone else saw anything."

"I wasn't hallucinating. I was standing right there." Em gestured at the rail, but didn't approach it. "He went right past me. I didn't believe it at first, then it sank in." She cringed; "sank" was not a word she meant to use.

A phone, or maybe a radio, beeped on Sobecy's belt. He turned away from Em before answering it. She eavesdropped on a conversation of only a few words: "You have? Deck nine? Right. I'll bring her down." Sobecy holstered the handset and faced Em again. "Would you mind coming below with me?"

"You found something?"

"Shoes and jewelry pretty much directly above here."

The deck doors were automatic. They opened when Sobecy strode in front of them. Em set out to follow him, but the effort left her lightheaded. She tried to steady herself with a hand on the door, but the door was moving, and she might have fallen into its path if Sobecy hadn't reacted quickly and caught her by the arm.

"Are you all right?" he asked, guiding her to one of the plush, interior chairs.

"Fine," she insisted while shaking her head. "He's dead. I just watched a man jump to his death."

Sobecy wasn't listening. He was talking to his handset again, and this time Em couldn't hear what he was saying. She took deep breaths and bent forward until her head touched her knees. A few moments and the panic had receded enough for her to raise her head.

"Ma'am?"

"I'm all right now. Where are we supposed to be going?" She stood up, slower than usual, but in command of herself.

"I've called for the ship's doctor. She's on her way."

"No. I've swallowed my shock. I'll be fine now." Em took a step to demonstrate her steadiness. "They're slowing the ship," she realized when her foot did not land precisely where she'd expected it to. "Turning it."

Sobecy nodded. "You don't happen to know how much time passed between when you saw what you saw and when you called?"

Em shook her head. "Not more than a minute."

Sobecy got back on his handset, giving Em time to consider how far the *Excitation* could travel in a minute and how much farther it would travel before it got itself turned around. "Easier to find a needle in a haystack."

"That's about right," he agreed.

They went through one of the "Crew Only" doors and along corridors that were narrower and considerably less luxe than the passenger passageways. Em made a comment about needing bread crumbs to find her way home. Sobecy laughed.

"You'll get an escort. We used to give little hats to the kids who wandered in—until we found the Web sites advertising them as secret perks and realized that parents were losing the kids on purpose."

Em started to laugh, then the missing man's face fell through her memory, and her laughter became a wave of nausea. *Motion sickness,* she lied to herself. She'd been born with a tourist's constitution and never come close to motion sickness. The wave passed. Em caught up with Sobecy before he disappeared down another narrow corridor.

Their journey ended in a room suitable for small conferences or quick meals. Two men and a woman were already seated at the table. Both men wore pseudo-military whites. One of them—the elder of the two, a man in his late forties or fifties—had three fingers of gold on his epaulets. His demeanor made him the authority in the room. Em wondered if he was the *Excitation*'s captain, though somewhere she'd read that captains had four golden bars. The other man's epaulets were unrelieved black, and he was clearly the junior officer in the room. The woman wore whites, too, and a doctor's name tag. They all stood until Emma had seated herself. The three-stripe man, who gave his name so quickly that Em never had a chance to remember it, assured her that their meeting was informal.

Until that moment, Em hadn't considered the possibility that it could be anything else. All the tales about a captain being the ultimate law aboard his ship at sea clamored out of memory, and she sat straighter than she had in months.

"What, exactly, happened? What did you see?" the man who might be captain asked.

The man with unadorned shoulders made a note on a clipboard pad.

"It was a little after two; I couldn't sleep, so I decided to go to the promenade deck. I'd been standing at the rail, just watching the water, when—suddenly—he went past."

The captain's tone turned accusatory. "You told the operator that he jumped."

Em's heart rate soared. "I—I did," she admitted. "I don't know. I didn't see him—" The memory replayed. "There wasn't any panic. His arms—I remember them now—were folded over his chest. And he was quiet, not screaming, not flailing or trying to save himself, and feet first. If he'd fallen by accident or been—" She considered criminal possibilities then remembered what Sobecy had said: "You found his shoes, didn't you?"

Sobecy and the captain exchanged glances, with Sobecy getting the sharper look.

The captain's radiophone buzzed. He answered its call, and though he was no more than six feet away, Emma couldn't make out a word he said until he returned the phone to his belt and told the room, "We've lowered a searcher." There was no optimism in his tone, merely the righteousness of a man—a ship—following the rules.

Emma dared a question, "Has anyone been reported missing?"

"We know who it was," the captain admitted stiffly. "He was part of the crew . . . shouldn't have been up on that deck at that hour."

Em wondered if the rules were different for out-of-place crew: a smaller search party, a shorter search? The captain wasn't saying, and if he wasn't, none of the others in the room would volunteer the information. A clock on the wall showed five after three—or five after fifteen; there was an extra set of digits on the perimeter for anyone on twenty-four-hour time. Em hid a yawn behind her hand. The yawn itself was a false alarm, a reaction to the clock. She knew herself too well to think she was going to fall asleep before dawn. But the yawn served a purpose, signaling that all the necessary notes had been taken. The meeting was over, and it was time for Sobecy to return her to the *Excitation*'s passenger side.

Emma took one step into the corridor outside the conference room and locked eyes with a familiar face: the young woman from the dining rooms, the young woman with a curse. She had a two-person escort, one a white-clad, two-striped young man like Sobecy, the other, an older woman who looked as if she'd been rudely awakened and hurriedly dressed in whatever came first in the closet. None of the three bothered to smile at a misplaced passenger. The young woman, still clad in her black-and-white Chelsea's Place costume, looked smaller than life and clearly terrified.

Putting two and two together, Em reached an uncomfortable conclusion: The girl knew the jumper. The sum was unexpected, but not surprising. A successful curse, like any successful parasite, kept its host alive while it spread its misery far and wide. And, knowing there was a curse involved, Em couldn't assume it was mere coincidence that put her on the promenade deck at just the right—wrong—moment. Where curses and hunters were involved, there were no coincidences.

"This way," Sobecy said, touching Em's arm and guiding her in the opposite direction.

She heard the conference room door close, nothing more.

"Try not to take it too hard," Sobecy advised when they emerged in the elevator lobby of Em's home deck. "When something like this happens, it's usually something that's been planned for a long time."

Emma got the hint that suicide by cruise ship wasn't unprecedented. "I imagine you're right," she replied, because Sobecy couldn't be much more than half her age and was so obviously trying to say the right thing to a passenger whose dream vacation might have been compromised. "It's not like I could have reached out and hauled him in beside me."

"Yeah," he agreed eagerly. "You know, he probably

didn't drown. From up there on the sports deck, the fall alone would have been enough."

Em couldn't stifle an ironic smile quickly enough, but kept the similarity of their thoughts to herself. She shook Sobecy's hand and headed down the corridor.

Once she'd heard the "Crew Only" door click shut, Em reconsidered the wisdom of locking herself in a dark room. Then again, she was none-too-eager to go walking on the promenade deck, either. She stuck her plastic passport in the appropriate slot and pressed down on the door handle.

"Is that you, Emma?" Eleanor asked from darkness.

"It is."

"You've been gone a long time."

"Not really. A little over an hour."

Em carefully bypassed the bed in favor of the sofa in the sitting area. She sank into it with a poorly repressed sigh.

"Is something wrong?"

"The curse has struck and killed."

"It's just your imagination working overtime. You can't possibly—"

"I was standing on the promenade deck—thinking about what you'd said about Blaise—and a body fell right past me."

"My God. Right in front of you? But still—"

"I called nine-one-one. It works, even on a ship in the middle of the ocean. I wound up being led through the bowels of the ship—I met the captain, I think, one of them, anyway. The night captain. And after I'd told him what I'd seen—when I was leaving the conference room—I nearly bumped into the girl from the dining room. I looked into her eyes, Eleanor; the curse had a hold on her life, and she was lost in there."

The sheets rustled. The light came on.

"You're serious?"

"The captain said the jumper was a crewman."

"You can't be sure that he jumped."

"He left his shoes behind, and he wasn't struggling. Our eyes almost met as he fell past. He meant to be alone when he died, and I intruded. Damn! I should have intruded sooner. Eleanor—a man's *dead* because we didn't want to take the risk of mooting a shipboard curse."

"An unacceptable risk, the way this ship can move through the water."

"We weren't moving through the water all day today. We could have mooted it instead of going ashore."

Eleanor swung her legs over the side of the bed. "If you feel so strongly, we can moot it on Wednesday—"

Emma lost patience. "Eleanor! A man's *dead* because of that curse!"

"And we'll moot it."

"Fat lot of good that's going to do the crewman," Em's voice rose in frustration. "He's *dead*. There's no way I can intervene. We're not talking the seventeenth century. I can't *change* anything that just happened. Yesterday's not going to be resilient tomorrow; it's not going to change. We can moot that curse six ways from Sunday, and that crewman's staying dead," she snarled.

"You never know—"

"I *do* know. Maybe the fact that a crewman jumped off the *Excitation* isn't going to show up on CNN—though if it's a slow news day, there's no telling what's going to make the crawl—but it's already been written down and reported. Too many people know about it already. . . . Hell, it's practically my fault that so many people know." Em paused to consider how quickly knowledge could propagate. "The way things are going with technology and instant communication, we all may find ourselves out of a job before long: There won't be any resilience left; nothing to play with. Everything's going to be recorded . . . set down in stone, or at least on digital media. There won't be anything we can change. Curses are going to have a field day!"

Eleanor fished a leather-bound hip flask from her drawer. She offered it to her daughter. "Have a swallow and calm down. First off, you don't know there's a curse involved. Second, there are thousands of curses, and they're not nearly responsible for all the misery and all the deaths that humankind suffers every day. *We do what we can,* Emma."

Emma opened the flask. She expected scotch, her mother's booze of choice, and got brandy instead. The fiery liquid left her coughing and watery eyed. Once her lachrymal pump had been primed by the brandy, Em began to cry in earnest. It had been a good six months since her last attack of the weepies: the sudden upsurge of tears that had marked her grief after her father's death. Once the dam broke, her inchoate tears came in torrents, sweeping words and thoughts aside. She scarcely noticed when Eleanor sat beside her and took her hands between her own.

Comfort was not a watchword of their relationship. Emotions, because they were hopelessly unresolved, were routinely denied. Em resisted the human urge to respond to human closeness, human warmth, but shock and exhaustion had stolen her strength. She leaned against Eleanor's shoulder and sobbed loudly when her mother's arm slipped around her shoulder.

Amid the sobs she managed to say, "I can't take it any longer."

"The responsibility."

Emma nodded, showering them both with tears. "I try. I try, but there are too many of them and not enough of me—"

Eleanor *shhsh*-ed her, like a mother would a small child.

Em shook her head and tried, feebly, to escape. "Not now," she murmured.

"Let it go. Let the responsibility and everything else go. There's no better time—You're not beholden to anyone."

"No," Em insisted and freed one hand from its gentle prison. "Not now. I don't want to talk about it now. I'm not myself."

"Then come back to bed."

That, suddenly, was an attractive idea. Em kicked off her shoes and crawled into bed with her clothes still on. She heard Eleanor sigh before the light went out.

F*ive*

E*mma made the* White Elephant mistake—as in "don't think about a white elephant"—when she resolved not to think about the jumper once her eyes were closed. Predictably, the doomed man was locked on every screen of her mental multiplex. In an effort to void her error, Em committed another one, when she reminded herself—

It's not like it's the worst you've seen.

The falling images broke apart, like the facets of a bug's eyes. Everything about the crewman kept its place, but now there were all the other horrific memories: brutal murders, gruesome punishments, and fatal accidents. They were nearly all vicarious, picked up in the course of tracking curses to their moment of inception and mooting them there. Some were so remote that her memory had recorded them in stark black-and-white. But monochrome or faded color, Emma had told herself the truth: A man leaping to his death was far from the worst she'd seen.

Em found herself helpless as images of death vied with one another before her mind's eye. Physically turning her head was no use; the scenes were on the inside and followed her. For one quick moment, Emma considered taking a walk.

That idea stifled itself in irony.

She wrapped her arms around one of the spare pillows forming a Maginot Line down the middle of the king-sized bed and clutched it close.

"Emma?"

Em bit her lip and said nothing.

Let it be morning. Another day, another day of memories and this *will start to recede.*

She opened her eyes and focused on the darkness, because real nothing was stronger than the memories. Em had no expectation of falling asleep, but darkness—intense, concentrated darkness—was a powerful soporific. Her eyelids fell and though there were fleeting dreams in surreal black-and-white, Em slept until the smell of coffee woke her up.

Eleanor stood at the foot of the bed, a tray in her hands. "When the cabin pixie didn't wake you up, I figured you needed your sleep."

Em raised her head then let it fall back to the pillow without saying thanks. Waves of pain radiated around her right eye, the worst of them looping behind her ear before burning her nerves to her elbow. Of all her headaches, and Emma Merrigan knew headaches the way Eskimos knew snow, the worst was the one that circled an eye while she slept. The least change in angle or altitude set her head to throbbing. Instinct said *don't move,* but experience had taught that the closest thing to a cure waited on the tray.

"Coffee," she croaked, hoping to strike a tone of good humor.

There were two kinds of migraine sufferers, her doctor had said years ago when he diagnosed her condition: the ones who needed to avoid caffeine at all costs and the rarer ones who needed their jolt every morning. Back then, Emma had gone cold turkey, enduring three months of daily pounding, until the doctor was convinced that she was indeed one of humanity's rare specimens.

"Coffee . . . please?"

"That bad?" Eleanor asked while putting a cup on the bedside table.

"Worse." Emma levered herself up awkwardly, raising her shoulders first, her head last. She savored the coffee's aroma before putting the cup to her lips.

"You got almost a full night's sleep. It's after nine now—we've got forty-five minutes before we have to catch our excursion in the disembark lobby."

Em's eyelids sank, the rest of her also. She'd forgotten their commitment to tropical kayaking.

"You're not going to funk out on me, are you?"

That was before I watched someone commit suicide, Em retorted silently. Aloud, she said only, "I've got a headache."

"Can't you take something for it? Something stronger than coffee. I saw you unpack your pills."

Em took another swallow. It burned on the way down and felt like paradise. Already the pounding had retreated to dull *thuds,* the kind of pain she'd learned to live with— until she thought of the Bahamian sun. She did have medicine to force the migraine into deeper retreat, but nothing really cured a migraine except time. At best she'd be nauseated, out-of-focus, and sensitive to sunlight. All of that together wasn't as ominous as an argument with Eleanor, and pain, real throbbing pain, pushed everything else out of her thoughts, even the image of a young man plummeting to his death.

"I'll be ready," she promised after another swallow.

"I didn't know what you'd want to eat, so I brought you a Danish and some cereal, a half grapefruit and some cantaloupe—"

"Any protein?"

"A hard-boiled egg, bacon, a sausage, and some cheese

squares: Cheddar and Swiss and something with black and red specks."

Emma peeled the egg and ate it plain, one bite quickly following another. Eggs might not be the best food for her heart, but like caffeine, they were good for headaches. Cheese was a bit dicier. She stared at the cubes, letting her eyes perform a litmus test on behalf of her gut. The nausea didn't worsen; she popped a Swiss morsel into her mouth and headed for the shower.

Thirty minutes, another cup of coffee, a variety of headache medications, and the rest of the cheese later, Emma and her camera were ready to face her tropical commitments. She and Eleanor mingled with about twenty other *Excitation* excursioners, all but a few of them kayaking veterans with a plethora of specialized clothing and gear hung around their bodies.

"We're outclassed," Em whispered to her mother.

"We are *not* chickening out. There's nothing to worry about. The brochure says everything will be provided. All we have to do is show up."

The smiling tour guides arrived five minutes late. There were four of them: three perky State-siders and a token Bahamian. They collected vouchers, passed out more information, told a few jokes, and led their charges from the ship into a maze of stalls and buses. Their bus was small, brightly painted, and, unfortunately, having a few problems with its air conditioning. Em felt her headache reorganize itself as she climbed the steps into the passenger compartment.

"Just open the windows and feel those fresh, cool Bahamian breezes," the Bahamian guide urged.

It was hard to tell if the guide believed his own words or was deeply steeped in sarcasm, but if Freeport's breezes had been cool or fresh, there wouldn't have been a need for air conditioning in the first place. The windows opened a few inches at best—just enough to admit the outflow from an exhaust that surely would have failed a stateside carbon monoxide emissions test. Breathing improved somewhat once they were out of Freeport-proper, though Em's relief was tempered by anxiety, as the bus swayed around the hairpin turns. The Bahamas, she recalled from high school geography class, weren't flat islands built by energetic coral polyps but the remains of substantial mountains, and though she once or twice flashed on an image from the promenade deck, there was always another gut-jolting turn to banish it again.

The bus deposited them in front of an open-air information center, where, while sitting in the shade, they got basic instruction in kayaking.

"We're going downstream. The river will do all the work. All you have to do is sit in the middle and use your paddle the way you'd use your arms."

Their kayaks were one-apiece, pastel-colored little things that drew wrinkled noses from the more experienced members of the group. Eleanor got the last of the lilac models; Emma's was bright turquoise. Both colors clashed with the mandatory bright orange life vests.

There was a zero-current lagoon beside the information center where they tested their paddling skills after stowing their perishables in industrial-strength plastic bags. Em's problem wasn't with her extended arms but with her eyes. Despite optician-recommended sunglasses and a wide-brimmed hat, there was enough ambient light that her face was locked in a constant squint. She washed down another handful of anti-headache pills with bottled water and pronounced herself as ready as she was ever going to be.

Minus the headache, the two-hour excursion would have made a beautifully memorable trip along crystal-clear waters through at least three distinct ecosystems. With a headache, Em could only hope that her camera had focused better than her eyes and captured a hundred or so images that she could enjoy in the weaker light of Bower,

Michigan. As for the actual kayaking part of the trek, she'd gotten the hang of her paddle quickly and had skimmed effortlessly from one patch of shade to the next all the way down the river.

Eleanor had fared less successfully. When she wasn't propelling herself into the riverbanks she was getting herself turned completely around and drifting backward. Tom, their lead guide, wound up paddling most of the trek beside her. Of course, in addition to being an expert kayaker, Tom was easily the best-looking unattached man under the age of thirty they'd seen since boarding the *Excitation.*

"How much trouble were you really having out there?" Em asked when the on-the-water part of their excursion had ended and they were waiting for the beach-side barbeque to begin.

"The damn thing had a mind of its own," Eleanor insisted. "No matter what I did, it wanted to wind up in the weeds and roots."

"All that personal attention from Tom had nothing to do with it?"

"Distraction. Pure distraction. I'd've done better without him. Hell, I tried sending him your way—"

"Looked in the mirror this morning? You're the one with the student's body. I probably look like his mother . . . *older* than his mother."

Eleanor pulled a sulk that lasted until someone calling himself Capt'n Modie drove up in a decorated jitney with boxes of steaming barbeque and other picnic trappings. On or off the ship, Fantabulous Cruises made certain its passengers were well fed. The island barbeque sauce was like nothing Em had tasted before, but it instantly became a favorite. She managed to forget her headache while eating every morsel, then stretched out in a shaded hammock with two other sun-dodgers while everyone else tanned and swam on a dazzling, white-sand beach. Her headache retreated as far as it would with heat all around her and sunlight nearby. Em opened the book she'd brought from the ship. The print was small, the plot uncompelling, but she kept the pages turning.

A different bus, one with a functioning air conditioner, came to collect them at three-thirty. Emma took a few last pictures, including one of Eleanor with her arm around Tom, the tour guide, then climbed into the blessedly cool bus. Migraines were fickle creatures, notorious for rebounding just when Em thought they'd run their course. The change in temperature and humidity, however welcomed by the rest of her, refueled the ache. She felt every bump and twist in the road between the beach and the ship and begged out of the late afternoon wine-tasting session that had been one of the items on her "must do" list.

"I've got to lie down," she explained on the short walk between the bus and the ship.

"Can I get you something?"

Em shook her head; even that made the pain worse. "No. I'll be better once the sun's set—"

"You'll miss the show, and dinner, too. Tonight we're in Xanadu. You don't want to miss Xanadu."

Emma agreed that she didn't want to miss anything, but she didn't want the headache to entrench itself, the way some migraines could, and hang on for three or four miserable days; and that was the direction the ache was headed, if she didn't retreat to someplace dark and quiet.

"I sprained my wrist once," Eleanor said while she was changing and Em was making a nest in the pillows. "Hurt like hell. I kept on respraining it until my doctor wanted to put it in a cast for six weeks. I thought, *this is ridiculous*, and went to the Netherlands instead. It wasn't hard . . . not as hard as letting go of one's self and becoming another. You could try it with your headaches. There's no reason to suffer: just imagine yourself without them."

"Not right now."

"Of course, not right now. When we're back in Bower. What about your pills? Can you take more pills?"

"I've already taken too many. I'll be all right. Come and get me when it's time to get dressed."

"Don't you want to watch us leave port? That's at five."

"All right," Em didn't have the will to argue. "Come back before five, or call me, but let me rest now."

Once Eleanor had left and Em was alone in the cabin, she considered her mother's words. Could she shed her migraines in the wasteland? For that matter, was the headache truly a product of too much sunshine and overnight stress, or had she succumbed to wasteland withdrawal? She had an hour and a half before the *Excitation* was scheduled to get under way again, an hour before Eleanor was likely to touch bases. And Eleanor was likely to come through the door or at least pick up the phone. If there was anything to Eleanor's fear of moving objects, Em wouldn't be putting herself at much risk.

She stretched on her back, making full contact with the bed and the ship, which was silent, perfectly motionless. The wasteland was a thought away. Then, before Em could grasp the thought, the suicidal crewman fell through her mind and, instead of a spinning coin or the way-back stone, she saw the haunt-eyed face of the girl with the curse. It didn't take a true-believer to recognize an omen when it loomed in front of her. Emma rolled onto her side and gave herself to the heartbeat rhythm of her headache.

The ringing phone jolted Em out of a gray daze. She'd sat up and grabbed the receiver without a thought for her aching ear.

"It's a few minutes after five," Eleanor said. "The band's playing again, and I think they're getting ready to untie the ship. If you're feeling up to it, now's the time to come watch us leave Freeport. Are you feeling up to it?"

Emma asked herself the same question. The headache was hiding in a corner of her mind, a shadow of its former

self. She thought of bright light and a lively band; it didn't
rise to the bait.

"Yeah, I'm feeling up for it. Where are you?"

"The pool deck. The port side—no, the starboard . . .
I'm looking down on the dock. There! Someone just untied
another rope and threw it at the ship."

"Okay, stay there. I'll be up in a few minutes."

The port at Nassau, even the one at Canaveral, had been
tailored to the cruise industry's demands. Not so the port
of Freeport, which was more thoroughly industrial than
Em had guessed from the short walk between the *Excitation* and the excursion bus. The scaffolding of a good-sized
container operation dwarfed the cruise facilities and beyond them—but by no means hidden from view—a row
of mothballed cruise ships. Through her camera's tele-
photo lens, Em made out the names still painted across
their sterns.

"Bankrupt," Eleanor said after Em recited the name of
the largest ship. "Too old. Too small. Too small," she said
in response to the other names. "The *Excitation*'s half
again as big, and she's not as big as the boats the cruise
lines have on order."

"Too bad," Em replied, clicking off a few shots. "Those
over there look like *ships,* not floating shoe boxes. My one
complaint about this ship is that it may be the fastest thing
on the ocean, but it has the silhouette of a margarine tub."

"A tub with three swimming pools, basketball and ten-
nis courts, and a driving range. Gotta give the passengers
what they want—and it's not like they want to get to Europe in record time. Records went out of style with the *Titanic*. These ships are all about creature comfort and
having a good time."

"It's a shame that—" Em began, then let a pithy comment on the importance of esthetics and the artificiality the
floating cities had foisted off on places like Freeport and

Nassau go unfinished, as the *Excitation*'s main engines came to life.

There was no sound, at least none that could be heard above the band—which might explain why there was always loud music playing whenever the *Excitation* left port—and the vibration was nothing that would have shaken a cocktail glass off the teak rail. That was the point: The engines were steel layers away, and yet their quickening could be felt on the highest decks. Then the *Excitation* began its improbable slide sideways into the channel—a slide that left the water's surface undisturbed.

"I'd love to see what this ship is doing under the water right now."

Eleanor laughed and said, "You sound just like your father. He said the same thing when we left Le Havre."

Em gripped the rail tightly and said nothing. Someday, but not today, she'd ask Eleanor about the brief, long-ago days when she'd been Arch Merrigan's wife.

The gap between the *Excitation* and the wharf widened slowly for about ten minutes, then the ship paused. Em imagined the engine-room crew had to do *something* to switch the ship from sideways to forward ho. She listened with her feet and thought she felt a faint lurch as the forward motion began—but that could just as easily have been a reaction to the ship's horn, which blared out its signature hoot at the pivotal moment.

"Let's eat!" Eleanor said, heading for the stairs and the hors d'oeuvres spread that, in three short days, had become a habit.

Eleanor drank wine. Em stuck with coffee, because of its caffeine, and tried unsuccessfully to limit herself to three shrimp and a single slice of proscuitto-wrapped melon.

Back in the cabin for a quick change into their dining room clothes, Em complained that she'd need to go on a diet when she got back to Bower.

"—And if I ever do a cruise again, I'm bringing slacks with an elastic waist!"

It was their third evening aboard the *Excitation,* their third visit to the plush theater, where, for a change of pace, instead of lavish musical numbers they got a stand-up comic—a one-man show with a one-man band. Comparing the bare stage to the glitzy overproduction of the previous two evenings, Em lowered her expectations—needlessly, as it turned out. With a smooth patter and his collection of parodies and improbable instruments, the comic expertly won the house. After a sing-along encore, the audience funneled through the ship's shopping arcade to the appropriate dining room.

Xanadu, the third and last dining room Em and Eleanor would visit, was the *Excitation*'s showplace—the dining room that scored the largest photo in the Fantabulous brochures and photo spreads. *Exotic* was the adjective most often applied to its glass mosaic walls and swag lighting. The colors were rich, and the overall effect made Em think of medieval cathedrals by way of the Arabian Nights. Draco handed them oversized menus with entrées almost as exotic as the decor. Eleanor had a desperate look on her face until she found a fairly plain steak-and-potatoes entrée buried on the second page. Em went Indian with a sampler of curries, kabobs, and korma. She knew of no wine that particularly complemented Indian food and gratefully ordered a tropical-fruit iced tea instead.

Em's tablemates noticed the exception, and Gracie guessed that she had a headache.

"Migraines!" the older woman said with a shake of her head when Emma admitted to one. "Had them until I went through the change. Best thing that ever happened to me, wasn't it?" She turned to her husband who smiled and nodded right on cue. "Do you get the auras?"

"No," Em admitted. "I'm common, not classic. None of

the fancy stuff, just banging and throbbing until it hurts to look straight ahead."

She got a round of sympathy she didn't need—on a scale of one to ten, her migraine had shrunk to fractional levels, and she was avoiding alcohol out of precaution, not necessity. On the other hand, she had an excuse to let the dinner conversation swirl past her, limiting herself to quick interjections when Eleanor told the tale of their excursion, portraying herself as the ultimate kayak klutz.

"I spent so much time fouled up on banks, I could have gotten out and walked to the sea faster!"

"Don't be fooled," Em warned her tablemates. "There was only one cute guide, and he spent the entire trip showing you how to paddle."

Eleanor hooted—she was on her third glass of wine.

The meal was a success, the best so far despite the faint migraine. They told Draco that Xanadu would be their last dinner.

"Tomorrow we're going to eat in Gondolas," Eleanor explained.

"Excellent choice," he replied in his flawless English. "The veal piccata is my favorite, but the osso buco is the house specialty. You'll have an excellent meal."

Draco made recommendations for both entrées and desserts. Moments later Em caught him whispering to Mitya and the other minions. Maybe they were talking about something else entirely, but it seemed to Emma that for the rest of the meal their normally attentive service kicked up a notch, as though the staff were making sure that she and Eleanor remembered who was who when the time came to allocate tips at the last breakfast.

Emma had noticed Draco's side conversation because it occurred while she was looking over the dining room, searching for the girl with the curse. Em was ready to swear that the girl wasn't in the room when she appeared with a dessert tray balanced against her shoulder. Their eyes met across the width of the room, and the girl looked away so quickly she almost lost control of her tray.

"You're staring," Eleanor whispered a few minutes later.

"I've got to fix her in my mind. We won't likely see her again."

"Let it go for now. When the time comes, you'll be able to do whatever needs doing."

But Emma had become a dog with a bone and though she was stone sober, as she hadn't been after her previous dinners aboard the *Excitation,* curiosity finally got the better of her on the way out of the dining room. Without a warning word to Eleanor, Em veered to the left and marched toward a meeting, maybe a confrontation. The girl saw Em coming. There was no surprise in her face when Em came to a halt just out of arm's reach. She read the girl's name, Donetta, from her name tag and that she, like Draco, was from Croatia.

The girl spoke first, "Yes? May I help you?" Her English was more accented, less fluent.

For a moment Emma was paralyzed by embarrassment. The only words she could think to say were: *Do you know you're harboring a curse?* and she couldn't very well say those. Where was her mother-voice when she needed its cold advice most? (Em knew where her mother was: a half-step behind her left shoulder.) She had to say something; she and Donetta were drawing the sort of attention Em had always dreaded. She opened her mouth, not entirely sure what she was going to say until the words began to flow.

"You seem so familiar. I'm sure I know you from somewhere."

"You have been to Croatia? Dubrovnik?" the young woman countered.

Emma shook her head. She felt calmer now that she'd proved one of life's fundamental laws: You can't actually die of embarrassment. "You haven't been to school in America . . . in Michigan?"

"Never to America or Michigan. Maybe someday, I hope."

"I'm sure our paths have crossed."

That, at least, was the honest truth. Their paths had crossed in the small hours of the morning, but there was no flicker of recognition in Donetta's eyes. Instead the girl betrayed a growing sense of panic, glancing desperately to her right, trying—Em realized—to attract the attention of someone who could rescue her from a mad passenger.

Emma felt a tug on her arm. "There, I told you. She doesn't remember, and you're mistaken," Eleanor said, keeping a grip on the sleeve of Em's blouse.

"No," Em insisted, shaking free. She'd gone too far to retreat without sating her curiosity. Without warning or invitation, she reached for Donetta's right hand and cradled it between her own. "I can help you," she whispered.

In an instant the expression in the girl's eyes went dead cold from wide-eyed anxiety. She said, "I need no help," and sought to free her hand.

"Emma!" Eleanor said sharply as she tugged again.

Every neuron of logic and wisdom in Emma's brain fired simultaneously and with a single message to her hands and fingers: Let go! Em fought her better judgment. She squeezed Donetta's hand tighter.

"Don't give up hope," she urged, meeting eyes that grew rapidly colder and menacing.

Suddenly a jolt like an electric shock struck her hands, driving them apart, freeing the girl and more. There were new memories in Emma's head, memories of places she'd never been, scenes she'd never witnessed. The third time Eleanor pulled on Em's sleeve got her moving like the drug-addled Coleridge himself crossing the Alph on his way out of Xanadu.

"Have you lost your mind?" Eleanor hissed.

"Maybe."

Eleanor had them aimed at the elevator lobby. Em wanted nothing to do with crowds pressing against her, not while she was making sense of what, for her, seemed like a dream but were likely memories stripped from Donetta's life. She turned toward the stairs and bounded down the six flights to their cabin deck. Eleanor, who was wearing sling-back heels to Emma's soft-soled flats, kept up, but barely.

They were both out of breath when Em dropped the plastic passport into the door handle. She waited until Eleanor was inside then bolted for the bathroom, dropped to her knees, and offered her entire dinner, back to the melon-wrapped proscuitto, to the porcelain god.

"Are you all right?" Eleanor shouted from the far side of the closed door as the toilet did its high-power vacuum flush.

Emma sagged sideways, drawing comfort from the cold tiles trimming the shower. The question was so foolish, so obvious, she initially refused to answer it, then Em imagined her mother barging into the tiny chamber.

"I think I've solved the problem."

"Can I get you anything? Crackers? A glass of milk?"

The mere thought of dairy products was enough to send Em leaning toward the bowl again. She got her breathing under control and realized the headache was back.

"It's just not fair."

Em found her toothbrush and covered it with a healthy squirt of toothpaste. Peppermint flavoring settled her mind as much as her stomach. She did feel better, except for the headache, which had climbed above the low numbers on the one-to-ten scale but remained well short of a number-ten headbanger.

"Sorry about that," she said emerging from the tiny bathroom.

"I don't want to say I told you so, but, Emma, whatever possessed you to grab that girl's hand like that?"

Emma shrugged. "Damned if I know. *Possession*'s not a bad word. Something hijacked my better judgment. That was pretty obvious." She sat on the bed, keeping as much distance between herself and her mother, who was sitting on the couch, as far apart as the cabin's geometry allowed.

"You knew better, and you went ahead and did it anyway?"

Another shrug. "Forget hunting; it's not ever good form to start grabbing the flesh of total strangers. I've got to admit, I surprised myself. It really was as though my impulse control had gone on vacation—but why those particular impulses got through is a mystery to me."

"The curse drew you in."

Em gave her mother a cockeyed stare.

"Have you bothered to *read* those books you've got?"

The books were the two handwritten curse-hunters' guides that Em kept beside her chair in the living room. "I've tried. The one you left behind is just a tad incomplete, and the one I got from Harry is just the opposite. I don't recall anything about getting drawn in by a curse."

"I know I left you a warning. It's in the chapter on keeping safe."

"There *are* no chapters in the one you wrote. Just a page of writing here, another there, and half of them listing ingredients for potions that would get me arrested if I tried to make them."

"You always dwell on the negative. One never makes direct contact with a cursed person on their turf. If direct contact is necessary—and it shouldn't be for a plunger like you—lure them into your space, or at least into a public space."

"A dining room isn't public enough?"

"Apparently not. You gave yourself away. The curse

knows what you are and who you are. We'll have to take precautions."

"Precautions?"

"We need to seal this room—make it our own. I can do it—no, better, I'll show you how to do it." Eleanor shared a thought with herself and sighed. "I should have done it as soon as we came aboard—as soon as we knew there was a curse. It's not unheard of for them to sense us before we sense them." She went to her half of the storage space and began rummaging through a drawer.

Recalling her mother's written recommendations for concoctions that included unhealthy amounts of laudanum, Em snapped, "What did you have in your luggage!?"

"Nothing for you to worry about." Eleanor brandished a bottle of perfume. "There's nothing like a little scent to mark your place in the world."

"Good grief . . . are we on a par with dogs?"

Emma didn't get an answer but watched as her mother shook a few drops onto her fingers. Then her mother traced the door frame, paying special attention to the hinges and latch.

"There are too many openings in the bathroom," Eleanor explained as she closed the bathroom door and began anointing it with designer fragrance. "You'll have to remember that the bathroom isn't ours." She stepped back and gave their porthole a critical glance. "It's probably sealed watertight, but it won't hurt to be certain. Do you want to do the honors?"

Em hesitated, shaking her head. "This is too weird for words, Eleanor," but she took the bottle. "Shouldn't we double-dose with my perfume?"

"If you want."

"I don't *want* any of this. I'm trying to be cooperative in a process that makes less than no sense to me. If I drew the curse, then why use your perfume?"

"No reason—" Eleanor began, then changed tack. "Belief. I believe in what I do. I believe I can seal this room against a curse; and I used my perfume because I knew where it was. It didn't occur to me to go looking for your perfume. Go ahead, use yours—if you brought any. I've never noticed that you use perfume. You're one of those all-natural types from the Sixties."

For reasons that Emma couldn't fully parse, her mother's accusations about her perfume choices—or lack of them—burrowed deep, especially as they were unjust. There was a perfectly good travel-sized bottle of cologne in one of her drawers. Granted, it wasn't a carriage-trade designer scent, but she bought a bottle twice a year— Christmas and Mother's Day, when it was packaged in add-on gift boxes—and had dutifully splashed it on before dinner, despite her lingering headache.

"I've about had it with 'belief.' For two years everything I believe has been shaken by the ears and hung out to dry. If belief were all that powerful, then my not believing should count for something. How about, 'I don't believe in curses'?" she snarled. "What if the whole Atlantis Curia got together and talked itself out of believing in curses . . . if belief is what it takes, we could wipe them all out."

Eleanor retreated, physically and verbally. Her voice was cowed when she said, "It's not like that."

"Then what is it like?" Em pressed, barely restraining the temper she hadn't completely lost since she and Jeff had finalized their divorce. "What do I have to believe in now?"

"Magic," Eleanor admitted softly, finally using the word that curse-hunters worked so hard to avoid. "Curses are real. You have to believe in our magic if we're to have any weapons against them."

Victory tasted sour. Emma shook a few drops of perfume onto her fingertips and ran them swiftly around the porthole's rubbery seal. "There—I believe that will keep us safe from curses. Does that cut it?" She offered the bottle to its owner.

"I don't know."

"Good grief, Eleanor—"

"I don't want to fight with you, Emma."

"We're not—" Em began, then resisted the urge to add a lie to the evening's transgressions. "All right, we *are* fighting . . . arguing. We disagree; it's not the end of the world." Though arguing—incessant, pointless carping— had been the downfall of her second marriage. "It's not altogether your fault. I should know better than to get started in discussions like this when I've got a headache. I'm not fit for human consumption."

"I so much didn't want to fight with you. I wanted this trip to be about friendship and bonding."

Emma felt her temper slipping again. "What bonding? A cruise isn't glue. We're not two halves of a broken plate! Think about it: If we bumped into each other right now or two years ago when you were still calling yourself Eleanor Merrigan—what, exactly, would we build a friendship on? We've got nothing in common. Except, we're mother and daughter, only, look in a mirror, and which one of us is which? I hardly know where to start with you."

"That's why I thought a vacation . . . and it would have worked. I know it would have, if we hadn't crossed paths with a curse the first night out and it hadn't given you a headache. Oh, Em, I know it's too late to be your mother, to really be your mother, but, if only we could be friends— if you trusted me with your friendship."

"There's no magic elixir for friendship, especially when the friendship is going to be based on something as fundamentally odd as hunting curses and growing younger. You think it's all in those books. Trust me, it's not. I don't know half of what you take for granted."

"You do," Eleanor insisted. "All right, the books are a kind of code, and maybe you haven't found the key. But, we're hunters, Em, *hunters*—not amateurs dressed in funny clothes chasing Bambi across cornfields, but bred-in-the-bone predators. We know our prey the way cats know mice and birds . . . *You* know it. Listen to your instincts. You know that curse drew you in."

Emma knew nothing of the sort. If anything, from the memories she'd unexpectedly ingested, she'd have said the opposite, but her instincts, such as they were, advised against opening another thread of discussion. She stuck to the argument at hand: "Instincts, schminstincts! What I know is that most of the time I still feel like some little kid thrown into the deep end of the adult pool —even if I look like that little kid's grandmother compared to you. I don't think you can imagine how unsettling it is to be in the middle of your fifties and find that everything you know about life is up for grabs."

It was a trite remark—a statement of what Emma considered the obvious, but it brought her mother up short. Eleanor took several moments to recap her perfume and stow it away before saying, "I can— I grew up outside, remember? When my parents died, I got shipped off to my father's relatives, and none of them had the *wyrd*. I was in my teens when I began to hunt; and I was nothing like you. You do some things so well. You have such confidence when we're in the Netherlands, it's hard to remember that you're young, really and truly young."

Suddenly tired, Em sat down on the sofa. Eleanor quickly sat beside her.

"Whatever you think," Eleanor said earnestly, "you *are* going on instinct, not experience. And, I'm afraid I'm not much of a teacher."

Eleanor took Emma's hand. Em wanted to pull away, but the dynamics of their argument were winding down. Pulling away would crank them up again, and she didn't want that to happen.

"You're your father's daughter—no surprise there,

right? You want to know why, and I don't know why. I didn't ask a lot of questions when I was learning. They just didn't occur to me, honest. Rosalie—she was my teacher—told me what to do when you didn't want a curse crossing your path. I did it, and the curse stayed away, end of story. After that, whenever I've needed to fend off a curse, I've done what she told me to do. I wish I could make learning as easy for you as Rosalie made it for me."

Em found a spark of conciliation and surrendered to it. "Nobody could . . . not even Harry."

"Harry!" Eleanor laughed. "Harry doesn't teach. Harry lectures."

Em was about to say that she learned quite readily from her stepfather's lectures—if she could keep him focused on the question she'd asked—when Eleanor added.

"The hunter you need is Red Longleigh."

The name stirred memories, none of them particularly pleasant. Red Longleigh was the head honcho of the Atlantis Curia of curse-hunters. Over and above the warnings Em had received about the curia—warnings she'd received from Eleanor as well as Harry—Longleigh's behavior during their first and only encounter the previous fall remained the primary reason that she kept herself apart from his organization.

"We're not going there, Eleanor," Em said, extracting her hand. "Longleigh and a headache definitely do not mix, and I've already said things that I wish I hadn't."

"I've forgotten them," Eleanor said, a trifle too quickly.

"Don't," Emma warned. "I said I regretted them; I didn't say they weren't true. We've got a long row to hoe—but we'll manage. Now, assuming it's safe to leave our cabin, if there's someplace on this ship that's quiet, we can go there and experience some bonding."

"There's a piano bar . . . it's adults only."

Six

The piano bar was a good place to unwind for a few hours. Background noise was steady, but not overpowering, and the pianist understood that her job was to produce a soothing break from all the other shipboard activities, not add to the excitement. Emma stuck to non-alcoholic beverages, as cold as possible and cracking with ice. The headache eased, allowing her and Eleanor to indulge in the "bonding" she had acidly dismissed in the cabin.

Emma described in all its ill-fated glory her only previous visit to the Caribbean—

"It was one of those all-inclusive island resorts—seven days on the far side of Guadeloupe Island. You used beads instead of money . . . or credit cards. Nancy couldn't come, so I let the tour-group match me up with a roommate . . . she spent five out of seven days sick in bed with the curtains drawn. It was like staying in a cave."

For her contribution, Eleanor revealed the year she'd spent in South Africa—

"Rosalie thought we'd be more comfortable there. And we were, but we couldn't get used to chilly Julys and baked Christmases, so we went back to France. Big mistake."

Eleanor was careful not to menton a year or any other chronologically distinct detail. Em got the idea, though, that they were talking about the 1930s and wondered if someday she'd find herself having a similarly veiled conversation about the 1960s. It wouldn't be with a daughter, of course. There were no *wyrd*-ing children in Emma's past, and she was confident that there'd be none in her future. Confident, but not utterly certain: The future was a bitterly cold wind that time-walking curse-hunters did not—could not—brave.

For all its frenetic activities, the *Excitation* was a family ship, a wholesome ship. Its version of paradise emphasized sunlight and sweat over all-night carousing. The pianist packed up her music and tip jar before midnight. Last call came not long after. Eleanor ordered scotch to finish off an evening of wine. Emma asked for ice water. They left the bar, glasses in hand.

"What about a walk around the ship?" Eleanor asked when they came abreast of the dark-wood doors leading to the promenade deck.

Emma hesitated. She hadn't returned to that deck and wasn't sure that she wanted to, though she realized, belatedly, that the rail where she'd watched the *Excitation*'s Freeport departure couldn't have been more than a few feet from the jumper's final perch.

"It's not going to happen again," Eleanor advised, proving that she did have some insight into her daughter's thought processes. "And, even if it did, you've always got to get back on the horse, and the sooner the better. If you let yourself get away with saying 'I don't want to go there again,' your world starts shrinking."

Em could have asked if that advice sprang from personal experience and, if it had, why Eleanor wasn't doing more to get herself back to the wasteland on her own power. But, maybe, what Eleanor had gone through when the curses held her was far worse than the passing memory of one man creating his own death. She put her shoulder to the wood and emerged into the tropical night breezes.

Eleanor, politely, didn't ask where the event had occurred. The women walked past it twice without pause or mention. By the second time, muscles deep in Emma's neck were beginning to unknot.

"You were right," she admitted as they left the promenade.

"Even a stopped clock is right twice a day."

"I didn't mean it that way. I'm glad we walked. I'll sleep better now," Em said with confidence that proved unfounded.

Back in the cabin with the lights extinguished and only the engines' faint rumble to distract her, Emma simply couldn't find the off switch. Her thoughts churned, careening from one notion to the next. She forced them to center on her job at the library and found herself editing scenes from the summer. But splicing in the clever, decisive retorts she hadn't delivered in real time didn't get Emma closer to a good night's sleep, and Maggie Patrick, for all her irritations, wasn't the pea beneath the mattress that was keeping Em awake.

"Eleanor?" she whispered loud enough to be heard but not loud enough to awaken.

"I'm awake."

"May I ask you a question?"

"Shoot."

"Two questions, really—are curses contagious, and can we catch them?"

The linens rustled. Eleanor sat up but didn't turn on the light. "I think of curses more as parasites than viruses. They're not catching the way colds are. Being downwind of a curse isn't going to get you cursed. There has to be direct contact—and you'd have to be a better host than the one it's got, and we're not good hosts. Think of hunters as having exceptionally vigorous immune systems—that's one of Harry's analogies. It takes a lot to wear us down. A pack of curses, that's another story."

Eleanor's voice faded. Em knew that story. A pack of curses hadn't been able to wear Eleanor down, though, heaven knew, they'd tried hard enough. Emma regretted raising the subject.

"Sorry. I was thinking of the girl's curse—the girl in the dining room."

"It didn't strike me as a curse on the verge of rogue-dom—which isn't to say it's not dangerous. The rawest curse can mess with your head, same as it messes with everyone else's." Moments passed before Eleanor asked, "Why do you ask?"

"Tonight, when I went over to the girl. You said it was me drawing the curse. But it wasn't. I'd stake anything on it being just the opposite. And when I took the girl's hand, it was like I got a jolt of her memories."

"Not good, but not the curse jumping from her to you, if that's what you're worried about."

Emma sighed. "Exactly what I'm worried about."

"Jus' messin' with your head," Eleanor lapsed into a pseudo-street dialect. "Nothing to worry about, really," she added, returning to her normal intonation. "When you think about it, that's all a curse is: screwed up memories. Want to tell me what you got?"

"Not really."

"If they're keeping you awake, you'll be better off airing them out."

"I'm not even sure that they're what's keeping me awake. And I'm not sure I can even describe them. They're not like a movie, or even a trailer. Think of a few newspaper pictures blowing past and you trying to make up all the day's news from them."

"Give it a try. Harry says that all the proof we need that

we're related to monkeys and apes comes from the fact that we communicate better to each other than we do to ourselves."

"Sounds like Harry."

"So, give it a try."

Em sat herself up among the pillows. "It might help if I knew something about Croatia other than that it used to be part of Yugoslavia and that it's predominantly Catholic as opposed to Serbia, which was and is predominately Orthodox."

"I don't know, you obviously know more than I do."

"Mostly what I know is that while there was a Yugoslavia, Serbs and Croats and everyone else in the country managed to get along, but once Yugoslavia broke down, the Serbs fought the first of their ethnic wars with the Croats . . . and I think what I got from Donetta were flashes from that war—"

"Ah," Eleanor interrupted. "Now, say someone with a curse gets killed in a war, and the curse had nothing to do with it. The death's just another statistic, and sometimes the curse disappears too, or it pops back up in the Netherlands and has to scramble to find a new host. But sometimes there's enough discord and horror to go along with the dying that the curse can generalize quickly and take up with a survivor. At least according to what the watchers think, and the combined curias assigned special watchers for all that bloodshed in the Balkans. They figured it was going to be a bad one. They're all bad ones, really, and with some of them, we don't even know *where* in the Netherlands to set the outposts. Africa's still pretty much the Dark Continent for us. The watchers argue whether the curse makes the transition direct or round-trips through the Netherlands—it's all about as interesting as eating rags or watching paint dry. All that matters is that curses persist and strengthen in war zones."

Emma nodded in the dark. "She had a bad time of it. I

see bodies—bodies of people I know or that I would know if these were my memories. Men and women, some children. I count ten, but that's me, Emma Merrigan, doing the counting. Donetta—that's the girl's name, and they're her memories—her curse's memories—she knows them, but can't count them because they're mutilated." Em twisted the sheet between her hands. "I hate this part, Eleanor. I led a quiet life . . . the worst thing I'd ever seen was a house on fire and dead animals on the side of the road. I'd never witnessed a bad accident, never seen a dead body. I'd only had stitches once in my life and that was when I was in college and, frankly, I don't remember that as well as I remember the sights I've inherited from others.

"When some news announcer said 'mutilated' I didn't have a picture to put to the words, but now I do. God, I don't know which side I'm flashing on, good guys or bad guys, but—" Em began to tremble. "You'd think we'd learn that somewhere between the caves and last week we humans would have burned out the *need,* if not to kill each other, then at least the need to savage a body. It wasn't the curse that—that—" Emma couldn't summon the words to describe the sacrilege seething in her mind. "The curse was a witness, that's all, and Donetta—she soaked it all up like a sponge."

Eleanor's cool hand slipped around her arm to squeeze gently. "You took the curse's measure?"

"Yes, I took its measure," Em snapped. "I could plunge the root in a heartbeat." She referred to her specific curse-hunting *wyrd* to not only isolate the exact place and moment when a particular curse had surged into existence but to enter, and change, the mind that had given rise to it.

"You can't. You won't. The ship is moving, Em. You'd never find your way back. Promise me you won't. Promise me!"

Em shook her head, a pointless gesture in the dark. "I won't, not yet, but I will, Orion's Children will, as soon as we can. It's not a rogue, not a fast-cycler. It's just a plain-vanilla curse."

The images churned. There was one in particular—a woman. Her clothes were torn rags clinging to her arms and legs, which had been twisted into grotesquely sexual poses. She might have been pregnant; her belly had been sliced open, and her breasts had been sliced off. One of them bled between her legs. Emma began to weep.

"Forget curses," she said between sobs. "What about post-traumatic stress? I don't know how long I can live with some of these memories."

"There are ways to forget." Eleanor released her daughter's hand. "You can forget anything, if you try hard enough. The bad thing, though, is: I can't tell you how—"

"Good grief, Eleanor, not more secrets, not now. Now is not a good time for dangling strings in front of me."

"No secrets. I can't . . . because I can't, that's all. I know how to do it, not how I do it. It's not something I remember learning, like walking. Try telling someone how you walk . . . how you walk to the Netherlands. Oh, Emma, so much went wrong. These are things you should have learned ages ago."

"Fat lot of good that's doing me." Em wrung the sheets tight. Compared to the images floating in her mind, the sight of a man jumping calmly to his death would have been quiet and restful. "I need a crash course in something, and quickly."

"You're not going to like this, but there's only one place where you can get a 'crash course,' and that's Atlantis. You need to be around other hunters. I can't teach you anything. Harry, well, learn too much from Harry, and you run the risk of becoming Harry. And Blaise—" Eleanor let her opinions of Em's lover go unsaid. "There are children at Atlantis, part of the time, anyway, and students—youngsters with talents that need honing. If you spent some time with them, you could pick up the pieces you missed."

It took one bad taste in her mouth to tame another. Em wiped her tears. "You're right about one thing—I don't much like the suggestion; and I can hardly believe that I'm hearing it from you . . . twice in the same night. We're not exactly on good terms with the inner circle of the Atlantis Curia. Redmond Longleigh and I agreed, barely, to disagree on just about everything, and you've all but accused Sylvianne of murdering her mother who happened to also be your sister. Sorry, but I can't see myself dropping in for a quick visit or Remedial Hunting 101."

"Even if it meant getting rid of a curse's haunting? You *can* forget. We all do it, for lots of reasons."

Em weighed the question. "No, and *not* because I couldn't swallow my pride and accept ends that justify their means. As tempting as punching a few, well-placed holes in my memory sounds right now, I'm thinking it's not a good long-term solution. You never know when you're going to need something. With my luck, I'll punch a hole in something I'm desperately going to need someday." She paused because, beside her in the darkness, Eleanor had gone very still. "What's wrong?"

Eleanor replied, "Nothing," and Em took her at her word.

"What I'd *like*, in a perfect world"—Emma reached deep into her heart and dragged up a wish—"is a way to defang the memories, the visions whenever I find them. I'd like to make them old and harmless and stuff them in an attic someplace—but someplace where I could find them again, if I needed them. God knows, I don't want to need what Donetta, or her curse, dumped into my consciousness, but I've got to believe that if I did need it, I'd really need it. There'd be no substitutes. Seriously, forgetting—full-scale wiping the slate and setting your neurons back to zero—has to be risky. The cure could be worse than the cause."

"Only you can decide."

Suddenly, in the midst of her own self-pity, Emma knew what had happened to her mother's ability to transfer herself in and out of the wasteland.

"And if I don't, would you go by yourself, to learn new things, or relearn old ones?" Em asked, implying Eleanor's secret without challenging it.

"What do I need from Atlantis?" Eleanor retorted. "But you—you learn fast, truly you do. You could visit, learn everything you need, and be gone again before anyone was the wiser. Longleigh would split himself in two to entertain you, you know. Ever since you stopped taking his calls, he's been pestering me, asking me to intercede."

"Good lord." Thoughts of Redmond Longleigh pestering her mother dragged a magnet through Em's mind, banishing everything that didn't adhere to an unpleasant pattern. "Why didn't you tell me? He laid down the gauntlet for fair when he told me he'd 'take care of me' if I mooted another curse . . . which I've done a thousand times over. We're *not* friends, Eleanor; and as far as taking his calls—they don't make a pole long enough for me to go near him again, here-and-now or elsewhere."

"He says he wants a fresh start."

"He can want whatever, I'm not interested. When I'm desperate for expertise, there's always Harry."

"Harry's not a hunter. You've lured him into more hunts with Orion's Children than he's been part of for the last two hundred years."

Em questioned the certainty in her mother's voice. "He's got to spend time in the wasteland—he doesn't look like he's four-hundred years old. If he's not hunting curses, what is he doing? Not visiting the Atlantic drawing room; I'm willing to bet on that."

"Investments. He does his investment research from the Netherlands—and don't ask me how. He's never shared that tidbit with me. All I know is that he reads the paper every day, religiously, at the same time and in the same place. God forbid if anything gets in his way. But, I swear, in all the years we were together, Harry Graves didn't *hunt* a curse except by accident. If it's hunting skills you want, then Red's your man. He's not head of the curia by accident, Em. If anyone knows how to defang a haunting, it's him."

"I'm not listening, Eleanor. I burnt the bridge with Redmond Longleigh's name on it. There's no going back. If I can't learn from you or Harry or Blaise, then I learn on my own. Just knowing it should be possible to defang an acquired memory gives me hope."

Eleanor fell silent long enough that Em thought the conversation was over. She slid down between the sheets again.

"You need to listen," Eleanor said just as Em shut her eyes. "For Harry's sake."

That was a plea Emma could never have anticipated. "Exactly *how* does Harry fit between me and Redmond Longleigh?"

"Everyone knows what Harry does. They put up with his—his eccentricities because he keeps their identities safe and makes them rich at the same time. He's the goose that lays the golden egg. But he's not laying as many eggs as he used to—at least, that's what Red implies when he talks to me. Look—Red's figured out that Harry's hunting with you, and I don't think he's happy about it. He wants Harry doing what Harry's always done and, right now, at least, he's willing to make peace with you to bring that about."

"What?"

"He hasn't said it in so many words, but I think he's deeply impressed with what you've done with Orion's Children and wants to bring you into the curia on your terms. He has said that you're the first real innovator in a generation."

"You *think?* I'm sorry, Eleanor, I *think* I know you bet-

ter than that. What, exactly, has Longleigh told you, and
what have you promised him?"

Emma could always count on her mother to jerk her
mood around. Now, anger was replacing horror and despair as her dominant emotion.

"Nothing. I haven't promised him anything—except
that when the time was right, I'd talk to you."

"So you waited until tonight? Good move, Eleanor.
Smart move." Em larded her voice with bitter sarcasm. "If
this is your idea of a good time—when I'm rocky from a
curse—God spare me your notion of a bad time." Then a
betraying thought stabbed her consciousness. "You
planned this . . . from day one. You planned this whole
thing. Or Redmond Longleigh did."

The time had come for Eleanor's tears. "No. Not for a
minute. I didn't know there was a curse here; I couldn't
have. And the cruise, this was my idea from the start—I
swear it—to bring us together. I never even told Red we
were going. He's probably left a dozen messages on my
answering machine by now."

"Great. Just great. Now he thinks I've kidnapped you,
or vice versa."

"Emma—he's a powerful man, a dangerous man, and
you can't be a hunter anywhere in North America and not
have a relationship with him. Yours is a shambles. I
thought—prayed—that I'd find a way to make you see
that. I've made mistakes. Harry's made mistakes. I wanted
it to be different with you. You can take the curia on your
own terms."

"How convenient: We crossed a curse, a young man
killed himself, and it's a good time for me to chum up with
Redmond Longleigh!" Emma heard herself and swallowed
her anger. "Eleanor, I barely survived high school, and this
feels an awful lot like high school. I don't want to go back,
and I'm not having a 'relationship' with Longleigh. End of
drama."

Eleanor's answer was damp silence.

"It's not the end of the world . . . trust me, I've been through two divorces. I know what the end of the world looks like, and, thank heaven, this isn't it. On the other hand, I am grateful for this conversation. Sometimes I have to wander pretty deep into absurdity to recognize the territory."

"I'm sorry," Eleanor insisted.

"Don't be. Nothing sorry-able has happened. Let it go. Take Longleigh's calls when we get back to Bower—if you want. Tell him I'm intransigent and you're not a go-between. Or, don't take his calls and let him figure it out for himself. Until then, let's enjoy the vacation we've got left—which will be easier if we get some sleep."

Emma punched up her pillow and snuggled into the sheets. Her headache had retreated—a sure sign of stress reduction—and, confident that she'd laid a ghost or two, if not a curse, she looked forward to a good night's sleep.

Em's eyes were shut when Eleanor said, "I tried ignoring Red once, right after I left Bower . . . and you. I thought I could get along just fine without him. For two years, I lived in the shadows, then I realized I was paying too high a price. Of course, I had to negotiate my way back, and my starting position wasn't good. You don't think I would have spent half a century with Harry Graves if I'd had a choice, do you?"

"I don't know, Eleanor. He's a bit of a blowhard, but, I don't know, now that I've gotten to know him, he's not the ogre I pegged him for in the beginning."

"He's not much of a man, either."

"Hard to say—it takes all types, Eleanor. He seems genuinely fond of you . . . of both of us."

"Fond, yes, but fondness isn't enough, is it? You'll be better off if you mend your fences with Red, especially when he wants to make a good impression. Let him be helpful for a while. Lord knows, it's a dangerous business, feeding tidbits to a lion, but if you're good—and, Emma, you *are* good—you'll keep your fingers."

Eleanor hadn't said a word about sex, yet Emma had the unshakable impression that sex was now the subject. She had the impression, too, that Longleigh already had a paramour—a jealous paramour—who was also Emma's cousin. Mention of Sylvianne Skellings' name was almost guaranteed to set Eleanor off on a tirade. Since Em wanted to sleep, she kept Sylvianne's name to herself and, without a response to keep the words flowing, Eleanor fell quiet.

Fondness, though, really wasn't enough. After three straight nights of sleeping in the real world, Em yearned for the wasteland—for plinking curses and Blaise Raponde. Thoughts of him were a thousand-fold improvement over the images that had been haunting her consciousness, but they were just as destructive of the sleep impulse. Em lay on her side, listening to the faint echo of engines as the *Excitation* plowed through the Caribbean. She wouldn't take her mother's advice where Redmond Longleigh was concerned, but she wasn't ready to ignore Eleanor's warning about translation from a moving ship.

Two more nights, she consoled herself, *tonight and tomorrow, and I'll be on dry land.* Em resorted to the integer math games that were her crutch for sleep. Somewhere between a sequence of prime numbers and the sense of Blaise's hand caressing her back, she lost track of everything until the ceiling pixie summoned her to Fantabulous Cruises' private island.

Eleanor was already up, dressed, and sitting on the sofa.

"I couldn't sleep," she explained. "Tried your trick of going for a walk on the promenade deck. Nothing happened, though. I watched us dock here—the ship turns around in open water and *backs* itself in. A crewman told me about it. I came down to get you, but you were sound asleep. You going to want breakfast before we go ashore?"

Em stretched and sat up slowly. She'd awoken without

her headache, but she couldn't declare an official victory over her latest migraine until she got her spine vertical without reigniting the ache. "Coffee," she said when her head was upright on her neck. Her nerves were quiet; clearing the air with Eleanor—clearing it with herself—had solved more than one problem. "And something light. Don't want to overload. We've got a busy day planned."

She watched Eleanor's face closely for signs that today would be Eleanor's day under the weather, but her mother's makeover had been thorough. Eleanor shrugged off a sleepless night the way Emma herself had back in her college days.

By ten-thirty they were pedaling rented bicycles along a shaded macadam path to the islet's windward side. Despite the burden of sunglasses, plastic helmet (replacing her straw hat, which hung temporarily on a lanyard between her shoulder blades), and a thick layer of sunscreen, Em was enjoying herself. There seemed to be some truth to the adage that you never forget how to ride a bike. Years had passed since she'd sat on a bicycle seat, yet before her feet had completed one revolution, she'd relocated her balance. She stood up for power-pedaling up one of the islet's many hills and stayed upright to catch all the breeze on the way down.

Eleanor fell behind and didn't catch up until Em stopped at the trail's extremity: a fenced-off bluff overlooking blue green ocean and, in the distance, another pair of islets, both apparently deserted. A stiff wind blew across the water, whipping the waves into whitecaps and wicking away sweat. Emma took pictures until another couple pedaled into their private paradise. They exchanged cameras, took pictures for each other, and went their separate ways.

The return route was longer and sunnier. Emma plunged her hands into the ice cooler at the bike-rental station and ran her chilled, dripping fingers through her hair. After a moment's hesitation, Eleanor did the same and immediately pronounced herself ready for the row of pseudo-beachcomber shacks. According to the *Secret Guide,* there were only five permanent residents of the private island. When the *Excitation* or her sister ship came in, it was up to the ship's crew to hawk the private island's exclusive merchandise. For Em the choice was between shopping in the shade and a self-guided nature hike to the highest point on the island.

"I'll meet you for lunch," she told her mother after deciding that the chance to take a few more digital pictures was more attractive than towels, T-shirts, and racks upon racks of enameled trading pins.

Eleanor nodded an answer. Her eyes were already focused on some souvenir in the depths of one of the shacks.

The trail was deserted. Quiet walks in the noonday sun apparently weren't high on anyone else's to-do list. Em set a slow pace, reading all the trail cards and capturing dozens of images. At the top of the trail Fantabulous Cruises had mounted a veritable Stonehenge of old-fashioned stanchion-mounted tourist binoculars. They were hot to the touch from the sun, but free to use, and worth the momentary pain Em got from peering through them. Gazing north, she got lucky and spotted a school of porpoises skimming through the jewel-colored water. She stood in the sun watching them until they'd swum out of sight, regretting only that there'd been no one to share it with.

Next time, I'll talk Nancy into coming, Em thought as she began the descent and realized, with some surprise, that she already assumed that her first cruise would not be her last. Of course, Nancy would want John to come along. Not that John wasn't good company—John would have appreciated the porpoises, and the hike to see them; Nancy would be prowling the gift kiosks with Eleanor. But cruises—at least tropical island cruises—were inherently romantic, and odd numbers, inherently awkward.

Eleanor made for an even number. Emma was getting

used to the idea that Eleanor was family, even if her thoughts of Eleanor as *mother* still had an edge on them. Em could see herself and Eleanor taking vacations together, sating the urge to travel while doing nothing for romance. And Eleanor, Em realized with a start, wouldn't deny herself romance. She'd already laid claim to Matt Barto and wasn't at all subtle when she cast her net across the *Excitation*'s decks. When push came to shove, Eleanor would pair up and leave her daughter out in the odd-number cold.

Emma put her back against one of the binocular stanchions and slid down until she was sitting on the children's rung.

In Bower, where Em's life was filled with habit, having a ghostly lover had seemed an efficient use of available time and energy. She had the best of two worlds. Blaise was there when she wanted to see him and *there* was tucked away in the most private corner of her life. On vacation, where, by definition, habit played no role, her decision to fall in love with a ghost—if it had been a conscious decision and Blaise could be classified as a ghost—showed its downside.

A lot more downside. Emma Merrigan had never mastered the gentle art of dating men by the handful. Early on, a pop-psychology test had diagnosed her as a serial monogamist, and the label had stuck. Worse, ending her affair with Blaise Raponde—even cheating on him in the here-and-now—would bring a chilling load of guilt.

Em chided herself for slipping into man trouble of the absurd kind . . . again. That it was a moot situation—there was no here-and-now man waiting in her wings—only heightened the absurdity.

Em's mother-voice wafted out of the increasing depths of her thoughts. *First rule of hole digging: When you find yourself in one, stop digging immediately!*

She stood up, brushed off the sand, and began the return

journey. Before Em reached the beach area, a double blast
of the ship's horn signaled that lunch was being served in
a series of open-air pavilions. She picked up her pace and
caught up with Eleanor before the first of the hamburgers
had gone cold. Em asked for hers without a bun, then
threw caution and diets to the wind with generous helpings
of every salad on the lengthy buffet.

"I'll walk it off once we're back in Bower," she insisted.

"Don't forget they've got a make-your-own sundae
setup under the next roof."

Emma passed on the desserts, lo-cal and otherwise.
She'd agreed to an afternoon of snorkeling and parasailing,
both of which she thought would go better on a dairy-less
digestion. Leaving Eleanor to pile on the hot fudge, nuts,
and cherries, Em changed into her spare bathing suit—a
skirted, floral relic from a university-sponsored aquatics-
exercise class that had never become part of her weekly
routine—and went ashore to the shade of a palm-tree-
shaped umbrella rising from the sugar-sand beach, where
the better part of two thousand tourists were claiming their
fair share of the Caribbean sun. In addition to the towels
she'd claimed at the changing cabana, Em's duffel bag
held an extra-large bottle of the strongest waterproof sunscreen sold in Michigan. She squirted a dollop into her
hands while waiting for Eleanor to join her, and set about
protecting every jot of vampire-pale flesh from the sun's
rays.

Despite Eleanor's indulgence at the dessert bar, there
could be no doubt that she cut a more striking figure when
she emerged from the changing cabanas in her near-bikini.
Heads turned when she strode across the white-sand beach.
Em waited until her mother was within the palm tree's
shade before offering the bottle of sunscreen.

"Quick—before you turn into a lobster."

"'SPF-50'?" Eleanor complained, reading from the bottle. "But I *want* a tan."

"Bright as this place is, we're still likely to turn into crispy critters before the day's through, regardless of the SPF."

Reluctantly, Eleanor began squeezing and smearing.

They rented snorkeling gear from a superficially disreputable pirate named Samson who looked suspiciously like one of the other table captains who served alongside Draco in the *Excitation*'s dining rooms and locked their valuables in one of his many "treasure chests."

"Have you done this before?" Em asked belatedly, as she struggled with her bright-pink (the better to find them when they fell off?) flippers.

"Once. In Hawaii. It's idiot-proof. You don't even have to spit in your mask; just slosh a little saltwater around."

Eleanor confidently led the way into the crystal clear water. They were headed to an adults-only sandbar and the cultivated tourist reef beyond it. Em knew she was in trouble before they were halfway to the sandbar. Since leaving Port Canaveral she'd survived the sunlight only by virtue of her prescription sunglasses with the ultra-dark lenses that were currently locked in one of Pirate Samson's treasure chests. With her eyes naked to the light, Em couldn't squint tight enough to blunt the sun's power. Her vision deteriorated into bright blobs of color. She thought things might get better when the water got deep enough to put her masked face down into it, but even in her own shadow, the light was too bright and the damage had been done.

When they reached the sandbar she declared defeat.

"I've spent too many years in the Great North Woods. My eyes have atrophied; I can't take the light. Honest, Eleanor, this is way more than I can handle."

Em stripped off her mask. She sank into one of the webbed chairs bolted into the cement underlying the sandbar and braced herself for an argument. Her face felt like a prune. Massaging the tight muscles helped, but true relief wouldn't come until she could hie herself into some deep shade—preferably the deep, air-conditioned shade of their cabin.

"Honey, if you feel as bad as you look, you'd better get yourself back to the beach."

Emma was a little unsettled by Eleanor's swift agreement, but the beach wasn't the destination she craved. "I'm going to go back to the ship."

"But the parasailing? We've made reservations. We've already paid for them."

Em was miserly enough to feel the loss, but it wasn't enough to shake her resolve. "Parasailing will be worse— I'll be that much closer to the sun. You go ahead and take both rides, if you can. Really—I just want to get someplace where it's dark and cool."

"You're sure you're okay? You can get back to the ship on your own? I can go with you."

How bad, Em wondered, *did* she look, all pale and squinting in the sunlight?

"I'll be fine. You go ahead and have fun without me."

Em tripped over her pink flippers getting out of the web chair. She skinned her knee on the cement reef but otherwise damaged nothing more vital than her pride. The fall erased from her mind any last vestige of doubt that she was out of her element.

Eleanor gave a final, "You be careful, then," and slipped into the water as if she'd been born there.

Emma was past caring about her mother or anything else. She snorkeled into the shallows, returned her gear to Pirate Samson, and made her way back to the *Excitation*.

Seven

Refreshed by a misty shower and grateful that the cabin was on the *Excitation*'s shady side, Emma stretched out across the bed and let herself dry in the chill breeze descending from the air conditioner vent. She'd been lucky. Aside from a certain redness around the eyes, Em was as freshly pale as a winter's day, and the headache she'd been nursing for the last two days remained in the background of her thoughts.

Em rolled to her feet and got as far as a layer of underwear before deciding that there was no good reason to get fully dressed. The oversized T-shirt she wore to bed was more than enough clothing for a self-indulgent lounge with her largely unread book. She wasn't going anywhere until Eleanor got back and the ship was prepped for its last departure.

After a few minutes sitting on the sofa and staring at a prose-filled page that refused to resolve itself into an interesting story, Em decided there was no good reason to read, either. She closed the porthole drapes and went back to the bed, thinking that she might nap until Eleanor's return. The cabin was quiet enough. Save for a gentle *whirr* coming through the air conditioning ducts there wasn't a sound she could hear, a vibration she could feel.

Buoyed by water and secured by its hawsers, the *Excitation* was perfectly calm, perfectly still—not moving at all. And it wouldn't move until six forty-five, nearly four hours hence and a full hour after all its passengers had said good-bye to their island paradise. Four hours could make for a long nap or a long visit to the wasteland where time, generally speaking, flowed at a more compact pace. An evening in the wasteland, curse-hunting and private time at the bolt-hole included, had a memory time of five or six hours but rarely clocked in at a body time of more than two. Even if wasteland time took one of its inversions and raced ahead of here-and-now clock time, Eleanor would come straight to the cabin once she'd reboarded the ship to shower off layers of sweat, sand, and industrial-strength sunscreen.

There was always an element of risk associated with a wasteland visit, but just now, in a locked cabin with a certainty that she'd be awakened well before the *Excitation* began its return voyage to Port Canaveral, Em easily convinced herself that the risk was no higher than it was from her Bower bedroom.

She let her thoughts slip free of the here-and-now and focused her mind's eye on a spinning, falling coin.

Heads, she thought as it passed through her mental vision, and heads it was. The bedspread's polished cotton texture became the wasteland's parched hardpan. The air-conditioner's *whirr* passed from Em's consciousness, and when she opened her eyes, the sky was a swirling, but familiar, magenta. Rising to her knees, she found the way-back stone in its proper position, but the tug deep in her gut that pulled her toward the bolt-hole was missing. Emma had to stand and deliberately stretch her awareness to the horizon and beyond before she had a sense of it.

"Well," she muttered to the emptiness around her.

"Place and distance really do matter. I don't know where the heck I am, but it's nowhere near my usual starting place."

The concordance of points in the here-and-now with points in the wasteland had been the subject of several of Harry Graves' prepackaged lectures. Harry believed—though he couldn't prove—that there was a one-to-one correspondence between not merely places but times as well, which, were it true, would make the wasteland theoretically larger than the known universe. Emma's engineering gene considered that an impossibility, which had given rise to several esoteric debates between stepfather and stepdaughter.

The next time their paths crossed, Emma would have to apologize. Though she still couldn't accept a wasteland that was larger than the universe, real-world distance plainly mattered, or she would not have wound up a good hike's distance from the bolt-hole. Setting out at the fastest pace she could comfortably maintain, Em wondered if she'd even get there before Eleanor came through the cabin door.

In absolute terms, the wasteland was no brighter than deep twilight. By habit, Emma had surrounded herself with a faint aura without which she would have been shrouded in shadow. The same sort of urban paranoia that would guide her in an unfamiliar city led Em to absorb her aura. She could sense the way-back stone's presence behind her but could no longer see it. By the same token, in theory at least, she was less visible to the occasional curse packs that heaved across the horizon as she strode toward her bolt-hole.

At a certain point in their evolution—if they weren't snuffed out first—curses appeared to lose interest in causing mortal misery. They banded together in predatory packs consuming anything they encountered, be it curse-hunter or curse or their own pack brethren. Months ago,

Em and Blaise had watched a pack turn on itself in a cannibalistic frenzy that lasted, literally, until there was only one fiery pillar left standing. Then she and Blaise had annihilated the survivor.

When they worked together, a pair of curse-hunters were a match for just about any solitary curse. Alone as she was, Em was less confident and didn't want to attract attention. She ignored the fingerlings she passed and made herself small whenever something large appeared. Her strategy was successful. The larger curses passed her by, and the sense of the bolt-hole grew slowly stronger.

She'd gotten her aerobic exercise for the week by the time the sense was strong enough for Emma to guesstimate the distance to the bolt-hole and allow herself the worry of whether or not she was on a fool's quest. There was no guarantee that she'd find Blaise at the bolt-hole. He knew she'd gone on vacation—correction, he knew she'd gone on a journey.

The inexplicable processes that allowed them to communicate in what sounded, to Em's ears, like perfectly normal twenty-first-century American English had faltered on the notion of a vacation. Travel for pleasure was not a concept that took root easily in Blaise Raponde's mind—though he had traveled somewhat during his lifetime, visiting several regions of France and the Venetian Republic before that fateful day when a vengeful lover had plunged her knife into his body's heart.

Judging by the number of times Blaise had wished her luck and safe journey, Em had come to believe that there were few things more dangerous in seventeenth-century France than leaving the safe confines of Paris. And no gentleman—to the extent that Blaise was a gentleman—would have allowed his woman to make a solitary journey, even through the streets of Paris.

The love they shared definitely represented a longer, harder journey to understanding for Blaise than it had for

Emma. Then again, he'd had greater incentive. When they'd met—when he'd come to her rescue at the very start of her curse-hunting career—he'd been talking to himself for more than three centuries. He'd let it slip, once, that he believed he'd go mad if he had to face that loneliness again.

Once again, Em fretted over the ethics of falling in love with a ghost and the guilt she would have to swallow if she ever let a real man into her life. When the bolt-hole was no longer a sense in the pit of her stomach, but the real thing set in the bottom of an orange-wedge depression, she approached the door with a sense of dread.

Her fingers met resistance when they closed on the latch. The door was bolted from within. She couldn't remember if there *was* a bolt on the bolt-hole's door and didn't waste time considering the circumstances that might have inspired Blaise to add one. After calling Blaise's name, Em knocked twice on the wood and gave the heavy door a shake on its hinges.

"It's me, Blaise—Emma. Are you in there?"

Silence.

There was another way out of the bolt-hole—the casement window to anywhere, anywhen. Blaise didn't use it much, preferring usually to limit his real-world activities to the city and century he knew personally. But he could use it. He could put his ghostly self on the here-and-now streets of Bower, if he chose to. Emma had made certain of that. With her off on a journey, might Blaise have gone walking down the street where she lived? Might he have gotten himself into trouble in those unfamiliar surroundings?

"Blaise?"

It was Emma's bolt-hole, too. More hers than his. She needed only to twitch her thoughts in the right direction, and the inside bolt would melt away. Another few seconds, and she did twitch. The latch lifted, she pulled the door open, and found herself staring at the smoldering bright lump of amber that served as the pommel-stone of Blaise's very serviceable sword.

They both swore, and Blaise sheathed the weapon in the leather-bound scabbard on his side.

"*Pardieu,* madame! I did not expect you."

"I knocked," she complained and caught sight of an hourglass sitting on the table in the instant before it disappeared.

"But you said eight days. It has not been eight days."

There was just a hint of doubt in Blaise's voice, which, when coupled with the vanished hourglass, was enough to propel Emma into her lover's open arms.

"I said 'maybe eight days.' I didn't want you to worry if I got all caught up in vacation activities and didn't make it back. But I couldn't wait eight days."

Blaise's sword-wielding fingers tightened around Em's arms and held her at arm's length.

"Where have you come from?" he demanded. "Are you still away from your home? Are you still on that *ship*?"

She nodded.

"Go back! Quickly! It is too dangerous to be apart from your body when your body is moving."

"I'm not moving—not aboard ship and not out of this room!"

"Your physical self is truly on board the *ship*? Madame, I beg you—go back. A ship in the water, it is always moving."

Emma rolled her eyes and freed herself. "This one isn't. It's sixty-thousand tons of steel that's not going anywhere that the Earth doesn't take it."

She expected him to swallow her arguments. Blaise was a reasonably well-educated man for his time. He hadn't heard of Galileo and accepted infinity as a theological, not scientific, concept; but he believed in a spherical Earth that orbited its sun and in the reality of movement he couldn't physically feel. When his hand fell to his sword, she realized that the stumbling block wasn't astronomy.

"Steel?" he muttered. "*Pardieu,* steel does not *float.*"

Em could have explained that the wooden boats he was familiar with didn't float, either—else they would never have sunk and he wouldn't regard all sea voyages with morbid suspicion. But that would have taken all the time she had until Eleanor came to wake her body up, and Blaise still wouldn't have believed her. She'd have to use the window to take him to a modern seaport where he could see an *Excitation*-sized steel ship with his own eyes and feel it with his hands.

Blaise could do that—interact with the past eras they visited. Emma's skills in that regard were far more limited. For her the past was uniformly solid and inert. Walls were impenetrable obstacles, and so were doors, unless someone else opened them. She made do with other talents— the ability to backtrack a curse through time to its moment of inception and to influence the mortal mind that spawned it.

Emma pried her lover's hand from the sword. "All the more reason to believe me when I tell you that I'm not moving. You know me; I'm not that reckless."

"You cannot be too careful."

"That's what Eleanor said—no curse-hunting while we were at sea."

"You should listen to her. *Pardieu*—if your body were to move while you were *au-delà,* you might never find it again." Blaise shrugged. "Of course, if someone has plunged a knife into your body, not finding it could be, perhaps, a blessing."

Emma cocked her head, anticipating further information.

"It is the simplest explanation of how I came to be here: There was a struggle—sufficient movement before she slew me—that the death of my body was not the death of me."

"I have no murderous enemies aboard the *Excitation*—none that I'm aware of, anyway—and the door to our cabin is locked. There is a curse aboard, but Eleanor insists there is nothing we can do about it, which hasn't stopped her from working some hoodoo around the doors and windows." Emma paused, watching Blaise's face for signs of confusion. There were none; "hoodoo" had passed the comprehension test. "I don't know whether it's the curse or something as simple as the sun giving me a headache. We've had a good time and all, but I've been getting seriously frayed around the edges. I don't know if you can believe this, but ships have become very romantic places, and I've missed you."

The words cheapened the air between them. Em let go of her lover's hand.

"It's been almost two years now," she confessed. "I guess I've gotten used to being able to come here to be with you. I've been so careful about staying put in the ship, I haven't been sleeping right."

Blaise retrieved Em's hand and used it to pull her back into his embrace. "And I do not sleep at all when you do not come *au-delà*."

Emma relaxed. In the wasteland, Blaise was fully substantial. His heart beat, his right arm was heavy around her shoulders, his left arm welcomed as it slid around her waist. They kissed; and there was nothing at all ghostly about the heat their lips kindled. Em put all her own strength into an embrace, and Blaise, in turn, very nearly squeezed the air from her lungs before sweeping her off her feet and carrying her to the bed.

They made love, but even as they did, a part of Em remained detached, observant of her passion. She could split hairs over the nature of curses, even the nature of the wasteland itself, but there was no escaping her love for this man. She cherished him—*needed* him—in the ways she'd sworn to herself after divorcing Jeff that she would never need a man again. Worse, the very ghostliness that had allowed Blaise Raponde to glide beneath her radar left her with a schizophrenic division in her heart: He was too perfect, too *safe* to be good for her mental health.

"What's the matter?" Blaise asked when she lay still with her arms lightly around him.

Surely he had not been so attentive of his lovers' moods in the days and nights of his life, but he'd had three lonely centuries in which to master sensitivity.

Empathy was the last thing Emma wanted from her lover just then; it would only complicate her turmoil. In silence, she shook her head against his chest and held her eyes shut.

"Is it Eleanor? I do not believe she was entirely honest with her reasons for this wandering journey."

"Not entirely, but mostly she was. She wanted time alone together—without you or Harry or even Matt. She's given me advice I have no intention of taking."

"About what?"

Em hesitated then admitted, "About the Atlantis Curia and its leader, Redmond Longleigh. She'd have me mending my bridges with him—something I'm not interested in doing. But, overall, we've gotten along fine. I guess we've managed to 'bond,' like the pieces of a broken teacup. No, if there's a problem, it's that there's a curse on the ship, clinging to a girl who waits tables in the dining rooms, and I can't get it out of my head, where it's causing a headache that won't either quit or explode."

"Explode? You *want* your head to explode?"

She shrugged and rearranged herself to see his face more clearly. "My headaches reach a point where they have to get worse before they'll go away. Didn't people have migraines in your day? Throbbing headaches in just one side of your skull, with a little nausea on the side and, sometimes, a bright aura just as they're getting started. I always thought the word itself was French."

"I knew a young girl once, she'd pound her head against a wall to balance the pains, she said."

"Doesn't work; I've tried. I've got some pills that work. Back in gray, dreary Michigan they do a pretty good job of knocking out the pain. On the ship, we're sailing in the tropics, and the sun's so bright—light triggers them, triggers them for me, anyway. Light and the curse. In my nauseated gut I know the curse has something to do with it."

"Then moot it and be done with it," Blaise suggested with the simplicity inherent in his half of the species. "If it's safe enough for you to visit me, then it's safe enough to moot a curse."

Em attempted a counterargument, "Eleanor says—" but left it unfinished. She was already ignoring her mother's advice.

"Haven't you taken its measure?"

"Pretty much." She sat up, grabbing an armful of linen and blankets for warmth. They'd neglected the hearth, and the bolt-hole had grown both chill and dim. "I made contact with the cursed girl. Eleanor fairly accused me of declaring a war I couldn't fight, much less win. Anyway, I got a sense of how the curse grabbed her—nothing like a little civil war to give a curse a chance—but my sense of how the curse came into being is still a little fuzzy. Memories within memories. I haven't taken time to sort them out."

"Ah—that's unfortunate. You'll have to do what? Seize her again? Could be tricky."

"Maybe," Em equivocated. "Or maybe I just have to sit back and let the memories unfold."

Truth to tell, Emma did most of her hunting in the wasteland and plunging into whatever slice of the past that held a curse's root. Her experience with here-and-now curses was limited to a handful of encounters, but when it had come time to track the curse to its origin, she hadn't needed physical contact with the curse's here-and-now victim. Her handclasp with Donetta should have been more than enough to fuel her curse-hunting *wyrd*. She asked herself the question, What had she missed? and scarcely noticed Blaise leaving the bed. He'd pulled on his clothes and poured himself a goblet of wine by the time she had her answer.

"I was right: There were other times and places buried in those memories. There's a cycle that repeats itself, practically in the same place—which, since the place is the Balkans, isn't hard to believe. And, frankly, the trappings of peasant life don't change all that much in a few generations. But, I think I've isolated the first moment—can't say exactly where or when, but there's enough texture that I should be able to project it through the window."

"Wine first?" Blaise offered her his glass.

Emma said no and rummaged through the bed linens for her hastily discarded clothes. "I'm muzzy-headed from the migraine and the medicine I take to dull the pain, or I wouldn't have needed someone to remind me that if I could come here I could moot that damned curse."

When she was decent again and her shoes were tied, Em stood in front of the window. The image she'd found among the memories she'd received from Donetta was visually vague, little more than a dark night with a sense of distant mountains, nearby fields, innocents asleep. The view beyond the window darkened to match the memory, but when the moment came to open the casement, Emma found herself unwilling to lift the latch.

"I'm not sure," she admitted. "I'm a little out of the habit of doing things for the first time—"

Blaise chuckled. "My Madame Mouse throwing herself toward caution rather than away from it?"

With a wry, defeated smile Emma said, "This time, yes. I'm not at home. My body's on a ship nursing a migraine;

and there's nothing in this vision I've borrowed to tell me what's where or when on the other side of this glass. I think I'd rather try tracking this one the old-fashioned way."

"Old-fashioned?"

Curse-hunters had certain talents in common. The talent to slide from the here-and-now to the wasteland was chief among them; and the one that allowed them to manifest a raw power that could destroy—moot—their enemies. Some hunters, and Blaise Raponde had been among their number while he lived, possessed only the common talents. There were uncommon talents, though. Watchers were sensitive to the passage of curses between the wasteland and the here-and-now. Trackers could follow a curse like a bloodhound across the wasteland. Delvers could track a curse through historical time. Plungers, who were the rarest hunters, could not only track and delve a curse to its chronological origin, they could possess the minds of the innocents they found there.

Emma Merrigan was a plunger. Once the taste of a curse was in her mind, she could track it across the wasteland and into the past. Then, by possessing an innocent mind or two, change the history that gave rise to it. Emma was also an inventor; that talent came with the engineering gene she'd inherited from her father. The bolt-hole's window did away with the need to march across the wasteland, tracking a curse to its root moment in the past; but the talent to track a curse was in her blood.

"We'll walk our way to this curse's origin. I'll feel safer that way."

"Safer it is," Blaise agreed, laying his hand on his sword hilt. "You are forearmed?"

Em held up her right hand where her grandmother's ruby ring shone unnaturally bright in the dusky wasteland light.

"Then we are off."

Tracking made use of the nonvisual memories Em had received from her contact with Donetta. The stillness of the night, the air of doom within it, even the faint smell of decay were all reference points in her mind. Standing on the verge of the bolt-hole's depression, Emma closed her eyes and spun slowly. She tuned her borrowed memories like an antenna, and when the signal had strengthened, began walking.

Blaise thought to make conversation as they walked. Em silenced him.

"This is harder than I thought. I've always had extra information—library information—that pretty much pinpointed my destination in history. This time, all I have is what I picked up from Donetta. It's enough, I'm sure of that, but it's hard. I have to concentrate, or it just melts away."

"If I can help?" Blaise offered his hand.

Em took it, thinking his touch would improve her concentration. A mistake. She lost all sense of the curse's origin and, when she found it again, they were pointed some ninety degrees clockwise of their original direction. He gave her a questioning glance.

"There's a correspondence—I proved that myself walking from where the ship lay to the bolt-hole. But it's not an exact correspondence, or even a consistent one."

If Blaise didn't understand her statement, he had the good sense to keep his doubts to himself. They released hands and walked the new heading for a mile, give or take. A solitary pillar, thicker and taller than any Em had spotted on her way from the *Excitation*, flamed its way above their left-side horizon. Together they might have taken it down. When it came to the sheer focus of destruction, Blaise lived up to his homophone. And any other occasion, Em would have welcomed the challenge.

"We don't have time," she said softly, as if the curse

might have ears to hear her and join the battle on its own initiative.

"Suddenly, there is a limit to our time?" Blaise asked with a cocked eyebrow.

He did not lower his voice. He was accustomed to their meetings when Bower was her starting point and she liked nothing better than to fall asleep in his arms.

"I told you, I'm not home; I'm based on a ship."

"But you say it is firmly anchored. You would not deceive me."

I would, Emma admitted to herself, but to her lover she said, "Firmly, for a few hours."

"Pardieu!" There was an edge to Blaise's voice. He had a temper and pride to match. He especially didn't like surprises that took him where he did not want to go. "Hours are slippery here. You can have no sense of how much time has passed. Madame, this is the height of foolishness. We must return—*you* must. We can uproot this curse some other time when nothing is at risk."

"There's no risk, nothing greater than usual, anyway. I've arranged it so I'll have plenty of warning before the ship disembarks."

Blaise pressed his lips together, but his tone was calmer when he said, "You have Eleanor watching beside you."

It was not a question, and Em knew a lie would be smarter than the truth; but their love was already complicated by forces she could neither control nor compromise. She answered his questions truthfully, even when the answers worked against her.

"Eleanor's ashore, doing things you can't imagine, but she's got to come back aboard the ship before it sails— well, not *sails,* literally. I told you, it's steel; it has engines, like a car." He'd seen cars when they walked the more recent past. "We'll have to use the window."

"Your mother does not know what you're about?"

Em shook her head. "Odds are she's parasailing right now, and I'm the farthest thought from her mind."

As she'd predicted, parasailing did not parse. Em had to describe the sport in simpler words. Blaise blanched and was momentarily speechless.

"A *bird*?"

"*Like* a bird. More like a kite, really, a huge kite towed behind a fast boat. Technically, you're not flying, you're gliding . . . sailing through air."

"Not I, Madame. And if this is what your mother is doing as we speak, I would not be so certain what she will do afterward. What if she falls? What if this *kite* of hers tangles in a tree?"

Emma didn't bother trying to explain that parasailing was safe enough that inexperienced tourists were allowed to risk it. Instead she tried to explain about sand, saltwater, and a layer or two of stale sunscreen. "After a day out in the Caribbean sun, she'll want to shower—bathe—as soon as she's back on the ship—and she'll want to tell me what a wonderful experience I missed."

"And she is convinced it is wonderful to cling to a kite?"

"Absolutely. I would have done it with her, except that the sun was too bright for my headache. It's the exhilaration of soaring forty, fifty feet or more above the water with the wind in your face."

"If you had not had a headache, you would have chosen this *parasailing* rather than visit our bolt-hole?"

"That wasn't the choice, but, yes—I wanted to try. It's really very safe. There are all kinds of straps and harnesses holding you and the sail together. You get a five minute safety lecture, and that's enough. Hardly anyone ever gets hurt."

Blaise gave Em the look that said he'd understood every word she'd uttered and still thought the world had gone mad in the centuries since he last lived in it. Em recognized a lost cause when she saw one and started walking—in a new direction.

"We're getting closer," she promised.

And, indeed, the congruence strengthened as though the tumblers of a complex lock were falling into place one by one until the image in Emma's mind was an unbearable weight. She sank to her knees, right arm reaching for her lover's hand.

"This is the place."

Blaise scanned the horizon. Emma couldn't imagine what he was looking for. The way-back stone had obediently followed her from the bolt-hole, but Blaise couldn't see the small, half-polished boulder that was the only landmark in her field of vision, and she couldn't see whatever intrigued him.

The wasteland was a subjective realm—subtly different for every hunter who walked across its parched surface. Most hunters agreed on a few things, that the ground was drought-dry and the sky was a seething vault of magenta clouds that never broke for sun, moon, or stars. But what was magenta? A shade of red or blue? Blaise thought Magenta was a Venetian city in the north of Italy; he said the seething sky was purple.

And there simply were no words to accurately describe the translation from the wasteland to the historic past. When Matt or Nancy pressed for answers, Emma spoke of falling from one level of reality to another, but, subjectively, it was the landscape that shifted, not the observer. All that mattered was that they made the translation from the wasteland to an impenetrably black night in the middle of nowhere.

"Do you know this place?" Blaise asked.

Em could see him—a silver-limned ghost in the darkness—because they'd brought the wasteland's self-lumination with them. She was surrounded by the same pale light. It extended about an arm's length around them. They could quench that light—and would, if they attracted company. Everyone knew that some people could see and hear ghosts.

"Haven't a clue," Em admitted. "We're on a road, both facing the same direction. We can stand here and wait or start walking."

Blaise always favored activity to ambush. They moved carefully. Being in the past produced a kind of sensory numbness that lasted until a hunter put his—or *her*—foot in a chuckhole and went crashing to the ground. Emma saved herself once by grabbing Blaise's arm.

"This has got to be the darkest night ever—no moon, no stars, no way to figure out at least *where* we are. I've been studying the stars, you know, so I'd have a hope of orienting myself in places like this. A lot of good that would do. It's so dark, you've got to wonder if there's a storm coming. Can you tell? Can you guess the season?"

Blaise tilted his head back and inhaled deeply. He was better at this. "Summer. The air is green; and you might be right about the storm. It's thick enough and not a breath of wind. Maybe this one's an outcry against the Lord God Himself?"

Emma let the theological question pass unanswered. She needed all her concentration for the road, which had begun a wide, clockwise, and downslope turn. They went from six o'clock to about eight and into sight of a pair of small, stationary lights. The lights flickered slightly, leading Em to decide that they shone from lanterns of some sort and not electricity. Donetta's curse had rooted in a village that was pre-twentieth century, yet well enough off to leave lamps burning through the night. She was probing the landscape with her dulled senses for other clues to the curse root's when-and-where, when Blaise seized her arm and pulled her onto the bank of ditch that paralleled the road.

"Quench yourself. Company's coming."

Hunters weren't immovable objects when they roamed the past. They regularly violated any number of Newton's laws, especially the one about two bodies—two *human* bodies—occupying the same place. If Emma had known for certain that one of the light-bearing visitors coming toward them from the hilltop was bound to Donetta's curse, she might have stood directly in his way and let herself get swept up in his—she took it for granted that the visitors were male—physical being and his mind.

Certainty would come later, after they'd watched the root rise from a safe distance. For reasons not even Harry Graves could explain, time was resilient. Hunters could observe a moment any number of times before deciding to intervene with a small change that would moot a curse without materially altering the cause and effect of time's arrow.

As the visitors drew closer Em counted two horsemen, each supporting a pole and lantern against his leg and an unknown number of footmen surrounding them.

"If we're in Europe," Em whispered, "we can't be farther back than the eighth century. Great—that narrows the window down to about thirteen hundred years."

The visitors were silent and seemed sober enough for serious work. The riders wore the uniforms of an unrecognizable army: long padded coats over pale, baggy trousers tucked into calf-high boots. Em thought she saw swords, but, even if she had, she couldn't pin a sword style to a century. The dozen or so footmen wore tunics and shirts of several styles. Their trousers were dark and indistinct. Most were bearded, unlike the officers—Em tagged the riders as officers—who were clean shaven. A few of the footmen carried clubs; the rest were technically unarmed. The whole cadre had a disreputable air to them, and Em imagined they were all proficient brawlers with their fists.

Em eyed them all, looking for the telltale aura that would betray a curse's presence. They were sour, brutish men, but none of them displayed an aura or harbored a curse.

Blaise waited until the last footman had passed before asking, "How can you claim to know anything about the time or place by looking at a column of irregulars?"

Emma had climbed out of the ditch before she noticed his hand poised in front of her. It wasn't that she couldn't have seen it—now that the riders were some forty feet ahead of them, Blaise had made himself faintly visible— she simply had never developed the habit of looking for chivalry.

"Stirrups," Em explained as they fell in step behind the riders. She spoke with confidence both of her facts and that the riders couldn't hear them. "Assuming we're in Europe—and judging by the faces we saw, I think that's a good assumption—we're looking for a curse that's wound up attached to a young woman from Croatia, which is in the Balkans, which is in Europe. And, in Europe there were no stirrups before the eighth century. Stirrups came in with one wave of Central Asian barbarians or another: the Huns, the Magyars, I don't know which, but before the Mongols.

"Actually, I'd bet we're quite a bit beyond the eighth century—I didn't notice anything remarkable about their saddles or anything else, and I think I would have, if they were eighth-century vintage. My guess—because they were riding horses and carrying lanterns—is we're somewhere between your time and about a hundred years before mine."

The riders doused their lanterns while they were still a good way from the village. They sent their footmen ahead to scout out obstacles and open the village gate. Blaise and Emma scurried forward, passing through the gate only a few feet behind the riders who, in any event, did not order the gate closed behind them.

"I've got a bad feeling about this. We could be seeing

the start of some sort of pogrom. Then again, I wouldn't expect a root to pull us back to a birthday party."

Blaise didn't respond to the signal word, but he knew enough about human nature to share Em's wariness. "Wait here," he advised. "I'll follow them from here. This tracking of curses through time may be new to me, but trouble keeps the same face. No need for you to witness this."

More chivalry. Em shook it off a second time, though not from a lack of habit. Blaise could possibly moot a curse with nothing more than his ability to manipulate historical objects, but this kind of mooting most often required plunging into someone's mind, and only she could do that; and only after she'd personally studied the circumstances that gave rise to the curse. Odds were that she was going to witness another death, another murder, no matter that the victim was long gone and forgotten.

"I've got to watch," she said, pushing ahead of her lover.

To the extent that Emma could see the buildings around them, they seemed well built. The lanterns they had spotted from afar hung beside the doors of two of the larger buildings. The irregulars Emma and Blaise followed moved past the first one and seemed headed toward the second. The illuminated buildings were two stories tall with mortared stone walls for the ground floor and wood-framed stucco above. Em studied the architecture, in the hope that it might be distinctive enough for research when she got back to Bower—if she couldn't find a way to moot the curse on the spot.

The riders dismounted. One of them pounded his fist against a closed door. He shouted words in a language Emma didn't recognize, though it had the soft, slurring consonants she associated with Slavic languages, which would be consistent, she thought, with a Balkans village.

Moments passed with no response from the inside of the house. The dismounted rider pounded harder and shouted louder. Emma, who was standing near the door of an otherwise shuttered and darkened house, heard movements within it but nothing from the lantern-lit house until a crack of light widened beneath the lantern. A man's face appeared in the crack. Fifteen feet away Emma could see the terror in his face. She checked for a curse's aura and found none, though she wouldn't expect to see anything in the essence of an innocent, even an innocent on the temporal verge of emitting a curse.

The rider put his fist to the door and shoved it open. Light from the interior spilled out of the house, stopping everyone in their tracks. Em made a beeline through the men and horses to get a look inside the house. There was a peasant-dressed woman standing by the hearth with something—maybe a poker—in her hand. That alone could get her killed, especially if the curse was rooted in the age of gunpowder and pistols.

During the frozen standoff between the invaders and the residents, Emma watched the hands of the dismounted riders. Both of them slung swords from their hips. A sword might not be much of a distance weapon, but Em had learned from Blaise to respect its deadliness in close quarters.

The standoff thawed. Em didn't catch the word or gesture that broke it, but suddenly there was movement. The invaders were across the threshold, and the residents were screaming. Blaise gripped Emma's wrist and pulled her away from the door. Em didn't need his caution. She knew what was going to happen: Someone was going to die and his—or her—death was going to give rise to a curse. Knowing was enough; she didn't need a front-row seat.

They got one anyway. After a few moments of chaos, the invaders emerged from the house with a prisoner—a disheveled woman, barefooted, loosely gowned, and probably pulled from her bed. The prisoner put up a fight. Her nightcap went flying, and a pair of thick, pale braids fell down her back like enraged serpents.

Emma expected rape, which repelled her more than the thought of murder. But the men didn't attack the prisoner's clothes, and she was neither pretty nor young. Her face was deeply creased, and, though it was hard to be certain, her mouth seemed to have the shrunken shape that meant she'd lost most of her teeth. The words *witch, crone,* and *old* filled Em's thoughts until the mother-voice quenched them with—

Do you think you *would look any different? Any better?*

Shamed, Em turned away before she looked for an aura. She missed the first blow that dropped the woman to the ground. The invaders, riders and footmen together, formed a circle around the fallen woman, and it became impossible to know if the woman was already cursed or about to give rise to one. The irregulars lashed out with booted feet. Ever the gentleman, Blaise tried to gather Emma against his chest, but it was too late to turn away. She stood firm and watched as, miraculously, the battered woman broke free between two of her attackers.

The woman lunged for her home, which had shut its door. She screamed. A plea for help or a curse on the family that had abandoned her? Her scream ended abruptly when a man clubbed her head from behind. By the way the woman went down, Em guessed the club was loaded with a good-sized rock. She hoped the blow had crushed the woman's skull and ended her terror. At any rate, the woman stopped fighting and was limp when one of the horsemen seized her by the ankle. He began dragging her toward the horses.

Em felt a wind gather at her back—a wind that did not affect anything in the village—and braced herself for the hot whirlwind that signaled a curse's creation. Her mind had already begun to work on the problem of where to intervene. But the wind blew steadily as the riders mounted and did not quicken into a curse.

"We must follow," Blaise whispered and took a step in that direction.

Em resisted. "It's here," she countered. "The wind blows toward the house. It's not the old woman. There's something else going on here."

The irregulars departed, dragging the old woman behind them. Blaise put his weight against the house door. He rattled it on its hinges, but the door was bolted from within, and none of the residents was brave enough or curious enough to see what was left outside. Emma retreated to get a better view of the house she was going to have to revisit—getting inside wouldn't be a problem; she'd simply mingle with the irregulars as they stormed it. She measured the wind with her available senses and looked up.

There were windows up on the second floor, a pair of them. They were small and masked with dark shutters; and one of them sealed itself with a slight movement as Em watched.

"We'll be upstairs," she told Blaise.

He joined her as the wind strengthened and penetrated the shutters as though they weren't there.

"Who?" Blaise asked.

"Couldn't see. I'm guessing it's someone who knew what was going to happen and did nothing to stop it—the very definition of evil, if it comes to that. Maybe it's the someone who put it all in motion: 'My grandmother's a witch'—"

"A child, you think?"

Em shivered. She'd imagined an adolescent—the emotional turmoil of their years was prime curse-making material; the image felt right. It took a death, though, to make a curse. Would the household turn on the betrayer, or would the betrayer repent and commit suicide?

The wind at their backs howled. It thickened and be-

came an obscuring darkness between them and the house.
They waited five minutes, or maybe fifteen, then the wind
died: The curse had been created. Emma looked at Blaise.

"A bad one," he agreed. "It lingered. Do you want to
moot it now or come back another time?"

"Another time. There's enough here; we can find it
through the window. I've got to get back to the ship.
Eleanor's coming."

"You've got a sense of her?"

"No," Em admitted. "But *tempus fugit*."

Ignoring what was going on above them and what had
happened where they stood, Em leaned up to kiss Blaise's
cheek. He responded with a less-chaste embrace.

"I'll be on dry land tomorrow," Emma promised when
they separated.

She didn't need the way-back stone to translate herself
from the shadowy past to the here-and-now. A simple act
of will was sufficient. She rolled over and looked at the
clock.

Six-fifteen.

The ship hadn't begun to move, but where the hell was
her mother?

E *ight*

I *t was six-thirty* and Emma was putting on her makeup when Eleanor breezed into the room. She was still in her swimsuit and looking a bit lobsterish from the Caribbean sun. Emma didn't have to ask to know that the parasailing adventure had been a success.

"I was *flying,* Em," Eleanor announced. She spread her arms like wings and spun her collection of tote and shopping bags onto the bed. "Flying! Can you imagine it? All my life I've dreamed of the wind holding me up. You don't feel the sail. There's no weight or strain of holding it up. It's just there around you—a frame for steering. You almost feel you could let go and just float."

"You didn't try that?"

"One hand," Eleanor confessed. "I thought about lifting both hands—you're not supposed to, but it's not like your hands are what's keeping you beneath the sail. I was wearing a harness." She pointed to red lines on her shoulder and midriff where the webbing had chafed her skin. "But—" Eleanor grinned conspiratorially and halved the distance to her daughter's ear. "You know how we have to walk in the Netherlands? How we *can't* make it easier on ourselves and fly like Superman? Well, I think I've got a solution. You've got to be able to imagine flying—really imagine it in all its details: the wind, the lightness, everything. I can't wait to try! The next time you go, I want you to take me with you. Maybe I can't translate by myself, but I can learn to *fly!*"

"What about the sail holding you up and the boat towing you across the water?" Em quibbled.

She was more intrigued than she was willing to admit. The first thing she'd done when she'd arrived in the wasteland—one of them, anyway—was ask why they had to walk, why couldn't they bolster themselves on imaginary wings and fly? Eleanor's explanation then and her proposed solution now made sense—but, since Emma hadn't absorbed the entire parasailing experience into her own memory, there was a good chance that Eleanor's solution wouldn't work for any hunter but Eleanor. There'd be a run on parasailing equipment among hunters, if Eleanor's theory held water.

"All right, maybe there're still some things I've got to work out, but, I'm on the right track. I don't need to *feel* the boat, not the way I'll need to feel the air floating past. Emma, you can't imagine how free I was. You've got to try it yourself. Anything that's weighing you down, it just falls away, and you're on top of the world."

"Maybe I will." Em returned her attention to the mirror and her lipstick. "It sounds like you had the high point of the whole trip—literally."

"Oh, I wish you could have been there with me!"

Eleanor gave Em a hug from behind. Fortunately she'd finished with her lipstick.

"Sorry I missed it. I took a nap. It wasn't very exciting"—Em decided not to mention her own adventure—"but just what I needed. I'm glad you got to go—twice."

"Once," Eleanor corrected. "I sold your reservation." She immediately rummaged among the vacation debris for her wallet. "It worked out very well, if I say so myself. Kinsey didn't decide she wanted to 'sail until she saw what fun everyone else was having, especially her husband. By then all the slots were filled—yours included. Selling yours to her just seemed like the right thing to do." She found the wallet and removed a wad of folded cash. "I sold it on the up-and-up, no profit. Harry'd never approve, but I figured you would."

Em did. "You could have given it away."

"That wouldn't do . . . we're having dinner with them. Hope you don't mind? They wanted to have a last night dinner at Gondolas, but they were late there, too. No separate tables left. I was able to get them added to our reservation—we had to give up our window seat in the San Marco section. I know that's what I told you to get, but we're in the Piazza—should be almost as good. You have to know how to treat those people—that's one thing Harry was good for: dealing with maître d's and their ilk. And I swapped us out of that Festivo thingy . . . chocolate volcanoes? Em, what were you thinking? A nice glass of Sambuco—that's the way to end an Italian dinner. Just give me a moment to shower and change—we're going to meet them on the pool deck for departure at seven fifteen."

"That's a little late for departure, isn't it?"

Eleanor shot her a puzzled glance. "Where were you for the storm? Don't tell me you slept through it? Thunder, lightning, raindrops the size of golf balls, and the wind to fire them at you like bullets. It blew up in a hurry and was over just as fast, but *impressive* while it lasted. The crew rounded us all up in a hurry and stowed us in the pavilions where we ate lunch. Then, when the sun came out, they said the captain had authorized a change in departure so we could get our hour back. Everything—dinners, the shows, even last call has been pushed back an hour. This ship can fly through the water, you know. I met Kinsey and Jack in the pavilion. And you slept through it?" Eleanor concluded with evident disbelief.

"Must have," Emma said with a wan smile, then she covered herself with a bit of misdirection, "You know how you've been saying I shouldn't hunt while the ship's moving, well, I'm thinking I didn't do such a great job sleeping while it was moving either. I feel like I've finally gotten some decent rest and for the first time since we left Florida—no headache."

None of which was a complete lie. Her body had soaked up sleep while she and Blaise spied on curses. She felt good enough that the prospect of dinner with strangers wasn't a downer.

Eleanor showered with admirable speed and changed into a fashionable, lingerie-style dress that suited her twenty-something self—a style that Emma wouldn't have dared wear on bet and which left her feeling old in a discreetly patterned blue silk shirt and tailored trousers. To make matters worse, Eleanor didn't waste time with a hair dryer or styling brush. She simply tousled her two-toned beaded hair with a towel and left it for the air to dry. The cabin was a mess—towels, tote bags, and shopping bags strewn everywhere—but Eleanor was perfect.

"Someday you'll have to show me how you do that," Em mused as they left the cabin.

"You'll learn; you're young yet."

The Whetlons, Kinsey and Jack, proved to be a late-thirties couple, nearing the end of a delayed honeymoon meant to celebrate what was, for each of them, a second marriage. At first, Emma couldn't interact with them without thinking of her own second marriage, the one that had begun so optimistically and ended with so many psychic scars. There were other similarities—Jack had custody of his first-marriage offspring, Kinsey had none of her own. But the Whetlons had done something Emma and Jeff had discussed just once and dismissed out of hand: They'd had a child of their own. Jack's two sons and the year-old little girl were back home, in the care of their paternal grandparents, while Jack and Kinsey rediscovered why they'd committed themselves to the particular insanities of a stepfamily.

While the *Excitation* eased away from its private island, Em found herself dredging up anecdotes from the good years—tales she hadn't thought about for years, much less shared with her own mother. The retelling was unexpectedly cathartic. The stories were still funny or wise, according to their foundations, and, at least as she retold them, Em could forget the hostilities that followed.

The *Excitation*'s entertainment crew had saved the best theatrical show for the last night. A fire-breathing magician got the ball rolling for an imaginary journey that was both more and less than it seemed. Emma's engineering gene fastened onto the special effects—lasers, fog, trapdoors, and the usual magician's bag of tricks, including doves and rabbits and an eight-foot-long snake.

"You've got to wonder what would happen if it got loose," she whispered to Eleanor during a scene change. "Think of all the places it could hide."

Eleanor gave a dramatic shudder and ignored her daughter for the rest of the show.

Dinner at Gondolas was all that a premium dinner should be, from the ring-binder wine list to the intricate desserts and the superb view of the western sky, sunset included. The restaurant was adults-only, meaning that the child-friendly cuteness of the ship's other dining rooms had been left behind. The room merely suggested Venice in its decor—except for the antipasto, which arrived at their table on a gondola-shaped platter. By then the foursome had shared enough stories, not to mention a glass of wine while waiting for their table. They laughed about the gondola plate and the weight they had all surely gained since leaving Port Canaveral, then proceeded to devour every mushroom, olive, and sliver of red, ripe tomato.

Sunset occurred between the antipasto and the pasto. A hush fell over the restaurant as red orange sunlight cast a fiery, coppery glow across every surface. Spontaneous applause erupted from a table over in the San Marco section, but—as the *Secret Guide* had promised—the view was almost as good from the Piazza. The foursome saluted the sun with their glasses and settled in for some serious eating.

They dragged the meal out as long as they could with espresso and Sambuco, then, unwilling to abandon newly forged friendships, made their way to the nightclub where the last trivia game was being played for another all-expenses-paid cruise aboard the *Excitation* or her sister, the *Marvelocity*. Kinsey declared herself a useless partner in trivial pursuits—"I never remember names or dates or movie titles"—while championing her husband. Eleanor suggested that Jack pair with Emma, adding, "We can figure out a way to split the prize, if they win." With Jack filling the gaps in her pop-culture knowledge and Em covering the historic and international bases, the Merrigan-Whetlon team sailed through round after round, until Jack missed a question about the director of *Wings,* the first movie to win the Academy Award for Best Picture.

Sharing the shipboard credit they won was simple. Spending it, less so. The arcade of souvenir ships and duty-free boutiques had less than a half-hour of shopping time left before they closed for the final time: Their cruise vacation was winding down.

Emma bought a bottle of French perfume and spent her change on a final glass of wine to drink with her new friends at a quiet table as close to the *Excitation*'s bow as they could manage.

"I wish we could stay on board and leave again tomorrow," Kinsey said when the time had come to return to their cabins—packed suitcases had to be outside the cabin doors for the invisibles to haul away by one thirty A.M.

Somewhat to her surprise, Emma agreed. Despite sun-induced headaches and the horror of a suicide, she'd enjoyed her *Excitation* cruise and looked forward to taking another—possibly with a less-sunny itinerary. Alaska sprang to mind. She might have trouble getting Eleanor to sign up for an Alaskan cruise, but Nancy would go.

The last stop was the purser's station off the atrium where they dutifully charged gratuities for Draco, Mitya, and all the other crewmembers who'd been charged with their comfort during the cruise. Eleanor's *Secret Guide* provided generally acceptable and specific amounts. Eleanor doubled them; Em added 15 percent and received her own receipt plus five formal-looking envelopes, each filled with a credit slip made out to a crewmember. As with everything else, Fantabulous Cruises and the *Secret Guide* had all the details nailed down.

Back in the cabin, they got ready for their final night aboard and started packing. The job went quickly with cruise clothes on the bottom and ultra-comfortable, ultra-casual theme-park clothes on the top.

"Don't forget to leave out your clothes for tomorrow," Eleanor advised.

Wordlessly, Em peeled off a pair of jeans and an *Excitation* T-shirt from the top of her suitcase and zipped it shut.

Their luggage disappeared moments after they set it out in the corridor. Emma stood at the porthole, watching moonlight play with the waves.

"You were right," she admitted. "I needed a vacation, and this was a good one."

"I keep telling you, it's not nearly over yet. Tomorrow we drive over to the Magic Kingdom and set out on three days of theme-park adventure."

Emma liked amusement parks, and Orlando's were the

best in the world, but they wouldn't compare to the view through the wide porthole. The lights were out, and Em was settled on her pillow before she remembered Donetta and her curse. Their wonderful Gondolas dinner had meant that their paths were unlikely to cross again. It didn't matter. Whatever else happened tomorrow, they'd be on solid ground tomorrow night, and Donetta's curse would have been mooted out of history.

"Thinking about that girl?" Eleanor asked through the darkness.

"Everything's under control on that front."

"You can track it from the theme parks' hotel."

"Already have," Em admitted before she could censor her wine-loosened tongue.

"During your nap?"

Em nodded, a pointless gesture in the dark cabin.

"Lucky for you that I came back to the cabin before the ship started to move."

"Not luck. I knew you would—and, anyway, I had nearly four hours. How often does it take more than four hours to track a curse?"

"Did you moot it?"

"No, we wound up watching the wrong hand. We'll have to go back and do it right. It shouldn't be too difficult. There's an open door."

"And Blaise, I suppose, can handle any that aren't. He can be handy to have around. Where and when did you track it to?"

They had a quick discussion about cloudy skies and the architectural similarities in peasant villages from one end of history and the Eurasian continent to the other. Eleanor managed to mention Blaise's name three times before Emma stopped counting. The two of them were like children—or cats—squabbling for her attention. She wished her mother a good night's sleep and settled in herself. One by one Emma loosened the strands of her conscious thoughts until her world was quiet and serene.

Then, with no sense of transition, Em was walking across parched ground beneath a dark, menacing sky. A check to her right side revealed what she already knew: The way-back stone had gone missing. She was stranded in the wasteland with no sense of the bolt-hole, the absolute present, or her touchstone. At least there were no fiery curses whirling on the horizon and no tiddlers clamoring for her destructive attention. But there was a dog barking somewhere in the distance.

From her first tentative steps in the wasteland nearly two years earlier, Emma had been haunted by a dog—a big dog to judge by its bark and the few glimpses she'd gotten of it both in the wasteland and around her Bower townhouse. She'd told no one about the dog—as if keeping it a secret could negate it. The last time she'd heard it baying in the distance was the night before Gene Shaunekker announced that he was headed east to the Ivy League.

Coincidence, Em told herself, without conviction. The whole canine phenomenon was coincidence, even though she'd come to believe, in all other respects, that there were no coincidences where curses were concerned.

She stood on tiptoe, as if an extra inch or two of altitude could expand her horizon or let her catch sight of the baying hound. For all the powers granted to curse-hunters in a subjective reality, their ability to reconnoiter an area was severely limited. If Eleanor were onto something and the experience of parasailing could translate into a new way to navigate the wasteland, there'd be a revolution in curse-hunting strategies to equal the day when Redmond Longleigh organized the first curia.

The dog had gone quiet, passing out of earshot, losing interest, or stalking her like prey. Emma squelched her anxiety and concentrated on the bolt-hole. However faint it became, she'd never before wandered beyond its strangely magnetic influence, but she had this time. No matter the direction Em faced there was nothing that said "follow me home."

Wait—the mother-voice, the voice of reason, struggled to be heard. *A curse-hunter cannot possibly be stranded in the wasteland. Even without the way-back stone, there're a dozen ways to get home.*

A dozen might be an exaggeration, but there were options, and the first one that came to Emma's mind seemed worth a try. Em's tracking talent let her trace a curse to the exact time and place of its origin, but there was a mappable association between any spot on the wasteland ground and real-world history. All Em had to do was close her eyes and, using her delving talent, ride that association to somewhere, someone. She didn't use the way-back stone to get out of the past, and though she relied on Nancy to provide her a fast exit from their Friday night rogue hunts, that was prudence, not necessity.

Eyes closed, Emma sank to her knees and beyond. A different hardness manifested itself beneath Emma's knees. She let out a sigh that was deeper and more ragged than she expected.

"Where?" she asked softly as she opened her eyes.

The past was often pale and misty, but this time Em had settled herself in a veritable pea soup fog. She could see the ground—dark stone—beneath her feet and precious little else. Her senses of sound and smell, never sharp in the past, were completely useless.

And unnecessary. All Emma had to do was relax and think of her body, and she would feel her own flesh around her again; but curiosity, the frequent bane of Merrigan existence, struck again.

"There has to be some clue other than dark, old granite," she muttered, though common sense said that most of the time most of the places in the real world had been untouched by human civilization, and her knowledge of geology was not good enough to differentiate between old granite and really old granite.

Emma struck out in the direction she happened to be facing and walked a good twenty paces before the fog thickened into a wall the same color and texture as the stone she stood on. She couldn't be sure of the wall's height—taller than she could reach or see, that much was certain. Turning right, she followed the wall and came to an empty bench.

"Nassau?" she asked, remembering the rock-cut park. "Of all the times and places, and I come back to a place, at least, where I've visited before?"

A chill rattled down Em's spine and gave her enough contrast sensation to know that the fog was steamy and the place very likely *was* Nassau. And there were no coincidences in a curse-hunter's reality—a fact that was driven home when Em heard a dog baying behind her. Two barking howls, and the sound had grown stronger. Whatever its origin or purpose, the dog could track Emma more easily than she could track it.

Without a second thought, Emma skirted the park bench and jogged away from the dog. She had a fifty-fifty chance of emerging onto the sometime streets of Nassau where she hoped for choices and a chance to rejoin her physical self. But Em had left her luck behind. She faced the solid rock steps of the Queen's Staircase instead and tried climbing them two at a time. Near nightly exercise mooting curses kept Em in good shape. She might be a bit winded when she reached the top of the staircase, but she should have been able to get there without feeling her legs turn to leaden jelly.

Long before the end was in sight, Emma slowed to a step at a time and used the iron handrail to pull herself along. Something was terribly wrong. There couldn't be more than a hundred steps in the Queen's Staircase and by twos or by ones, Em had climbed at least that many. Gasping for air that seemed as breathless as she was, Em hung on to the handrail with both hands. The dog continued to bay. She was sure it was already on the steps.

I don't understand, she complained, but there wasn't time for analysis. Em pulled herself up another step and resumed her exhausted climb.

She couldn't have said whether she came to the wrought-iron gate at the top of the staircase ten steps later or a hundred. What mattered was that the gate was shut—latched and bolted—and she was trapped against it with the dog drawing closer by the heartbeat. The truth was that Emma didn't know for certain that the dog was an enemy; it had just never seemed prudent to confront its mystery. And it didn't seem prudent just then, either.

Desperate, Em grabbed a pair of metallic curlicues and gave them the mightiest shake she could imagine. The gate actually rattled on its hinges—which was a whole lot more effect than she usually had on objects, but far short of the effect she needed. With her back to the wall, Emma sank into a fetal ball.

This can't be happening! This is like a bad dream come true. It can't be—

Like a bad dream . . .

The thought returned to Em and with it, the solution to her predicament. She hadn't gotten stranded in the wasteland. She wasn't dog meat at the top of the Queen's Staircase. She was asleep on a boat and putting herself through the agonies of a *dream.* Years earlier, long before Emma had stumbled upon her curse-hunting heritage, before she had gotten out of junior high school, her father had convinced her that it was possible to bring the weight of logic to bear on a dream gone bad. With the dog so close, she surely could have seen his tongue and teeth but for the fog, Em put Arch Merrigan's lessons to good use.

This is a dream. I can peel it off like a pair of gloves or a wet bathing suit. I can crumple it into a ball and toss it far away. I can wake up in my own bed—

Emma's own bed was aboard the *Excitation*, king-sized, and shared with her mother. But the very ability to recollect those details gave Emma the strength to separate herself from the dream—from the square landing at the top of the Queen's Staircase where her dream-self had succumbed to exhaustion and couldn't have stood up or fought the dog if her life had depended on it.

It's a dream *and it's over,* Em insisted.

The details fell away one by one: the fog, the stairs, the stone, the dog—until only the exhaustion remained. She willed her eyes to open, but nothing happened. There wasn't a part of her that wasn't too tired to move, too tired to feel. Wisps of panic licked the edges of Em's thought. She truly didn't know if she was awake or asleep, only that she was numb—paralyzed—where she should have been moving.

Paralysis—now that was something to worry about. Then, before she could marshal her forces for a solid panic attack, the numbness had passed. Her eyes popped open or, rather, the lids tore themselves apart—there was no denying the sense that they'd been stuck together and that it had taken effort to pry them apart. Not heroic efforts, but enough, perhaps, to account for that horrible moment when she'd been awake but unable to move.

The moment was over, though, and slipping into the fog of spent dreams, barking dogs, and unending staircases. Emma propped herself on an elbow for a view of the clock: 3:00 A.M.

All was well, and the good ship *Excitation* was charging through the water en route to its Port Canaveral home. Em lulled herself to the engines' faint vibrations and slipped into a less tumultuous sleep.

The pixie voice in the ceiling speaker adopted a no-nonsense tone for its six thirty A.M. wake-up announcement—a clear indication that Emma and Eleanor were *departing* passengers whose dream vacation was over and who were expected to get themselves off the ship promptly ... but not without breakfast.

"You can have the bathroom first," Em offered. "I'll get dressed out here."

Which she quickly did, zipping into the jeans and T-shirt that would take her through Orlando's far-more-casual theme parks. She pulled the porthole drape open and was absorbing a last glimpse of the Atlantic, when Eleanor stepped out of the bathroom.

"Your turn."

Emma turned away from the view, and Eleanor screamed—not quite a bloodcurdling scream, but a scream all the same. Em spun back to the window, expecting to see a mushroom cloud or something equally catastrophic between the glass and the horizon.

"No! It's you. Emma, it's you. My God—it's your eyes. What's happened to your eyes?"

"Nothing."

Emma couldn't see clearly, of course. The last time she'd seen the world clearly first thing in the morning had been sometime during the summer between fourth and fifth grades. Sharp vision required her myopia and astigmatism-correcting contact lenses, which she hadn't yet inserted. But she could see faces clearly enough, and there was no denying the horrified sincerity of her mother's expression.

"All right," Em grumbled. She grabbed the short-order toiletries kit she'd left out of her luggage and, shouldering through the narrows at the foot of the bed, made her way to the bathroom mirror.

"Shit." The expletive escaped before her lead foot cleared the marble threshold. She followed it with a softer, more heartfelt, "What the hell?"

The problem was obvious: Where her right eye—her

dominant eye—should have been a uniform white color, it was, with a tiny white exception near the tear duct, a bright, bloody red. And she hadn't suspected a thing. She'd been up for a good fifteen minutes, dressing, staring out the porthole, with nary a clue that her eye resembled a maraschino cherry with a pupil. Knowledge brought discomfort of the psychological kind. The red eye didn't hurt, didn't feel at all out of the ordinary, but looking at its reflection brought tears to both Em's eyes.

She strode closer to the mirror in time to assure herself that, whatever was going on with her eye, her tears remained clear, unbloodied.

"Does it hurt?" Eleanor demanded from the doorway as Em winked her left eye shut.

"Doesn't hurt. Doesn't feel as though there's anything odd at all. And I can see everything the way it's supposed to be. The world the way it looks when I haven't put my lenses in. It's not like I'm looking out through red sunglasses."

"You're sure?"

Em grimaced and reopened her left eye. "I wouldn't have known anything if you hadn't said something— wouldn't have known until I got in here." Overcoming aversion, she skimmed a fingertip lightly against the bright-red sclera. There was no sudden pain and no blood, either, on her fingertip when she examined it. "I don't understand."

"What about a fever? Are you running a fever?"

Obediently, Em felt her forehead. "Nothing. I'm fine. I'm fine everywhere except my eye. I've seen pictures like this of people who've been in accidents or fights and they've got great, big swollen black eyes to go with the red. But here, there's no swelling." She probed the bony ridge around her eye to reassure herself. "And I haven't been in any sort of fight or walked into a door . . ."

Emma paused as she remembered her dream and its aftermath, particularly the paralysis and the tearing sensation as she finally opened her eyes. For her life, she couldn't remember if she'd felt it more in her right eye than her left, but she seized on it as an explanation—*the* explanation—for the eye looking back at her from the mirror.

"It can't be healthy," Eleanor stated the obvious. "We've got to do something."

Em shook her head. She carried a little bottle of artificial tears in her full-sized toiletries kit—the one she'd dutifully packed in the suitcase long gone from the corridor outside the cabin. The best she could think of was the wetting solution she normally used with her contacts, but, somehow, that didn't seem like a viable idea. Nor could she talk herself into inserting a fingernail-sized dome of plastic into her blood-colored eye.

"I don't think there's anything I can do."

"The ship's doctor," Eleanor suggested.

"No time," Emma countered. "We've got to be off the ship by eight thirty. Even if we could find him by then. No, I'll just have to put up with it until we get to Orlando. Maybe an emergency room?"

She didn't like the sound of the words she was using. An emergency room seemed too panicky for a complaint that had produced only the appearance of blood and no pain at all. Yet it was her eye she was thinking about, and of all her dreads, a loss of vision was the disability she feared most. She'd slipped into a two-day depression after her last visit to the eye doctor when he'd announced there were cataracts growing in both her natural lenses.

"Nine o'clock," she murmured, building a plan in her mind. "Nine o'clock. My eye doctor's office opens at nine. I can call information, get the number, and call his office. I'll tell him what's happened, and he'll tell me if I need to go to an emergency room. Maybe he'll even recommend a doctor in the Orlando area. Sometimes they know people—"

"Don't be foolish," Eleanor chided from the cabin depths. "This is your *eye* we're talking about. Your vision! You can't be taking chances."

Emma followed Eleanor's voice out of the bathroom. She found her mother with her cell phone pressed against her ear. When their eyes met, Eleanor put a warding hand between her mouth and the phone.

"Reception's lousy—all this metal, I guess. But it's ringing. Someone will answer."

"Who? Who are you calling?"

"The Atlantis emergency number."

"Atlantis!" Emma failed to suppress a disbelieving shudder. "We're going to Orlando."

"And a doctor we don't know from Adam? Not a chance. Shevaun will set up an appointment with one of their doctors. Late afternoon should be fine. We can get up there by three, if we push it. And, believe me, we're going to fly."

"But we've got plans . . . reservations at a hotel!" Em had been less enthusiastic about the theme-park portion of the vacation, but anywhere sounded better than dead-center in the Atlantis Curia.

"Plans! How can you even *think* of doing the parks with your eye looking like that? You can barely handle the sun under the best of conditions. Going to the parks would be like going to the beach when you've already got a sunburn. You can't seriously be thinking of doing it."

Put that way, Emma had to agree, though things were happening so fast—before she'd had the chance to absorb them—that she felt as though she'd been caught in an undertow. "Who's Shevaun?" she asked belatedly, never having heard the name before. "I just don't know about Atlantis, Mother." Emma knew she was in trouble any time she referred to Eleanor as capital-M Mother.

"One of us," Eleanor assured her. "She's good, Emma, in every sense of the word. Shevaun's the one who really runs Atlantis—makes sure the bills get paid and there's food on the table. She keeps Red and everyone else in line. That's why she mans the emergency line."

The ringing, apparently, had drawn someone to the Georgia end of the cellular transmission. Eleanor identified herself as Eleanor Graves, which was apparently sufficient. She didn't construct her conversation in a way that allowed Em to guess the name of the person to whom her mother was speaking. After a moment of annoyance for the oversight, Em returned to the bathroom where she washed her face and brushed her teeth, all the while watching herself in the mirror. Her cherry-red eye drew attention the way sugar drew ants. She'd have to wear her sunglasses when she left the cabin, regardless of where she wound up going.

And the mere fact that she admitted destination doubts meant that she'd probably be headed for Georgia, not Orlando. Eleanor's urgent concern was contagious. Even the mother-voice's steady message of *Don't panic* and *If your vision were at stake, there'd be additional signs,* fell short of permission to continue a vacation. She checked her watch—five past seven. Way too early to think about calling her Michigan eye doctor, but moving toward late for breakfast in Rocaille.

Emma tucked her toothbrush and other toiletries into the small case and returned to the cabin to tuck the case into the duffel bag she'd be carrying to breakfast and off the ship. By the sound of Eleanor's voice, the conversation was winding down and cooperation had been secured. Em waited until Eleanor pushed buttons to end the call before asking,

"What's the good word?"

"Shevaun will take care of getting you an appointment. I told her any time after three thirty. Figure we'll be on the road by nine, that gives us six and a half hours, most of it on the Interstates, between here and Atlanta—that's just about what it took coming down, and we weren't pushing time then."

"We better cancel our Orlando reservations, then."

"You're right," Eleanor nodded.

She dug into her purse, looking for the itinerary Emma had printed up before they left Bower. With or without a reddened eyeball, Emma could recognize a lost cause when she saw one. She fished an identical piece of paper out of her own purse and spotted her own cell phone in the depths.

"I'll call," she volunteered, and in five minutes, plus cancellation fees, rerouted the second half of her vacation from central Florida to somewhere in Georgia. "You *do* know the way?" she asked her mother as they closed their cabin door for the last time.

"Well enough," Eleanor insisted in a tone that did not inspire 100-percent confidence. "I know the way once we're in town, and the main roads. We'll just follow signs until we're northeast of Atlanta, then we'll hope for the best. Worse comes to worst, we'll call again for directions. We've both got cells and plenty of minutes, right?"

Em didn't argue—it took most of her concentration just to see where she was going in the *Excitation* corridors while wearing her industrial-strength sunglasses over nonexistent contact lenses. Faces on the far side of the breakfast table lost their sharpness. Em excused herself and inserted a contact lens into her left eye. That helped, but only a little; Em's right eye was her dominant eye. Her brain was accustomed to paying more attention to its signals and rebelled against switching its priorities.

She drew concerned questions from her dining table companions and stern warnings to get herself to a doctor when she reluctantly gave in and lowered her sunglasses. Only Gracie offered encouragement.

"Subconjunctival hemorrhage," she decreed. "Popped a little blood vessel, that's what you've done. I got at least one of them with every pregnancy. If you're not headachy or seeing double, there's nothing to worry about. The blood'll get reabsorbed in a couple of weeks, and you'll be as good as new—though you'll probably have a new little, red line in the white of your eye."

In point of fact, Em did have the shadow of a headache—the familiar right hemisphere headache she'd had off and on for the whole cruise—but if migraines could cause popped blood vessels, one or another of her eyes would have been bright red for the entire last year of her marriage to Jeff. She was the only one at the table, though, who took heart from Gracie's diagnosis. The rest were unanimous: Even Draco and his crew, lavishly attentive on account of the generous gratuities they'd reccived, believed that a mad dash up the Interstates to Atlanta was the only sane course.

All Em needed to complete the morning's chaos was a face-to-face encounter with Donetta and her curse. Fate smiled, or perhaps it giggled, and set the two women on a collision course when Emma and Eleanor were leaving the dining room. Em's attention was riveted on her mother's two-toned, bead-enhanced hair. She ignored her flanks until it was too late. Circling a left-behind chair when she'd have been smarter to shove it back toward its table, Em brushed shoulders with the cursed Croatian.

Emma recognized the young woman at once, but—thanks to the dark glasses and T-shirt—there was no glint of recognition in the opposite direction.

I know where your curse is rooted, Em thought as the girl continued her rush toward some unknown destination. *I'm going to moot it tonight.* Then she hurried to catch up with Eleanor who hadn't slowed or noticed.

Fantabulous Cruises' efficiency bogged down in the final moments of the voyage. Their luggage had gotten separated, with Eleanor's suitcase winding up properly in the taped-off terminal warehouse area corresponding to their cabin deck and Emma's hiding out with suitcases harvested from a more exclusive deck. By the time they'd located it, they had the customs inspectors mostly to themselves. Thanks to their less-than-satisfying shopping expedition in Nassau, neither of them had anything to declare and the cruise ended anticlimactically on the terminal sidewalk where passengers for the turnaround cruise had already begun to mass.

"Keys," Eleanor said with her hand out.

"Pardon?"

"Your car keys. You can't drive, and we're not going to drag these suitcases all the way to the parking lot."

Em felt her cheeks turn red as her right eye. Sure, she couldn't read the signs on the far side of the road, but that hadn't stopped her from thinking she'd be driving the Integra up to Atlanta. Meekly, she fished out her keys and gave Eleanor instructions for finding the car.

"While you're doing that, I'll call my eye doctor and get his opinion."

It never ceased to amaze Emma, who'd learned her telephone etiquette in the days of stiff, cloth-wrapped cords and rotary dials, that she could carry on a thousand-mile conversation from a crowded sidewalk and a lump of plastic no bigger than the palm of her hand. She still had to stifle the urge to cup her hand around a nonexistent mouthpiece or talk loudly to be heard. Fortunately, the staffer in her optometrist's office was a patient woman who bore with Em's technological awkwardness and gave her the same diagnosis that Gracie had over breakfast.

"Sounds like a subconjunctival hemorrhage. They're almost always nothing to worry about as long as there's no pain or blurring or any other symptom. We see them, sometimes, in conjunction with high blood pressure. Yours isn't, is it? We wouldn't necessarily tell you to come in for an examination, if you were in town. Don't be surprised if it gets bigger before it gets smaller or turns brown—or even greenish—before the blood is fully reabsorbed."

Emma swallowed hard, grateful for that bit of information but hardly pleased by it. She could imagine her horror if she'd awoken one of these next few mornings to find that her red eye had turned olive-drab.

"And that could take three weeks. If it takes longer than three weeks, or there's anything else that concerns you, once you're back in Bower, don't even make an appointment. Just stop by the office, and someone here will take a look at it for you."

"What about my contact lenses?"

The staffer paused a moment before answering, "Oh, I wouldn't recommend that. Stick to your glasses for a few days, at least."

Em failed to suppress a sigh. Her five-year-old, emergency-only pair of glasses were safe in the top drawer of her Bower dresser.

"It probably wouldn't hurt." The staffer responded to the sigh. "But go easy. You can't see it or feel it, but your eye's a little swollen, a little blistered, and you really don't want to do anything that might aggravate the situation. If you don't already use them, you'll probably want to invest in a fresh bottle of artificial tears—your eyes are apt to feel drier and scratchier than usual for the next couple of days."

There was no arguing with wisdom. Em promised to take good care of her eyes and to stop into the office once she got back to Bower, assuming she wasn't well on the mend by then. In the back of her mind she was already bargaining with the advice she'd been given: She'd endure twenty-four hours of reduced acuity, then, if things were looking better—or at least no worse—she'd give her contacts the cleaning of their plastic lives and get her vision back to normal.

Until then, though, she was going to be a passenger in her own car and facing the mysteries of Atlantis with considerably less than twenty-twenty vision.

Nine

Eleanor drove into the terminal entrance area and waited in the idling car while Emma wrestled their luggage into the Integra's trunk. The lid shut on the first try, to Emma's surprise. She tossed their overnight bags into the back and settled into the passenger seat.

"Did you get ahold of your doctor."

Em nodded. "Gracie was right. Somehow, during the night I managed to give myself a subconjunctival hemorrhage. Unless it hangs around for more than three weeks, it falls into the 'just one of those things' category. I'm leaving my contacts out for a day and dosing myself with artificial tears—once we stop and I buy a fresh bottle of them. I'm convinced it's nothing to worry about, but, by the same token, you're going to have to do the driving and the navigating, 'cause without both my contacts, I'm not seeing worth a damn."

"Not a problem," Eleanor said as she accelerated out of the loading area. "If it's one place I know how to get to, it's Atlantis. I promise. I may have to watch for the signs, but the closer we get, the more I'll recognize." She glanced at her watch. "We'll have to make up some time. Can you wait to buy your tears until we stop for gas?"

Emma said she could wait and added nothing about the three-lane crossover her mother pulled to get them headed for I-95. Maybe it wouldn't have looked as reckless if she'd been seeing things clearly. So far, her body had reported nothing untoward with her right eye, but partially corrected vision was making her crazy. There was a stubborn temptation to blame Eleanor for noticing the hemorrhage, though that, Em realized, would have been unfair. Even on her most autopilot mornings, she would have noticed the big red splotch in her eye when she went to insert her lenses, and she wouldn't have finished the insertion ritual. At least Emma thought she'd have returned the lens to its storage case. She didn't know what she would have done if she'd been by herself and faced with the long drive back to Bower.

"I really appreciate that you're here to do the driving," she admitted to her mother. "I'd be in a real mess if I were alone."

"Hell, Em—if you were alone, you'd be home in Bower. Did your doctor say what might have caused it?"

"I didn't really ask. She mentioned high blood pressure. That's probably what caused Gracie's. Nancy's blood pressure went through the roof with Alyx. Otherwise, it could have been anything. Who knows? Maybe even a dream."

"Did you have a high-blood-pressure dream?"

Em changed the subject. "Watch the signs," she advised and leaned forward for a better view of the red-white-and-blue markers. Her brain was doing yeoman's service to adapt to unbalanced information she was getting from her optic nerves. Mile by mile, her vision was getting better, though it remained way short of what she'd need to drive. "We're getting near the Interstate. We want to go north."

"North to 10, west to 75, and north again to Atlanta—I've got the routing covered, Emma. You just sit back and try to relax. I figure we can put on a hundred and fifty miles before we need to stop for gas. That should get us near the Georgia border—can you last that long?"

"No problem," Em replied and tried to take her mother's advice.

Whatever her brain was doing to make sense of her vision, it was exhausting work. Every few minutes Emma felt the need to close her eyes. The lens she had in her left eye wasn't rated for sleeping or napping. The doctor who'd fitted her for her first pair of lenses back in the Sixties had given her a lecture on all the horrible things that would happen if she left her lenses in while she slept. After all the intervening years, the warning was as fresh as ever. There was no way Em could relax with one lens in and the other out.

"Is it okay with you if I try to take a nap—I'm not getting much in the way of useful information from my eyeballs right now."

"I'm fine," Eleanor assured. "Just don't go getting any bright ideas about fixing yourself in the Netherlands. If time's all you need to get your eye looking normal again, you can borrow some tonight at Atlantis."

Emma brought herself up short twice in one statement. On the one hand, she hadn't considered that she could accelerate her eye's healing in the wasteland, but more significantly, she'd somehow overlooked the likelihood that she'd be spending the night in the enemy's lair. Suddenly all she could think of was Blaise's oft-told tale of how an unhappy lover had slain his body as he slept. She removed her left contact lens and tilted the passenger seat back for a nap she very much doubted she'd take.

In her wildest paranoia, Em didn't think she had to worry about Redmond Longleigh sneaking into her bedroom, knife or pillow in hand. By all she knew of the man, Longleigh was too confident of his superior abilities as both a curse-hunter and a human being to stoop to murdering someone who happened to disagree with how he ran his curia. But Red Longleigh wasn't the only enemy that sprang to mind. Emma had a cousin, Sylvianne Skellings, the daughter of Eleanor's sister—Eleanor's deceased sister.

Sylvianne had the blond, horsey grace of a true-blue aristocrat, and, if Emma were to believe the tales her own mother told, Sylvianne had lived out the full Electra complex, murdering her mother in order to become her father's lover. Granted, the rest of the story was that Sylvianne's mother had pulled a fast one and Sylvianne was not genetically her father's daughter, giving her a technical bye, at least, on the charge of incest.

All of Em's sources agreed that a curse-hunter's talents were largely inherited. Daughters got their *wyrd* from their mothers, sons from their fathers. Eleanor and her sister had apparently turned out more talented than their mother. That, in turn, had attracted Red Longleigh's attention. He'd proposed to Eleanor—*Let's make new, improved curse-hunting babies*—but she'd turned him down. He'd been more successful with Eleanor's sister, at least in the wooing, wedding, and bedding department.

The couple had fallen short of the begetting goals, though—all that shifting back and forth between objective and subjective realities was apparently hard on the gonads. A curse-hunting woman had to give up her *wyrd* for the duration of her pregnancy, and maybe a couple years before it, too. Em didn't know what a curse-hunting man had to give up, or whether Longleigh had made any sacrifices. Suffice to conclude that Eleanor and her sister had both chosen *wyrd*-less men to be the fathers of their daughters.

For the better part of a year, Eleanor had insisted that Sylvianne would do anything to safeguard her position as Longleigh's right hand and consort, and the eventual mother of his supremely talented children—anything up to and including doing to her first cousin what she'd already done to her unfortunate mother.

There was nothing like the unknown mixed with a little paranoia to muddy up a nap. The awake, but not necessarily mature or rational, part of Emma wanted to grill Eleanor about every aspect of Atlantis, from its history and appearance to another round of rumor and bias about its regular residents. She kept that part stifled as her car purred along the Interstate. It was just as well Em couldn't read—or see—the speedometer from the passenger seat; Eleanor had to be taking the 70-mile-per-hour speed limit as a guideline or even a starting point for the race to Atlantis.

Emma was less successful when it came to her own imagination. She'd visited the wasteland reflection of Atlantis a few times a little less than a year earlier when she'd been hot in pursuit of what had turned out to be a pair of persistent curses. Redmond Longleigh's version of her bolt-hole was a village-sized warren of large, dark-paneled rooms, Persian carpets, and candelabra that everyone called "the bunker." Em tried to imagine the real-world Atlantis as a cross between those Victorian-themed rooms and Scarlet O'Hara. They were, after all, headed for the remnants of the plantation country clinging to the fringe of Atlanta. But her mental conjuring led to an interior much closer in spirit to *Wuthering Heights* or, even, a *Dracula*-esque vision of stone walls and stairways that went down, never up.

Em abandoned her nap. She cranked up the seat back and watched the blurred landscape whiz past. They pressed on to Lake City, where I-10 crossed I-75 and truck stops and hotels cluttered the north Florida landscape. Emma despaired of finding her artificial tears, but dry eyes were apparently a common enough problem among Interstate travelers. They didn't need lunch, not after the way they'd been eating on the ship, but the scents of hamburgers and pizza drew them into a fast-food arcade.

"That should do us," Eleanor decreed. "Nothing like heavy fuel: sixteen ounces of coffee in a sippy cup, a bag of cheese curls, and two chocolate bars. We won't touch the ground again until we're under the porch at Atlantis."

"Under the porch?" Em countered, juggling her own stash of snacks as she opened the passenger door. The Atlantis of her imagination had three-story white columns, black shutters on a myriad of windows, but no porches at all.

"I guess they call it something else, something fancy. Everything has a fancy name up there, but when it rains buckets—which it usually does—you'd have to swim from your car to the front door without that porch. Maybe they call it a portico. Porch, portico—I get mixed up."

Emma began editing her vision. "It's white, isn't it? I can't imagine a big, old southern plantation that isn't white."

"Oh, it's not a Civil War plantation." Eleanor arranged her personal fuel around the driver's seat and started the car. "There *was* a Civil War plantation—they call it the Great Rebellion—but it got burnt out in the war. Sherman, I think, or someone like that. Don't ask! When it comes to that house, Red can talk Harry into the ground. All I know is that, except for the kitchen, the current house was built in the 1880s and considerably remodeled in the Twenties. The kitchen's older, I guess. Maybe it dates back to the original house. Not that you'd know it to look at it. Only the best in kitchen equipment for Red's Atlantis. You could run a restaurant out of it, if you wanted to."

Em got as far as a massive stainless steel range and refrigerator—the sort of appliances that showed up in photo spreads of mansions and four-star restaurants—set against specifically red-brick walls. But it was all speculation, and she tried to put it out of her mind as Eleanor got the car up

198 * Lynn Abbey

to speed again. They talked about the weather and how autumn was still several weeks away from Georgia; and they talked about the cruise. Emma conceded that, despite the way it had ended, she'd be willing to take another cruise.

"Maybe a longer one, with days at sea instead of tied up at a dock. It's nice to travel with your hotel instead of packing and unpacking every day."

"If we timed it right," Eleanor replied enthusiastically, "we could book a transocean passage—when the ships are headed from the Caribbean to the Mediterranean. I'd love to sail across the Atlantic again."

She couldn't mean "sail" in the literal sense, Em decided. Eleanor was old, but not *that* old. "It's something to think about, depending on how my vacation schedule works out next year."

That was the first thought she'd given to the library and Maggie Patrick in days. It wasn't a pleasant experience. Work hadn't been a pleasant experience for months, and it looked even worse from the far side of a vacation. The notion of retirement crept into Em's mind. She was too young to start collecting her pension or Social Security—Harry had warned her to be careful with her Social Security. He wanted to handle her transition from working stiff to full-time curse-hunter himself. Mistakes involving the government could cause problems for every curse-hunter in the U.S. of A.

Harry was old enough to have literally sailed to the New World on the Mayflower. Emma wasn't so sure about Red Longleigh. Eleanor or Harry—she couldn't remember which—had once said that the whole concept of the Atlantis Curia was rooted in Longleigh's experience running the Northern blockade of the Southern ports.

Em was back to thinking about Atlantis again and watching the mileposts flick past, too quick and hazy for her to make out the numbers. It had been a good year for kudzu. Then again, every year was a good year for kudzu.

It covered the landscape like some alien liquid flowing from the roadside into every field. It defied gravity to surge up trees, telephone poles, and anything else that got in its way. Here and there, they'd pass a house with a yard where the kudzu feared to tread. Emma imagined the owners defending their precious grass from the green onslaught morning, noon, and night. She wondered if they dared take vacations, or if Georgia homeowners hired kudzu wranglers to patrol their lawns.

"How far?" she asked an hour later, when even the endless shapes of kudzu had become boring and she didn't care that she sounded like an impatient child.

"Two hours, maybe two and a half—depends on the Atlanta traffic. If it's moving, staying on the Interstates is quicker, even though it's longer, but if it's jammed up, it's just longer all around."

"Should I put my one contact back in to help you with the navigation?"

"No, I know the way. You just rest your eyes. Take off your sunglasses—let me see how it looks."

Emma regretted her obedience when she saw her mother frown. She lowered the sun visor and gasped at her reflection in the mirror on the visor's back. The nurse in her Bower eye-doctor's office had warned her that the hemorrhage might grow before it shrank, and it had. There was red all the way around her iris now, and she looked like a creature from a horror movie.

"Has it started hurting?" Eleanor asked.

"Nope, thank heaven. It still feels completely normal. If I didn't look in the mirror—" Em shuddered involuntarily. "I guess I am glad that I'm going to get to see a doctor today. Do you suppose that woman—what was her name?—was able to get an appointment?"

"Shevaun. Shevaun Morrison." Eleanor goosed the accelerator. "She promised, and Shevaun's promises are money in the bank."

They had to be doing eighty on a road that was starting to pick up lanes of traffic. Emma started to say something about their speed, then put her sunglasses back on instead.

"Should we call ahead—to find out for sure and let this Shevaun know how we're doing time-wise?"

"Once we're on the loop around Atlanta. See if you can find us a radio station that's doing traffic reports."

Emma did her best, but it was the middle of the day, the middle of the hour. The radio bands seemed equally divided between music neither of them liked and call-in shows whose repartee they liked even less. She switched back to CDs and, spurred by the commentary they'd avoided, began discussing the world at large. When it came to politics, at least, Em could carry on a conversation with her mother without wondering where it might wind up. And, to her modest surprise, she could let her mother drive her car through the tangle of Atlanta's freeways with the same freedom from care.

In good time, the razor-sharp high-rises of Atlanta's skyline were visible only through the rearview window. Eleanor said it was time to call Shevaun Morrison. She recited the number from memory, and Emma tapped it into her cell phone—two calls in one day, she was sure that was a new technological record. Shevaun Morrison proved to have a soft-spoken voice that radiated calm and confidence.

"Not to worry about a thing. I've just put a fresh pitcher of tea out in the sun. You'll have plenty of time for a glass and to get to the doctor's once you've arrived."

"She sounds nice," Em said to Eleanor after she'd ended the cellular call. "She's making tea for us."

"Real tea . . . I'm not at all a Southerner, except when it comes to iced tea."

They left the Interstate for a Georgia state road that wound through hills of green leaves and orange red dirt. They passed farms where fresh produce was set out on honor-system tables—choose your own corn, onions, or tomatoes, then put your money in a box with a rock sitting atop it. From the state road, they turned onto a country road that took them through a series of little towns, some of them hanging on by their fingernails, others gentrified with antique shops and restaurants by Atlanta refugees.

"I'll bet this has all changed a lot since you started coming here."

"It's changed a lot since I last came through. Creeping suburbs, if you ask me. It's good for Red, though; at least it should be. Once you've got enough yuppies and dinks, the bed-breakfast-and-catering business starts to take off."

"Bed and breakfast?" Emma asked in disbelief. None of her imaginings had tended in that direction.

"If nothing else it's cover for all our comings and goings. He does some catering, too—wedding receptions and the like. It helps pay the bills—not that Red *needs* help, but it's always better for a man to *look* as if he's working for a living."

Emma was still digesting those revelations when Eleanor pointed the Integra down a country avenue lined with full-grown, impressive oak trees and newer, but still impressive houses.

"In the beginning, everything between the house and the state road belonged to the plantation. It's been shrinking ever since. A big chunk went after the Civil War, another just before World War One. Red sold off his portion back in the Seventies. He swears he'll never sell another acre to developers, and maybe he won't. He doesn't want neighbors closer to the house, but there's still lots of property to the north."

Eleanor drove out of the clutch of 1970s houses and into sight of a neatly painted navy and white sign welcoming them to Atlantis. The lettering was large enough, and Eleanor was driving slowly enough, that Emma could read that Atlantis had been "established in 1847. A jewel of the

Old South. Bed and breakfast. Available for parties, receptions, weddings, and graduations." The sign included a phone number that Em failed to recognize. Then they were past the sign, and the plantation house came into view through the avenue.

Atlantis-proper was a large white structure with pairs of two-story white columns flanking the black door of a three-story-plus-attic house. Em immediately guessed that the house had been built, or rebuilt, in sections. The largest section was centered formally and symmetrically around the front door. The windows sported black shutters that might still be functional and decorative woodwork that struck Emma as a bit too elaborate for an antebellum plantation. To the right of the main section a two-and-a-half-story outrigger took several windows to slope down to a one-story screened-in porch belted with flower boxes. To the left, two layers of screen porches, one for the ground floor, the other for, presumably, second floor bedrooms, had been attached to the house. The driveway passed in front of the columned front door, then continued onto a large portico extended out from the layered screen porches.

Though the sky was cloudless and blue as it could be, Eleanor drove past the front door and brought the car to a stop beneath the portico.

"Welcome to Atlantis."

White-painted cement lions worthy of a European castle defended the shallow stairway between the black-top driveway and the porch deck, which had been painted battleship gray. Close up and out of the sun, Em could see that the trim wasn't black but dark navy blue like the sign. She supposed that nautical colors made a certain amount of sense, what with the name *Atlantis*.

It was an imposing house, perhaps the largest house she'd ever visited that wasn't given over totally to commercial use or a historical society, but it was far from the breathtaking beauty that might lead a visitor to imagine that she was stepping backward in time.

A copper cowbell hung from a rope on the driver's side of the portico. Eleanor gave it a good shake before opening the trunk. She hauled her suitcase out and set it upright on the blacktop. The handle came up to her hip.

"There's a dumbwaiter to get the suitcases upstairs to where the bedrooms are—if these suitcases will fit in it."

Emma grabbed hers and heaved. "That's what the wheels are for."

"On Red's polished wood floors? You're kidding yourself."

Before Em could respond, they heard the sound of a house door opening. Em looked through the screens and realized that the house had a side door, too. A tall, African American woman in business-casual, rust red slacks and an autumn-print tunic stepped onto the porch.

"Eleanor?" she asked.

The woman was looking at Emma, and Em felt an instant appreciation for the special difficulties curse-hunters might have in recognizing one another after appearance-changing absences.

"Shevaun!" Eleanor corrected as she ascended the porch steps.

The two women renewed what looked like a sincere friendship with a hearty embrace.

There really was no reason that Eleanor should have mentioned that Shevaun was African American. No reason at all—except Emma was shamefully relieved to have a few moments to shed her white-bread preconceptions and chase all her unnecessary questions about ancestry and relationships into a closet at the back of her mind.

"And you must be Emma," Shevaun declared the probable when she and Eleanor had broken their embrace. "Welcome to Atlantis. We're glad to have you here."

Smiling broadly, Shevaun held out her hand.

Few things were more pointless than guessing a curse-hunter's true age. Shevaun looked to be in her mid-thirties but if she were even a decade or two older than that—if she matched chronology with Emma herself—then she'd grown up in a time when a black woman of Georgia did not grasp a white woman's hand or meet her eyes equally.

"I'm glad to be here, finally," Em replied and realized, to her considerable surprise, that she hadn't lied.

"May I take a look at the problem?" Shevaun asked, and Emma lowered her sunglasses. "That is an angry-looking mess, but I'm sure Doctor Santirez will know just what to do about it. You made good time getting here—good enough that there's time for you to come in and freshen up a moment and enjoy a glass of tea."

Emma watched Shevaun's not-so-subtle appraisal of her comfy jeans and T-shirt. The outfit would, no doubt, have served her well in an Orlando theme park, but she was in the civilized part of Georgia now, where a doctor's office visit, even under near-emergency conditions, was not a jeans-and-T-shirt occasion. After returning her sunglasses to the bridge of her nose, Em slung her carry-on around the extended handle of her suitcase and rocked it onto its wheels.

"Enough time for me to change?"

"Barely." Shevaun led the way into the house. "You can use the dressing room behind the kitchen stairs where our brides freshen up. There's room enough in there for you and an army."

Shevaun set a good pace through two rooms, either one of which was the size of Em's kitchen, dining room, and living room combined. Yards of drapery damask, lace, and filmy white chiffon hung around all the windows, tempering the bright Georgia sunlight. Between the shadows and her sunglasses, Em didn't have attention to spare for the decorating details, though both rooms seemed heavy on the antiques and potpourri. After descending two steps into a restaurant-sized and -equipped kitchen, she wheeled her suitcase into a room that was small only in comparison to the rooms that had preceded it.

"I'll go call Red," Shevaun said from the doorway. "It'll take him a few minutes to get here."

Em tried not to react—of course the owner of the house would want to greet his guests. She shouldn't have expected otherwise, not from a longtime Southerner. If anything, she was grateful that she'd have time to change into something a little more appropriate. Not that the contents of her huge suitcase were all that much help. Business casual wasn't the order of the day, either aboard a cruise ship or at a theme park. She settled on a silk shirt she'd worn to dinner one night and the pair of all-purpose black slacks she'd tucked into a suitcase corner but hadn't worn on the *Excitation*.

Her cosmetics case beckoned from the carry-on. It wasn't so much that Emma felt the need to make a *good* impression on the problematic Redmond Longleigh as she wanted to avoid making a *bad* one. By the looks of things, he was surrounded by people—and rooms—that took their appearances seriously. This was one place where having aubergine fingernails was a plus.

Then again, she was headed to an eye doctor. Surely no one expected her to powder her eyelids or any other part of her face before a doctor started dribbling drops into them? Em finished her quick-change toilette with a brush of her hair and her teeth.

She zipped her luggage shut and returned to the kitchen, where Eleanor and Shevaun were sipping tall glasses of iced tea. A third glass waited on a faux marble counter beside the refrigerator.

"Where should I leave all this?" she asked with regard to her luggage.

"Oh, you can leave it right there," Shevaun said with another smile. She cast a sidelong glance Eleanor's way.

"We haven't settled on your rooms for the night. There's no one else here right now. They're all available, including the Wisteria. Will you be wanting separate rooms?"

"Separate," Emma said quickly, and the other two women exchanged obscure looks. Did they know something she didn't? Had she made a mistake? She tried to cover for herself. "I have the feeling that I'm going to want to go to bed early."

By the expression on Eleanor's face, Em had broken the cardinal rule of hole digging. Then a completely different thought burst into her mind: The varied glances the other two women were exchanging and casting toward her had little to do with her as a socially awkward person and everything to do with her as the owner of a freakishly blood-red eye. Without another moment's hesitation she retrieved her sunglasses. The kitchen went dark, subtle expressions vanished, but so did her current deformity.

What if it *weren't* temporary? What if Gracie and the nurse in her Bower doctor's office were wrong? What if this Doctor Santirez took one look at her and said *Get used to it*? Emma prided herself for her tolerance, but she'd never needed to seek tolerance from others ... from strangers passing on the street.

That something she could neither see nor feel—something that, so far, had no impact on her physical sense of self—could so utterly transform her life shook Emma to the core. She grasped the third glass of iced tea with the sense that she had never felt cold, sweated glass against her flesh before. The tea was refreshing, lightly spiced with cinnamon and lemon. A few swallows grounded her again. She could face the people who knew her, but she didn't remove her sunglasses.

"It's delicious," Em said, breaking the silence that had permeated the kitchen. She was spared the need to find another subject for conversation by the sound of a car horn coming from the portico. After another quick sip of tea, she set the glass down and said, "I guess I'd better go."

Eleanor and Shevaun followed Emma through the antiqued rooms. Had she seriously thought the first face-to-face, real-world meeting between herself and Redmond Longleigh could pass unwitnessed? She crossed the second room with her attention riveted to the Aubusson-style carpet beneath her feet. Her hand shook when she reached for the screen-door's handle. It took willpower, and quite a bit of it, to look straight ahead—

What the—?

Emma's attention shot past the man standing at the top of the steps to the car idling on the far side of her own. They could have been twins—fraternal twins. Em's Integra was silver, never her first choice in car colors, but she'd been desperate for a car after Eleanor had wrecked hers last year, and at least it wasn't red or yellow or some other primary color. The car beyond hers, though, was also an Integra, maybe a year or two older, and as black as every other car Emma had owned since college.

She couldn't suppress a backward glance, meeting Eleanor's eyes through a shield of dark green plastic. Had Eleanor known? Had *Harry Graves* known? They'd both been instrumental in steering her toward the silver car—a car whose power and handling she'd come to love. Emma had an instant answer for her second question—Harry's relationship with Redmond Longleigh was prickly enough that he wouldn't have been caught dead recommending one of his rival's preferences. But Eleanor? Eleanor who'd driven unerringly through the maze of Atlanta freeways and right to the door of Atlantis—Eleanor who chatted so comfortably with Shevaun and had a favorite among the house's many bedrooms—?

Eleanor *had* to have known. The complete lack of expression on her face bespoke guilty knowledge, if not outright conspiracy.

"Emma?" Longleigh's voice shattered Em's reverie.

In life Redmond Longleigh's face was longer and narrower than it had been in the wasteland bolt-hole he called the curia's bunker. He was a tall man, not as tall as he seemed in the wasteland, but six feet, give or take an inch. There was a bit of lantern to his jaw and a fine net of wrinkles around his eyes and mouth. No doubting he was older than the rest of them, Longleigh had a fine-edged look to his face that belonged on currency. His eyes were pale blue, almost gray; and his hair was, as Emma had known it would be, vibrant, flaming red.

His body was lean, hard, and clothed with the same precision of style that marked Harry and Blaise, the other two cursing-hunting men Emma knew well. Longleigh's style was his own: a dark blue dress shirt worn open at the neck and tucked into snug twill trousers. It was no stretch to see in Longleigh the once and future plantation master or a walking advertisement for a line of expensive American men's sportswear.

"Shall we?" he asked. "Time's wasting. I wouldn't want you to have come all this way and miss your appointment."

Why, Em thought as she nodded, did that sound as though it had nothing to do with an eye doctor? She disdained the hand he extended toward her, and descended the porch steps.

The black car sported the luxury package for its model: leather seats, wood burl veneer on the dashboard, an extravagant sound system. Em made a point of adjusting the seat before buckling her seat belt.

"Shall I close the sunroof?" Longleigh asked as he eased into the driver's seat.

Em thought a moment. The rectangular opening let in sunlight, fresh air, and a sense of freedom. Closing it would seal her into the passenger compartment with a man—a human being and a curse-hunter—she did not trust. But she heeded the warning she'd gotten from her Bower eye doctor.

"I'm not supposed to let my eye get dried out."

"Very well, then." Longleigh touched a button, and tempered glass slid over the opening. He touched another, and the flow from the car's ventilation ducts was halved. "We're off."

He put the car in gear; like hers, it was a standard transmission with a fancy wooden knob atop the gearshift. Hers was stitched leather, polished smooth by someone else's hand. Somehow, she doubted Longleigh had bought his vehicle used.

They took the curves of the long Atlantis driveway at a faster speed than Em would have dared.

"Relax. I know where we're going. I'll get you there in time."

Emma said nothing.

He slowed the car down a notch before adding, "In one piece."

Longleigh said nothing else until they reached the state highway leading to the Interstate. "Does it hurt? Your eye, I mean."

What other part could he have meant? "No. I wouldn't know there was a problem if Eleanor hadn't noticed it this morning. Well, I would have, eventually, when I looked in a mirror, but only because it looks so ghastly. It feels completely normal. Not that I can see particularly well. Normally I wear contacts, but it didn't seem like a good idea to put them in this morning." She was babbling, the way she did when she was in an uncomfortable environment. She'd never mastered the art of idle chitchat. "I called my doctor's office this morning. His nurse said there was probably nothing to worry about . . . and that the eye might get all weird looking before it healed up . . . weirder, that is."

Her nervousness finally got a stranglehold on her

tongue. They sat in silence as the Interstate on-ramp came and went. Emma had no idea how far they had to go and was keenly aware that she had no idea where they were. She had her cell phone. If worse came to worst—and she could imagine myriad ways that might happen—she could call Eleanor.

After turning onto another state road, Longleigh asked, "Did you have a pleasant cruise?"

Give Longleigh credit—he was making a near heroic effort to be social. At that moment, though, thoughts of the cruise were thoughts of the crewman plunging past the promenade deck.

"Pleasant enough," she replied without enthusiasm.

"Santirez is a good doctor," Longleigh announced after another long silence. "A few years back I made a fool of myself with a chainsaw out back of the house. Wound up with an eye that probably looked worse than yours does. Plus, it *did* hurt, and I was seeing double. Santirez got me through it —far enough through it that I could do the rest myself. Do you practice restoration?"

Restoration—that had to be Longleigh's word for Eleanor's *transformation* and her own infrequently practiced ability to heal cuts, burns, and bruises, some of them not so minor. "I've done it—not on a grand scale, not with something I couldn't see or feel." She'd restored herself out of her gray roots, but saw no need to mention that.

Without warning, Longleigh's right hand grasped her left. "You'll be fine," he assured her, squeezing her hand before releasing it. "I knew a man who lost an eye in the war." He didn't say which war; she didn't interrupt with chronological questions. "He got it back. Took him a decade for the eye, and another for the vision in it; but the main thing is, he got it back. And, by what you say, you're in no danger of losing the eye."

"Fortunately," she agreed. The thought of regrowing an eyeball horrified her. Em imagined it half-finished then she, who never got carsick, fought a wave of nausea. She brought her hands together over her seat belt.

"Just shut up and drive?" Longleigh asked.

Nothing would have made Emma happier, but her father had done too good a job of raising his only child for her to have said yes.

"I'm worried," she admitted. "It's my eyes. So much of what I enjoy doing depends on my eyes." There was more to her anxiety, of course, but civility did not at all require honesty.

"We'll be there in about twenty minutes. We could have taken the Interstate. It's faster, but quite a bit longer. At this hour of the day, on this road, you gain more by shortening the route than you lose from the lowered speed limit."

Not that Longleigh was paying all that much attention to any posted speed limits. Although Em couldn't see the speedometer from this passenger seat, she confidently guessed they were doing seventy on a nearly empty two-lane blacktop road through hills and lush, green farmland. That was faster than she would have taken them, even had they been the familiar roads around Bower, but she felt less endangered than she had all day beside Eleanor.

The predicted twenty minutes lengthened to a half hour when they picked up the local traffic of a town whose welcome sign had whizzed by too fast for Emma's compromised vision. Between the traffic, the landscaped sidewalks and streets, and the generally prosperous look to its storefronts, she judged it to be a town that had gotten a second lease on life as the Atlanta suburbs oozed toward it. Her judgment seemed confirmed when Longleigh pulled into the parking lot of a professional complex tricked out in "plantation miniature" style, complete with columns, shutters, and oak trees struggling in the median buffers.

Em got herself out of the car, but Longleigh beat her to the door and held it open for her. She mumbled gratitude she didn't honestly feel and strode into a well-appointed waiting room. Checking in with the receptionist, she learned that her appointment was an imprecise thing.

"Doctor Santirez will see you between patients or afterward. His last appointment today is at five thirty. He should get to you no later than six."

Em knew better than to argue with a receptionist. She explained the situation to Longleigh who had seated himself in one of the many overstuffed chairs weaving through the room.

"So it could be an hour-and-a-half wait. I don't know if there's anything else you could be doing, but there's no need to sit here and wait with me."

"Waiting's not a problem. I will call back to Atlantis, if you don't mind, and tell them to make their dinner plans without us?"

Em would rather have waited alone; she'd rather just about anything that didn't keep her side by side with Redmond Longleigh. She especially didn't want to set herself up for a private dinner with the de facto boss of all the North American curse-hunters, but there didn't look to be a good way out of it. "That sounds right," she agreed. "There's no telling, really, how long this is going to take."

She could have chosen the chair next to his, but selected one that put a magazine-covered end table between them. The magazines were an assortment of out-of-date news weeklies, paens to Southern style, and sports monthlies, one of which Longleigh already had in his hands. Em spotted the corner of a six-month-old *New Yorker* peeking out beneath the Southern comfort magazines. She extracted it from its pile and, wishing she'd thought to extract her book from her luggage, settled in for the duration.

Longleigh left the waiting room, sleek, little cell phone in hand. He returned a few minutes later to say that everything was taken care of and they needn't worry how long it took Santirez to see Emma.

Doctor Santirez ran his practice with admirable efficiency. Patients emerged from the examination rooms, settled their accounts, left the office, and were replaced by new arrivals, about one every twenty minutes. If there was a cancellation or bottleneck, Em couldn't detect it. She pored through every article in the *New Yorker*, even the reviews of restaurants she would never in a thousand years visit, and started in on the old weeklies.

At six fifteen, when the waiting room had emptied and her inconsiderate stomach had begun to growl noisily, the receptionist called Emma's name.

"Good luck," Longleigh offered as Em stood up. He winced, as though he'd forgotten something and added, "Did anyone tell you, Santirez isn't *adrêsteia*?"

Emma needed a moment to place the word. She'd scarcely heard it in over a year, but she'd heard it first from Sylvianne Skellings in her own Bower living room. It was a Greek word that meant inevitable, irresistible or some such. Longleigh used it as a label for the curia's members; Em preferred just plain hunters or Orion's Children.

No one had told Emma that the doctor was ordinary, but she'd guessed as much, not unless everyone who'd passed through the office during the hour-plus they'd spent cooling their heels in the waiting room were Orion's Children.

"I'll mind my manners," she assured Longleigh before following the nurse into an examination room.

The nurse's questions, once Em had removed her sunglasses, were perfunctory. Her problem was obvious and more cosmetic than serious. Santirez himself proved to be an intense young man, who peered through his instruments as if he could see the formula for world peace written on her retinas.

"No damage where it counts," he announced in TV-perfect English. "Any idea how it happened?"

Emma shook her head before saying, "I'd been on a cruise since Sunday, so I'd been out in brighter sunlight than someone from Michigan is normally accustomed to . . . and I've been fighting a headache off and on since the cruise started. A migraine."

"Still got it?" Santirez asked, swinging his brushed-metal-and-black-plastic technology back into place for a second look into her eyes.

"A bit . . . on a scale from one to ten, it's definitely down to a two, and it was never really worse than an eight, but my gut tells me the headache had something to do with the mess I'm in." Actually, it didn't; her gut said she'd burst a blood vessel struggling against the paralysis that infested the previous night's wasteland dream.

Santirez asked a few more questions about Emma's migraines and, apparently satisfied with her answers, told her not to worry about her eyes or her vision. "You may have a tiny red streak for a couple months, maybe even a couple of years, but it's nothing to worry about."

"Contact lenses? The gas permeable kind."

"Can you go without? Do you have glasses with you?"

Em shook her head. "They're back in Michigan, to which, by the way, I'm returning no later than Monday . . . driving."

It was Santirez's turn to shake his head. "I'd like to see you go a week without your lenses. Your eye doesn't need any extra stress right now. But—honestly—make sure they're religiously clean, don't leave them in overlong, use a fresh bottle of artificial tears to keep things lubricated. If you can stand having them in, it's not likely to make any difference to the healing. Be careful; use your head. You'll know if you're doing something you shouldn't do."

Em smiled and said nothing. She told herself that she *would* know and she wouldn't risk her vision. But her life had gotten so much riskier in ways Doctor Santirez couldn't imagine. At least she hoped he couldn't.

They shook hands. He pointed the way to the billing desk where his nurse-receptionist had packed away everything except one very thin chart. "I tried calling your insurance office—" the woman began.

"Just let me pay you now, then go ahead and submit it to them. I'll handle the arm wrestling from my end." The U's health insurance was as bureaucratic as it was comprehensive, but Emma had friends on the inside. She handed over her credit card with confidence. "I can't tell you how much I appreciate the way you stayed late to take care of me."

"Mr. Longleigh's been coming to see Doctor Santirez since he opened his office—not that he needs to; he's got perfect 20/20 vision. He sends us patients, though." The nurse looked at the chart. "You're number twenty-seven."

"I can't promise that I'll be back, but if I hear of someone headed down this way, I'll make sure they know the doctor's name."

Another handshake, and Em was opening the door to the waiting room.

Ten

Redmond *Longleigh was* on his feet and closing in before Emma had cleared the waiting room threshold.

"What's the verdict?" he bantered.

"I'll live."

"Medications? Prescriptions to take to the pharmacy? We'll do that now; there aren't any pharmacies out in the sticks by us."

Emma shook her head. "Nothing like that. A little non-prescription TLC, and I'll be back to normal in no time."

By his brightening smile, Longleigh was either a good actor or genuinely relieved. "Dinner?" he asked graciously.

Dinner. Emma knew the invitation was inevitable. Why else had Longleigh called back to Atlantis? She'd been hungry when he'd made the call and was ravenous now. In all likelihood, Longleigh felt the same. Dinner somewhere in this little town—she still hadn't caught its name—was the only sensible option. Yet Em hesitated. Sitting down to a meal with someone implied a degree of peace and alliance.

Longleigh stopped an arm's length away. Em could

fairly see him weighing the wisdom of repeating his question. If it had been cold enough for a coat or jacket, Emma had a certainty that Longleigh would have held it for her. He held the outside door instead. She hesitated, then walked out of Santirez's office without saying yes or no to dinner for two.

Emma wasn't, she assured herself, *afraid* of Redmond Longleigh, and though she conceded that she was nervous around him, her flutters could just as easily be blamed on the months—no, make that years—since the last time a man had, for any reason, asked her to dinner.

Social rustiness, not fear was the root of her hesitation, then—notwithstanding Eleanor's contention that Longleigh was intimately involved with Sylvianne Skellings, the woman whom he'd raised as a daughter, at least until the truth had leaked out of his wife's diary; or that the erstwhile daughter had been responsible for the leak and, through means unspecified, for her mother's untimely death. (Was any hunter's death ever *timely*?)

Eleanor, after all, was the erstwhile daughter's aunt, the sister of the deceased mother. Not to put too fine a point on it, but Eleanor was biased against both Sylvianne Skelling and Redmond Longleigh; and Eleanor had been known to tell a lie when it suited her purposes.

No, Emma had prudently decided to form her own opinion of the curia's founder, and he'd given her a prime opportunity the past autumn when she'd been hot on the trail of a pair of curses leapfrogging through a family that didn't need any extra bad luck. From the porch of a nineteenth-century home, soon to be enveloped in a firestorm, Longleigh had handed Em a pair of ultimatums: If she wouldn't toe the curia's line, then she should stay away from hunters who did and, especially, stay out of the past.

Emma had flaunted both dictates. Far from avoiding curial hunters, she'd included her mother and Harry Graves among Orion's Children; and they were both, by their own admissions, card-carrying members of Longleigh's Atlantis Curia. As for staying out of the past, for the better part of a year the Children had spent their Friday nights flushing rogues out of their historic lairs. Longleigh knew what Emma was about; she'd been careful not to cover her tracks.

He would have to call her to account. The man she'd met last autumn couldn't ignore a challenge to his authority, especially one that came from family . . . or almost family. Em judged his genial charm an act that would have to end. So, better to end it in a restaurant—a public place with the hope of witnesses whose presence would keep both of them on their self-censoring toes? Or should she get into the car for the long ride back to Atlantis and a longer night under his roof? Suddenly the choice didn't seem so difficult.

"Dinner would be nice."

"There's a nice, little place just outside of town. It may not compare to what you got used to on the cruise, but I've never had a bad meal and their kitchen's open until nine."

"Sounds good to me."

They got in each other's way beside the black car. Em caught herself reaching for the door handle a hair's breadth after Longleigh had begun his reach. She dropped her arm with a stifled sigh. The problem was that Longleigh pulled back too and they were both left standing with their arms at their sides. So, they reached again. Em couldn't have said who reached first, but he got the handle first and she felt like a fool.

Before Longleigh could turn the key, she admitted, "I don't mean to be rude to your Southern courtesy—it's just—well, I've gotten so used to doing for myself, and it's different up North. I really hadn't realized how different."

"Not so different, not now, anyway," Longleigh countered, guiding the car out of its parking spot. "Times have changed in these parts, too. I'm old-fashioned, and proud of it."

Another man could have said that and Em could have thought up a reply. When Blaise Raponde said it, they both laughed. But when a man who'd lived through the Civil War said he was old-fashioned, Emma was left speechless. Silence reigned inside the car all the way to the restaurant where Em, thinking she was conforming to Longleigh's civil standards, sat still in her seat after he got out of the car only to have to scurry to catch up with him because he had not come around to open her door.

The restaurant was small, tastefully decorated in dark colors and wood paneling, and filled with delicious odors. The maître d' hailed Longleigh as a regular and valued customer. He gave Em and her sunglasses-after-sunset fashion a more critical stare. She was tempted to lower her glasses and return the stare.

That would be childish, her mother-voice sniffed; and, as usual, the mother-voice was right.

Em walked between the maître d' and Longleigh, following a path that led to a table for two in a quiet corner with a good view of the parking lot. The early evening light streaming through the window was almost bright enough to justify her sunglasses.

The business of ordering drinks and food was quickly accomplished. Longleigh ordered a single-malt scotch, neat; Em hoped one would be enough—she was decades past her tolerance for drink-and-drive indulgences—and ordered raspberry iced tea for herself, claiming medical concerns for her abstinence. Their waiter recited the night's specials before heading for the bar. When he returned with a glass of improbably colored tea, Em ordered a chicken breast in mustard sauce and a house salad. Longleigh proved he was a hard-eating, as well as a hard-drinking, man by ordering a slab of steak, rare, and baked potato with extra butter.

In habit, Longleigh reminded Em of her mother, but it would probably be a bad idea to mention the similarities to either of them.

The waiter departed, and they were alone. Longleigh raised his glass.

"Shall we toast to second chances?"

No question that Longleigh was pouring on the charm, or that he was quite good at it. Emma couldn't come up with a reason to refuse his request quickly enough and clinked her taller glass against his.

"We got off to a dreadful start, didn't we?" Longleigh said, more statement than question.

Em nodded. She couldn't forget their initial encounters, but wouldn't be the one to start rehashing them. Now that she was seated opposite the curia's leader, Em couldn't imagine a subject that she wanted to discuss with him—or, more accurately, her head swam with dozens of questions, all of them too pointed and personal for a public dining room. She sipped her tea—which was surprisingly flavorful, despite its garish pink color—and let Longleigh make the first move.

He surprised her with a series of questions about the inner workings of a university library. Em started slowly with short answers, but Longleigh's curiosity was persistent, and gradually she grew more expansive. Midway through her explanation of the typical acquisitions process, Emma deliberately contradicted herself— a test to see if Longleigh was merely skilled at the art of conversation or if he was truly paying attention to what she said.

Longleigh frowned at once and interrupted to ask, "Didn't you say that the various departments set their own book-buying budgets?"

Emma's breath caught momentarily in her throat, and she hoped the twilight through the window had grown dim enough that Longleigh wouldn't notice her embarrassed blush. *Serves you right,* the mother-voice chided. *Stay hon-*

est and stick to the high ground. She fumbled for words. "Well, yes, but we keep a running total and notify them when they go overboard"—as if she had the time to do the bookkeeping for the English department or anyone else.

Her gaffe marked the end of the first round of casual conversation. Their dinners hadn't arrived and weren't emerging from the kitchen. Emma felt the burden of small talk settle around her shoulders.

"Why Atlantis? Did you—?" Em caught a chronologically inappropriate question before it escaped completely. "Is there a connection between the house name and Atlanta?"

Longleigh sighed and shrugged. "Atlanta, Atlantic, Atlantis. There was a sea captain from Savannah who'd sailed through one too many storms and thought he'd build a house somewhere where the sea couldn't harm it. Or so the story goes. These old plantation homes, you know, they each come with their own set of myths. Maybe there was a sea captain. I couldn't say, I'm just the caretaker, you know." He smiled furtively and winked. "The whole place is under a trust agreement. It's managed by some suspendered financial type up in New York City."

Another half-smile and Emma tried to recall if she'd ever seen Harry Graves wearing suspenders.

"It's touch and go all the time," Longleigh continued between sips of his single-malt scotch. "We've got a few Indian sites in the woods that keep us in good stead with the historic societies, but nothing from the more picturesque periods. The captain built his house in the 1840s only to rebuild it again after a fire in 1852. It burned again when Sherman came through. Except for the wall behind the kitchen stove, there's nothing that dates back before the 1880s, and most of what's standing wasn't built until 1920. Another few decades—if any of us live that long—and Atlantis might turn quaint. Until then it's bed-and-breakfast weekends for city folk out of Atlanta and whatever weddings and receptions we can manage to attract."

Emma stared across the table, uncertain how much of Longleigh's spiel she should believe. Most of the details, she decided; the house had an Edwardian, early twentieth-century look to it. But she discounted the touch-and-go finances. She knew Harry too well to think that anything he dipped his fingers in was financially unstable.

"You'll have to let me show you around the old place. The house might not be anything special, but we've scrounged up a few choice antiques. There's a wing chair up in one of the upstairs bedrooms you might find interesting. The upholstery fabric was hand embroidered in Paris . . . I hear you're a collector yourself."

"Not really," Em stammered, wondering where and how Longleigh had acquired that bit of misinformation. Her passion for embroidery had led her to buy a few pieces, but it fell far short of a collection. But Eleanor—the clue had to have come from Eleanor, and clearly Eleanor had kept in closer touch than Em had reckoned—wouldn't have realized that. "I'd like to see your chair all the same."

Longleigh sat back in his chair as if some major issue between them had just been settled.

"I admire you, Emma Merrigan," he said when he leaned forward again, but the waiter chose that moment to appear with Emma's salad.

Longleigh had disdained the salad course. Em found herself stabbing lettuce when Longleigh resumed his flattery.

"You've got a talent for innovation. When we met—that disastrous first meeting! I do hope we can put that behind us and start over—I admit I misunderstood what you were about. The world is rife with amateurs poking their noses into dangerous places. Better to scare them off before they hurt themselves or someone else, I've always said. But you're no amateur; you're pure *adrêsteia*. Your instincts are top drawer. You've gotten Harry Graves out into the field again; no amateur could have done that. The old man's kept strictly to himself as long as I've known him. Doesn't trust anyone at his back—except you, and not just because he says you're proving his theories. Those theories only matter to him. I've always said that it's enough to know something works without muddying the picture with a truckload of hows and whys."

He paused. Emma swallowed and nodded. "Harry Graves," she offered cautiously, "has been around a very long time. When it comes to whys, I don't know why he works with me, only that he shows up when I need him, most of the time, anyway." She marveled at how easy it was to talk curse-hunting business without leaking details that ought not be overheard.

"He does more for you than he does for anyone else, including Eleanor. If getting Harry Graves off his butt was your only accomplishment, I'd still be interested in working more closely with you, but you've done more than that. I hear you've created a space of your own—a stronghold in the middle of nowhere. A very unusual place, for sure, with very unusual windows."

Em swallowed tea. "Not exactly by myself," she corrected, ignoring Longleigh's comment about the bolt-hole's window. Surely that was another leak she could pin on her mother. And, probably, Eleanor had leaked about Blaise Raponde, too. Emma didn't want to bring Blaise Raponde into this discussion if she could avoid it.

Longleigh nodded and let the subject drop without comment. He told her tales about Atlantis, the big white house, not the curia. He referred to them as myths. Emma imagined a British lord might have told similar stories to the tourists visiting the family estate he'd opened to the public for the tax write-off. The ghost stories she chalked up as pure fiction, but the others about the slow, frugal times before Atlanta had become the phoenix of the South, had the ring not merely of truth but of personal experience.

But before Em drowned in the charm of a man who'd had the foresight to establish a one-room school for the children of the neighborhood's sharecroppers, she reminded herself that he'd almost certainly been the same man who'd outright owned their grandparents and great-grandparents.

A man has to adapt himself according to the rules of his time, especially if he doesn't want to draw attention.

Emma didn't deny the wisdom flowing from her mother-voice, but she didn't embrace it, either. Conversation had flagged by the time the waiter brought their entrées. It was dark outside by then, too. The waiter lowered the drapes, blocking the view from the parking lot. He lit the table's small hurricane lamp and after the obligatory "Is everything all right?" retreated to the far side of the dining room.

The area around their table had grown too dark for Em's sunglasses. She couldn't distinguish her chicken breast from the nearby mound of rice pilaf without removing them. Longleigh winced when he got a close-up view of her bloodstained eye. He looked elsewhere, and, in sympathy, Em did too.

She counted four occupied tables other than their own in a room that held a good two dozen. The nearest ears were twenty feet away, while soft background music provided a layer of white noise that was protection against casual eavesdropping.

"What are you looking for, Emma?"

Em blinked and thought, for a heartbeat, that Longleigh had noticed her studying the geometry of the dining room. "Nothing," she insisted, then realized he'd asked a far more personal question. "I'm not comfortable talking about these things—about what we do."

"Hide in plain sight. It's been good advice all *my* life.

As long as we don't argue—We're not going to argue, are we, Emma? We're starting over with a clean slate. There's no reason for you to avoid me . . . us any longer."

Em resisted the easy answer, the answer Longleigh wanted. "What was that expression from the Cold War? Coming in from the cold? I've been outside all my life. I'm happy where I am; I don't notice the temperature."

"I'm sorry I threatened you. That was my mistake. I regret it, and I apologize for it. What else can I do so you'll lay down your suspicions—your fears—and become part of my curia? What do you need to know? What assurances can I give you that you'll be making a wise decision?"

Emma laid down her knife and fork. "You know, I don't believe everything Eleanor tells me, but she is my mother, and, sometimes, just to keep me on my toes, she tells the unvarnished truth—"

"Your mother knows where her home is. Whatever she's said, she brought you to us today, when you needed help, didn't she? We've had our differences, nothing serious, nothing beyond repair. Eleanor trusts us . . , trusts me. You can, too. I ask nothing in return."

"She ran away . . . to my father in Michigan; and you hounded her there so she panicked and bolted for God knows where, and when she surfaced again, you frogmarched her into marrying Harry Graves."

Longleigh had the grace to look embarrassed before he stiffened with indignation. "Eleanor does not do well on her own. Good lord, Emma, you've seen her in action; you know I'm telling the truth. And, where better to place her than under Harry Graves's wing? She was safe . . . comfortable. She didn't suffer, if that's what you're thinking. I know what it's like to grow up without a mother, but I'm not the one who uprooted her from your life. When it came to abandoning the family she'd created, Eleanor was all on her own. When she resurfaced, I told her to go back to Michigan, at least until her child came of age. She *owed* you that much, not to mention what she owed your father, but *owing* is not a thing Eleanor handles well."

Longleigh's words were so plausible, Emma wondered why she hadn't thought of them herself. From the beginning plausibility had been her problem: Eleanor, Harry, Blaise, and now Redmond Longleigh all had solid, sensible explanations for things she couldn't verify on her own. Well, she could, but using one's time-walking ability to poke around another hunter's back pages was risky—even roguish—business. She'd been tempted, and rarely more tempted than by Longleigh's bald assertion that her motherless childhood wasn't his fault, but she hadn't yet succumbed.

After a moment's thought, Em said, "Eleanor's left out the part about you telling her to go back to Bower," and went back to carving morsels from her chicken breast.

"We all make mistakes, don't you think? And we edit our memories afterward. For years we all believed you'd died in childhood, then suddenly you appear, roving the Netherlands, attracting curses. Could we have found you? By all accounts, you changed your first name, not your last, and for fifty years, your father lived in the same house Eleanor had walked out of. Of course we could. Harry and I could find anyone who breeched the Netherlands, if there'd been a breech. The *wyrd* does sometimes arise spontaneously. The watchers are always alert for the signs of a teenager streaking to the Netherlands for the first time. We kept special watch those years when you would have been in high school. Those are the prime years; the mind just isn't ready before that. But you weren't among them, and by the time you would have been in your early twenties, Eleanor was adamant that only death could have quenched your *wyrd*."

Em nodded, though when Eleanor spun the tale, it was Harry who'd come to the conclusion that Merle Acalia

Merrigan had died before stretching her curse-hunter wings.

"Shall I apologize for that, too?" Longleigh asked as the silence lengthened. The faintest whiff of acid laced through his Southern gentleman's charm. "That I believed Eleanor when she said the only possible reason for your failure to trip the watchers was that you'd died before the age of fifteen or so? The watchers don't miss, and no one born with the *wyrd* had ever failed to use it the way you did."

Later, when she had the time and privacy, Em vowed she'd replay the conversation to determine exactly how she'd been maneuvered onto the defensive. Until then, she was content to shake her head and pointedly change the subject to the weather.

"I seem to recall that you had an unusually wet summer. Weren't there pictures of flash floods and stranded dogs on CNN?"

"Northwest of Atlanta, not around here," Longleigh replied, but he got the message and let conversation remain on neutral ground until the check was paid—he deflected Em's attempt to cover her share with cash, and she didn't put up a fight.

They emerged from the restaurant into a warm—to a Michigander's senses—early autumn night.

"Too bad it's so late," Longleigh said as he opened the passenger door. "There's a scenic route back to Atlantis—scenic by day, anyway. May I assume that you'll stay on for a few days? Surely there's no great rush to get back to Bower. Since you were driving, you couldn't have planned to be back at work before Monday. You were going to spend how many extra days in Florida?"

"Three," Em admitted.

"Then you'll stay and let me show you around some."

Em hedged. "I'll have to talk to Eleanor. She's the one

who's going to get stuck with the lion's share of the driving."

"I'm sure she'll agree," Longleigh said with enough confidence to keep Emma quiet pretty much the whole trip back to Atlantis.

Despite the silence, the return to Atlantis seemed quicker than the outbound trip had been. An ornate and massive electric lantern slung beneath the portico provided ample light to see them into the house where the level of light was lower, and Longleigh moved quickly to disarm the security system.

"Are you in the mood for a tour? As I said, there's nothing outstanding about the architecture, but some of the furnishings are worth a closer look."

"I need to talk to Eleanor . . . if she's here. It doesn't look like she is. She wouldn't just take off—"

Emma's Integra hadn't been parked under the portico. She felt her heart muscles tighten before she recalled seeing a silvery rear bumper and a Michigan license plate in the lantern's peripheral light. Her first thought was to return to the portico, but Longleigh was headed through a door beneath the main stairs, and she followed him instead.

They'd entered an office with two desks—one impressively large and uncluttered, the other more utilitarian and papered over. Family pictures adorned the smaller desk and the walls around it, marking Shevaun's territory. A good-sized whiteboard hung directly above the smaller desk. On it someone, presumably Shevaun, because the writing was legible and Eleanor's only rarely achieved that distinction, had written in two-inch-high letters.

Gone to dinner with E—Thinking about a movie afterward. Back by midnight. Gary called after you left. The mower's fixed. He'll drop it off tomorrow morning.

"They're old friends," Longleigh offered as he erased the writing.

An array of lights on Shevaun's phone was blinking, each with its own rhythm. Emma could never have turned her back on them the way Longleigh did, or walked past a working computer, its monitor in screen-saver mode, without checking her e-mail.

"About that tour?" he asked.

It seemed the least intimate of the likely options, so Em agreed. They started with the downstairs rooms: the dining room with its huge, dark wood table, big enough to serve a sit-down dinner to thirty guests, followed by the Edwardian music room with its clutter of overstuffed chairs and a grand piano. The music room opened into both the living room Emma had seen earlier and a full-blown ballroom.

"We built this just a few years ago. Thought it would help with the wedding trade. It looks exactly like the ballroom that old sea captain wanted for his daughters— which means, of course, it's totally out of step with the rest of the house now, but the brides like it when they come to check things out."

There were genre paintings on the walls —life-size and larger portraits of men and women, all of them genuine antiques but none of them related to each other or to Redmond Longleigh. With their stern, flat faces, they lent the ballroom an unearned air of antebellum authenticity. The carpets were new, copied from period textiles, as were the drapes and upholsteries. Longleigh had commissioned the chandelier from the same Parisian firm that had made the nineteenth-century fixtures. Em couldn't be certain, but she thought the chandelier bore dramatic similarity to one she'd seen in Longleigh's wasteland bunker complex.

She couldn't resist a jibe. "For a plantation with no distinguishing features and one that's hanging on by its wedding receptions, you seem to have gone to great lengths to recreate a bride-ready room."

Longleigh's eyebrows rose. "We needed a ballroom if we were going to compete for the larger weddings. Why settle for anything less than the grandest room ever to rise on this site? Do you want to see the kitchen, or shall we go directly upstairs?"

Em chose the kitchen with its sole surviving original wall and an array of appliances worthy of a haute cuisine restaurant.

"Do you eat in much?" she asked.

"Most nights—but not here. I don't actually *live* here. This is all business—the ones that everyone knows about and the *adrêsteia* affairs that we keep secret. I live in the caretaker's cottage out back. There are three cottages on the grounds. They're all older than the house. You haven't asked, but your cousin—or is it aunt?—stays in what used to be the grooms' quarters adjoining the stables when she's here. They've been completely redone, of course. Sylvie's not here tonight, by the way. Do you ride?"

Em let the allusion to Sylvianne pass. "Not since high school, and not well then."

"Pity. We've got six horses right now: three of our own and three boarding. It's a challenge keeping them properly exercised. If you change your mind, let me know. There are several trails round and about. Sylvianne's always looking for someone to show them to. I imagine Eleanor will go riding . . . if you decide to stick around for a few days."

With Sylvianne? Emma stifled the question before it got close to her tongue. Dealing with Redmond Longleigh was challenging enough. She didn't want to add Sylvianne to the mix if she could help it and counted on her mother not to go kicking over hornets' nests. Of course, counting on Eleanor was often a fool's speculation.

There were five bedrooms on the second floor, each decorated to a specific theme or image. Eleanor's luggage had come to rest in the Wisteria bedroom—a confection of lavender murals, eyelet lace, and a four-poster bed complete with a canopy. Em found that she'd been put in something called the Tuscany bedroom, where the walls were a lemony beige and all the wood had the deep patina that came from a century's worth of furniture polish. A huge bouquet of autumnal silk flowers sat in front of the fireplace. The arrangement softened the room without feminizing it. A man could stay in the Tuscany room.

"Shevaun must not have figured you for the romantic type."

"This is perfect," Em agreed.

There were four doors attached to the Tuscany bedroom. One led to a many-angled closet, one to a bathroom that appeared to retain its original plumbing. The one that Longleigh had opened to show her the room, was at the top of two right-angle, three-step flights. Directly across the room, the fourth door opened onto the landing of what appeared to be a full-length set of stairs descending into darkness.

"This room—this whole part of the house—is older than the rest," Em guessed.

Longleigh nodded. "It's over the kitchen. I'd venture most of the wood and plaster dates back to the first postwar rebuilding. You've got your own personal stairway"—he gestured toward the fourth door—"to the kitchen if you get the late-night munchies. The larder's heavy on things that come in boxes and cans, but Shevaun keeps it well-stocked. We never know when a paying customer might show up . . . or one of our own. The key's in the lock; don't lose it." He closed the door and reinserted the old-fashioned skeleton key into the keyhole.

"I'm not the midnight raider type," Em assured her host. "Once I turn the lights out, I stay put until the alarm goes off."

"Your body does."

"My body, yes," she agreed.

Another four bedrooms awaited on the third floor with the attic above that. Emma was vaguely interested in the Pompeii room (erotic murals on the walls?) and the sewing room up in the attic, but in neither case was her interest strong enough to ask Longleigh to show them to her. She already felt she was falling behind in the calculus of favors granted, and the stress of a long day worrying about her eye and relocating herself from the world of the *Excitation* to that of Atlantis was making itself felt.

They descended the formal stairs to the foyer where Emma thanked Longleigh for his help, the dinner, and the tour. He was gracious, as she expected he would be, but didn't make a move toward the front door. Maybe he didn't want to leave her alone in the big house?

That suspicion seemed borne out when he asked, "Brandy? We have an excellent selection in the music room. Will you join me for a nightcap?"

Well, she could understand a caretaker's reluctance to give an unproven guest unbridled access to a house filled with antiques.

"A tiny nightcap."

In addition to the piano and a discreet wet bar housed behind mahogany doors, the music room housed a state-of-the-art sound system, which Longleigh tuned to a public broadcast station that was airing a program of rhythm-heavy world music; the same sort of program Em might have listened to in Bower. He poured brandy from a crystal decanter into big-belled glasses; a splash for her, rather more for himself.

Emma had barely settled into one of the smaller, leather-upholstery chairs when Longleigh asked, "Don't you have any questions? I'd find it hard to believe that you didn't have questions about me, about the curia, the price of tea in China. This is as good a time as any to get them answered."

She hadn't expected the offer and, though she did have questions—dozens, if not hundreds, of them—the only one that sprang quickly into her mind was so basic she was almost embarrassed to ask it:

"What's a curse?"

Longleigh drew back, as if he'd been struck. "A curse is a curse," he answered gruffly and didn't sit down.

"Actually, it isn't," Em countered, intrigued by his reaction. "There are big curses and little curses. Curses that persist and curses that wither away almost as quickly as they come into being. Some manifest as fire, others as little wisps of smoke rising from the ground. And that doesn't begin to cover the rogues. What do they have in common? What makes a curse? What drives it?"

"That's more up Harry Graves' line."

"And Harry says no one agrees with him. So, I'm asking you, because if you're the head of the curia of curse-hunters, you must have a pretty firm idea of what business you're in and what our responsibilities are. Just two days ago, I swear I watched a curse kill a man right in front of me."

Redmond Longleigh raised a single eyebrow, his left.

"One of the servers in the dining room was cursed. Eleanor and I both spotted it . . . and did nothing about it, because, according to Eleanor, one doesn't moot curses from moving boats, or moving anything. Somehow—I don't know the exact details—that girl and her curse contributed to another crewman climbing over the rail and jumping to his death. The fall, they told me, probably was enough to kill him; he didn't need to drown."

"That must have spoiled a vacation or two."

"I was standing on a lower deck, the right place, the right time, or the wrong one, depending on your point of view. I watched him fall."

"My condolences. There was a time when I thought of curses as demons—devils that lurked everywhere and took possession of unwary souls. I suppose I still do."

"Where do they come from?"

"Inside. Everybody has a curse inside, waiting to burst free. Maybe it does, mostly it doesn't; thank God for small blessings. Once it's loose, it looks for a kindred spirit and merges with it. The more it finds, the stronger it gets. What drives it? The need to survive and reproduce, like all things. Being a parasite, it needs a host; and once it's found a host, then what else to do but secure the release of other curses? Your suicide, I wonder did he possess a spark of futility strong enough, at the last, to free his curse?"

"And us—the hunters? And the wasteland? And rogues?"

"The wasteland?" Longleigh quizzed Em with his eyes before nodding his head. "You mean the Netherlands. I knew a man who thought they were one of Dante's circles. You're aware of the story—more of a legend, I suppose— that the *adrêsteia* surrendered our immortal souls in exchange for immortality of the flesh and that we hunt curses in the hope of regaining God's favor?"

Em had heard the first part from Blaise. The hopeful part was new to her. "I take it as a myth, a way of explaining something otherwise inexplicable; I don't take it for— you'll excuse the expression—gospel. What about rogues?"

"Ah, a rogue is Shakespeare's Iago: motiveless malignity incarnate. A rogue is a curse raised to its highest power or a hunter gone bad; or maybe there's a rogue inside all of us . . . all of the *adrêsteia*, at least. Could be all three or something I can't even guess. Rogues are like pornography—I might not be able to define one, but I can smell one across a room—across a town, if the wind's right."

Longleigh's face transformed when he spoke of rogues. The blasé charm faded, replaced by an ice-eyed fury that Blaise Raponde might understand or even envy. He glowered at one of the windows, seeing something there that Em could not.

She sipped her brandy. It was the good stuff: smooth,

warm, deceptively easy to swallow. Her glass was empty before Longleigh relaxed.

"I believe there's a choice," he said slowly, "a moment before the rogue has become completely rogue: a last chance for honor."

"What happens if honor wins?" Emma asked timidly. "Does the rogue moot itself?"

"Better to ask what happens to the hunter who abandons his honor."

"What does happen?"

Longleigh refreshed his brandy and splashed another finger's breadth into Em's glass. He was less than an arm's length away and towering over her when he said, "The easiest thing for any hunter is to go rogue. Go back far enough—before my time, but not, I assure you, before Harry's, and the only difference between us and rogues was what, and how, we hunted. Ask him, if you don't believe me."

Emma squirmed in her chair, gaining another inch or so of distance from those hard, blue eyes. "What I'd like, someday, is to have you and him and Eleanor and any other hunter who happened to be available all together, in one place, so I can watch you react to one another."

"You know the way to the Bunker." Longleigh blinked. He took a backward step and the temperature in the music room rose perceptibly. "Day or night, there's always someone there, sometimes even Harry. Not Eleanor, not for the last several years. She has a problem, doesn't she?" The last question had the tone of a guardian inquiring about a wayward ward.

"She's a little phobic," Em admitted. "No great surprise after what happened to her. You want to talk about choices and honor—she went through hell not choosing to be a rogue."

"There's never been a question about Eleanor's honor."

Em had a few, all of them fifty-plus years old and not

worth asking, but since they were talking about Eleanor now, she risked a very personal question. "Did you once ask Eleanor to marry you?"

"We get to the meat, at last. Yes, most definitely, yes. She was—and is—a very beautiful woman, your mother; and I was a widower."

The statement took Emma by surprise, and the brandy let her emotions radiate. Longleigh twisted his mouth into a wry grin and began to pace.

"For the record, like you, I've married twice. The first time was for love and to a mortal woman. I realized the risks, but any fool could see there was a war coming and a bullet could kill a hunter as easily as any lesser man. At least my sons would be like me—you do know, don't you, that the trait is sex-linked: mothers to daughters, fathers to sons?"

Emma nodded. "I wouldn't be here if I'd been born a son."

"My wife and I had no sons, only daughters. Four of them—and my wife died giving birth to the last of them. I watched them grow—beauties every one of them. They married and wore themselves out bearing children for the Struggle. The last one was twenty-seven when she died. Twenty-seven! It was easier, then. If you lived long enough, you just rode away to a town where no one knew who you'd been. Then, after a while, if your heart hadn't been set free, you changed a bit here, a bit there—you've watched Eleanor do it—and you came back.

"I foreswore women and formed the curia instead—as much to build a community for us as to wreak havoc on curses and rogues. Before the curia, the *adrêsteia* had no *families*. It was an unnatural state. No wonder the line between rogue and hunter was so faint. When you sensed someone coming toward you, the smart man assumed a rogue and fired first. I made *changes*. Where there was suspicion, I made families—for everyone except myself.

"Then, along came Eleanor Baker and her sister." Em said suggestively and just a bit sarcastically.

Longleigh shook his head. "Just the sister. Jeanette Skellings, then—she'd adopted her mother's maiden name—but not Eleanor. I didn't know about Eleanor when I met Jeanette. Eleanor was a surprise—a bit like you, I suppose. There were three sisters, you see: Jeanette, Eleanor, and a third, Katherine, who died in infancy, or maybe childbirth. The details are fuzzy; I don't pry. But Jeanette grew up in her grandmother's house thinking that her parents and sister had been taken by the Spanish flu.

"Jeanette and her grandmother and a maiden aunt would come to Atlantis in the winter—they lived in Massachusetts where the winters were brutal. She was young— naturally young—and among the first to grow up without fear that the first hunter she met would be the death of her, no different than a rogue.

"I'd been trying to wring the magic out of the *adrêsteia* for decades; Jeanette brought it back. She was fey—all the Skellings women are. I was hardly young, but I was captivated—captivated by her charm and, yes, by the thought that with her I wouldn't have to watch my daughters die.

"Tell me Emma: Have you ever fallen in love with precisely the wrong person?"

Em thought of her two husbands, especially Jeff. She'd spotted all the traits that would eventually destroy their marriage their first weekend together. At the time, though, she lumped them with the rest of his charms, and they'd only fueled her passion. She answered Longleigh's question with a nod.

"Then you know what happened. I proposed to Jeanette, she accepted, and for—what?" Longleigh raised his eyes toward the ceiling. "Five years, five lovely years, then it was over. I don't know which one of us fell out of love first, but out of love we fell. Separate bedrooms, separate lives, but keeping up appearances, always keeping up appearances for the *adrêsteia* and, especially for our daughter, Sylvia Anne.

"Make no mistakes, Emma—I loved my daughter long after I'd stopped loving my wife. I grieved for our early years after she had her accident, but I admit, I did not grieve for long. The year, if you're interested in such things—and I can see by your face that you are—was 1946. She's buried in the family cemetery; I'll take you there if you'd like.

"Your mother showed up about a year later. I knew she was coming. My curia idea had caught on. The European *adrêsteia* had formed similar alliances, mostly along national lines. Out of courtesy, the French let me know there was an American in the midst, when she'd married an American officer, and when she was coming home.

"When I met Eleanor she spoke French better than English; she's forgotten that she ever knew that language—but that's Eleanor, always living in the moment. She keeps her youth—you know that. It was like meeting Jeanette again, but—what do they say?—once bitten, twice shy? And she was married . . . to an ordinary man. And I am a gentleman. She was *adrêsteia*; I invited her into the curia, showed her the ropes. She wasn't interested, so I told her the door would always be open and she could come back whenever she was ready."

Longleigh paused for a sip of brandy.

Emma asked, "And a few years later, when she was—?" to get him talking again.

"She wasn't; that was the whole problem. She got herself in trouble, crossed paths with a rogue or some such, and couldn't find a way out, so she ran. When a Skellings woman runs, Emma, she leaves a wide track behind her. We tried—what did you say at dinner? We tried to bring her in from the cold. You'd have thought, she *did* think, Atlantis was a greater enemy than the rogue. It wasn't true, but—" Longleigh shrugged. "We couldn't have someone with her *wyrd* running around, behaving like some mind-less baitfish before every rogue in creation!"

"So you packed her off to Harry Graves." A statement, not a question.

Longleigh heaved another masculine shrug. "She's Peter Pan, for Pete's sake. She lives in never-never land, and she has no intention of growing up. No one—no one at all is better at striding down the up escalator. In her own way, Eleanor's an inspiration to every one of us who's ever wondered what's next, but whenever she's tried to make her own way, it's been an unmitigated disaster—for her and for the innocents around her. Think of yourself! What kind of woman up and walks out on her husband and in-fant daughter? She needs a special sort of guardian. Surely you've seen that yourself. You've had a front-row seat for the last year or so. Where would Eleanor be without you? Harry Graves owed me a favor, rare enough but true."

And the root cause of Harry's oft-repeated advice: *Don't get in debt, any kind of debt, with Redmond Long-leigh's curia?*

Emma's face must have been transparent. Longleigh said, "It's high time he stirred himself to a child or two, but no matter how many times you lead a horse to water, there's no guarantee he'll take a drink. He looked on her as a ward, a work in progress. They weren't an unhappy cou-ple, Emma. They stayed together far longer than I bar-gained for. They'd be together still, I wager, if you hadn't come along. They had a high degree of tolerance for each other. She'd have her little flings, he'd have his, and it never got messy. Not messy enough to show. They were better at it than Jeanette and I. They'd never been in love; there was nothing to fall out of."

Em supposed she shouldn't have been surprised, much less shocked, but she was and covered her embarrassment with her brandy glass.

"Aren't you going to ask the other question?"

"Which other question?"

"What about Sylvianne Skellings? You can't be your mother's daughter and not be primed with questions about Syl. I can scarcely imagine what Eleanor has told you. If I'd any idea that Eleanor had relocated to Bower last fall, well I'd never have sent Syl up to visit. You *can* have Eleanor, Harry, and me in a single room, if you'd like, in the flesh. We gather here for New Year's; bad for the catering business, good for the ties that bind. You got an invitation, if you recall. You and Eleanor, both. But you can't put Eleanor and Syl in the same room. They repel each other like the opposite poles of a magnet. Force them together, and bad things happen."

Em drained her second small glass of brandy. "All right, since you raised the subject. What about my cousin?"

"Your cousin, who no longer believes that she's my daughter," Longleigh said with spectacular bluntness. "All right—from the beginning. I wanted children, as many as the house could hold, and, all right, that was selfish of me, and that's where the trouble started, even before Syl was born. We had trouble. You've got an inquiring mind; you know how ignorant we are, of necessity, about ourselves, about our *differences*. It's not as if we could have gone to some enlightened fertility clinic—if there'd been any fertility clinics back when we were trying. It seems to be a woman's problem—no political incorrectness intended. At a minimum, it takes a year of abstinence for a woman to bring a child to term. It was worse for Jeanette. Call it an incompatibility that neither will nor effort could overcome until, finally, we did. I thought we did: Sylvia Anne. She inherited the *wyrd* from her mother, of course, and looked more like herself than either of us, though I fancied she had my eyes in her mother's face. I didn't intend to raise an only child, but that's what we did—and we did it well, despite our separate lives.

"Jeanette had an accident, pure and simple. There'd

been a storm. The roads were dark and slippery. She missed a curve, and it was over. As simple as that—regardless of what Eleanor or Syl believes. As for the diary—I assume Eleanor has told you that I found a diary detailing Jeanette's indiscretions. Yes, there was a diary, and yes, there were indiscretions that no husband wants to know about—but proof—*proof!*—that Syl's some country doctor's daughter? There's no proof.

"I should have burned it. I should have burned it the night I found it. Can you imagine the nights I've wasted, wishing I'd destroyed it? We can change the past, but not when it matters most. But I left it out on my dresser. Syl found it, and she confronted me.

"I told her that we should forget we'd ever seen it, but she'd have none of that: honesty or nothing. That should be written on the Skellings' family crest, never mind the carnage. My daughter went off—another Skellings trait—and when she returned she was Sylvianne with ultimatums, prices to be paid for failures she blamed entirely on me.

"She comes and goes as she wishes and drives much too fast along the same roads that killed her mother. We get along. Underneath it all, Syl has never forgiven me. I doubt she ever will—and ever, as you know, can be a very long time.

"How Eleanor got worked back into all this is something I do not understand. Eleanor seems to think the diary is not merely a forgery, but Syl's forgery and that Syl somehow had a hand in setting up Jeanette's fatal accident. This assumes I wouldn't have known my daughter's writing from my wife's and that accidents don't happen. But I've learned my lesson. I do not argue with Skellings women, nor do I try to broker peace between them.

"That said, Syl and Eleanor despise each other as only blood kin can. I don't think Syl's spite extends to you, at least not yet and not completely. You, after all, were betrayed and abandoned by Eleanor. You might be an ally, or become one . . . although, equally, you might consider the proposals that Eleanor had rejected—"

Emma pricked up her ears. What manner of proposal did Longleigh have in mind? A *proposal* proposal? Was he making moves on *her*? She listened for the mother-voice's sarcasm and heard silence in every corner of her mind.

"—and, in that case, I doubt Syl would regard you favorably. Vengeance is a jealous lover . . . and, notwithstanding Eleanor's rather too frequent accusations, an unrequited one. I still regard Syl as my daughter—my beautiful, brilliant, and fixated daughter, who I someday hope will find her way back to a healthier perspective on love and family. I would lay down my life for her, but I don't live by her rules or her wishes."

Em spun her brandy glass, wishing there were one more drop she could sip. "It's all perspective, all subjective, just like the wasteland itself. The individual facts tally, but the interpretations differ. Have you ever told Eleanor your version of events?"

"More than once—for all the good it's done. As I said, one doesn't win an argument with the Skellings women."

"And I'm a Skellings woman, aren't I?"

"It remains to be seen if I can stay on the right side of you. Have we started over?"

The man was good—both charming and sincere, a dangerous combination. "There's no such thing—" Em began, only to be spared her conclusions by the sound of the front door opening.

"We're back!" Eleanor's voice boomed from the entryway to the music room, but the words were not followed by an appearance in the doorway.

Em glanced at her watch: eleven thirteen. "I don't cultivate enemies, and I'm not really interested in who did what to whom, so long as they don't do it to me," she told Longleigh. "Behave like a friend, and I'll treat you like a friend."

Footsteps echoed from the stairs. Shevaun called, "I'll be in by ten tomorrow. *Don't* touch anything on my desk!" and shut the door. Longleigh's eyes registered momentary interest then returned to Emma.

" 'Like a friend?' Nothing more?"

A hit, a palpable hit. Emma unwound from the leather chair and carried her empty glass to the bar. Had she grown so rusty around men that she couldn't separate the wolves from the sheep? It was possible, depressingly possible. "Not tonight," she said between a sigh and a yawn. "One thing I learned in two bum marriages—no serious discussions after eleven."

"A wise lesson, no doubt. Are you ready to call it a night?"

Em nodded and added, "I can find my own way." She truly did lose a good twenty intelligence points at the stroke of eleven, fifty by midnight.

Longleigh flared his hands in her direction. "I wouldn't think of standing in your way."

She felt foolish and beat a retreat toward the door.

"But—" Longleigh caught her in mid-stride. "There's business to attend to. I know, I know—I should have taken care of it earlier. Will you come to the office?"

Business? When she'd just demonstrated her complete lack of acuity? Em was tempted to say no, but resisted the temptation and followed her host to the two-desk office where Longleigh produced a one-page form for her to sign.

"What?" she demanded before taking it from his hand.

"A release. Atlantis is neutral territory. No probes, vendettas, or cross purposes. There's a lock on your door. You use it. The bedroom is your private space. Yours alone. You want to talk to someone—even your mother—you knock on her door; she knocks on yours. You talk in the hallways or meet in the Bunker. Humor us, Emma, the *adrêsteia* have not always been a trusting bunch. You can sleep undisturbed safe in the knowledge that anyone who violates the privacy of your bedroom—past or present— will be found out and hunted down, mercilessly, here and there. There are no midnight assignations in Atlantis." He finished with a deprecating smile.

Emma thought it was absurd and unspeakably rude for Longleigh to spring such nonsense on her at the last minute when she had no choice, really, but to sign her name or sleep in her car. But she smoothed the paper on his uncluttered desk and signed by the boldface **X**.

Eleven

In the guaranteed privacy of the Tuscany bedroom Emma eased her suitcase onto its side in the middle of the floral-patterned carpet at the foot of the bed. The bedroom was large—easily the size of her living room in Bower—but none of the pieces of heavy Victorian furniture could handle the cruise suitcase's bulk. She thought about unpacking a day or two's worth of clothes and underwear, but settled on a nightshirt and the toiletries before pulling the big zippers shut and standing the suitcase like a sentinel beside the door to the kitchen stairs.

When she'd finished her evening rituals, including an examination of her benighted eye, which looked worse but felt no different, Emma climbed into the high bed and arranged the pillows behind her. She'd intended to read another chapter of her novel, but lingering concerns about her eyes' welfare kept the small print from coming into focus. That, and Longleigh's version of a story she'd heard first from her mother.

"*Rashomon,*" Em whispered the name of a movie she'd never seen but whose title had become synonymous with conflicting viewpoints.

The engineering gene, not to mention a career in the orderly confines of library science, craved neat sequences of causes and consequences: Event A brought about event B, with clear consequences that were apparent like moving balls on a pool table or books properly placed on their shelves.

Life's not like that, the mother-voice chided. *Could you and Jeff agree on anything when your marriage was falling apart? Did you even believe it collapsed for the same reasons?*

The answer, of course, was a sadder-but-wiser no.

Alone in the unfamiliar room, Emma faced the reality that as interesting as it was to dig out the intricate stories of the long-lived hunters, it was also pointless. She'd never amass enough information in advance. A smarter course was to take the words she'd said to Longleigh to heart: If he or any other hunter behaved well toward her, then she'd return the favor.

A strategy that focused on the future rather than the past lifted a great weight from Emma's consciousness, a weight she'd carried so long she'd forgotten it. She yawned and nearly rubbed her eyes. Her fingers were inches from the night lamp's switch when she heard scratching sounds on the hallway door.

The lock! Em thought. After signing Longleigh's paper, she'd forgotten to turn the key. Damn.

The scratching continued. Warily, wearily, Em threw the covers back and headed across the carpet.

"Who's there?" she demanded softly.

"Me . . . your mother."

A sigh sank Emma's head toward her shoulders. "What do you want?"

"You had dinner with Red. You were still with him when Shevaun and I got home. I want to know what happened."

"Nothing."

"Six hours of *nothing*?"

"That's about right."

Eleanor rattled the doorknob gently. Fortunately, the latch was stiff, requiring a good twist and a liberal application of shoulder power before it would swing open.

"Hey! You're not supposed to be doing that. I signed some damn paper saying I'd stay in here *alone*—neither a visitor nor a visitee."

"Then come out here, and we'll find someplace to talk."

Em looked wistfully at the bed, then reached for the doorknob.

The hallway was pitch dark except for small nightlights outlining the stairs up and down. Eleanor, still dressed in the clothes she'd worn off the *Excitation,* carried a flashlight.

"I feel like I've wandered into some Agatha Christie mystery, or a parody of one," Em complained.

"Don't be silly. Red's locked up for the night and gone home, but you *know* someone's watching. We start turning on lights, and we'll have company."

"So we stand here by flashlight? Or slink off to the Bunker, where all the watchers hang out? You've got to admit it's pretty absurd."

"Nonsense."

Eleanor took Emma by the hand and led her another ten or twelve feet to the end of the hall and a door Longleigh had not opened during their guided tour. Without hesitation, Eleanor turned the doorknob and flipped the light switch on a huge, but decidedly old-fashioned, bathroom.

"You're in the only bedroom with an attached bath— not counting the family bedrooms. It's take a number and wait when the house is full, but we'll do fine here. And no one's going to come prowling after a bathroom light. Too common."

"If you say so," Em agreed without enthusiasm.

She looked around for a place to sit. There was the toilet, of course: a big, white porcelain throne with a stylish burgundy cover tied over its lid. Burgundy was clearly the accent color for the otherwise black-and-white room. The curtains bracketing the frosted-glass window were burgundy, ditto the numerous towels—Em counted ten, not including facecloths—and the throw rug covering the black-and-white check tiles in front of the sink. There were burgundy silk flowers in what she assumed—hoped— was a plastic vase atop the toilet tank, dustless burgundy swags outlining the walls from hooks in a ceiling that had to be at least nine feet above the floor, a burgundy show curtain and—the pièce de résistance in Em's opinion—an ornately gathered burgundy skirt completely circling the deep, free-standing bathtub.

"A person could drown in that thing."

"The men love it because it's a full six feet long. They can really stretch out."

Eleanor availed herself of the toilet seat, leaving Emma to perch—uncomfortably—on the bathtub's curved rim.

"My rear end's going to fall asleep on this thing."

"We can switch before it does. What did you and Red talk about at dinner?"

"Don't you want to hear what the doctor had to say first?"

Eleanor flustered and took a moment to mutter, "You'd have said something when we came in if it wasn't okay news. You or Red. It was okay news, wasn't it?"

"It was, thank you. He's advising against my contacts for a few more days—advising against, not forbidding. It's all cosmetic, like a bruise, albeit, a very obvious one."

"The blood's spread, you know. There's no white left. Your eye's completely crimson. Quite impressive, in a creepy way."

"Thanks again. You already know what Longleigh and I talked about; you can guess, anyway. He wants us to start over—"

"What did you tell him? Did you agree? What did he offer?"

Em shrugged. "Starting over's just a metaphor. Real people can't start over. They can't just forget—" Except that's apparently what Eleanor had done with her knowledge of French and who knew what else. "It's out of the question, for me, anyway. My memory isn't something I can flush like a computer's—" she shook her head at her own choice of metaphor and hid behind a hand. When Eleanor didn't immediately say something sarcastic, Em tried a different approach. "Longleigh sees things differently, and he describes them differently. I don't think he told any whopping lies, but—well, he believes Jeanette died in an accident, pure and simple, and, if you scratch below the surface, he believes that Sylvianne's still his daughter, his delusional and maybe psychotic daughter, but his daughter just the same."

"No. They're lovers, Emma. You haven't seen them together. That woman guards him like Fort Knox."

"You might be right. You all may be right. Short of going back and watching that night and days that followed like I was tracking a curse, there's no way to know for sure. It's all a matter of perspective, anyway. Sylvianne might well think she's destined to be the mother of Redmond Longleigh's children. Longleigh nearly admitted as much, but Longleigh himself isn't on board. For one thing, he seems to think that Sylvianne blames him for whatever went wrong between him and Jeanette; and that she despises him . . . despises him almost as much as she despises *you.*"

"Nonsense. I've heard that before, and it's all lies, all an act."

"Now you're sounding like the one with the obsession. Look, he's pretty much convinced me that there is no *act.* He's just a father who loves his daughter—and not in an improper way."

"Red's not her father. That woman had tests done. It's a proven fact."

Longleigh hadn't mentioned paternity tests. But did it matter? Not really. "I don't think Longleigh believes it, not really, not in his heart—and, isn't what one believes all that's important for a hunter? You get used to living with subjective reality the way we do, and DNA testing just doesn't pack the same punch anymore."

"You can't be serious."

"I don't know. Check with me in fifty years or so. Longleigh says when the two of you first met you spoke French better than you spoke English, and that now you've forgotten it."

"I—I had no need to remember the language. I'd come home, for better or worse."

"And you don't think Longleigh could manage to forget the results of a silly medical test, if that would give him back his memories of his wife and his daughter? As long as she's playing the daughter wronged, he can't forget, but I'll bet in the back of his mind he's thinking that if his belief is stronger than hers, eventually he will be able to forget. And, heaven knows, when people around here think about 'eventually,' it has a whole new meaning."

"I still say, nonsense."

"He calls her Syl."

"What does that prove?"

"Syl, for Sylvia Anne, the name Longleigh and Jeanette gave their daughter. I bet nobody else calls her that. Even you—when you bother to use her name—call her Sylvianne."

"Means nothing."

"Okay, try this one on: Longleigh hit on me. Me! I know, it's not as if you hadn't warned me, and I suppose it's not entirely illogical. He's got me pigeonholed as one of those 'Skellings women.' But, all things considered, I don't think he'd be making moves in my direction—*and* warning me to be wary of his daughter—if the two of them were in bed together."

"You're mistaken."

"Rusty, yes; mistaken, I don't think so. The old goat seems to have a thing for women who don't fit in. There was a moment tonight when I'm sure, if I'd wanted, he'd have led me off somewhere for a night of passionate sex. And, you know, if it happens again, I just might consider it—for the sheer experience of it, like parasailing."

For the first time since she'd shown up on Emma's doorstep Eleanor was speechless.

"All right, I'm exaggerating. It would be a big mistake to get involved romantically with Redmond Longleigh. God love him, but he's one of those men who craves children, and there's no way I can go down that road."

"Good!"

Emma grimaced. "I don't think you understand. Even if the spirit were willing, the flesh has had it. I'm not like you, Eleanor, making myself young decade after decade— or Sylvianne herself, who's got to be older than she looks. I've crossed the reproductive divide. My biological clock stopped ticking about three years ago. All those teeny-tiny eggs crammed into my ovaries have turned to white, undifferentiated mush. Poor, old Longleigh might just as well be chasing a mule for all the good I'm ever going to do him. I could remake myself to look like my college graduation picture, but there's no way I'm getting my eggs back."

This time Eleanor's mouth was gaping and silent. "You know too much. Knowledge hems you in, takes away your freedom. You'd have to forget what you know to . . . to . . . *refresh* yourself when the time comes."

"Then again, maybe I'll just stay the way I am."

"But—"

"I'm *old?* I'm me. If I reshaped myself the way you have, I wouldn't be me."

"How do you know? You haven't tried."

Eleanor had Em there. "All right. I don't know what I'll want to do five years from now, but right now, I'm not adding extra variables to my life. I am interested in getting some sleep, and my rear end's starting to get numb from sitting on this ridge. If you guys meet in the bathrooms around here, why haven't you moved in a chair or two? There's enough room."

"We don't meet in bathrooms . . . usually. Red's whole security thing works because we meet in the Bunker. But—well, you caught me by surprise when you said separate bedrooms. Meeting in the Bunker isn't an option, not from separate bedrooms."

"Do you feel the need?" Em asked dutifully. It had been nearly a week since she'd last escorted her mother to the wasteland, and Eleanor was fastidious about her appearance, if nothing else.

"No, not yet—" Eleanor's eyes lost their focus; she was changing her mind. "Maybe from here. All the roads lead to the same place. If I knew you would be waiting for me—there'd be a way back."

Em tried to piece the fractured logic together. "You want to try the transition on your own . . . with me waiting for you? What, do you think it will be easier because so many hunters have come and gone from here?"

"Something like that."

Emma didn't ask for further explanation. Her thighs were starting to tingle where the bathtub rim was cutting off circulation. She stood up and began to pace. The bathroom was so large she could get three good strides between the tub and the sink before turning around. Eleanor complained that Em was making her dizzy, but she didn't renew her offer to change perches.

"Okay. I'll sit on the floor." Em eyed the burgundy throw rug. "That'll be easier on my rump."

"Oh, don't be silly! We'll each go back to our rooms—

we won't be more than, what? Twenty feet apart? That's close enough. Call me—call me *hard;* and give me fifteen minutes to make it through. That's all I ask, then do what you want, if you want."

Emma agreed because she didn't have the energy to argue. Returning to the Tuscany room, she carefully locked the door, turned out the light, and pulled the sheet and lightweight blanket close around her. She envisioned her spinning coin, called it, and effortlessly made the transition from the Victorian bedstead to the wasteland.

Something was different—not ominous, merely *different.* Em felt a change through her feet and fingertips before she opened her eyes. It wasn't the ground, which was as parched and crumbly as ever, or the weird wasteland light. She stood and turned right.

No way-back stone! Ignoring a heartbeat of panic, Em stretched her perceptions to their limit. She found the stone, out of sight, but not impossibly far away; and the bolt-hole which, even at her utmost, was faint and distant. Well, she knew, even before she walked up the *Excitation's* gangway, that there was a skewed correlation between starting points in the real world and entry points in the wasteland, though it was strange that her bolt-hole seemed farther from the Bunker than it had from the Bahamas.

For a moment the engineering gene wrestled with notions of wasteland geography, distance, and orientation, then Em pulled her attention back to the job at hand. Em didn't have to stretch too far to locate herself on the perimeter of what Longleigh had named the Bunker. The parched ground was more textured around the Bunker. There were dozens of small steep hills marking the locations of who-knew-what. The largest hill, at the center of everything, contained the entrance to Longleigh's fully detailed bolt-hole, but the nearby smaller ones were more than adequate for Em to climb and call her mother's name, not with her voice but with her mind.

Time was always tricky in the wasteland, and for all Em knew, time was different in Longleigh's neck of the woods. She stood atop a mound until what her father had called her "think muscles" were sore and exhausted. Nothing that might have been Eleanor Graves had crossed her perception, though she had observed another hunter—no one she knew or recognized—phase into the wasteland. That had been interesting, even informative, to watch. The hunter's presence began as a sheer star-white blob and had, over the course of several moments, darkened and solidified into a human shape, definitely not Eleanor, but probably female.

The newcomer ignored Em, and Em saw no reason to announce herself. She might have said something if the hunter had still been visible when she conceded that Eleanor hadn't conquered her phobias and wasn't coming through on her own, but the hunter had disappeared behind one of the hills.

Without Eleanor, there was no good reason to stay in the wasteland either, and at least one good reason for heading back to Atlantis. Most of the time Eleanor's failures were simple and unspectacular; she hadn't managed to take the first step out of mundane reality for months, but sometimes frustration got the better of Eleanor and she worked herself into a state bordering hysteria.

"I should be there to calm her down," Emma counseled herself, then thought of the locked doors. "Oh, well. She knows the rules better than I do."

Em climbed down the hill. By all she knew, there was only one straightforward way out of the Bunker complex, and it lay deep in Longleigh's bolt-hole. With a little luck, Em thought she could find her way there, but she didn't feel like wasting luck when her own way-back stone was a palpable presence in her mind. She fixed her course with a twist of her neck—Em had discovered she could sense the change in intensity with that small a movement—and began walking.

The watchers' perimeter lay between Em and her way-back stone. Em's path brought her within a hundred feet of a lean and older woman seated full-lotus style on a raised platform. To Em's surprise, the woman broke her meditation to speak.

"Who are you?" the watcher asked in unaccented English. Then again, Blaise spoke unaccented English. Wasteland magic made communication simple.

"Emma Merrigan," she replied, seeing no reason to lie. "And you?"

"They call me Rosalie. Where are you going?"

Em frowned and pondered a moment. Rosalie . . . Rosalie, she knew that name, but couldn't place it; and why did asking a simple question in the wasteland always produce a complex answer? Who were *they*? Other hunters? Was it common for a hunter to have a shared name and a private one? Or, was that something peculiar to watchers?

Rosalie was waiting for an answer to her question. Em strove to make it truly simple. "I have a stone waiting for me just over the horizon. It's my way back to my body."

"Surely, the Bunker—?"

"I wanted to walk."

Oddly, that seemed a perfectly satisfactory answer. The watcher placed her hands palms-up on her knees; her open hands were filled with colored pebbles. Em knew enough yoga to realize the other woman was headed back to meditation. She could have walked away; instead she asked, "Anything out there I should be wary of?"

The watcher blinked and stared down at the pebble pattern on the platform in front of her. "Nothing in front of you. All the major activity is in the fourth quadrant, minus. Don't go there, and you'll be fine."

Em nodded, as if she knew what the fourth quadrant, plus *or* minus, was. "Thanks for the heads-up."

"Good hunting," the watcher said and closed her eyes.

"Good watching," Em replied and continued on her way toward the way-back stone.

She found her stone right where she expected it to be, and a tiddling curse hunched close to the ground not twenty paces away. It lurched to its full height as Em approached.

Em snarled at its flames. "You're nowhere big enough to threaten me." Then dropped fluidly to one knee and pasted it with a jet of light from her grandmother's ring. When it was reduced to another dark shadow on the landscape, she moved close by the way-back stone. Curses came in pairs and sometimes in packs. She'd proved that the hard way and had always tried not to make the same mistake twice. With the way-back stone in easy reach, Em could scoot homeward in a heartbeat, if she needed to. But, as time lengthened without another curse popping up for another try, that didn't seem likely.

She stood up, still wary. One thing to remember about curses—they got smarter as they got bigger, and the smartest of them could curb their more ravenous impulses. Em stayed close to the stone. She couldn't have said why she hadn't placed her hands on its smooth surface and made the transition back to her body, except her adrenaline was pumping, and she figured she'd wake her body up returning to it.

Better to do a little hunting to calm herself down.

Better still to find Blaise. They could hunt together then retreat behind the door of their bolt-hole. But the bolt-hole's tingle was still at the limit of Em's senses. Her gut—the best forecaster of wasteland time and distance—said she could walk until dawn and wind up no closer to Blaise. It wasn't logical—she'd walked from her bolt-hole to the Bunker the first time she visited it, and Harry had no trouble joining Orion's Children on Friday nights. Logic, though, didn't rule the wasteland.

Something Eleanor said echoed in Emma's mind—"All

roads lead to the same place." The Bunker might be the wasteland equivalent of a gravity sink, pulling every visiting curse-hunter toward itself. Em vowed that she'd solve the mystery, but from Bower, where she was the dominant hunter. In the meantime, she set out to plink off a few curses, her way-back stone following, in its usual way, a few paces to the rear and the right.

Rosalie the watcher hadn't been kidding when she said there was nothing out front; and, though hunting lore was adamant that every rogue and whirling inferno had begun its existence as an easily plinked fingerling, the vast majority of newly emerged curses withered into the wasteland dirt without a hunter's assistance. Em chased down a few curses, all of them fingerlings and tiddlers. She didn't have the sense that her predatory skills had spared the real world much future misery.

She settled on the way-back stone—it made a better seat than the skirted bathtub—wide awake and bored. A bad combination. Her idle thoughts quickly skewed to the one curse she knew she could find, the curse she had promised to moot her first night back on dry land: Donetta's curse.

Never mind that she'd tracked the root of Donetta's curse starting from her now-distant bolt-hole; once the idea of mooting it took hold of Em's imagination, she knew exactly which direction to turn and how far she'd have to walk. She wasn't wrong, either. Her talent for plunging curses was as reliable as a dog's nose and, if she believed her mother, equally sharp.

Emma came to the place, no different from any other place, and knelt down. Plunging started with delving, which was a little like transferring, only easier. Instead of a spinning coin, Em concentrated on a collection of specifics—not quite a unique scent, but almost—and let her *wyrd* take over.

The night, the rutted, muddy street, the gang of irregular soldiers and their mounted officer: Everything was as it had been when she and Blaise had witnessed the old woman's death. Watching it happen was easier the second time around; Em knew when to turn away. After the irregulars had completed their brutal murder and walked or ridden away, Emma set about "rolling up time." It was her own trick for getting to the absolute root of a curse and unique to her, so far as she knew. Eleanor didn't know how to thrust herself backward through time, moment by moment; and Eleanor was the only other plunger among Em's acquaintances.

The process was simple enough, though, like so many wasteland processes, it defied logic and explanation. Em imagined the flow of time from past toward future as a steady wind and strode against it. There was a *Through the Looking Glass* quality to her efforts: The harder she strove, the more time she rolled up, the less ground she covered. Choosing an oblique approach, she started rolling time about ten feet from the cottage that had been the murdered woman's home and was still a good five feet away when the officer marched up and *through* her toward the door.

For a heartbeat Em was linked to the simple, cruel mind of a man who lived by his duty and his prejudice, untroubled by any wider empathy or conscience. Em took an instant dislike to him and, if it would have mooted the curse, she would gladly have cut short his contribution to humanity's evolution. But curse-hunting didn't work that way, and the resilience of time made it practically impossible to weave anyone with a future into the mooting of a curse. Emma wrenched free and, when a dark-bearded man opened the door, her insubstantial self darted beneath his outstretched arm.

She didn't need to know a word of the peasants' language to recognize an ultimatum when it was delivered or to read the emotions on the faces of the four adults and three half-grown children in the cottage's single downstairs room. They weren't cowards. They wanted to fight for their honor and defend what was theirs, but they weren't martyrs, either; and against the irregulars they didn't have a prayer of success.

The stand-off lasted thirty seconds, no more. One of the adults—the woman who would die on the street—said something, and the man at the door began to lower his arm. The woman was prepared to die, to surrender herself for the preservation of her family; no wonder her death, brutal as it had been, hadn't given rise to Donetta's curse.

The officer didn't have time for the woman to make a dignified last exit from her home. He barked a command, and as many of his men as could squeeze themselves through the doorway rushed in to seize her. Adding insult to injury, the irregulars trampled or broke as much as they could. They knocked the bearded man down; his head struck hard on the packed earth floor, and he didn't try to get up. A woman, younger than the doomed woman, dodged punches and kicks to kneel by his side, while the children cowered and the fourth man, the youngest of the adults, made the mistake of taking a swing at the irregular who'd decked the bearded man. He, too, wound up motionless on the floor. The largest of the children, a girl of perhaps ten or twelve, had the presence of mind to shut and bar the door when the officer and last of the irregulars had withdrawn to the street.

Neither of the men was dead, or, if they were, their deaths were not responsible for the curse Emma hunted. Like a ghost, she threaded through the horror-numbed family and climbed the stairs to the second floor, which, she discovered to her dismay, was divided into rooms with doors.

Doors and other mundane objects were no problem for Blaise; he could lift a latch or turn a key with ease. For the last year or so, he'd been trying to share his secret, but his ability to interact physically with the past seemed as specialized as Emma's talent for plunging to the root of things and merging into the minds she found there. She even suspected they were contradictory talents: If she'd been able to *feel* the past, then how would she be able to walk into a stranger's mind?

And how would she be able to moot Donetta's curse, if the mind she needed to influence was on the far side of a closed door? She could roll up time again. Eventually the door would have to open. But rolling up time was exhausting work, and before she threw herself against another wind, Emma decided to learn what she could from the situation as she'd found it.

There were three doors. Two of them were firmly shut and leading into rooms that seemed vacant. The third, though, was slightly ajar and lit from within. Em couldn't budge the door and didn't particularly want to. Some innocents could see curse-hunters going about their work, and a vision at the wrong moment could change history the wrong way. Odds were that the root of Donetta's curse was on the far side of the door, and Em didn't want to risk scaring her—at least not prematurely, not until she had a chance to witness the way history had unfolded in its own time.

Em measured the candlelight yellow crack. It was no more than a quarter-inch wide. Surely a hunter who could roll up time around her could figure out a way to squeeze through a crack? She tried thinking herself thin, *very* thin; that didn't work. She imagined herself to be as insubstantial as fog and tried seeping through the crack; that didn't work either.

Time—the particular slice of time and space surrounding Emma—was running out. There were screams and shouts out in the street. The crone was dying, and one of the unnameable senses Em had acquired when she began hunting curses tingled in anticipation of a curse's creation. Em took that tingling, reconceived it as the wind she felt against her face when she rolled time up, and surged against it.

The pain was intense, like nothing Emma had experienced before. Human flesh, even insubstantial flesh was not meant to flatten itself into a pie crust. She would have screamed from her toes, if she could have located either her toes or her mouth. But, when the pain ended, Em was inside the room.

A woman—no, a teenage girl, with dark, curly hair falling loose to her slender waist—rummaged single-mindedly through a wooden trunk. Emma scanned her for an aura and found none, which squared with her certainty that she'd come to the right time, the right place. The floor around the girl was littered with discards: folded paper packets, sprays of dried flowers tied in bunches, a red scarf, a disarrayed set of nesting bowls, a beaded necklace long enough to be looped several times around the wearer's neck.

The beads were crude ceramics of no intrinsic worth, unmatched in both size and color. Not the sort of thing anyone would mistake as jewelry, Em reasoned they must have had a different purpose. Combining what she saw with what she already knew about the crone's death, witchcraft seemed a likely explanation. Emma couldn't know whether the crone was a bitter, malingering woman who'd passed her time cooking up traditional (and ineffective) curses or a gentle soul whose homemade remedies were the closest the peasants were likely to get to medicine for another few centuries.

Based on the crone's innate dignity and the fact that her death wouldn't yield a curse, Em inclined toward the second explanation. She also had a hunch that she was watching the back of the person who had betrayed the crone to what passed for the local authorities. A betrayal from within the family. A betrayal for what purpose?

The girl had stopped rummaging. Em moved in for a

closer look. The girl had found what she was looking for: a small, brightly painted box with a hinged lid and an impressive wrought-iron lock, which popped open when the girl squeezed it in just the right places. Her face, which had worn a feral grin while she manipulated the lock, fell. If she wanted to know why, Emma, who couldn't see into the box, had no choice but to wrap herself around the teenager and merge with her thoughts.

A mass of small, dark coins, nothing glittery, filled the little box. Given the poverty evident in the cottage, they represented a small fortune for a peasant woman, witch or not; but they weren't what the girl had been hoping for. Disappointment and rage exploded in the girl's mind, leaving little room for anything else. Emma took advantage of the confusion to extract herself. Beyond a doubt the girl had the will and the self-absorption necessary to fuel a curse, a real curse and not the idle malice of ordinary anger.

But the curse was gathering, like lightning before the bolt, and that meant death was in the offing, too: the girl's death.

Em waited with one eye on the door. Her expectation was that one of the menfolk, having recovered consciousness and figured out the source of betrayal and tragedy, would come charging through the door to murder the girl. She'd begun to devise possible interventions that would keep the girl alive, or, at least, blunt the curse-forming power of her death, but there were no footsteps on the stairs, no fist against the unlatched door, only a final, high-pitched wail from the street beyond the shuttered window.

The girl dumped the coins on the floor. Their clatter, Em thought, would surely draw attention from below, but the last coin stopped spinning and still no footsteps. While Em asked herself unanswerable questions, the girl dropped to her knees. She fetched up a beribboned wisp that resembled a lock of pale blond baby hair from amid the tumbled coins. Her hand began to shake as she held it, and though Em couldn't guess the significance of the hair until she once again merged with the girl's thoughts, she began to formulate a new theory of the curse's origins . . . and, this time, the theory predicted the girl's actions.

Still clutching the lock of hair in her trembling fingers, the girl began to sob in great, almost silent gasps.

Whatever it is, now that she's found it, that girl knows she's made a terrible—fatal—*mistake.* And a mistake, lodged deeply enough in a heart of guilt and helplessness, could engender a curse.

The pieces and a strategy to moot the curse fell together in Em's mind. If she was right, she'd need to roll up a few minutes of the past, but that was no obstacle.

The girl's sobs caught in her throat. She turned and stared, not at the door, which Em would have expected, but at the dark corner of the room where Em had positioned herself.

Curse-hunters were not uniformly invisible when they walked the past. They could make themselves plainly visible to one another, and they were unpredictably apparent to ordinary folks. If Emma were visible, then, will she or nil she, she was already interacting with the past, changing the flow of time and history; but not mooting the curse. Its tingle grew palpably stronger the longer the girl stared. Whatever was happening—whether the girl could see her or whether Emma was already, and unintentionally, manipulating the fabric of time—the curse remained on course.

Emma met the girl's eyes; there was no reason not to. She watched as all emotion drained from the young face. When it had become as expressionless as a painted mask, the girl turned away. She strode purposefully into the darkest corner of the room, where Em could track her silhouette, nothing more. Em heard the clatter of crockery and glass then a few moments of silence before the girl reeled back into the lamplight. A muddy stain trailed from the corners of her mouth, and she held a small ceramic bottle.

The bottle slipped from her fingers. It cracked open on the floor, seeping dark fluid onto the wood. Then the girl dropped awkwardly to her knees, her empty hands searching for her throat.

Em drew conclusions. The crone had kept her nostrums close at hand, and among them must have been at least one potent, fast-acting poison, which the girl had found and swallowed in quantities that were both fatal and painful. The girl had fallen to her side. She writhed in apparent agony. Her mouth was open, but her screams were muffled by the dark, bubbling foam welling up from her throat.

The curse was ready. Emma smelled it like the scent of a storm on a sultry afternoon. The mysteries had all been solved. She didn't need to witness the girl's death or the curse's inception. With her teeth clenched in determination, she began to roll up time.

Generously, Em should have rolled up more than a few minutes. She could have searched for the moment when the girl plotted the crone's betrayal and tried to intervene before the tragedy commenced. The lock of hair, whatever its true significance, was a powerful talisman; perhaps, if the girl could have been made to discover it earlier, she might join forces with the crone rather than betray her. But that was moral calculus left over from the days when Emma knew nothing of curses or her own *wyrd*. Hunters weren't in the business of saving lives or improving the human condition. Their job—their only job—was mooting curses, simple and direct.

Emma waited just inside the crone's bedroom. When the girl entered, they collided, and Em was enmeshed in the girl's thoughts, where rage, greed, self-righteousness, and a leavening of adolescent confusion seethed together. She had to fight for the girl's attention. In the end, it was easier to guide the girl's hand toward the brightly painted box than to make it the subject of her frantic search.

Then, when the box was in the girl's hands, Em employed every trick in the super-ego book to focus the girl's attention on the lock of hair. The tumult in the girl's mind blocked specifics. Even when the lock was the only image in the girl's mind, Em discerned only that it was a memento from the funeral of someone dear to both the crone and the girl. The details didn't matter as Emma flooded the girl's thoughts with guilt and empathy.

She was doomed anyway. The resilience of time forgave small displacements in chronology or motive, but it would hardly allow this girl to live a normal, much less exemplary, life. The choice—as Emma rationalized it to herself—was between savagery and suicide. Thought by thought, she quenched the girl's rage and greed. She left the self-righteousness and confusion. Freed from their former anchors, those free-floating emotions attached themselves to the guilt and made it easier for Em to turn the girl away from the shelf where the poison vials were hidden.

There was resistance, and it came from *outside:* a hitherto unsuspected tug between the upstream curse and the girl's tumble toward self-destruction. Em would bring that phenomenon to Harry Graves' attention. Harry would spend months fitting a new puzzle piece into his understanding of curse ecology. For the specific moment, though, the presence of another pressure in the girl's mind meant only that Emma had to summon more strength.

The girl hesitated but did not return to the dark corner. She left the door open and made her way down the stairs, one hand on the banister, because Em wasn't completely confident of her control, though the external pressure had faded dramatically once the girl had left the crone's room.

They were on the right track.

The household's other children noticed their elder sibling coming down the stairway. They made moves toward

the woman who was probably their mother and definitely
the only fully conscious adult in the cottage. Emma didn't
have to add much to the glower the girl shot their way: It
was a rare teenager who couldn't dominate her younger
brothers and sisters with a single glance. The maternal
woman was too busy tending her fallen menfolk to notice
a wayward daughter slipping quietly to the door.

Latches were no obstacle for Em when she was in possession of an innocent's mind. The door creaked on its
hinges, drawing adult attention at last. But it was too late
for intervention. Laden with guilt and freed from external
pressure, the doomed girl embraced the fate Emma Merrigan had devised for her.

Em had nothing to do with the girl's decision to fling
herself at the officer, all shrieks and fists. The girl managed
to score that gentleman's face with her fingernails before
he flung her to the ground. For a heartbeat, the girl's
thoughts cleared, and she asked herself a question in a language Em didn't understand. There was, however, no time
or place for regrets. The girl fought off the irregular who
tried to seize her by the arms and launched another attack
on the officer.

She saw—and Emma saw—the man's hand drop to his
sword hilt. Em knew how quickly Blaise could draw and
use his weapon of choice; and she knew what death looked
like from the inside of a doomed mind. She withdrew into
herself and out of the girl the instant before the sharp steel
piece pierced her belly.

The girl bled out beside the crone, and no curse rose to
mark her death. The mooting had been successful. Emma
stumbled into the shadows of another house—not that
anyone could see her—and caught her breath. Once the
excitement of plunging into a stranger's mind died down,
and it always died quickly, she suffered a finer appreciation of a plunger's ruthless morality. Her stomach heaved.
She fought nausea with closed eyes and clenched fists.

When her private battle had been won, Em opened her eyes again.

The irregulars and their officer were headed home, leaving two corpses behind.

Somewhere nearby, a child was crying.

Twelve

E mma turned toward the cottage. She expected to see that one of the household youngsters had opened the door and, seeing the bodies in the street, was streaming tears at the sight. But the cottage door was tightly shut and, now that the irregulars were gone, there was no lamplight anywhere—even the few lanterns that had flickered before the incident began had been prudently extinguished. The neighbors, apparently, preferred not to get involved.

The sobbing, however, continued, and, though Emma's work in this ill-defined time and place was done, she stirred herself toward the sound. Her curiosity led her onto the narrow path between the crone's cottage and its closest neighbor. Near what had to be the rear of the cottages, clear white light spilled onto the path from a right-side alcove, the side opposite the home of the deceased women.

A twenty-first-century flashlight could have produced the sort of glow Em had her eye on, but since everything else she had seen in the village basked in flickering, preindustrial light, she ruled flashlights out. That left another hunter—a child by the sobbing, even though she'd always been told the *wyrd* didn't make itself useful much before the age of fifteen. A hunter or a rogue. Rogues could do anything a hunter could and go a step farther by disguising themselves as innocent men or women or children.

Time to go home, the mother-voice advised.

It was good advice, and Em consciously ignored it. A child was crying, and she was curious. Curious and just a little wary. She fondled her ruby ring before she took another step. Forget rogues for a moment; Blaise told tales of seventeenth-century hunters ambushing one another against the backdrop of his beloved Paris. Em's ears believed she was listening to a child, but her gut wished she had a sword as well as a ring. She inhaled her self-luminance, making herself as dark as the moonless village, and started down the path.

Refuse cluttered the ground. The two households must have used the path as a garbage midden. Em stumbled at every step, because the place was real to her even if she wasn't real enough to impact it. Bracing herself against the left-side wall, she made slow progress toward the light. She stopped before entering it and sought a vantage for seeing without being seen.

Despite her caution, the child—the sobbing came from a five- or six-year-old child sitting cross-legged in a pool of light—looked her way the moment she got a good look at him—him? Em's perceptions had leapt to gender conclusions. With shoulder-length golden curls and an all-concealing pale tunic about ten sizes too big, the child could have as easily been a girl as a boy. Add a pair of wings and he—or she—could have passed for an angel.

Because the child had noticed her, and because he was the source of the light in which he sat, Emma knew she wasn't looking at an ordinary innocent. The question, which she couldn't answer, was whether she'd come across a hunter too young to comprehend his *wyrd* or a rogue pretending to be such a child.

Emma had seen *The Bad Seed* during its 1950s theatrical release—her father's idea of children's entertainment because it had starred a child. The film had left lifelong scars—she tended to distrust beautiful blond children on sight. Much as she'd like to lend a hand to another hunter, Em assumed she was dealing with a rogue. She tightened her fist, expecting the unexpected, expecting anything but a renewed torrent of tears.

The Bad Seed notwithstanding, there was a chance she was wrong about the self-illuminating child.

With her thumb pressed tight against her mooting ring, Em stepped fully into the child's light. She'd soloed against rogues before. It was dangerous business, but beating a retreat was as simple as willing herself back to her body. She was good at that—good enough to offer her hand in friendship and aim the ruby ring at the same time.

"Why are you crying?" she asked, trying to sound maternal and hoping that the magic that allowed her to communicate with Blaise would work in a Balkans village.

"She's gone. She's disappeared. I followed her all the way, then she was *gone!*" the child said between sobs.

The child ignored Emma's hand. She lowered it partway and kept her thumb pressed against the gold.

"Who was she?"

"Mira. We were together, then she got sick and left. I followed her here. She went out in the street. A man hit her with his sword and she disappeared. I tried to stop her. I tried! But she wouldn't listen. She didn't even see me. Something made her—" The sobbing stopped. The child fixed Em with a stare straight out of *The Bad Seed*. His eyes hardened, and when he spoke again, it was an accusation. "*You* made her walk in the street. *You* made her disappear."

Emma took a deep breath. Plunging, she'd thought, was the ultimate invasion of privacy, but it was still a private act. She never imagined that there could be witnesses. She'd never imagined curses as companions, either. Yet, clearly, that was what the child described: His companion was the curse that Mira had birthed and Donetta had borne aboard the *Excitation*; and when Emma mooted the curse, she erased the companion's existence everywhere in time and place, except for the child's mind.

Rogues possess; curses infest, Em's mother-voice advised. *Donetta carried a curse. She wasn't a rogue. She didn't have a separate existence.*

Then what am I looking at?

The mother-voice fell unhelpfully silent, and the best Emma could come up with was that the child in front of her was a freak, like Blaise Raponde: a hunter caught between life and death. And what Em wouldn't have given to have her lover standing beside her. When it came to rogues, she trusted his judgment above all others.

Emma had fixed the time and place in her plunger's memory; she could go off in search of Blaise and come back to this precise moment, but the odds against finding the child again were long. Rogues and hunters, except for Blaise, were free agents, bound only by the absolute present. They moved through the past like worms through an apple.

Blaise might be able to pick up the child's scent; usually, though, he required direct contact with his prey before he could follow it to a lair.

The safest course—the course Em could imagine both Blaise and her mother-voice recommending—was to moot the child where he—*it*—sat. Hunters were their own judge and jury. No appeals committee gainsayed a hunter's mooting. If she painted the child with enough ruby-red light to reduce it to memory, she'd have only her own conscience to contend with.

Em raised her arm and lowered it again. The rogue—if the child was a rogue—had chosen its masquerade well. She could dehumanize and attack an adult rogue, regardless of its apparent sex, but she wasn't cold enough to blast a child without provocation.

She hadn't so much turned around as shifted her weight from her forward foot, when the child stiffened suddenly and snorted his tears away. He threw back his head and inhaled deeply as he turned first one way, then the other. After a moment of canine sniffing, he homed in again on Emma.

"I see you," he said. "I *see* you!" He balled his hands into fists that barely protruded from the over-long sleeves of his shirt and pulled his brows together in a ferocious scowl. Rogues usually employed talismans to focus their destructive energies, the same as hunters, but they could just as easily extend their power through open eyes, an open mouth, or an extended fist. (Hunters could do the same—Emma had in the very beginning. It was exhausting and inefficient, but far from impossible.)

She prepared herself for battle. Enclosed spaces weren't the best venues for fighting a rogue, but they were far from the worst. They were infinitely better than making a break for the street and giving a rogue a clean shot at her back. Emma tested her connections out of the past. With gentle effort she could feel her horizontal body sleeping in the Tuscany room and she could feel the pull of the wasteland, too. Her escape routes were wide open. She could be gone in less than a heartbeat.

Fortified with that knowledge and still reluctant to make the first move against a child, Emma made one last attempt to convince herself that the child was a hunter, not a rogue.

"I don't want to hurt you. I'll help you, if I can. Do you have a place where you belong?"

She meant a body and knew it was very unlikely that he did. Eleanor had survived a two-month separation from her body, but only because twenty-first-century medical technology had kept that body alive. She could hope the boy was equally fortunate, at least until he shook his head.

"Mira's place. I went with Mira. She's gone. Gone! I'm alone again."

Again? Emma zeroed in on the boy's final word. It quashed her hopes, but spurred her curiosity. "You've been alone before?"

The child nodded solemnly.

"You were alone until you found Mira?"

This time the child shook his head. "Baba found me first."

Emma ransacked her store of linguistic trivia and recalled that in several of the Slavic languages the word *baba* was less a given name than an endearment bestowed on a grandmother. In this situation, there was only one candidate for grandmother-hood: the crone the irregulars had pulled out of the house, the crone who had seemed so dignified and whose death hadn't given rise to a curse.

Malice doesn't cause curses; futility and misery cause curses . . . Just because they're evil doesn't mean they're not innocent. . . . The victims of malice give rise to curses. The mother-voice recited from Harry Graves' black book.

Em sagged under the weight of irony: Mira might well have had good reasons for turning the old crone over to the irregulars, brutal and cruel as they were. The girl could have tried to get rid of one evil only to give rise to a greater, more persistent one herself.

"Where did Baba find you?"

"Out there." The child opened his arms wide.

"Out where?"

"You know, out where it's empty. I got lost, and she found me."

"Baba found you and brought you back here?"

"Where it's safe. It's not safe out there."

"Out there" had to be the wasteland, but for some reason the linguistic magic wasn't conveying any of the usual synonyms. Could it be that the boy didn't know where he'd been when the crone had found him? There were in-nocents who could see hunters—and, presumably, rogues—as they wandered the past, but Em had never heard of an innocent making it all the way to the waste-land. For that matter, she'd never heard of a hunter under the age of fifteen translating to the wasteland—

Yes, you have, the mother-voice corrected. *Where do you think you were the instant before the night terrors woke you up?*

The boy had the logic and behavior appropriate to his appearance. It was so tempting to believe that he wasn't a rogue. Then again, a master mimic would recreate a child's behavior down to the last overly simple answer. All rogues were master mimics; they assimilated the complete per-sonalities of the innocents they claimed.

"So Baba kept you here? Kept you safe?"

The boy nodded quickly before volunteering the addi-tional information: "I did chores. I came when she called."

"Did you like that?" Em asked, struggling to keep her voice calm. She wasn't happy about the direction this seemed headed: a child—a hunter not yet in command of his *wyrd*—caught in a night terror the likes of which she could all-too-readily imagine, waking up in the wasteland instead of a warm bed with no understanding father to re-assure him the way her father had reassured her; and get-ting caught in an old woman's web.

He shrugged, pressing his ear against his shoulder and hiding his hands in twists of his roomy shirt. Em recog-nized those evasive moves from her days as a stepparent.

"You didn't like it?"

More writhing followed by, "I had to. Baba had—" The boy unwound his hands and shaped them around an imag-inary rectangle. "It *hurt.*"

"My God—" Em whispered, unable to keep her shock from showing. She definitely had misread the crone's dignity. That lock of blond hair in the box—it was the boy's hair, and the crone had used it to imprison him, to make him into her pet and slave. "But, you're free now. Baba's gone. Baba can't hurt you again," she said automatically. She was a patriotic American; she took it for granted that freedom solved problems.

The boy corrected her. "I'm alone. Mira's gone. Where can I go to be safe?"

Emma didn't have a long-term answer for that question, so she punted with a different question. "Do you remember anything from before Baba found you, from before you were alone for the first time?"

"No." He writhed the other ear against the other shoulder and admitted, "Not the first time. Lots of times. Lots of times like Baba. Not like Mira. Mira was my friend. We played games."

"Was Mira your sister?" Em asked.

It was a foolish question, in light of what the boy had just said, but he lowered his eyes and wouldn't answer.

"Isn't there someplace where you belong—someplace that was home, before you were alone? We could look for it together." Not that Em knew what she'd do if she found it; although Blaise spent a good deal of his time in the Paris he knew best, he most emphatically did *not* reunite with his body.

The boy nodded, but when she asked where and when, he gave her a blank stare for an answer. Then Emma recalled that boys inherited their *wyrd* from their fathers and asked the boy if he remembered his father.

"He disappeared."

"He abandoned you?"

The boy looked straight at her and snapped, "Disappeared!" as if Em were the one with limited comprehension. "Like Mira. Disappeared."

Mira's disappearance was tied in a way that Emma did not fully understand to the mooting of the curse that had arisen from her death. Could she infer that the boy's father had run fatally afoul of another hunter?

"Do you remember where you were when he disappeared?"

A nod and another episode of averted eyes.

Em worried that she was about to embark on a course that could backfire seriously, but her conscience wouldn't let her walk away from the boy, and taking him back to the bolt-hole was an absolute last resort. She'd survived stepparenting, knew all its pitfalls, and had no interest in taking an orphaned hunter-child under her wing.

"Give me your hand." She held out hers.

The boy retreated to the far side of the alcove.

"I'm not going to hurt you. I can take you back to the beginning—"

"No! You'll make me do things."

The crone was dead, and she died horribly, but for just one moment Emma wished she could have intervened to make the death worse.

"I won't, I promise."

With her hand out, Em moved closer to the boy. Her hope was to get a charge off the boy the way she'd picked up images from Donetta. It was worth a try; they were all part of the same curse. And if it worked, maybe she'd figure out something constructive for when they got back to the time and place where the boy had last seen his father. Or, maybe there was no alternative to taking him to the bolt-hole and enlisting Blaise as a babysitter until they came up with better strategies.

Hesitantly, the boy extended his hand. Emma took it. The hand was small, warm, and inert against hers. Em was disappointed, but not surprised that her plunging *wyrd* didn't work with mysterious hunters the way it did with innocents. She'd touched Blaise Raponde countless times and never once gotten a sense of his private life. Then again, she'd never really tried that, either. After a few mo-

ments of gentle pressure Em had a sense of narrow streets
and dark, tiny rooms with cluttered floors and casement
windows not terribly different from the one in the bolt-
hole.

European, but she could have guessed that much from
the boy's appearance, not modern, but not ancient, either.
Emma had gotten less from Donetta and managed to find
her way to this forsaken village.

When Em thought of Donetta, the boy began to struggle against her grasp.

"I don't want to go there!" he protested, tugging with all
his might. "I don't want to go back there."

He very nearly freed himself, but Emma held on.
"There's nothing to be afraid of. I need to see where you
come from so we can go back. If I don't zero in on the right
place—if it's not the place where you belong and want to
stay, we'll come back here."

Something she'd said made the boy stretch his arm out
to put the greatest possible distance between them.

"Trust me."

The boy's whole body went rigid. His eyes, which had
been puppy-like and pleading, narrowed down, like a dog
about to bite.

He's damaged, the mother-voice whispered. *Severely
damaged. The old crone wasn't the first who hurt him . . .
used him. What do you want to bet that his dear, old dad
was the first? Remember what Blaise said: He feared his
father and the rest of his relatives more than he feared
rogues.*

Emma didn't argue, or even disagree. Her position was
as simple as it was confining: *I can't moot him, and I can't
walk away from him either.*

*Even if you can stuff him back into his own time and
place, you won't be doing anyone any favors, especially
him. Look at his eyes. He's headed down the wrong path.*

When it came to the obvious, the mother-voice never

hesitated. It was less forthcoming with practical advice. For no good reason, Em recalled Longleigh saying that there was a curse inside every innocent and a rogue inside every hunter. With the boy, the rogue was very close to the surface, if it hadn't already spilled over, but she had to try.

"Close your eyes and follow where I lead."

Anyone who shone by their own light could handle the translation from the past to the wasteland. Em kept a firm clasp on the boy's hand and started walking. Two steps, she figured; one more than usual because of the boy trailing along behind her. She felt the air change first, then the ground.

"You can open your eyes—"

The boy shrieked. He tugged violently against Emma's grasp. Her thumb bent in a direction nature never intended, and the boy was free.

"Here!" he sputtered. "You brought me *here*!" He spun around in a complete circle, clearly watching the horizon. "They'll get me. They'll make me disappear, just like my father."

Rogues? Fiery curses like the ones that captured Eleanor? Emma began to analyze the situation, but hadn't gotten beyond her assumptions when the boy took off running.

Let him go. He's making himself into someone else's problem. You can walk away with clean hands.

But Em couldn't, not when she was responsible for dragging the boy to the wasteland. Worse, in a few short moments since their arrival they'd attracted more attention than Emma usually pulled in a dozen translations. In addition to her way-back stone, she counted four fingerling curses shooting out of their hidey-holes and two good-sized pillars coming in from different quadrants. With any luck, the pillars would go after each other and the fingerlings would go to ground. Absent any luck, they'd all draw a bead on the fleeing boy; and Em wasn't leaving anyone alone to face that sort of conflagration.

She took off after him, grateful for the strength and stamina she'd built up over the past two years. Her legs were longer than the boy's, her lung capacity was greater, and there was no doubt in her mind that she'd reach him before he got in serious trouble. She was maybe ten feet behind and closing fast when he went shimmery and disappeared like a blown-out flame.

"Damn!"

Emma stopped short on the spot where the boy had vanished. Other than a few indistinct scuffs on the dirt and faint tang of ozone lingering in the air, there were no easy signs to say the boy had been there a moment earlier. There was something more obscure, something that tickled Em's *wyrd* in unprecedented ways. She could follow the boy, if she chose.

How many signs do you need? the mother-voice carped.

Em scanned the horizon. As expected, the fingerlings had sucked themselves in, but the two pillars had been joined by a third, and though they were shedding sparks and embers at one another, they were all closing in on the spot where Emma stood.

Time to cut and run. Chalk this one up to bad experience and get yourself out while the getting's still good.

Em glanced at the cool, black depths of the way-back stone. She had only to kneel and touch its polished surface, and she'd be back in the Tuscany room at Atlantis. She'd mooted the curse, and as for Mira, the boy, and the crone— no one would know anything if she didn't tell them.

An arc of searing yellow fire leapt between two of the pillars. An atavistic roar echoed across the barren plain, and while two of the curses fought for dominance, the third dimmed and rushed closer to Emma.

Now, or never—

Emma squatted, but not beside the stone. She placed her

palms on the hard, yet crumbling, dirt and thought about the boy. A gray emptiness like nothing she'd seen before opened up in front of her. A trail of glowing footsteps drew a straight line leading from her to a fleeing point in the distance.

Fool!

I will not stand by and let the curses win. I won't let him suffer the way Eleanor suffered when the curses and rogues caught her; he wouldn't survive.

She took a deep breath and pushed away from the wasteland, into the unknown.

The line Emma followed was solid beneath her feet. It might have a plain as broad and featureless as the wasteland itself or an arrow-straight bridge through a featureless void. There was air to breathe, that was important, and she knew from her first stride that she was gaining on the boy, that was more important. He went from being a speck to a blob to a hard-running child wearing a too-big shirt. His hair resolved itself into a mass of bouncing curls, then the seams of his shirt became apparent.

Em reached out. She felt the cloth against her fingertips. The boy craned his head around as he ran. His mouth was open, his cheeks were red, and there was desperation in his eyes. He swung his head forward again and bent deeper into his stride. The gap between them widened, until Emma summoned her own reserves and in two strong strides got close enough to clamp one hand on the boy's shirt collar and the other on his shoulder.

"I'm only trying—"

The rest of Emma's benign assertion went unsaid as the ground gave way beneath her feet. She experienced the physical sensations of falling: the lack of anything tangible beneath her churning feet, wind pressure that came from below rather than in front, along with an overwhelming sense of helplessness. Her eyes, though, were no help. She might just as well have been standing still for all the visual difference apparent in the gray reality.

Emma tried to pull the boy close, hoping against hope that she could use her *wyrd* to pull them both to safer surroundings. At that moment, the middle of a curses' brawl would have seemed safe enough. But the boy would have none of her help. Even as they fell, he twisted and squirmed within the too-large shirt. Em struggled valiantly to hold on through a layer of shifting cloth. She clenched a handful of golden hair just as the pale sleeves went limp and began to flap against her face.

A foot thrust into her gut. Em hadn't realized, until it did, that the boy was wearing sturdy boots. The jolt made her wince and, worse, begin to tumble. She rotated up as the boy went down and, when he was directly below, he slipped out of his shirt altogether. The cloth furled up Em's arms. She lost her grip on the boy's shoulder immediately and her grip on his hair an instant later.

With nothing left to hold on to, Em thrashed the cloth from her face. It opened like a useless parachute above her and, for a few heartbeats, she floated face-to-face and just beyond her own arm's reach of the boy. If he'd extend his arm, their fingers could mesh.

"Take my hand!" she pleaded, still determined to save him before she tried to save herself.

The boy folded his arms tightly over his bare chest. "You made Mira disappear. I hate you."

And suddenly Em was falling faster than the boy. She rolled onto her back and saw him shrinking above her and, far above him, a patch of bright light that might have been the sun.

Think! Save yourself. Nothing falls forever.

Em tried. The way-back stone hadn't followed her into the gray, but there were other options. She sought a sense of her body back in the Tuscany room. Fighting turbulence, she oriented herself with her face to the light and her back flat against the wind. She could feel the sheets . . . almost feel the sheets.

*Now! Believe. **Believe!***

Between heartbeats, Em felt cotton all around her, but the sensation didn't last. She returned to the gray hole where she immediately tried to regain the safety of her body. Neither the second try nor the third were as close to successful as the first. She changed her focus to the bolt-hole and pulled herself into the crouched posture that was her usual arrival position. That only increased the speed at which she was falling.

On the edge of panic, Em screamed for Blaise Raponde, who had rescued her from equally dangerous and improbable situations in the early days of her curse-hunting career.

But not this time.

Emma had time for the classic near-death experiences, except that she was falling away from the light. There was a leisurely review of her life's touchstones: moments with her father, her husbands, her stepchildren, Nancy, and even the cats she had known and loved over the years. Sunsets and sunrises, each with all its memories and details attached. The Grand Canyon from the air the first time she flew from Michigan to southern California.

She was in the second tier of precious memories, when the wind pressure changed and she knew the mother-voice was right and nothing fell forever.

Thirteen

"**Y**ou took *her* away!"

Emma winced as something small and hard thumped into her shoulder.

"You made her disappear."

Another thump, this time across her arm and between her ribs. She had a thought to defend herself, but the thought didn't connect with any muscles, not even the little ones that would open her eyes.

"I hate you! I hate you! I hope you *die*!"

A third thump into her side of her head and everything went fuzzy for a while. Time was tricky here, wherever "here" was. Em knew it wasn't Bower, nor the antique bed in the Tuscany room. The more she thought, the more she knew, and the more she hurt. There wasn't a part of her that wasn't aching or throbbing, from the back of her head to her tailbone and her heels. She'd been face up when the final moment had arrived.

Em supposed she should be grateful for the pain. It meant she was alive and that she probably hadn't damaged her spinal chord. She tested her theory by moving the index finger of her right hand. The digit responded: up, down, and sideways, brushing a surface that was rough, textured, and harder than the wasteland's parched dirt.

Stone, Emma thought. She was stretched out on a slab of stone. There wasn't any stone in the wasteland. So where was she? A morgue? The metaphor was "laid out on a slab," but did morgues still have stone slabs? Hadn't they adopted stainless steel?

Maybe she needed to reconsider her basic assumption about life versus death. Maybe she needed to find the muscles that opened her eyes.

Gray. Pale, dense, foggy gray that had no distinguishing features yet was bright enough to hurt Em's eyes. She closed them and waited a few moments before testing the bones and ligaments of her wrists. Each movement was sharply painful at first but quickly settled into a dull, bearable ache. Em successfully wriggled her toes—the most remote part of her body. The movement met resistance in the confines of her shoes.

That was reassuring. Corpses couldn't wear shoes. Shoes were incompatible with toe tags.

Emma bent one arm, then the other, at the elbow. Both movements left her momentarily dizzy and worried that she might be bleeding internally. Her mind had cleared considerably. Her brain must be getting enough oxygenated blood to keep her neurons firing in logical sequences. With a little more effort she remembered racing through gray emptiness—

She opened her eyes again. The grays were different. The one she'd run through was darker, emptier than the gray that surrounded her as she lay on her back.

"Where am I?" she whispered, in part because she needed to break the silence and, also, to test her ears for deafness.

Em heard the question clearly, but the answer, for a curse-hunter, could be rather complicated, especially for a curse-hunter who wandered the past as well as the waste-land.

Her breath caught in her throat as she remembered her last visit to the past, the boy she'd found after mooting a curse, the boy she'd chased through the dark gray empti-ness, the boy who'd sworn at her as he kicked her in the shoulder, ribs, and head.

"Oh, lord, what have I done to myself?"

She'd performed all the little tests: fingers, toes, arms, and ankles. Except for the dizziness, which hadn't repeated itself the second time Emma had bent her arm, everything seemed to be in working order. The moment had come for greater risks: rolling onto her side and raising her head high enough to get a look at the hole into which she'd fallen. Rolling over hurt, but the pain was all on the sur-face. Em pulled her knees up and lay with her head resting on her upper arm, catching her breath and waiting for the aches to subside.

Gray stone and paler gray fog stretched as far as her eyes could see, which, given their altitude, was about fif-teen feet. Her free hand cast a shadow when she lifted it—an almost-straight-down shadow, meaning that the light source was nearly overhead. Em wasn't in the wasteland, but, somehow, she didn't think she was anywhere near Bower or Atlantis, either.

Emma planted her free hand in front of her waist and cautiously levered her upper body a few degrees closer to perpendicular. There was nausea, dizziness, and a throb-bing place the size of a saucer at the back of her head. She suspected she'd given herself a concussion when her head first struck the stone. The nausea passed quickly, and the dizziness didn't get any worse as she straightened both arms and swiveled on her hips until she was sitting cross-legged on the stone.

"Well, they say that God watches over fools and drunks.

I guess there's someone who watches over falling curse-hunters, too."

The light, despite the fog, was bright enough to hurt Em's eyes. Wishing for her sunglasses, she closed them and realized she could hear faint background noises: muffled conversations, the rhythmic pounding that came through apartment walls when neighbors cranked the bass up. She braved the light, looking for the source of the various sounds.

There were shapes in the fog—human shapes, big and small, thin and wide, with well-defined legs and legs obscured by skirts. Em's spirits soared on the hope that she'd managed to translate herself back to the here-and-now world before landing on her back.

"No," she chided herself, "I'm stuck in the past somewhere, some when. Stuck in the past. Stuck in a hole—" Though, come to think of it, distant music and the silhouettes of a dozen or more strangers made for a very large hole.

Emma's curiosity had survived intact. She *needed* more information, but her body—the body that felt more real than it was—wasn't ready for the effort, so she made do with twisting as far as her neck and shoulders would allow. The hole was big. As best Em could discern through the fog, it was limitless in two directions, but, face out, there was a change in color and texture that might be a wall while behind—she scrunched herself around without uncrossing her legs—there definitely was a wall the same color and texture as the gray stone on which she sat.

Between Emma and the wall was a park bench of a style she'd seen both in the here-and-now and in her dreams.

"The Queen's damn Staircase. What is it about this place?"

Outraged by fate, Em threw caution to the winds and stood up as quickly as she could manage, somewhat more quickly than was wise. The ground tipped and whirled at her feet. She held her arms out like a tightrope walker and staggered to the bench where she more fell than sat on the wooden slats. Emma's skin went clammy, her gut churned, and the only move that kept her from fainting was doubling over until her forehead rested against her knees. But when the wave of nausea passed, it took the dizziness and most of the lesser aches with it. She was left with a throbbing bump on the back of her head and the sense that she'd become the pawn of a cosmic practical joke.

When she lifted her head and opened her eyes, Em found that the fog had retreated somewhat. The rhythmic pounding she heard was just that: the sound of heavy hammers striking stone to the beat of a chantey sung in a language she didn't recognize. Cold sweat reformed on Emma's face and forearms, but this time the cause wasn't physical.

Long before Eleanor had told her not to translate herself to the wasteland from a moving platform, she'd been told not to let her travels in the past cross her real-world path through time. Eleanor hadn't been the only one to issue the warning. Blaise and Harry were equally adamant, and Emma had been, for once in her life, strictly obedient. But, sitting on a bench at the bottom of the Queen's damn Staircase, listening to the work songs of the men who'd carved the stone while a parade of humanity, colonial and modern, passed by, fairly convinced Em that she'd inadvertently committed curse-hunting's cardinal sin.

Emma had to be sure. The engineering gene made certain that doubt and dread were always worse in her mind than facing the truth, however unpleasant. With one hand on the bench for support, Em stood up, and when her balance had steadied, she began a clockwise circuit of the staircase park and the benches along its gray stone walls. Her worst fears seemed confirmed when she came upon her architect standing beside his young wife and her servant, drinking from a silvery cup, while laborers toiled on the unfinished stairway.

They didn't notice her, of course, even though Em dared to walk within a few feet of them before continuing clockwise along what was now the opposite wall. She saw Eleanor first, her bicolored hair unmistakable in the dewy light. Eleanor had a plastic sack hung on her left arm—her T-shirt purchase—and an irritated look on her face as she strode toward a shaded bench where a woman wearing tourist sneakers, slacks, and a wide-brimmed straw hat had leaned back for a catnap.

Em's first reaction was acute embarrassment for the way her other self—her truer self—sprawled on the bench with her arms limp in her lap and her legs carelessly crossed in front of her. She'd just never been one of those people who was always neat, always in place, like her friend Nancy who could fall in a snowbank without mussing her hair.

While Eleanor called her name, Emma eased closer to her dozing self. For all the warnings she'd gotten, no one had told her what happened next after a hunter crossed her own path or how to undo the damage. Maybe if she touched herself—if she merged into her own thoughts the way she plunged into innocent minds . . . Innocent. *Innocent* was the very opposite of what a curse-hunter was, meaning that a plunge into her other self's mind was probably the last thing Em should do.

She circled wide behind her mother and got another shock: Her dozing self wasn't alone on the bench. The golden-haired boy was sitting close beside her.

"You made Mira disappear, so I made you disappear. You're not so smart. You followed me right into your past."

Whatever else the boy was, he had the simple black-and-white worldview of a child. Em didn't think her logic would hold much water with him, but she tried—

"When Mira died, she made a curse. A curse, that's something that lives on after you die and makes bad things happen to other people—innocent people. I don't know how Mira managed keep her personality intact and attached to the curse—" Emma stopped short. A child, if the boy was truly a child, wouldn't understand personalities and attachments. She tried another tack. "Do you remember Donetta? The girl who lived and worked on the big white ship? She was carrying Mira's curse. She was very unhappy and bad things were happening to her and the innocent people around her. I had to set Donetta free from the curse she was carrying; that's my job. I'm sorry about Mira. She wasn't a bad person, but she made a curse when—"

The boy interrupted Em with a scowl. "We weren't hurting her," he insisted, folding his arms and wriggling the way he did when he dodged the truth. He seemed to have understood everything Em had said.

"Donetta had a friend, a man who jumped off the ship because of Donetta's curse—Mira's curse."

"Wasn't *our* fault," the boy insisted. "Mira said nothing would've happened, not for a long, long time, then you came along. You and her—" He pointed at Eleanor who, at that moment in the recent past, was repeating Emma's name and reaching for her daughter's shoulders. "You made the trouble. It's *your* fault. You woke her up, an' that changed everything. Mira had to push him away. Had to."

Emma filed the boy's statements for later reflection. In the meantime, she pressed her argument: "And he *died*. You can't kill innocents. I can't let you."

The boy's scowl deepened. He no longer looked particularly young, much less innocent. "You killed Mira. We never hurt anyone; we just made ourselves small. Nobody bothered us. Now, Mira's gone, and I'm all alone. And you're all alone, too. Serves you right. You've got to stay here . . . with me. It's not hard, if we stay small. You'll see; you'll get used to it."

Em blinked. The little boy was making threats—laying claim to her life and freedom. Well, she hadn't protested her way through college without learning a thing or two about defying authorities.

"Not a chance."

She backed away from the bench, the boy, and herself. It was no end of odd for Em to see herself at her worst: bedraggled by the tropical heat and berated by her mother. Even if the boy hadn't been present, Emma would have wanted to leave this slice of the Queen's Staircase in a hurry. As always, there were two possible vectors out of the past. One led to the wasteland, the other to her real-world body.

Or, the other path should have. Although the pull of the real world was often weaker than its wasteland counterpart, the pull had always been focused. Standing in the gap, meeting the boy's glower, Em felt the tug of countless tiny threads, each pulling in a slightly different direction.

So, that's what they're talking about when they say don't cross your path. The real-world side is blurred. You can't feel the absolute present and you can't be sure exactly where or when you've left your body. No problem—

Emma might not be certain which of the threads led back to the Tuscany room, but she had no such doubts about taking the fast track to the wasteland. She prepared for the translation, never taking her eyes from the boy's face. He shouted protests and leapt off the bench. His hands reached toward her; they entered the space where she stood, passing through her substance like fish through water—if water had the wit to feel violated. But there was no harm done. Em was on the move. The gray world of the Queen's Staircase became the familiar parched ground and magenta skies of the wasteland.

The first thing Emma did, after a self-administered hug

that satisfied an emotional need to know that she was whole and unharmed, was look to her right. Solid and shiny, the way-back stone waited in its customary place, ready to whisk her back to the Tuscany room. Em made a halfhearted attempt to orient herself relative to the bolt-hold or the Bunker. Neither location made itself felt in her mind, nor could she feel any remnants of the chill breeze blowing across the invisible divide between the future and the past.

But isolation didn't matter, so long as the way-back stone was in place. Emma had absolute faith in its ability to reunite her consciousness with her sleeping body. She knelt down, put her hands on the polished stone. Her body was *there,* sleeping peacefully, waiting for her return.

In a heartbeat, Emma was *there,* too, inside her own body, conscious of it and her sleeping self. That was a rare sensation, but not unprecedented. Though she usually used the way-back stone to return to an awake body, there had been times when she'd been so bone tired at the outset that her body, given even five minutes of respite, had fallen asleep. She'd learned the hard way to wake herself up when that happened unless she wanted to wake up with cramps in every joint. And, although Em was 99-percent sure that her body was stretched out comfortably on a firm mattress, it wouldn't hurt to pop open her physical eyes and make certain.

A little bit of applied willpower and, sure enough, she was in bed, in a thoroughly darkened room. Everything was in order until the covers shifted and someone sighed.

Without a conscious thought, Emma sat bolt upright and immediately wished she hadn't. The discomfort that had accompanied the boy reaching into her body's space was nothing compared to what she'd just done to herself. It was as though she'd been torn in half or, worse, as though her consciousness was a sticky layer between two objects as they were pried apart. Em pressed her palms against her abdomen and fought to keep from vomiting. The effort, which was successful, kept her from asking herself too many questions. Then, with her stomach quieted, she let her hands drop to her side.

She expected a fluffy blanket, smooth sheets, the sense of her hands resting against her thighs but got none of those things. Oh, there was *something* beneath her fingertips, but Emma could be no more certain of its composition than she could of any object she encountered while browsing the past.

I'm numb, Em told herself. *I must have been sleeping on my arms and now they've gone numb. Good thing I woke myself up—*

The positive analysis didn't work. In the back of her mind—the place where the strangely silent mother-voice usually resided—Emma knew her problem had nothing to do with numbness and everything to do with being in the wrong place, the wrong time.

Holding her breath, Em followed the contours she could feel and confirmed her worst fear—

I'm sitting. I'm sitting, and I'm stretched out sleeping, too. There's one of me from the hips down; two of me—

Em couldn't finish her thought. Horror had her in its grip, and she couldn't do a thing, not even open her mouth for a scream.

Nothing changed, nothing happened and, muscle by muscle, Emma regained control of her body—of her seated body—with the help of the curiosity she'd inherited from her father.

I'm breaking some fundamental law of physics here, one of Newton's or Kepler's. Two bodies aren't supposed to occupy the same space, or nearly the same space. There are two of me up here and just one from the hips down. This cannot be good . . .

Any movement that involved Em's spine brought a return of the tearing sensation, but she was prepared for it the second time and separated her selves completely.

"Obviously," she said aloud, confident that no one could hear her, "I didn't make it all the way back to the present." Talking to herself was a way of fending off panic. "I need to know where the stone *did* send me."

Arms extended and flapping as she took tiny, spiraling steps, Em explored her space. She had a good idea where she was—not that there was anything particularly good about it—but reserved final judgment until she groped her way around a corner and encountered the distinctive hardware of a bathroom door aboard the *Excitation.*

"So much for not being able to translate to or from a moving object," she muttered. "Or maybe that rule only applies if you know where you're going."

An oath or two did little to relieve Emma's sense of doom. She wished she'd asked more questions about what happened when a hunter crossed her own path and wished even more that she asked about strategies to undo the damage. The situation got the better of her, and she slid toward the floor with her back against the door.

"There's got to be a way back to me in the absolute present—"

A proverbial light went on in Em's mind: The past was the past whether she was looking at a potential curse or herself. She already knew how to roll up time to reach deeper into history; all she had to do was figure out how to roll up the past in the opposite direction until it and the present came together and hope her consciousness and her body would do the same. It was that, or return to the wasteland. Weighing the options for a moment, Emma realized she'd lost faith in her way-back stone and decided in favor of rolling up the past.

Regardless of the direction, rolling up the past was hard work. Best-case scenario was that she'd doubled up on herself while the *Excitation* was headed back to Port

Canaveral. That would mean about twenty-four hours of rolling, and she'd never rolled up more than a few minutes, and that was in the opposite direction. Worst case, the *Excitation* was outbound for Port Canaveral—

Em took a breath and held it, using pressure in her lungs to push the panic back. She'd faced tough situations before, situations when she didn't know how she'd manage to get from one minute to the next. In their own ways, the day she'd decided to divorce Jeff had been such a panic-stricken day, and the last time her father had called to say he wasn't feeling well had been another. Compared to them, a marathon roll up of an *Excitation* cruise didn't seem so daunting.

She started to stand, only to hear noises coming from the bed.

A whisper came through the darkness: "Eleanor?"

Emma sank back against the door. She had her worst case—the *Excitation* was on its way to its first port-of-call, and her in-the-past self had just awakened from a night terror with a rejuvenated migraine. A migraine and, as Emma ordered her memories, a sense of being watched. Watched, perhaps, by her disembodied self? Em rested her forehead against her knees.

No wonder I had a headache the whole time! If I roll up the whole cruise, there're going to be two of me. Three of me when I visit the Queen's Staircase. Good God, I've done it this time, really done it. I'm—

A host of words, all of them negative and destructive, presented themselves for Emma's selection. She leaned back and beat her skull gently against the wall, rejecting all of them.

Her other self had gotten out of bed and, much as the time-shifted Emma had done moments earlier, groped her way through the cabin in search of her migraine medication. Em had had one bitter taste of sharing space with her other self, she didn't want another. She scurried to flatten herself against the cabin's outside door, then waited until the other Emma had returned to bed, before preparing to roll up time toward the absolute present.

In the end, it was easier to charge through time toward the present—which was, at least, time's usual direction—than fight her way deeper into history. Em figured she compressed more than a half hour of historical darkness into about sixty seconds of breathless swimming with time's tide before her strength gave out and she needed to rest. After six cycles of rolling and resting, there was light in the cabin. A cheerful voice descending from the ceiling fixture announced the time as eight A.M.

Emma could have remained in the cabin, rolling and resting, ignoring the activities of her past-time self. She couldn't open the door or move anything else by herself, but that wasn't a critical concern, so long as she followed herself out of the cabin for Thursday morning's final disembarkation. Boredom wasn't a critical concern either, although Em feared for what was left of her sanity if she let herself be locked in the cabin for the equivalent of three full days. When her other self put her hand on the cabin's door, Em got as close as she dared—without coming into physical or nonphysical contact—and stayed close all the way to the breakfast buffet.

She tried rolling up time during breakfast and discovered that the act of rolling up forty-five minutes of Monday morning (practice had already improved her rolling ability) was no more difficult in a crowded dining room than it had been in the cabin. The downside, though, was that Eleanor and the other Emma hadn't lingered over their breakfasts for forty-five minutes. When Em paused to catch her breath she realized she'd become separated from them.

Em's first instinct was to take such advantage as she could of her invisible, immaterial status and try to catch up. She attached herself to a family group of six and squeezed through two automatic doors and an elevator before deciding that it was more important to return to the present than satisfy her morbid curiosity about the Queen's Staircase. Her rolling skills continued to improve. She'd wrapped up two cycles when her sweaty, distracted self emerged from the elevator and followed Eleanor to the cabin. Another cycle and Em caught herself going to and coming from the spa—the aubergine fingernails *were* noticeable, but nowhere near as noticeable as Emma had feared.

Emma stayed in the elevator lobby, rolling up another chunk of time, while her other self went to the Broadway revue, but when she'd finished resting after that exertion she went down to Chelsea's Place to assure herself that, if she'd done nothing else right, she'd at least managed to rid Donetta of her curse. Navigating the crowded dining room without letting anyone violate her space was a nerveracking, but ultimately successful, exercise. Successful on two accounts: She got to within an arm's length of Donetta, and one look into the woman's gray eyes made it clear that whatever troubles the young woman might have seen in her homeland, she was no longer haunted by a curse.

Em curbed her celebration, hoping against hope that after another few cycles of rolling and resting she might find herself standing out on the starboard-side deck watching nothing more than moonlight scatter on the waves. Time was resilient, not forgiving. Emma watched the young man plunge to his fate for a second time.

After that, there was nothing more Em's personal history could teach her. She kept her distance as her other self reached for the phone and, with a trembling hand, made an emergency call. When the junior officer showed up, she slipped through the door he'd opened before it closed. Back in the elevator lobby near their cabin, Emma began rolling the past toward the present with head-down determination. She'd pause when the rolling images revealed herself or Eleanor at the cabin's door; and she paused to avoid contact with the invisible crew when they made a cleaning pass through the lobby, but otherwise Em pursued the present relentlessly.

She'd perfected her rolling techniques and was cycling several hours at one shot when suitcases began appearing in the corridor. Rather than risk separation, Emma slipped into the cabin where she nibbled history in fifteen or twenty minute chunks. She couldn't see her other self thrashing through the nightmare that turned her right eye into a blood-red ball, but she heard it and couldn't escape the guilt that, somehow, her doppelgänger presence was to blame.

When Emma had bought the Integra, she'd never given a thought to rear-seat comfort; an oversight she'd never commit again. Eleanor kept her seat ratcheted close to the steering wheel, but the alternate Emma—the Emma who had originally lived these moments—pushed the passenger seat back as far as it would go, then lowered the seat back. That left Emma the time-walker with no alternative but to scrunch herself up in the available space and roll up the hours as Eleanor rolled up the road.

Em elected to stay close to her historical self and made good progress in her pursuit of the present until she and Longleigh finished dinner. At that point, which she reckoned was between six and seven hours from the convergence of past and present, she began meeting resistance. By the time Longleigh was giving her the guided tour of Atlantis, Em had become mired in an Alice-in-Wonderland squeeze where she was struggling just to hold her place in the time stream and her efforts to surge closer to the present were losing her almost as many minutes as she gained.

She stayed in the Tuscany room when her other self left with Eleanor for the burgundy bathroom, thinking that putting a bit of distance between her selves might make the process easier. It didn't. Pushing herself to the brink of collapse, Em got close enough to the present that she could feel two heartbeats, then, with reunion within her grasp, all hell broke loose. It was as though she'd been shot out of a cannon. A turbulent force engulfed her consciousness. It ripped her away from the Tuscany room, wrapped her in suffocating darkness, and hurled her into the utterly unknown.

In all her surreal wanderings, be they in the past or the wasteland, Emma had never had to fight for air. Oxygen had been hers for the breathing until, suddenly, it wasn't, and she was terrified. An instinct rooted deep in her inherited *wyrd* seized control of her thoughts and translated her to the wasteland where she landed face-down and gasping on the parched dirt.

With no thought except to flush her lungs, Em heaved onto her side. Her eyes might have been open or closed for all the attention she paid to the data her optic nerve carried to her brain. Then an image hit her consciousness: a pillar of fire near enough that she could distinguish between the whirling bands of flame and darkness.

Groaning, Em raised herself on all fours. She extended an unsteady right arm and realized with cold certainty that she didn't have the strength to drive off the predatory curse. If it were only a matter of driving off a single curse—but there were three of them closing in, and that was without turning around to see what might be coming up from the rear. Emma muttered a curse of her own and vowed to go down fighting, but the same instinct that had gotten her out of the frying pan and into her current fire pulled her eyes to the right.

There it was: cool, black, and polished—the way-back stone. It hadn't worked properly the last time, but beggars couldn't be choosers. Em dragged herself to the stone and plunged into its depths. If desire had counted, or the intensity of imagination, Emma would have surfaced, one mind in one body, in the Tuscany bedroom.

She missed the Tuscany room, but she did manage to propel herself into a bed, a bed she hadn't slept in for a generation.

"No!"

Em had returned to her childhood, to Teagarden Street and her high school bedroom with the Beatles posters hung on every wall. She'd given herself one of her infamous night terrors. Her father was awake. Emma heard his bed creaking. He'd never failed to come to her when she woke up screaming—

I can't! I can't face him. I can't see him. If I see him again . . . even once—

Emma closed her eyes and blindly returned to the wasteland.

The ground was dark. The sky was seething magenta. The way-back stone was just out of reach to Em's right. Never mind that she couldn't feel the pull of either her bolt-hole or the curia's Bunker, or that she had no sense of the absolute present; the horizon was blessedly empty. Crawling closer to the stone, she sat cross-legged and waited for an answer to the question, What do I do now? to make its appearance in her mind's eye.

Her options seemed limited. Since she had crossed her own path, the way-back stone had turned into a pipeline to various moments of her past rather than her present-dwelling physical self; and trekking across the wasteland without an inner sense of destination was an exercise in futility: The flat land went on forever when a hunter didn't know where she was going.

Not that Em didn't try walking. When she'd recovered from the rapid-fire shocks that had followed her failure to reconnect with herself at the convergence of the past and present, she chose a random direction and started walking. Emma walked until her feet cried out for rest, then walked some more. Subjective hours and miles of unchanging scenery flowed past her senses without leaving impressions in her memory. She could have logged more hours, more miles, but for a stray thought about water.

Curse-hunters did not need food or water when they walked the wasteland. Blaise Raponde had gotten along just fine with neither for centuries, although he'd admitted that learning to exist without sustenance had been the most difficult lesson the wasteland had taught him. He'd hinted that cravings had driven him mad more than once, and Emma, sensing that this was a sore subject, hadn't asked how or when her lover had regained his sanity. As thoughts of water grew more oppressive, she regretted her discretion.

She could force water into existence the same way she had drawn the bolt-hole out of her imagination, but the brimful bowls and bottles she produced lacked the power to quench her thirst.

"I don't believe in myself right now," she muttered, emptying her most recent effort into the parched dirt where it disappeared without a trace. "Faith is the key—"

The mother-voice should have had something pithy to say about that, but the voice had been silent since Em had fallen down the rabbit hole that ended with the golden boy at the bottom of the Queen's Staircase.

"I should have known right then that I'd stumbled into some lesser reality."

The sudden notion of a lesser reality led to a thought that she had translated herself to a lesser wasteland where neither the bolt-hole nor the Bunker existed. That thought was more disturbing than thirst. Between the two, Em could feel the pull of madness no matter which direction she faced.

"And I've only been stuck here a few hours. It's not even dawn yet back in Atlantis."

I won't wake up. Eleanor didn't when she got stuck in the wasteland. I knew something was wrong. I started looking. Blaise started looking, and he found her, too—

Eleanor had been captured by curses, imprisoned by them. She hadn't been lured across her own path.

"I am *not* going to die from stupidity!"

The words were a bold vow; and they got Em moving again, continuing the line of footprints she'd left in the dirt before her most recent attempt to slake her thirst, but she couldn't completely dampen the thought that stupidity had already done the deed. She soldiered on, walking because she didn't dare stop, while doubt and craving worked their double damage in her mind.

A fiery curse on the horizon was almost a welcome relief—something to fight, something to focus on—until it was joined by another pair.

"Shit on a shingle—I'm back where I started."

Fourteen

E mma's options hadn't really changed since her last visit to the wasteland, her last encounter with the pack of fiery pillars. She tried, but by herself she didn't have the firepower to divert, much less moot, three large-scale curses. In the end, the choices were annihilation or the way-back stone and, once again, the way-back stone won the toss. With her hands already sinking into the stone, Emma wondered how many round-trips she could stand before annihilation seemed a better deal.

Em made four round-trips between wasteland rings of virtually identical curses and desperation plunges into her historical life. Each time she sent her younger self into a fit of terror. After returning to the wasteland for the fourth time, she ran out of willpower.

"How many night terrors have I had? A couple hundred? And how many migraines . . . ?"

Em fell silent. At their peak, as her marriage to Jeff went through its death throes, the only way she'd known one headache had ended and the next begun was when the throbbing switched hemispheres. Surely she and Jeff bore the blame for the misery they'd inflicted on each other.

Every headache, every terror couldn't possibly be the result of an overconfident curse-hunter's monumental stupidity.

Or could it?

"I can't keep doing this to myself. There's got to be an alternative."

Paris.

For the better part of three centuries, Blaise Raponde had regularly returned to his favorite streets, favorite taverns, and, yes, his favorite boudoirs. If Em could find her way to Paris of the 1670s and 1680s, there was a chance—maybe a good chance—that she could cross her lover's path. Between the two of them, they'd manage to solve her problems.

The way-back stone beckoned. Emma knelt before it, thinking thoughts of Paris and Blaise Raponde. She imagined her lover's face in wondrous detail, his hands, his smells, the warmth rising from his back when she slid her hands between his shirt and greatcoat to give him a hug. She couldn't remember her own bedroom with such precision, yet when the moment came to put her hands on the stone, Em sat back on her heels instead.

"What if I'm wrong?"

What if Blaise didn't recognize her? What if he mistook her for a rogue and slew her on the spot? Worse, what if she missed Paris altogether and found herself on the far side of anything familiar?

Emma wrapped her arms across her chest and swayed from side to side. Tears threatened; she swallowed them before they escaped. Though Em believed the absolute present had advanced only a few hours into the future, the body her consciousness inhabited felt the strain of too many failed efforts and translations gone wrong.

Rest, she decided, was what she needed more than Paris, more, even, than Blaise Raponde. But where or how? Curse-hunters didn't take cat naps on the wasteland dirt. Such behavior attracted curses sooner or later, and in Em's case, sooner had become the rule. She needed a place to hide; she needed a bolt-hole. Bolt-holes weren't proof positive against curses. The bolt-hole she shared with Blaise had been trashed once by curses or rogues, but it didn't attract curses the way an exposed curse-hunter did.

Em set her imagination to forging a new bolt-hole . . . with a window. She'd never used the bolt-hole window to get back to herself and the absolute present; that didn't mean it wouldn't be worth a try once she'd gotten a few hours of sleep.

Everything felt right in her mind, but her spirits fell when she opened her eyes. Where she expected to find an orange-wedge hollow and a sturdy upright door, there was a mound of packed dirt about a yard high and flattened on one side by a rickety storm-cellar door with peeling gray paint and a metal latch plate, missing two of its four screws. The whole thing looked like it had come straight out of the dust bowl instead of her imagination.

"Better than nothing," Emma whispered shakily and grasped the latch.

The door creaked on its hinges, a very loud sound in the silent wasteland. A steep, packed-dirt ramp rather than stairs descended into unrelieved darkness.

Light, Em thought and held out her hand. She'd wanted a flashlight but nothing was going her way, and she got a flaming torch instead. Holding it at arm's length, she made her way down the ramp into a space that stretched the definition of the word *room*. The walls were dirt, the floor and ceiling also. There was no furniture and, needless to say, no magic window. Still, Em would have stretched out on the floor had the air not smelled faintly of ash and decay. Wasteland odors were as rare as wasteland sounds.

Try as she might, Emma couldn't convince herself that the scents of rot were a good omen. Her doubts strengthened when she brought the torch close to a wall and noticed that the dirt was flecked with shiny white globules of varying sizes up to about a sixteenth of an inch across. So far as Em knew, the wasteland's ecology consisted of two species: curses and hunters, with rogues thrown in as crossbreeds. There was nothing in her leather-bound books about parasites or their eggs, and certainly no one had ever suggested that such things existed in the barren plain. But once the idea had hatched in Em's mind, there was no way she was closing her eyes in this poor excuse for a bolt-hole.

The horizon was empty when Em returned to the surface. She couldn't count on it staying empty, not when curses had come flocking every other time.

"Someplace safe," she said to the way-back stone, like some desperate gambler pleading with his dice.

Em recalled the boy telling her that he and Mira stayed in safe places and how he'd panicked when she'd translated him to the wasteland. For all she'd been through on his account, Emma still wasn't completely convinced that the boy was a rogue. Rogues rested in the past, but they didn't hide there, not the way she was planning to hide.

"Someplace where I won't hurt myself."

She'd already given up trying for the Tuscany room.

Emma sank her hands into the way-back stone. She blinked and completed the translation. Once again, she was surrounded by darkness. Was there something about crossing her path that condemned her to nighttime translations, or was it that she'd never suffered a *day* terror? For sure, Em's historical self had just awakened from a terror dream. The stifled sobs defined the room for Em's conscious self. She did not recognize it.

She inventoried the bedrooms of her memory and thought she'd collected them all without matching the small room to which she'd translated herself. Standing up, Em spread her arms wide and searched for a wall. Feeling nothing, she took a step in the direction she happened to be facing. She stumbled immediately and crashed to her hands and knees. Agony flashed up her right arm—just her luck to break something—but her fingers worked, and so, after a moment's shock, did her wrist. Em willed that she'd done nothing worse than sprain her wrist and, sticking close to the floor, continued her exploration.

A metal post, about two inches square, rose from the floor to a horizontal bar curtained with the distinctive textures of a wool blanket and a dotted chenille bedspread. Following the horizontal bar, Em's fingers found a wall of cement blocks covered and smoothed by a thick coat of paint. Orange paint, she remembered as the aspects of her freshman dorm room came into focus.

She'd been so determined that she wouldn't be a townie, living at home while she went to college. Her father had gone ballistic over the extra expense, but after six months of relentless persuasion Em had won her case—only to end up in an orange room with an incompatible roommate.

"What's wrong now?" that roommate asked from the upper bunk.

Emma couldn't remember the girl's name, but she remembered the acute embarrassment like it was yesterday.

"Nothing," the historical Emma insisted bravely. "I'm sorry. I didn't mean to wake you."

The metal spines of the upper bunk mattress made alarming sounds. Em not only heard the sounds, she remembered them and the cringe that followed. Her migraines had started during her freshman year.

She apologized to herself: "I'm sorry, too."

But Em didn't translate herself back to the wasteland. There was room on the floor amid the books, shoes, clothes, and soda bottles—the outward signs of the war of style and will she and her roommate had waged for nine months. She found a wadded-up pair of jeans—no telling if they were hers or her roommate's—to use for a pillow.

The tile floor was hard, as expected, and cold. Emma pulled her knees up and tucked her hands beneath her arms.

She said, "It doesn't get much lower than this," and immediately worried that she'd tempted fate.

Her ex-husband, Jeff, and her father had both insisted that a man who couldn't sleep when he lay down simply wasn't tired enough. It was one of the few things the men had agreed upon. Emma had chalked it up as another bit of mythology both men had acquired in the army. There were any number of good reasons why someone on the brink of exhaustion could lay awake. A cold, hard floor was one of them, but a cold hard floor didn't keep Emma awake.

Em dreamt while she slept. She returned to the Tuscany bedroom, where she woke up to sunshine. She drifted, dream-like, to the music room, where she stared out the window, waiting for something to happen. Then the roommate's alarm went off and blared for a full two minutes until the girl with the long dark hair clambered down from the upper bunk to turn it off. Em knew it blared for two minutes, because she remembered timing it and because she could see the clock from the floor.

She watched herself pull the blankets over her head, then waited by the door for the roommate to grab her towels and toothbrush. No attached bathrooms back in the Sixties, all the girls had to troop down the corridor to the communal sinks, showers, and johns. The roommate didn't open the door very wide. Emma had to get close if she wanted to leave the room. Too close—their arms touched, and for a moment they were staring into each other's eyes.

Emma blinked first. *No wonder she hated me. I was weirder than I knew.* Em gave a little shove, and the roommate hurried into the corridor, letting the door slam. Em barely cleared the door. Bad enough to occupy the same space as a living person; she didn't want to share space with a varnished wood door.

Once in the hall, Em waited for someone to open the door to the stairwell. Girls came, but none of them opened the heavy fire-door much wider than was necessary. Emma chickened out of her first two opportunities, then shoved through with an inseparable pair named Marti and Martha. They looked at each other as Em slipped past and down the stairs. She had to wait for them at the bottom of the stairs.

If she survived this fiasco—if she made it back to a sound mind in a sound body, Emma vowed that she was going to get Blaise to teach her how to move things while she wandered through history.

The dorm's lobby was crowded, and its doors were open, letting in a blast of frigid air. Emma shivered, more from memory than actual need. An inch of snow had fallen overnight, just enough to freshen the winter landscape. Em walked on a virgin patch to assure herself that she left no footprints, then stuck to the middle of the sidewalks where salt and her dorm mates had already cleared a path.

The sun had barely risen—it was winter in Michigan, after all, halfway to the North Pole where the sun didn't shine at all. The sky was pink and blue in the east, gray in the west. There'd be more snow by the end of the day, not that Emma intended to be around to see it. Her plan—her need—was simpler: a walk through the university town where she'd been born and reared; and where she'd lived for almost all of her adult life.

If she couldn't find her way back to the absolute present and she couldn't find Blaise in Paris, then there were worse fates than returning to Bower, a ghost in the attic, to be sure, but a ghost in beloved surroundings.

Emma strolled down the diagonal walkway connecting one corner of the Old Quad with its opposite. The sun hadn't brightened enough to trigger the sensors in the cast-iron street lamps—walk lamps, really—that patterned the quad. Looking into their light Em made out a mist of minuscule ice particles, all of them glittering in the silvery light. It had to be January, and the ambient temperature couldn't be much above zero to create the ice-mist effect. She was cool, but not shivering cold in her usual hunting garb of jeans and a sweatshirt. If she could count on a similar buffering from reality in July—

"You're giving up." The mother-voice reemerged after a night's sleep.

I'm not. I'm going to keep trying. I'm going to try to find Blaise. He'll come looking for me—

She would have sold her soul just then—if curse-hunters had had souls to sell—for the sound of her lover's voice. Bower was a fine place to spend a finite future, but no future seemed appealing if she was going to have to face it all alone.

Em sat on one of the very empty benches. She'd overcome the panic she'd felt since—what should she call the period of time after she'd plummeted down the rabbit hole, before she'd gotten some sleep in her dorm room? Her gut called it yesterday, but what did her gut know? Whatever she labeled it, she'd reached a different emotional plateau. A slow, calm despair had replaced the panic. She was determined to make the best of what she found, because the mother-voice had touched the truth: Emma didn't believe she was ever going to find herself on the living side of Bower, Michigan, again.

Slowly she rose from the bench. *I'll walk to Teagarden Street. I'll take a look at the old house. Dad was on sabbatical my freshman year; he'd gone out to California for the semester. The place will be empty.*

Emma didn't have to think about which sidewalk to take, which streets to cross in which directions. Her feet knew the way without any help from her bleak thoughts. There had been cars to dodge near the campus, but the Teagarden neighborhood was quiet. Lights were on in some of the houses, but not in her house, which was locked up tight as a drum.

No sneaking inside to sleep on her own bed.

It was time to translate to the wasteland, to fight curses, find Paris, find Blaise Raponde. Em made her mental preparations and became aware that she was not alone on Teagarden Street.

A man stood on the corner beyond her house. He hadn't been there a moment earlier and, though he could have taken Reading Street to arrive there, Emma felt certain that he hadn't.

Blaise? He came looking for me!

The thoughts were irresistible, even though the silhouette was tall and slender where her lover was more compact and muscular.

Harry?

Harry Graves, though slender, was not particularly tall; and Eleanor was out of the question. Emma made a fist around her ruby ring—would it work here in the past? Blaise carried a sword for his Parisian fights.

The man had spotted her. He was coming toward Emma. She squinted hard, looking for footprints in the virgin snow. There were none. Bower in the Sixties wasn't Blaise's Paris. The curiae had risen. Hunters worked together. They trusted one another, recognized one another. Em held her ground for a moment but made mental preparations to return to the wasteland when the man had halved the distance between them.

"Emma!"

Her name sounded through the cold and stopped Em in her tracks. She took a tentative step toward the newcomer. He picked up his pace.

"Emma! Stay there!"

Three words were enough for Em to place the voice. She wouldn't have needed that many if Redmond Longleigh weren't wearing a Russian-style astrakhan hat over his red hair.

"You found me."

Emma unwound her fist and released a world of tension in a sigh. She started toward him.

"No! Wait there. Let me come to you."

Em couldn't imagine why that should matter, but she stayed put until they were an arm's length apart and Longleigh had grasped her hand within a leather glove of astronaut proportions. Longleigh's lips were pale, his cheeks were cherry red. Wisps of condensation wreathed his mouth when he opened it. The man was seriously cold and far more in tune with Bower's historic weather than she.

"You're a welcome sight," Em admitted. "You look like you've been waiting for hours."

Longleigh nodded and released her hand. "I've been trying to locate you. Your mother said look in Bower, because you'd circle back to your hometown, but I couldn't pinpoint the when of it. You've got a lot of years here, my dear." He shook his head. "You've given everyone quite a scare. Eleanor said you two were going to meet at the Bunker. When she couldn't muster her way through, she thought you might have gone to moot a curse instead   "

"I did. I mooted it and then everything went downhill in a hurry."

"Ah, we thought the mooting itself had soured. You racked up a lot of mileage, my dear."

"Not hardly. I tried to force myself to where me, the past, and the present converge. Once that didn't work, I've been cycling between wasteland and my own nightmares. But, you know, it's not like I've been that many places. If I come back to my past, I come back to Bower. That's the house where I grew up." Em gestured toward the empty house.

"Not many places, but different times. Usually, when someone gets tangled up, they tend to narrow down to a single strip of their life: a week, a day, maybe a single hour. I can find them easily."

"So, even when I screw up, I do it uniquely?"

"You could say that, I suppose. Are you ready to get back to business?"

Em was more than ready. Since Longleigh had touched her, she'd grown steadily more sensitive to Bower's weather. Her sweatshirt wasn't nearly enough insulation against January, and she'd started to shiver.

Longleigh took her hand again. "Allow me to lead."

Emma closed her eyes and opened them under magenta skies. A quick check revealed the way-back stone in its usual place. If Longleigh used a similar device for his translations, it was hidden from her subjective view. Longleigh had shed his winter gear in the translation in favor of jeans and a Georgia Bulldogs sweatshirt that clashed with his hair.

Emma extended her senses, searching for either her bolt-hole or the Bunker. The bolt-hole remained out of reach, but the curia's Bunker was equally absent, which surprised her. She would have thought Longleigh would bring her to his own front door.

Before Em could ask why he'd chosen to translate them to some godforsaken wasteland corner, he bent down to retrieve something small and invisible to her from the ground. He dropped the object, whatever it was to him, in a pants pocket.

"Breadcrumbs?" she asked.

He repeated the word and thought about it a moment before answering, "Yes, I suppose you could say so. You're up for a hike, I hope. We've got a ways to go."

"Fine by me. You lead. I feel like I've been here before. More precisely, since I got myself in trouble, every time I translated, I wound up in a place just like this where I couldn't sense a thing, not the absolute present, my bolt-hole, or your Bunker. I'm guessing you've laid some sort of trail back to civilization?"

They started walking in a direction that seemed utterly

random to Emma. She stole a quick rightward glance; the way-back stone was keeping pace, doing its thing.

"I didn't lay it," Longleigh countered. "You did, but I doubt you can see it. The *adrêsteia* who get lost rarely can see their own trail."

"But you can?"

"There are *wyrds* even more rare than yours, my dear. You can track and delve and plunge; I seek. It's a *wyrd* I'd hoped to pass along to my children, but—well, you know that story."

Longleigh was right about that. Grateful as she was for the rescue, Emma couldn't help but think she'd gone and done the one thing Harry Graves had warned her against: She'd gotten herself into debt with the curia, with Longleigh personally, and that unpleasant consequences were sure to follow.

When they'd gone about as far as a tall, sharp-eyed man could see from their starting place, Longleigh picked up another invisible object.

"What do they look like?"

"Shiny, black pebbles that catch the light like tittle beacons. Yours shine a sort of pale blue, if that interests you. The *adrêsteia* each have their own signature. I know them all."

Emma shivered, and not from cold. For the first time, she had a sense of the power Redmond Longleigh could wield. There was no hiding from a man who could track you by a trail you couldn't see to cover. After that revelation, Em scanned the horizon, hoping to regain her composure without drawing attention to the fact that she'd lost it.

"No need to worry. We're as safe here as we'd be on a country lane outside Atlantis. Curses and rogues don't get drawn into these pockets."

"If it's my pocket, then it's got curses in it. A good-sized pack of the tall, fiery kind. I've run into them every time I've translated. They're one of the reasons I've cycled back to Bower so many times. I can't stay in the wasteland very long without attracting notice."

"You imagined them. You can, you know. You can imagine just about anything and make it real enough to be dangerous, even a curse."

Could she have conjured those fiery pillars out of her own imagination? Not bloody likely, but Emma kept her opinions to herself. She concentrated on little black stones—miniature way-back stones—and blue-light specials, hoping to catch sight of the trail they were following. Concentration wasn't enough. She hadn't a clue what had caught Longleigh's attention when he picked up the third and, later, the fourth stones.

After the fourth stone, they changed their heading slightly toward what Emma would have called the east . . . if they'd been walking north before.

Longleigh cleared his throat lightly and said, "Curious. Did that curse you mooted put up much of a fight?"

Emma considered keeping the details of her embarrassment to herself, then decided that she might as well hear Longleigh's opinion of her misadventure. "The curse didn't, but as soon as I mooted the curse, I flushed something else out of the woodwork. I'm still not sure if it was a rogue or another hunter, but chasing it was how I got myself into this mess."

" 'Flushed something'? Tell me about it."

"It's a long story."

"We have quite a bit farther to go. If it matters, Eleanor has told me about the girl on the ship with the curse and your determination to moot it at the earliest opportunity. We presumed it was something of a wolf in sheep's clothing."

"No, mooting it was the easy part. I've been back to the *Excitation*. That curse is gone as if it never existed—the damage, that remained, but I got rid of the glue that held it together; and Donetta, the girl, has her life and fate to herself." Then Emma took a deep breath. "The problem wasn't really the curse. The problem started with the woman we—I thought was responsible for the curse."

Em started her story with her first delving of Donetta's curse, though she was careful, after her initial slip of the tongue, to keep everything in the first person singular and made no mention of Blaise Raponde. She described how moved she'd been by the old woman's dignity as she faced her death, a death that had not given rise to a curse; and how easy it had been to assume that Mira had earned the sacrifice Emma's plunging demanded of her.

"I took the shortest path, the quickest nudge. She was going to commit suicide and make a curse on her way out. In the final analysis, all I had to do was change the way she killed herself from drinking poison to throwing herself on the swords and clubs of the irregulars. It worked. There was no curse, but I can't help thinking I made a mistake."

"It's never a mistake to moot a curse. Never. But something happened after Mira met a quiet death?"

"It wasn't quiet. I heard a child crying—a boy, not more than six. I swear, he wasn't there the first time I delved the scene, and he wasn't there before I mooted the curse. It was like, moot the curse and out pops a little boy. I found him by his light; he made his own light, the way we do—"

"And rogues."

"The thought did occur to me."

Em repeated the conversation she'd had with the boy as accurately as she could reconstruct it. Longleigh scooped up another invisible pebble without interrupting. They changed direction again. Emma would have sworn they were headed back the way they'd come, but she shared her suspicions about the boy instead.

"The old woman had some kind of hold on the boy, regardless of what he was, rogue or hunter. He was bound to her, afraid of her, I have the feeling the boy was a mascot, maybe a familiar—I can't really say why. Heaven knows, there's nothing about mascots and familiar spirits in the books I've got. Maybe it was the lock of hair. When Mira found a lock of hair the same color as the boy's among the old woman's stuff, that's when her thoughts turned to suicide. But, when I plunged, I'd only seen the hair; I didn't know about the boy. I'm thinking, whether the boy was a rogue or a hunter, the old woman had a piece of him—a literal piece—and was able to compel him with it. Is that possible?"

Longleigh took several strides before answering. "Possible, not likely. How far back in time had you delved?"

"Between stirrups and electricity. The eighth century and the nineteenth. And the Balkans—Croatia. Donetta's from Croatia; I'm guessing she caught a homegrown curse. I couldn't make sense out of Mira's thoughts. She was running on emotion. There weren't many words to make sense of."

"They might all have been *adrêsteia* . . . or rogues, and not fully understood their *wyrd*. I've seen it, but not among children. The *adrêsteia* are born with their *wyrd*, but it stays hidden until they're old enough to command it. A child would be consumed—"

"I think maybe the boy was. I think that lock of hair was all that was left of him physically. Well, I didn't think that at first. My first thought was that I was going to reconnect him with his physical self. Don't ask me how; I hadn't figured that out. I managed to get him as far as the wasteland. He was terrified and ran away from me. I followed him; that was my big mistake, I followed him square across my path, like everyone's told me not to do. It was deliberate on the boy's part. He blamed me for taking Mira away from him—somehow he and Mira were connected through the curse that I mooted. The boy knew what he'd done. It was a roguish thing, but I still have doubts; it's also the kind of rough justice a child hands out.

"I can't shake the sense that I didn't do right by him;

and adults are supposed to do right by children, regardless of what children try to do to them."

"How noble," Longleigh replied with only a hint of sarcasm. "And how will you do right by this boy—who's probably older, in absolute terms, than you or I?"

Emma shrugged. "I haven't the foggiest. It's going to be one of those debts that hangs around. For all I know, he's gone like a mooted curse. He was so afraid of the wasteland. I think he relied on Mira to keep him safe, and now she's gone. Either he got scooped up like a newborn fawn as soon as I split from the Queen's Staircase, or he's gone into deep hiding."

"Count on the hiding. Didn't you say he'd been alone before he'd fallen in with the grandmother and the girl?"

"I did."

"Then count on his instincts being razor sharp. The boy can take care of himself. He might not cross anyone's path again for centuries . . . especially if he finds another Mira."

"Could I be right about Mira? Could a woman's personality piggyback on a curse? Could she have deliberately forged a curse so she could stay with the boy?"

Longleigh surprised Em with a quick, one-word answer: "Yes," which he immediately qualified. "If she were *adrêsteia,* especially if she were, without knowing what she was. You, yourself, during all those years when we thought you were dead, if the circumstances had come down to it, you could have embraced a curse and become a rogue; that the watchers would have noticed. But, say you came to an unfortunate end—the end that yields a curse—the theory holds that, yes, *adrêsteia* can yield a curse, but, also, that an essence of you would linger in the curse. The theory is nonsense, of course. We both know that without a physical presence in the absolute present, your essence would wither and vanish."

Emma looked at Longleigh and found him looking at her. Most likely he knew about Blaise Raponde and, maybe, she did owe Longleigh a few answers about her mysterious lover, but she'd wait until the bill came due and keep Blaise to herself until then. She blinked, slow and deliberate, before saying, "There was a lock of hair."

"After all these years?" Longleigh arched his eyebrows skeptically.

"If the boy was a hunter, and Mira was, too; and they believed they existed, maybe that was enough to keep them going until I came along and pulled the curse out from under them." For an instant Em envisioned that Blaise had a companion curse—and that some hunter might come along and moot it the way she'd mooted Mira's. "Or maybe we need a different theory altogether."

"We don't need a theory. We have the curia and the watchers. We find the ones like Mira and bring them into the fold." Longleigh stooped to pick up another pebble. "We're getting closer now. What do you sense?"

Em admitted that she sensed the same nothing she'd been sensing since their arrival in the wasteland pocket, but two pebbles farther along she picked a faint, chilly breeze out of the air.

"That way to the absolute present," she said, pointing in the appropriate direction.

"That way, indeed, if the absolute present were our destination. We need to return to the place where this circle began. Can you find it?"

The answer was in the question. Emma felt the tug of the Queen's Staircase like the twinge of an almost-healed sprain. "That's the last place I want to go."

"Think of it as breaking a spell . . . or mooting a curse."

Em wasn't convinced. She stayed put when Longleigh started walking again. He turned and gave her a disparaging scowl.

"You must face yourself . . . yourselves, if you prefer. It will work. I've done this more times than need counting. I call it 'pinching off the loop.' It is very much like mooting

a curse, only you're mooting a loop of your own life.
You'll remember what happened. We're not talking amne-
sia. Think of it as putting everything back in its proper perspective."

"I tried going back. It didn't work."

"You didn't have me beside you. Now, come on. We
have time, but Eleanor has been beside herself for three
days."

"Three days? I've been out of it for three days?" Em put
her own face on her memories of Eleanor lying comatose
in a Bower nursing home. The image sent a shiver down
her spine, but did nothing to quell her doubts about revis-
iting the Queen's Staircase. "I've got a bad feeling about
this," Em insisted, but she caught up and kept pace until
every nerve fiber twitched with the knowledge that her disastrous encounter in the Queen's Staircase was only a moment away.

Longleigh gave his final instructions. "Face what you
find. It's as simple as that."

"Where will you be?"

"Right beside you, but don't look at me, don't think
about me. I can't pinch off the loop; only you can do that,
by facing it. I give you my word: Mooting's never been
simpler. Take the step, get it over with, and you'll be on
your way."

Emma had never been one for jumping off diving
boards. She'd rather endure the torture of easing into cold
water one inch at a time than lose control. She took a deep
breath, held it, and made the shift—

"Open your eyes!" Longleigh shouted as the wasteland
fell away.

Thank heaven, all Em had to do was lift her eyelids. If
she'd had to turn around, she wouldn't have had the
strength. But they were all there in front of her: Emma-on-
the-bench, Emma-with-the-boy, even a wispy sense of the
Emma who'd dreamt herself into the gray-walled gap. The

scene repelled her emotionally, if not physically. She took
a backward step.

"Face them! Face whatever you can see."

Her lungs burnt; she couldn't take a breath, but somehow Em got her legs moving. She faced her third self, the
dreaming self. There was intelligence in those eyes when
Em met them, then the intelligence faded, and she burned
as if she'd swallowed fire.

"I can't do this!"

"You must! You can't give up halfway."

The other two selves were too close together for her to
get between them. Gritting her teeth, Em laid a shaking
hand on the shoulder of the self who'd followed the boy.

"Don't plunge!" Longleigh shouted. "Face them."

"There's no room. I can't move things—"

Even as Emma protested her inability, the self she held
twisted toward her. Their eyes met, and headache didn't
begin to describe what Em felt as she absorbed another
piece of herself. The pieces didn't fit together smoothly.
They warred with each other and would continue to war
until she embraced her final self. She expected the seated
Emma to be the worst, but she'd felt the wisdom of Longleigh's strategy and was up to the challenge.

"I've got it now!" she shouted without turning around.

"Good! Now, quickly, translate yourself to the Netherlands. I'll meet you there and show you the way home.
Hurry! You don't want to recreate the problem—"

"I'm coming, as soon as I'm done. There's one more me
to integrate."

Emma faced her final self. It *was* like mooting a curse.
She made changes to the past—squeezing between
Eleanor and herself, shoving Eleanor ever-so-slightly
aside—to make a better present. Em took her own hands,
met her own eyes—

That was all it took: An instant of eye contact and she

was whole again. No mental fireworks, just the sense of a breath held too long slipping away in a sigh.

She called to Longleigh, "Okay, I'm done. We're out of here—?"

When she'd finished turning around, Em found no sign of the red-haired curia master. She cocked a private smile. Chalk up another one for the perils of subjective realities: Longleigh wasn't omniscient. He clearly hadn't had an accurate Emma count and had cut out for the wasteland between Emma numbers two and three. No great matter. Per instructions, she reached for the wasteland.

And found herself in the blast zone of a fiery-pillar curse. Something grabbed her sleeve and spun her out of the heat.

"Stay back!" Longleigh shouted.

He held a sword, a curved, cavalry-type sword that cast a bolt of brilliant lightning from the length of its blade when he slashed with it. The lightning shock drove Em back another several feet and carved a dark gash—one of several—across the pillar's midsection. It responded with a primal roar and a flaming, serpentine arm. Longleigh slashed low to high, severing the limb and collapsing it into a shower of soot. With scarcely a pause, he delivered another cut that turned the gash into a barn-door tear. The pillar howled and shrank a good ten feet. It sprouted another arm; Longleigh sliced it off with the first of two slashes that opened a gaping hole in the pillar, through which Em could see the horizon.

Emma was properly awed by Longleigh's obvious prowess. Blaise and Eleanor together couldn't have cut down a towering curse half as fast or neatly. But she'd been through this attack before, and a single pillar was only the beginning.

"Company's coming!" she shouted.

Longleigh carved a slice out of the curse's flank and gave no indication that he'd heard Em's warning.

"I already count two more, closing fast!"

There were four by the time Emma closed her mouth. She glanced around for the way-back stone and found it, a few feet farther out than usual, but well within sprinting distance. Could she trust it not merely to get her out of an ambush but to take her safely back to her body? Hadn't Longleigh said something about showing her the way home?

"We've got to get out of here before it's too late!"

Still no response. The first two pillars were within Emma's range. Another few seconds and they'd be on top of her. Em had to make a fight-or-flight decision and, acting on instinct rather than reason, chose fight. She dropped to one knee and steadied her right arm with her left. Her will to vanquish curses wherever, however she found them opened her grandmother's ring.

Ruby light spilled out and wrapped itself around Emma's hand before leaping toward the curse, broader and more potent than any assault she'd launched before. It struck the fiery pillar some ten feet above the ground and drove it into retreat. Em was pleased—not to mention astonished—by her improved performance. Pride caused her attention to waver for an instant. The ruby beam fizzled at the same instant, and the curse surged. She'd surprised it, but hadn't seriously damaged it, and it sprouted a handful of boa constrictor arms, all of them reaching for her.

Em couldn't renew her attack on the first pillar; its twin had gotten close enough to smell. She blasted it, not quite as powerfully, but enough to drive it back a little and give her a heartbeat to deal with the longest arms from the first pillar. Somewhere there were two more fiery pillars . . . at least two more. They could be drawing down on her back, or Longleigh's, but Emma didn't dare look for them.

She blasted her first curse. Em thought it was the first. The way they were dodging and weaving, she was hard-pressed to keep her beam on target, any target. She faltered, and one of the curses closed in with gouts of fire. Instinctively, Emma raised her left arm. Coils of flame engulfed her arm from fingertips to elbow. The pain was searing, but, worse, the curse was dragging her close.

Emma drew on reserves she'd never suspected. She flailed with both arms. The ruby light arced uselessly wide and faded, but the coils around her arm went flying as well. Em was free *and* unscathed. She'd conjured up a defense, a soft glow only slightly more intense than the self-illumination that normally surrounded a hunter in the wasteland, but thicker and proof against a curse.

"I've got you now!" she whooped and brought the ring in line with the nearer of the two curses.

According to Harry Graves, the black books sitting on Em's bookshelf back in Bower, and every other bit of lore she'd been able to accumulate, curses weren't intelligent, but the pair Em faced were canny enough to sense that something had changed. They retreated out of range and twined around each other like referees debating a tough call. The battle wasn't over and, even with her newfound defense, Em wasn't foolish enough to think she had a sure win. If she was half as clever as the curses, she'd retreat to the way-back stone.

Longleigh, too.

Em spared a sidelong glance in his direction and almost wished she hadn't. Where Longleigh had been fighting one fiery pillar and winning, he was now facing three, and, despite his prowess, he was clearly hard-pressed. Emma shouted his name but hesitated to do more than that—one false move and the swarming curses would have them both.

One false move . . .

Heat seared Em's back. She spun around, left arm leading, right hand ready to blast whichever of her pair of curses had dared to sneak up on her. But there was only one fiery pillar. Emma's enemies had merged, consuming each other and renewing each other. It lashed out with three limbs at once and opened a maw the size of a garage door. She screamed and poured her will to survive, her predatory hatred of curses, down her right arm and into the ruby ring.

The streak of light it expelled drove Em backward. She collided with Longleigh—the last thing she wanted to do. She barely kept her balance and had no sense of what havoc her clumsiness had caused for Longleigh—but she'd vanquished the curse. There was a gaping hole through its maw, bigger than the hole Longleigh had wrought with his lightning sword. Dark cracks spread from the hole through the flames. Em watched breathlessly as the pillar began to collapse.

She couldn't savor her triumph. Slamming into Longleigh couldn't have helped his cause. She owed him, and quickly. Spinning around, Emma struck the nearest of Longleigh's three curses with the power of her ruby ring. It wasn't the powerhouse her previous strike had been, but it was enough to drive the curse back and keep it fleeing toward the horizon. She laid into what had been the middle pillar, the broadest, tallest one.

Faced with a combination of laser light and lightning, the middle curse tried to retreat. Longleigh's lightning sword had range over Emma's ring. He cut through the air, peeling off a bolt that pierced the curse from behind. Lightning danced between the sword tip and the curse, which writhed and shrank.

Emma attacked the third cause. Her arm felt like a lead pipe, and her aim was off. She nicked one of the limbs, creating an ember burst, nothing more. Groaning from the effort, Em braced her right arm with her left hand and lined up for another blast. The curse retreated before she found the will to energize the ring. Beside her the lightning sizzled and faded.

"Do something! It's getting away."

"Let it go." The tip of Longleigh's sword dropped to the ground. "You said you'd drawn a pack. I should have known you meant more than two." He heaved a sigh. "You realize I meant to impress you."

Em retreated. "You could have gotten killed. You could have gotten us both killed." She unmade her fist. Each finger quivered and burned as the blood flow returned. The left sleeve of her sweatshirt was soaking wet and dripping onto the ground.

"You're hurt."

"No—I don't think so." Em didn't *feel* injured, but in the wasteland's chancy light it was impossible to say whether the liquid soaking her dark sleeve was blood or water. She squeezed the cloth and studied her fingers. The liquid was clear. She tasted it: water. "I'm fine. Tired—exhausted, really, but fine. You?"

Longleigh sheathed his sword in a scabbard that disappeared as soon as he released it. "Better than I would have been without your help. You wield a mighty weapon."

"A desperate weapon. I admit, I outdid myself. I saw what you were doing with that sword. My teachers used to say I have a competitive nature." Em attempted a depreciatory laugh.

"We're quite a pair, then, aren't we? I try to impress you with the might of the Atlantis Curia; you impress me with—what? An improvisation?"

Emma shook her head, not because Longleigh was wrong but because she wasn't in the mood to talk about what had just happened. "You said you'd show me the way home."

"Show you or tell you, your choice. There's a chance you're lying in the same bed where you began this journey and your translation will be effortless. But there's a better chance that you're elsewhere in Atlantis. Three days have passed—three days when I last left. It could be longer now. You were restless. Eleanor agreed that it would be best if we let you move around—within Atlantis, of course, and never alone."

"Good grief, what have I been up to?"

"Very little. I liken it to sleepwalking. Eleanor talks about comas, but I don't think it's that serious."

Em recoiled from the thought of a coma in any form.

"I have found *adrêsteia* who've been lost for many more than three days, and they all woke up with no ill effects as soon as their minds reinhabited their bodies. I expect no less from you—*but,* if you're not sleeping in your bed, then you'll have to find yourself. Now, I can translate first and arrange for you to be in the Tuscany room, if not actually in the bed. The downside is that, should something go amiss, we'd be back where we were and I'd have to find you again. Or, I can guide your translation and stay beside you until you find yourself. The downside there is that other lost *adrêsteia* describe a sense of being underwater that can turn to panic if the reunion's delayed. You don't strike me as the panicky type."

Emma let the compliment go unchallenged. She'd never had much luck letting someone else guide her translation. Then again, she'd never had anyone but Eleanor acting as her guide. Whatever else Redmond Longleigh might be, he was competent . . . and they'd just saved each other's lives.

"I'll take door number two. You're my guide."

Longleigh extended a gentlemanly arm. "Ready?"

"Past ready," Em replied as she laid her hand across it.

The wasteland faded. Longleigh's translation ritual, apparently, was all in his head and involved nothing so mundane as kneeling in front of a shiny black stone. Emma's body, however, was not where her mind expected to find it, and being underwater scarcely described the sensation that followed.

Steady . . . steady. Let the current take you where you need to go.

Longleigh's voice seemed to rise from the far end of a long tunnel, but his arm was tangible beneath Emma's hand. She tightened her grip, and together they drifted downward, like bugs spiraling down the drain. Pressure bands tightened around Em's chest, squeezing what little breath she held from her lungs. Panic seemed a very reasonable option. Then the drifting current strengthened. Em released Longleigh's arm and dove downward—

Her forehead struck her knees. Her very real forehead against her equally real knees. Everything felt heavy, reminding Em of astronauts' complaints when they returned to Earth after a sojourn in space; but everything felt right, too.

"Look at her!"

The voice was Eleanor's, the hands, too. They closed on Emma's shoulders and raised her up to a seated position. Eleanor's green eyes were filled with tears. An eye blink later, and Emma was sobbing with her.

"I'm back. I made it. I'm really back."

Fifteen

"So, as soon as I could put one foot in front of the other I went upstairs to take a long, hot shower. By the time I was done someone, probably Shevaun, had put together a barbeque dinner. I ate, drank champagne, went to bed, and slept the sleep of the innocents. We left this morning and drove straight through. Tomorrow I go back to work. It seems like I've been gone more than ten days . . . more like a lifetime."

Emma signaled that she'd finished the oral version of "What I Did on My Vacation" by taking a long swallow of wine. She waited for Blaise to say something. He hadn't interrupted since she got to the part about arriving at Atlantis for the first time. If she hadn't caught him blinking once or twice, she'd have sworn he'd stopped moving completely.

The hearth-fire crackled, taking the chill and darkness from the air. A single candle sat on the table between Emma and Blaise, dancing to its own tune. A bowl of lime green Jell-O sat untouched on the table as well.

It didn't take a genius to see that Blaise wasn't happy. If length of silence was a measure of displeasure, then he was nearing a ballistic explosion. When he began twirling the stem of his wine glass, Em expected it to snap. Finally he began to speak in a voice so soft Em could barely hear it and her chair was only a few feet from his.

"You have indebted yourself to the Atlantis Curia."

"I pulled Longleigh's bacon out of the fire when he decided to show off in the wasteland. He admitted as much."

"He would not have risked his life if you hadn't crossed your path."

"A technicality. If he comes to collect a favor, I'm telling him that we're even and that's the end of it."

"I doubt he will agree."

"Oh, I doubt he will, either, but Longleigh's a Southern gentleman of the old school, and he won't quibble over honor."

The stem snapped. Em had forgotten, as she sometimes did, that her lover remained a student of a far older school where honor was concerned. Fortunately the goblet was empty when it broke. Blaise tossed the pieces into the hearth.

"I worry about you, Madame Mouse. A man's honor lies within his heart. It should not be quibbled with. You should not quibble."

Em set her goblet on the table, lest she become tempted to break hers as well. There was no shortage of wine glasses in the bolt-hole. If the cupboard was bare, all either one of them needed to do was close the door and apply a little imagination. Except for the Jell-O. Jell-O took more imagination. Emma had never seen Blaise turn his nose up at a bowl of Jell-O.

"What I shouldn't do is leave myself with debts to Redmond Longleigh. He's a man of surprises. You should have seen him with that cavalry saber and this business of *seeking*. If I believe what he said, he knows my 'signature' now and could track me the way you track rogues. I'm glad he found me, but it gives me chills now to think of the time he spent looking for me—roaming back and forth through my life. It's as bad as if he'd plunged inside my mind and ransacked my memories. I'll quibble my best with him, if it'll give me any advantage."

"He's a rogue," Blaise announced and took a swig straight from the wine bottle.

"In the ordinary sense."

"In *every* sense. He does what a rogue does. Better to kill a rogue than quibble with one."

"I don't think I need to go quite that far." Em engaged in a bit of quibbling and didn't mention that she wasn't sure Longleigh *could* be killed, at least not by the likes of her.

"If he comes nosing around here . . . or around you again, *I* will."

It was Emma's turn to be silent. Blaise Raponde, for all his charms and wit, would never understand that some battles were her battles, hers alone. She hadn't completely decided how she was going to handle Redmond Longleigh—other than standing firm on the principle that she owed him nothing—but she'd hoped to handle it without involving her lover.

Really, she should have known better. She should have kept the whole story to herself, or let it age in her memories a while until she could spin it out without so many loose ends.

Em went to the cupboard and retrieved a goblet identical to the one Blaise had broken. She filled it up and offered it to Blaise. He gave it a feline-suspicious stare then took it from her hand. She refilled her own goblet.

"I'll just have to make sure it doesn't come to that," she promised and held her goblet out for a toast.

Blaise tapped rim to rim. "That should be interesting to watch."

From the fantasy world of

Lynn Abbey

co-creator of *Thieves' World*™

Out of Time
0-441-00751-1

Taking Time
0-441-01153-5

Available wherever books are sold or at
www.penguin.com

Penguin Group (USA) Inc. Online

What will you be reading tomorrow?

Tom Clancy, Patricia Cornwell, W.E.B. Griffin,
Nora Roberts, William Gibson, Robin Cook,
Brian Jacques, Catherine Coulter, Stephen King,
Dean Koontz, Ken Follett, Clive Cussler,
Eric Jerome Dickey, John Sandford,
Terry McMillan…

You'll find them all at
http://www.penguin.com

*Read excerpts and newsletters,
find tour schedules, and enter contests.*

Subscribe to Penguin Group (USA) Inc. Newsletters
and get an exclusive inside look
at exciting new titles and the authors you love
long before everyone else does.

PENGUIN GROUP (USA) INC. NEWS
http://www.penguin.com/news